Also by Carrie Carr:

<u>Lex and Amanda Series</u>
Destiny's Bridge
Faith's Crossing
Hope's Path
Love's Journey
Strength of the Heart
The Way Things Should Be
To Hold Forever
Trust Our Tomorrows

<u>Other Titles From Carrie Carr</u>
Something To Be Thankful For
Diving Into The Turn
Piperton
Heart's Resolve

Beyond Always

Carrie Carr

*Yellow Rose Books
by Regal Crest*

Texas

Copyright © 2014 by Carrie Carr

All rights reserved. No part of this publication may be reproduced, transmitted in any form or by any means, electronic or mechanical, including photocopy, recording, or any information storage and retrieval system, without permission in writing from the publisher. The characters, incidents and dialogue herein are fictional and any resemblance to actual events or persons, living or dead, is purely coincidental.

Print ISBN 978-1-61929-160-7

First Printing 2014

9 8 7 6 5 4 3 2 1

Original cover design by Donna Pawlowski
Final cover design by AcornGraphics

Published by:

Regal Crest Enterprises, LLC
229 Sheridan Loop
Belton, Texas 76513

Find us on the World Wide Web at
http://www.regalcrest.biz

Published in the United States of America

Acknowledgments

I've worked with a lot of editors over the years, and learn something new every time. This book was no different but Nat Burns (a terrific writer, as well) is a step above. Thanks, Natty—you're awesome!

Great beta readers are hard to find, especially ones that will tell you the truth. I'm lucky to have found Kay and Kelly. They both helped in different ways, and I will always be in their debt.

For many years, my covers were done by a great artist, Donna Pawlowski. She was an even better person, and will be sorely missed. My heart goes out to her partner and family.

Dedication

To the woman who holds my heart, my beautiful wife, Jan. We've been together fifteen years, and every day seems like a honeymoon. I love you, sweetheart. Always and forever.

To Cher, our own little rat terrier. She rescued us when we found her at the animal shelter and her antics kept us laughing. Although we only spent ten years together, she'll always be in our hearts and live on forever in print as Freckles. Rest well, crazy dog. We'll miss you.

Chapter One

THE QUIET OF the master bedroom was interrupted by sudden music from a clock radio. Lex's bare arm snaked from beneath the covers and slapped near the offending object, which continued to blare. The song ended and a far too-cheerful voice took over.

"Good morning! If you haven't looked outside, better jump out of bed. We're a day late for a white Christmas, but it's beautiful anyway!"

A groan sounded and the blanket flipped back.

"What the hell?" Lexington Walters sat up and rubbed her dark-blue eyes.

"Did he say what I think he said?" asked her wife, Amanda. Short, reddish-blonde hair stuck out in every direction, and an attempt at brushing it with her hands didn't help.

"I dunno." Lex adjusted her T-shirt. "Did we forget to turn up the furnace last night?"

Amanda donned her slippers. "Sure feels like it." She stood and wrapped her thick, pink robe around her body as she shuffled toward the nearest window. "Holy crap."

"What?" Lex padded around the bed, wincing as her bare feet met the cold, wooden floor. She stood behind Amanda and peered over her shoulder. "Geez. Where the hell did that come from?"

The area between their ranch house and their housekeeper, Martha's, smaller home nearby was lit by a large guard light. In the pre-dawn gloom, an even layer of white snow rested undisturbed, giving the yard an eerie appearance.

"The weather forecast last night said we had a slight chance of precipitation," Amanda said as she snuggled into Lex's arms. She jumped when Lex's cold hands crept beneath her robe and nightgown. "Yeow!"

"Heh." Lex kissed Amanda on the neck. "Did they mention how long this slight chance would last?"

Amanda tilted her head as the kissing continued. "Mmm." She reached back to tangle her fingers in her wife's hair as the phone rang.

Lex placed a final kiss on her shoulder then walked around the bed and picked up the phone. "Walters."

The voice of Roy Wilson, her ranch foreman, crackled on the line. "Hey, Boss. I know it's early, but—"

"It's snowing."

"Uh, yeah." Roy sounded confused at the interruption. "I checked the forecast, and we could be in for some trouble."

All humor gone from her voice, Lex sat on the edge of the bed. "What do you mean?"

"They're talking about us getting at least a foot of snow today. Maybe more."

"We never get more than an inch or two," Lex argued. "Are you sure?"

"Yeah. The weather guy started spouting all sorts of gibberish about fronts and stalls, but from what I gathered, they're just as surprised as the rest of us."

Lex scratched her head. "Damn it. And we've got a couple of hundred head in the south pasture. All right. How many guys do we have here?"

"Just the skeleton crew, Boss. Not enough to move the herd quickly. The rest of the hands aren't due back until Monday."

"Damn, damn, damn." Lex stood and began to pace. "We've got to get those animals out of the low areas before they're buried up to their necks. Damned things aren't smart enough to do it themselves."

"Yeah, I know. Listen, Helen volunteered to ride with us, so if we can get a couple more, we should be okay."

Helen was Roy's wife, as well as the cook for the ranch hands. She had grown up around ranching and was an accomplished horsewoman.

"A couple more people. On the day after Christmas? Who the hell is going to come all the way out here and ride in this crap?" Lex stopped short when Amanda stepped into her path. "What?"

Amanda patted Lex on the hip. "We can ask Martha and Charlie to watch the kids and I'll go with you."

Lex thought about it and realized it was the best solution. "I'd like that."

When her foreman laughed, she returned her attention to the call. "Shut up, Roy. I don't see you telling your wife no."

"Hell, no. I'm smarter than that. We'll saddle up and be at the main house in less than an hour."

Lex slowly lowered the phone and looked into Amanda's eyes. "Are you sure about this? It's going to be cold and wet."

Amanda took the phone away from her and tossed it on the bed. She wrapped her arms around Lex's waist and leaned into her embrace. "I'm positive. Will we be enough?"

"I'd really like at least one or two more people, but we can make do." Lex kissed the top of Amanda's head. "I'd ask Charlie, but he's still fighting that nasty cold."

"And Martha would kill both of you," Amanda replied.

Their housekeeper, Martha, had been the mother figure for Lex as she grew up, and was now grandmother to their three children. Martha's husband, Charlie Bristol, had retired as sheriff of the county and now spent his days enjoying the grandchildren.

"Why don't you call Shelby?"

Shelby Fisher and her partner, Rebecca Starrett, were good friends of theirs. Shelby had been a bull rider on the rodeo circuit when she met

Rebecca, but a shoulder injury caused her to retire. They had a small parcel of land on the other side of Somerville, where they boarded horses for a fee. Rebecca worked at a western wear store in town and Shelby took on odd jobs to help make ends meet.

"She's got her own place to worry about, sweetheart. I'm sure she has her hands full right now."

"Have you talked to her lately?" Amanda pulled back and looked at Lex. "I mean, really talked?"

"We saw them day before yesterday, remember?"

Amanda swatted her on the arm. "I know that, doofus. Did you actually talk to her?"

"Yeah?" Lex shrugged. They had kept to their usual discussions about horses, cattle and their partners. But mostly about cattle.

"Ow." She rubbed the place on her stomach her wife poked. "What?"

"Rebecca told me that they haven't had any boarders for several months. She's been taking as much overtime as the store will allow her, but Shelby's going crazy trying to find work. She's even thinking about returning to the rodeo circuit, which scares Rebecca to death."

Lex sat on the bed and tugged Amanda onto her lap. "Damn. Why didn't she say anything?"

"Really? She's almost as stubborn as you are."

"No, she isn't." It took her a moment, but Lex finally realized she had been dissed. "Hey!"

Amanda laid her head on Lex's shoulder. "The point is, you need an extra rider and Shelby is looking for work. It's a win-win."

"Yeah. Now I just have to figure out the best way to ask without hurting her pride."

"I have faith in you." Amanda kissed Lex on the throat. Lex took a shaky breath. "Think you can dial the number?"

Lex laughed as she was flipped onto the bed and covered by her wife's body.

"In a minute." Lex trailed her lips along Amanda's throat. They had plenty of time.

BY MID-MORNING, THE snow was already six inches deep. The fat, wet flakes fell heavily, making travel hazardous. Posted by a gate, Amanda, astride a paint mare, shivered and hunched lower in an attempt to get warm. Her task was to allow the straggling Angus into the next pasture, without letting any escape.

"I m...mu...must be out of m...m...my mind," Amanda griped as her teeth chattered. She blinked the snow off her eyelashes and lowered her face. "S...st...stupid."

She hadn't seen any of the black cattle for quite some time, making her wonder if she needed to stay by the gate. She considered taking her radio from her coat pocket, but didn't want to remove a glove to do so. She closed her eyes and decided to wait a while longer. The brightness of the snow was beginning to give her a headache.

The arrival of a large, black stallion and its rider caused her horse, Stormy, to dance sideways. Amanda tugged on the reins to control her. "W...wh...whoa."

"Amanda?" Lex held her powerful horse in place, although he snorted his displeasure.

"I'm f...f...fine."

Lex edged Thunder closer. "No, you're not. Why don't you head for the house? I'll take on the gate duties."

"I can d...d...do it," Amanda forced out between clenched teeth.

"I know you can, sweetheart. But sitting still makes it worse. Chet was supposed to relieve you half an hour ago. Have you seen him?"

Amanda shook her head. Her entire body started to tremble.

"Damn it." Lex hurriedly dismounted. She waded through the snow and pulled Amanda off the mare. Amanda remained rigid as Lex unbuttoned her own duster and wrapped it around her. "I told you we should buy you something heavier for winter."

"W...wa...waste of money." Amanda snuggled as close as she could. "I'm n...n...not usually out...side for l...long, an...and it's rar...rare...rarely th...thi...this c...c...cold."

Lex growled and briskly rubbed Amanda's back. "Stubborn."

The echo of a gunshot startled them as well as both horses. Thunder stood wide-eyed as Stormy took off. Lex tossed Amanda to the ground and covered her with her own body. She raised her head and carefully searched the area before she rolled off her. "Are you all right?"

Amanda got to her knees and dusted the snow off her chest. "I *was* warming up. Was th...that a gunshot?"

"Yeah." Lex stood and helped Amanda to her feet. "Rifle. Not too far, either." She climbed into the saddle. "Come on. It was probably one of the guys, trying to move a stubborn heifer. But we can check it out. While we're at it, maybe we can catch your ride before she makes it back to the barn."

She held out her hand and tugged Amanda up behind her.

Amanda snuggled close and wrapped her arms tightly around Lex.

They rode in silence as Lex headed to where she thought the shot had originated. Within ten minutes, Lex pulled Thunder to a stop.

Amanda raised her head and tried to look around Lex. "What is it?"

"Tracks. Heading down into that gully."

Lex pointed to the single set of tracks being quickly covered by falling snow. She swung her right leg across Thunder's neck to climb down.

"Stay here while I check it out."

When Amanda refused the reins, she sighed. "Amanda, please."

"I think you've been kicked in the head by a horse too many times."

Amanda dropped to the ground beside her. "That's the only logical explanation for this bout of brain damage you seem to have acquired."

She patted Thunder's shoulder and moved closer to Lex. "Lead on."

Lex looked into the sky. "Give me strength." Amanda patted her on the back to let her know she'd heard her. "All right. Then at least stay behind me."

"Sure. It's easier to walk in your steps, anyway." Amanda dropped the reins to the ground, secure in the knowledge that Thunder was trained to stay in place. "Extra goodies for you when we get home, buddy," she told him.

"You've spoiled my horse. He's going to get fat and lazy."

"Yeah, right."

Two more shots rang out, this time from the direction of the gully.

Lex immediately squatted and pulled Amanda down with her. "We're getting close. I don't suppose you'll let me go first?"

"Hell, no." Amanda tangled her fingers in the back of Lex's coat. "You're not getting out of my sight."

"I was afraid you'd say that. All right. Stick close."

Amanda tightened her grip. "Like glue."

They waded through the snow-covered brush, Lex doing her best to keep them upright. Their descent became more of a struggle as they went, the deepening snow making the walk more difficult. Lex stumbled and would have fallen if Amanda hadn't grabbed the back of her coat.

"Thanks," she muttered.

"Are you okay?"

"Yep." Lex struggled past a large cedar and stopped. "What the hell?"

Chet Burns, one of the four regular ranch hands, stood at the foot of the gully. He turned toward her voice. "Boss! I was hoping someone would hear the shots."

Amanda looked around Lex. "Chet?"

He waded through the snow and met them halfway. "Hi, ma'am. I didn't know what else to do, Boss."

Lex looked around him. Amanda did as well. They saw the body of his horse. "What happened?" Lex asked.

"Found a hole and poor Shadow broke his leg. He was in such agony, I shot him." The chapped and moist skin around Chet's eyes showed how hard he took the horse's death. "I didn't know how long it would take help to get here, and I couldn't stand to see him suffer."

Lex patted his shoulder. "I'd have done the same. Why didn't you call out on your radio?"

Chet held up what was left of the device. "It broke when we fell."

"Damn. All right. Gather as much of your gear as you can, and follow us. We'll have someone meet us up there." Lex pointed in the direction they came from. "Thunder can carry Amanda and me, but I think he'd balk at hauling you, Chet."

He wiped his eyes on his sleeve. "Yeah." He took a few minutes to get what he could from the fallen animal. "I feel bad leaving him like this." Chet said as he straightened up with his hands full.

"Can't be helped." Lex flinched as Amanda prodded her in the ribs. "Uh, right. As soon as the snow lets up, you can come back with a couple of guys and a trailer." She turned to Amanda. "Okay?"

"Better. Chet, give me your saddle bags, at least."

Chet blushed as he glanced at Amanda. "No, ma'am, I can handle it."

He dropped the bags when he tried to pick up the saddle he had struggled to remove. When he bent to pick up the bags, his rifle scabbard landed in the snow.

"Not a good way to treat a gun," Lex deadpanned.

"No, ma'am. I know." Chet flipped the saddlebags onto one shoulder and tried to dig the scabbard out of the snow. He shook the scabbard clean, which caused the saddlebags to drop from his shoulder. Again.

Lex held out her hand. "Chet, we're gonna turn into ice sculptures at this rate. Give me the gun, hand Amanda the bags and you carry the saddle."

"Right." He did as she suggested, and soon they were slogging uphill.

When they reached the crest, they were greeted by two riders, Shelby and Roy. The latter casually leaned on one arm against his saddle horn. He tipped his black Stetson. "Hey, Boss Lady."

His gray mustache had pieces of ice along the edges and his heavy green coat was covered with snow.

Lex laughed. "Hey, yourself. Comfy?"

She handed him the scabbard.

"Been worse. We heard the shots. What happened?" Lex looked significantly at Chet with the saddle and it seemed the only answer Roy needed. "Damn."

He raised his voice and spoke to Chet. "Just leave your saddle here and you can double up with me."

Shelby spoke up. "I'll take the saddle, if you want."

Her thin frame was bulked up by the heavy jacket she wore and her brown western hat drooped from precipitation. Small strands of her shoulder-length brown hair peeked from beneath the hat.

Chet looked relieved. "Thanks, ma'am."

With a laugh, Shelby accepted the saddle. "I've been called a lot of things, but never that." Shelby nodded to Lex. "All the cattle have been moved and everyone else is on their way back."

"Careful, Shelby. We'll make a ranch hand out of you, yet." Lex tried to shake the snow from the bottom of her duster, with little success. She ended up using her hands to break up the clumps.

"Had worse jobs."

Roy helped Chet climb up behind him. "We'll see what you say in the summer when we have to clean the cattle pens."

"Is that a job offer?" Shelby asked, looking from Roy to Lex.

"Would you take it, if it was?" Lex said. "Shelby?"

"Yeah?"

Amanda had heard enough. "Really? Have you all lost your minds? I'm freezing my ass off out here, and you're playing word games." She patted Shelby's leg as she passed. "I'm sure if you show up Monday morning, Lex will have all the paperwork ready. Go home and get warm. That's what I'm going to do."

Lex followed her. "You heard the boss. Let's get out of this damned snow."

Chapter Two

THE GAS FIREPLACE flickered brightly, warming the petite woman who reclined on the nearby sofa. The wind howled against the house, causing Anna Leigh Cauble to raise her eyes from the book in her lap and shiver in response. She glanced at the grandfather clock near the doorway and placed her book by her feet. "Goodness. It's almost three o'clock. Jacob must have gotten lost in his work."

She slid her socked feet into light blue slippers before she stood and wrapped a crocheted blanket around her shoulders.

She continued to grumble as she walked through the house and out the door to the side yard. "Rushed right out this morning. Too busy to eat."

As was their usual custom, they had spent breakfast together in the kitchen. Her husband had barely touched his food, which she attributed to his mind being on new ideas for his woodwork. He had made Amanda a hand-carved laptop desk and had been thrilled at her exuberance on Christmas day upon seeing the gift. He had mentioned designing something for Lex, but hadn't said what it would be.

"I swear. That man would work past bedtime if I let him."

An enclosed breezeway protected her from the elements. She opened the shop door and hurriedly entered. "Jacob? You've worked past lunch again, my dear. And I was too busy dozing on the sofa to notice. Come in and we'll have an early dinner."

The blare of his favorite radio station made it impossible to hear him if he'd answered, so she headed toward the back of the shop.

Anna Leigh had to navigate stacks of wood as well as finished products, to get to where Jacob spent the majority of his time.

"Dearest? Where are you?"

She tightened the blanket around her shoulders and stepped around a large dresser. "Jacob, darl—"

Her voice stopped when she noticed the still form on the floor. He was partially hidden behind a table.

Heedless of the dirt, sawdust and spilled lacquer on the floor, Anna Leigh dropped to her knees beside her husband. He was lying on his side, his face away from her. She carefully rolled him onto his back. He appeared to be asleep.

"Jacob?" Her badly shaking hand touched the side of his neck, which was much too cool in the warmth of the shop. "Oh, my dearest. Why didn't my heart stop, as well?"

The man she had loved and lived with for almost sixty years was gone. Anna Leigh's heart, once filled with love and happiness, shattered as she lowered her face to his chest and cried.

She didn't know how long she'd lain there, covered in sawdust and tears. Feeling emptier that she'd ever thought possible, Anna Leigh sat up and lovingly brushed her fingertips across the damp spots on Jacob's shirt.

"I've made a mess of you, haven't I?"

She sniffled and wiped her eyes with the edge of the blanket she wore. "I have calls to make, dearest. But I don't want to leave you alone." She shook her head. "Now isn't that the silliest thing you've ever heard?"

Placing what she knew was the final kiss on his lips, she lovingly draped the blanket across Jacob's upper body and stood. "Wait for me, my love."

The cold air didn't faze Anna Leigh as she trekked from the shop to the kitchen. Only as she dialed the wall phone did she realize that somewhere she had lost a slipper, and her left foot was covered in sawdust. She stared at the littered wool sock as she waited for an answer.

"Hello?"

Anna Leigh noticed the sawdust she had tracked in. "I'll need to get the mop."

"Mom? Is that you?" Michael, her son, asked.

"Yes, I'm sorry. I need your help, Michael." Reality finally hit and she began to shiver. "Could you please come right over? Thank you."

She hung up the phone without waiting for his answer. Her body continued to shake as she slid down the wall. "What am I going to do without you, Jacob?"

She wrapped her arms around her waist and gazed sightlessly across the room.

LEX AND AMANDA bustled through the back door, giggling like a pair of children. They slipped on the wood floor as they jockeyed for position by the coat rack.

"Lexington Walters, don't you dare track that mud and snow through the house." Amanda sat on the bench and removed her boots. "Sit."

Lex grinned, but sat beside her anyway. "Woof."

She nudged Amanda with her shoulder and kicked off her boots. "I wonder where the monsters are."

"Maybe upstairs driving Martha crazy." Amanda looked up as Martha stepped through the kitchen doorway. "Oh. Hi."

Martha's face was blotchy and her eyes were red. "Amanda, honey, you need to call your grandparent's house."

Amanda stood and moved toward Martha. She put her hand on Martha's arm. "Are you all right? What's wrong?"

"I'll be fine. But you really need to make that call." Martha squeezed her hand and released it. "Why don't you use the office?"

"Um, okay." Amanda gave Lex a questioning glance before she headed down the hall.

Lex put both pairs of boots on a mat near the door. "What's going on, Martha? And where are the kids?"

"They're with Charlie at our place." Martha blinked the tears from her eyes and wiped her face with a handkerchief.

"What is it? What has you so upset?"

Martha shook her head and gestured toward the office. "You go on, honey. She's going to need you."

"I don't understand."

Martha gently brushed Lex away. "You will. Hurry."

Lex stared at her for a moment before she jogged down the hall. Her socked feet slid on the floor as she turned into the den.

Amanda looked up from behind the desk when Lex entered the office. "Hi."

"Hey, there. Mind if I join you? The kids are with their pawpaw."

"Sure." Amanda rose and twisted the office chair toward Lex, who obediently sat.

Amanda crawled onto her wife's lap and picked up the phone. She dialed the familiar number and pressed the speaker button. They were both surprised by the answering voice.

"Cauble residence," Lois answered. The formal, stilted voice caught Lex off guard. Lois had been married to Amanda's father, Michael, for many years, and was more of a mother figure to Amanda than her real mother had ever been.

"Hi, Lois. This is Amanda. Martha told me I needed to call. What's going on?"

Lois cleared her throat. "Hi, honey. Um, let me get your father, all right? I know he's been waiting to hear from you."

Amanda pulled the receiver away from her face and looked at it. "What on earth is going on?"

She glanced at Lex, who shrugged.

The sound of her father's voice brought her back to the reason she was calling. "Hey, Dad. What's going on?"

Michael sounded tired. "Hi, honey. Is Lex there with you?"

"Yes, she is. What's going on?"

Michael coughed, choked with emotion. "Sweetheart, it's about your grandfather. I...I'm not sure how to tell you this, but—"

"Is he sick?" Lex's arms tightened around Amanda. "Daddy?"

"No, baby, he's not sick." Michael's voice broke. "He's...gone."

There was a rustling as the phone was passed to Lois.

"No, that's not possible." Amanda shook her head. "We saw him yesterday and he was fine."

Lois sniffled. "I'm so sorry, honey. But your grandfather has passed on."

"I don't understand." Amanda handed the phone to Lex. "They're not making any sense."

"Hello?"

"Lexington, honey. I'm so sorry. But Jacob passed away a short time ago," Lois gently said.

"Oh, God." Lex used one arm to pull Amanda close again. "How is Gramma?"

"Numb, I think. Honey, I know the weather's dreadful, but—"

Lex cut her off. "We'll be there as soon as we can, Lois. Thanks for letting us know."

She hung up the phone and wrapped both arms around Amanda. "I'm so sorry, sweetheart."

"But we saw him yesterday," Amanda repeated. "He was okay."

"I know." Lex struggled to keep her emotions under control. Amanda needed her and that was the most important thing. She'd find time later, in private, to mourn.

Amanda stared into her eyes for a long moment. "Gramma's going to need us."

At Lex's nod, she fell forward and buried her face against Lex's neck.

LEX PARKED THEIR Ford Expedition in the Cauble's long, gravel driveway, behind an older model Cadillac sedan and a black Ford Explorer. She hurried around to assist Amanda from the SUV, keeping her arm around her waist as they waded across the yard through the snow.

As they trudged up the steps, the front door opened to reveal Michael, dressed in a pair of dark slacks and a red sweater. He opened his arms and embraced Amanda, who clung to him as if her life depended on it.

"Hey, Dad." Lex joined them and put her hand on Michael's shoulder. "I'm really sorry about Grandpa Jake."

"Thanks, Lex." He kept his arm around Amanda and led them into the house. "Lois is in the kitchen with Jeannie and Mom's resting upstairs."

He explained that his older daughter, Jeannie, had driven to the house as soon as he called her. Releasing Amanda momentarily, Michael awkwardly patted Lex on the arm. "I'm glad you're here, too."

Lex cleared her throat. "Where's Rodney?"

Jeannie's husband, Rodney Crews, ran a medical practice in town.

"He's finishing up at the clinic. The kids are at the Skimmerly's."

Amanda moved to give her father one more comforting embrace before she stepped back. "That's sweet of them."

Wanda Skimmerly had worked for Anna Leigh, and then Amanda, at Sunflower Realty before it closed. Wanda and Dirk's daughter,

Allison, was a few days older than Lex and Amanda's eldest child, Lorrie. The Skimmerly's youngest, Penny, was in their daughter Melanie's class. Amanda looked at the staircase. "I should check on Gramma."

"Do you want me to go up with you?" Michael asked.

"No, thank you. But maybe we could talk, later?" Amanda held her hand out to Lex, who immediately grasped it. "Will you be okay down here?"

Lex kissed the back of her hand. "Don't worry about me."

"I always will," Amanda whispered, cupping her wife's cheek. She pulled away as if finally realizing her father had witnessed their intimacy. "Um, I'll just head upstairs."

Michael studied Lex, as if noting the weariness in her features. "Cup of coffee?"

"Yeah, that would be good, thanks."

With a final glance toward Amanda's ascent, Lex followed him to the kitchen.

As they crossed the threshold, Lex felt her heart break at how miserable Jeannie appeared. Amanda's sister held a special place in Lex's heart, since she was Lorrie's birth mother. She was barely in the room before Jeannie rushed into her arms.

"I—can't—believe he's gone," Jeannie stammered as she clung to Lex.

"I know, sweetheart. Me, either." Lex made eye contact with Lois, who held Michael's hand. "Is there anything I can do?"

Michael scooted his chair nearer to his wife's. "Not that I can think of. Mom's still in shock. She, uh..." his voice broke. "She found him collapsed in his shop. Too late."

Jeannie stepped away from Lex and squeezed her hand. She wiped her eyes with the heel of one hand before she turned toward her father. "Do you think it would have mattered?"

"Not according to the paramedics. There was a gash on his head where he had fallen, but it barely bled."

He took a tissue from the box on the table and blew his nose. "They said it was likely a massive heart attack. Even if Dad had been in the hospital, they couldn't have helped him." Unable to continue, Michael stood. "Excuse me."

He escaped through the back door.

Lois scooted her chair away from the table but stopped when Lex raised her hand.

"Let me," Lex offered quietly. She squeezed Lois' shoulder before she followed Michael.

Even with the relative protection of the porch, the cold wind cut across Lex's face.

"Where did he..." She noticed footprints leading away from the porch to the backyard. "Damn." She tucked her hands in the front pockets of her jeans to keep them warm and stepped onto the snow.

Michael was across the yard, leaning against a large oak tree with his back to the house.

With another muttered curse, Lex trudged through the snow until she stood directly behind him. "Michael?"

When he didn't answer, she softened her voice. "Dad?"

"Go back to the house, Lex. I...I can't—"

"You don't have to say anything." She put her hand on his shoulder. "Look, I know I'm not the greatest conversationalist, but if you need to talk, I'm here."

He lowered his head. "This whole thing feels like some sort of terrible nightmare." Michael slowly turned and looked into Lex's face. "I'm at a loss, Lex. What are we supposed to do? When Mom called me, she sounded so damned casual, as if she needed me to run an errand for her. Not like my father had just died."

Unable to keep his composure, he put his hands in his pockets and coughed. "I don't want to believe it. And I feel like such a failure. I couldn't even go into his shop to see him. Now all I'll remember is a lump on a stretcher, hidden by a damned sheet!"

Lex tried to put her arm around him, but Michael angrily brushed it away. She swallowed hard from the hurt it caused. "No, Dad. You'll remember him like I will, laughing on Christmas Day as his great-grandchildren played hide-and-seek in the living room."

"I hope." His voice faded into the wind. It took a moment, but he seemed to be able to picture the scene. "Melanie did look silly, hiding beside the tree. And the squeal Eddie let out at 'finding' her, did tickle Dad." He grasped Lex's arm. "I'm sorry."

She shrugged. "It's okay. Why don't we go inside before we freeze? Amanda will have my hide if you get sick."

"Not to mention what would happen to you, right?"

Lex grunted, but didn't argue.

UPSTAIRS, AMANDA'S SENSES were on overload as she experienced the accustomed sights and smells as she walked the carpeted hallway. Her childhood summers had been spent in this house. She ran her finger along the small table that always held a lovely arrangement of flowers. Today, the silk wildflowers seemed faded in testament to the family's loss. The familiar aroma of vanilla tickled her nose. She was never certain where it came from, but it soothed her frazzled nerves.

At the end of the hall she stopped in front of the open door to her grandparent's room. She had been cuddled on Saturday mornings and comforted from bad dreams and protected from the real and imaginary monsters while in this room. She saw her grandmother, the woman whose strength always held the family together, curled up in the middle of the king-sized bed. She looked like a child.

Anna Leigh lay atop the covers with a patchwork quilt draped across her. She was wrapped around a pillow and appeared asleep, but her eyes opened when Amanda walked in. Without speaking a word, she held out a hand and beckoned Amanda inside.

Amanda rushed to the bed. She sat beside her grandmother and put her arm around her. Unable to express her grief in words, she found herself held as she broke down in Anna Leigh's embrace.

"Ssssh, dearest." Anna Leigh brushed her hand down Amanda's hair.

"This is so unreal. I can't wrap my mind around it, Gramma."

Anna Leigh kissed her head. "Neither can I."

She held Amanda close. "I keep expecting him to come in, covered in sawdust and varnish." Her voice turned wistful. "You were such a gift to him, Mandy. We missed so much of your sister's first years, and we were not about to make that mistake a second time. We flew out to Los Angeles the moment your mother went into labor. I remember, not hours after you were born, when Jacob held you. He was so smitten." She laughed lightly. "Those big, strong hands were so gentle."

"When," Amanda took in a shaky breath. "When I would stay here in the summer, I used to pray at night for you and Grandpa to be my parents."

"We would have loved that. Your visits brought such joy into our life." Anna Leigh sat up and wiped Amanda's cheeks with her fingertips. "Your mother was determined for you to have the best education, and she refused to believe that you could have received that here."

The bitter laugh from Amanda was loud in the dark room. "Right. Not to mention the fact that she wanted both her daughters under her thumb."

Anna Leigh touched her knee. "I'm sure it was her way of showing her love for you."

"Yeah, right. My mother only loved one thing, and that was herself."

There was a soft tap at the door. Lex stood in the hall, looking uncomfortable. "Uh, excuse me."

"Come in, Lexington." Anna Leigh patted the bed. "Join us, please."

"I didn't mean to intrude, but Reverend Hampton is downstairs to see you." Lex edged into the room, but remained standing. She cleared her throat. "I'm so terribly sorry for your loss."

Anna Leigh crooked a finger at her. "Lexington, come here."

Looking like a chastised child, Lex trudged to the bed. "Yes, ma'am?"

"The loss is all of ours." Anna Leigh held out her hands, which were immediately grasped. "Thank you for being here."

"No other place I'd be, Gramma."

Lex grunted in surprise as she was hauled onto the bed and pulled into a group hug.

SNOWFLAKES DAMPENED HER head as Martha navigated the concrete walk to her home. She smiled when she saw the salt sprinkled beneath her feet. "Looks like Charlie and the kids have been busy."

Her smile faded as she thought about the three children. "They'll be heartbroken when they hear about Jacob."

Once Martha reached her front porch, she shook the snow off her head and shoulders, and stepped inside. Before she could remove her coat, a small blur wrapped around her knees.

"Mada!" Eddie released his grip and patted her slacks. "Eww."

"I know, honey. Mada got wet walking home."

She hung her coat on the hook by the door then picked up the toddler. "Have you been a good boy for Pawpaw?"

He wriggled happily in her arms. "Good, Pawpaw."

Martha laughed at Eddie's enthusiasm. "Come on, cutie. Let's go see what folks are doing."

A loud snore greeted them as they crossed the threshold to the living room. Charlie was stretched out and sound asleep in his recliner. On the sofa beside him, Lorrie had her nose buried in a book, with small, wired headphones tucked into her ears. Her MP3 player was never far away. In fact, it was usually stowed in the back pocket of her jeans. It had taken her several months of saving her allowance, along with handling extra chores, to pay for the device. She appeared to ignore the world around her, as well as Martha's entrance.

Someone else noticed, though.

"Mada!" From her position on the floor in front of the television, Melanie rolled and got to her knees. "Did you know that alacapacas spit? And so do llamas?"

Lorrie looked up from her book and pulled one earpiece out. "Alpacas, dummy."

"That's what I said."

"Girls, no fighting. And Lorrie, don't call your sister names."

Martha placed Eddie on the floor beside his sister. "How long has Pawpaw been napping?"

The snores abruptly stopped with a snort and Charlie opened his eyes. "I wasn't asleep."

He sat up and closed the footstool of the recliner. "We were watching..."

He looked to Melanie. "What channel was that again?"

"Animal channel. We was learning about llamas and...," Melanie glared at Lorrie. "Alacapacas." She turned back to the television.

"Right." Charlie adjusted his glasses and cleared his throat.

"Everything okay?" he asked his wife.

Martha nodded and sat on the end of the sofa closest to him. "As okay as it can be." She sighed heavily when he held her hand. "I'm not sure what we can do to help."

"Mada!" Eddie waved his arms in the air in front of her.

Charlie stood and picked up Eddie. "How about we put some snacks together in the kitchen?"

Grateful that they could talk without their conversation being overheard, Martha nodded. She silently followed him to the kitchen.

"Yum!" Eddie celebrated being set in his high chair by slapping the plastic tray. "Yum!"

Martha handed him a toddler cookie as Charlie filled his bright green sippy cup with milk.

"Thank you, honey," she said. "Have the kids given you any trouble?"

He kissed her cheek before taking two coffee mugs from the cabinet. "Not at all. I don't think Lorrie's said more than a couple of words all afternoon. I know she suspects something is up, but she hasn't asked."

They doctored their coffee and sat at the table, one on each side of Eddie. "Before they left, Lex told me that they'd speak to the girls when they got home," Martha said. "But I don't know. Maybe it would be better if we told them."

"I don't think so. We shouldn't interfere."

Martha waved her hand. "Pshaw. You know as well as I do that the girls are going to be exhausted by the time they get home. We'd be doing them a favor."

Chapter Three

THE SNOW HAD stopped earlier, but visibility was still a problem due to the winds that swirled and kicked up what had already fallen. Lex struggled to see through the windshield since the headlights barely cut through the mess. They had stayed until after sunset, stuck until they could find the owners of the vehicle that had blocked them in.

"Maybe we should have spent the night." Amanda saw the white-knuckled grip her wife had on the steering wheel. "It's just that I really wanted to get home to the kids."

"I know what you mean. The house filled up pretty quick. And to tell you the truth, all those people were starting to get to me. Where did they come from?"

Amanda rubbed her temples in an attempt to alleviate her headache. "The Historical Society, the church and I think the Ladies Auxiliary. I didn't realize Somerville, Texas had that many people in it."

"Neither did I."

Lex cursed as the Expedition skidded toward the right side of the road. Although the snow-covered ditch appeared level, she knew the drop off was dangerous. "Damned black ice."

She carefully got the vehicle under control. "I was half-tempted to bring Gramma back with us. I think the good intentions of the town folks were beginning to get to her."

"I tried. She promised that she'd let Dad run everyone off if it got to be too much. But you know how she is."

"Polite to a fault."

"Mmm hmm."

Amanda breathed a sigh of relief as Lex turned onto the road to the ranch. It had been freshly graded and was much easier to navigate. "Looks like Roy's been busy."

"He called me earlier. Said Chet was out the door the moment the snow stopped."

Lex reached across the center console and took her wife's hand. "How are you holding up?"

Amanda wiped at her damp cheeks with her free hand. "I think I'm still in shock." She turned to Lex. "I keep having all these what-ifs go through my mind."

"What-ifs?"

"Yeah. What if we'd asked Grandpa and Gramma to spend an extra day with us at Christmas? What if he hadn't gone to work in his shop? Would he still be alive?"

Amanda ignored the tears that fell. They tracked down her cheeks to the collar of her sweater. "I can't even remember if I told him I loved him on Christmas."

Once they crossed the old bridge, Lex stopped the SUV. She unbuckled her seatbelt and exited, slipping a couple of times before she made it to the passenger side. She opened Amanda's door and pulled her crying wife into her arms.

"He knew you loved him." She whispered words of love and comfort, until a cold gust of wind blew snow into the vehicle.

"You're going to freeze." Amanda tugged at Lex's shirt. "Get back in here."

"Yes, ma'am."

Once they arrived at the ranch house, Lex turned to her. "Why don't you go inside while I run get the kids? No sense in both of us being out in the cold."

Amanda shook her head. "I'll go with you. I...I don't want to be alone."

"All right." Lex took her duster from the back seat of the SUV and put it on as she walked around to help Amanda. She grinned as Amanda kissed her hand. "Ready?"

"I think so." Amanda took a deep breath and got out.

Holding hands, they walked along the cleared driveway toward the two-bedroom house that Martha shared with Charlie. The guard light was on, causing the undisturbed snow around them to sparkle.

"It's so beautiful," Amanda commented quietly.

Lex turned her head so that she could see her. "Absolutely stunning."

"Well, it's pretty, but..." Amanda realized where Lex's eyes were. "Lex."

"I stand by my statement."

"You're biased."

"Not a bit."

Lex stopped and gave Amanda her full attention. "Would you like to know what I see when I look at you?"

Amanda blushed, but nodded.

Lex took off her gloves and cupped Amanda's face. "I see the most beautiful woman I've ever known, an answer to a prayer I never realized I made." She kissed her lightly on the lips. "You are the mother of my children and the reason my house is a home. And the one reason I wake up every morning and thank God I'm alive." Her next kiss was more involved, but just as gentle.

Once she could breathe again, Amanda said, "I spent our first couple of years trying to get you to say more than a word or two, and now you've turned into a poet."

"Nah, just stating the obvious."

Lex put her arm around her. They both turned their heads when the door to Martha's home opened.

Martha waved at them from her doorway. "I was beginning to wonder if you were going to come in or sit out there and moon at one another all evening."

Lex snorted, but didn't move her arm. "You're just jealous."

She stomped her boots on the porch to remove any excess. "How are the kids?"

"They've been little angels." Martha swatted Lex on the rear as they passed her.

"Ow! Are you sure you're talking about our kids?"

Martha ignored the snarky remark and hugged Amanda. "How are you doing, sweetie?"

Amanda closed her eyes and absorbed the love from the older woman. Her eyes burned from the tears brought on by the light kiss on her cheek. "I'm all right."

"Well, come on inside and get out of the cold." Martha kept her arm around Amanda as they moved down the short entry hall to the living room.

On the far wall, the gas fireplace flickered, sending shadows across the toddler stretched out asleep on the floor. The adjoining wall held a flat screen television, which played an animated movie. Across from the television, Charlie sat in the middle of the floral-patterned couch, a napping girl on each side. His head was tipped against the back of the sofa and his eyes were closed.

Lex stopped a few feet away. "I see their pawpaw is enjoying the movie almost as much as the kids," she whispered to Martha and Amanda.

"Hush." Martha poked Lex in the ribs. "Why don't you let them stay the night? I can see how exhausted you both are."

Amanda shook her head. "No. I mean, thanks, but—"

"It's okay, honey. I understand."

Martha watched as Lex knelt and scooped Eddie and his blanket in one movement. "He finally crashed about fifteen minutes ago, so he may be down for the night."

Lex kissed a small blemish on the toddler's forehead. "Took another tumble, little man?"

At fifteen months, he felt he had mastered walking and was impatient to explore the world around him. Unfortunately, his enthusiasm exceeded his agility.

"You'll find a matching one on Lorrie's chin. She tried to catch him and didn't quite get there."

Amanda sat beside Lorrie and brushed her hand across her head. "Hey, sweetie."

"Mom?" Lorrie blinked her eyes opened and yawned. She curled into Amanda and closed her eyes. "Is it morning?"

"No, honey. Let's go home so you can sleep in your own bed, all right?"

Amanda laughed as Lorrie mumbled into her shoulder.

Lex handed Eddie to Martha. "If you'll hold him for a minute, I'll wrestle with Melanie." Their seven-year old was almost impossible to wake once she fell asleep.

Charlie opened his eyes and looked around. "Uh, hi there." He straightened his glasses and sat up. "When did y'all get here?"

"A few minutes ago." Lex raised a limp Melanie into her arms. "Mel, sweetheart. You need to wake up."

"Mmm." Melanie put her arms around Lex's neck. "Don't wanna go to school."

The adults all laughed and Charlie stood. "Do you need any help getting them home?"

"No, we'll be fine." Amanda kissed Lorrie's head. "I'm afraid you're too big to carry, honey."

Lorrie opened her eyes and grinned. "Bet Momma could carry me."

Amanda pinched her lightly on the nose. "Only if she wants to get in trouble with me." Lex's back had healed from an injury the previous year but Amanda was still very protective of her.

"Ha!" Lorrie hopped off the couch and stood in front of Lex. "You're afraid of Mom."

"You betcha." Lex ruffled Lorrie's dark hair. "And if you're smart, you would be, too."

Amanda stood and wrapped Eddie in his blue flannel blanket. "Thank you, Mada."

"Sure thing, hon." Martha touched her lightly on the shoulder. "You let me know if there's anything I can do for you."

Unable to answer without breaking down, Amanda nodded.

Lorrie stared at her for a moment. "What's wrong?" She turned to Lex. "Momma?"

"We'll talk about it when we get home, all right?" Lex gave her what she hoped was a reassuring smile. "Can you gather up your brother's stuff for me?"

"Okay." Lorrie looked into her eyes, which Lex knew were red and swollen. "But—"

Lex shook her head. "I promise we'll talk about it when we get home."

"Yes, ma'am."

Doing as she was told, Lorrie quickly gathered the few toys that Eddie had scattered around the room. She tucked them in his blue-striped diaper bag and hefted it to her shoulder.

Martha handed Lorrie her coat. "Don't forget this."

Lorrie set the bag down and put on the coat. "Thanks."

"You're welcome, honey." Martha bent down and cupped Lorrie's cheek. "You're such a wonderful young woman, Lorrie. I'm so proud of you."

The girl blushed and tried to lower her head. Lorrie had recently turned eleven, and the accompanying hormones were confusing and hard to handle. She mumbled something incoherent and picked up the diaper bag.

Once the goodbyes were said, Lex and Amanda took their little family home.

Lorrie led the way while each adult carried a sleeping child. She held open the gate and had to fight off a very excited dog. Freckles danced around her, nipping at her jacket. She was smart enough to stay on the walkway, which someone had cleared.

"Freckles, no!" She cried and closed the gate after her parents passed. "Silly dog."

When Freckles barked, Melanie raised her head from Lex's shoulder. "Momma?"

"It's all right, sweetheart." Lex opened the door for Amanda and held it for Lorrie. "Let's get upstairs and into our pajamas."

Melanie kept a tight grip around her mother's neck. "Where were you today? Mada said you had business in town."

Lex set her down and stretched. "Yep. You're growing too fast for me. I don't think I can carry you around much longer."

"I'm getting big," Melanie agreed. "One of these days I'll be as tall as Lorrie." She yawned. "I'm sleepy."

"So am I, kiddo. Come on."

Lex turned her around and gave her a light pat on the rear. "Let's see who can get ready for bed first."

Melanie grinned, her earlier fatigue, gone. "I'll win!" She took off toward the stairs, her older sister on her heels. "Come on, Lorrie, hurry!"

With a long-suffering sigh, Lorrie glanced at the adults before she followed. "Yeah, yeah. Whatever. Let's go, Freckles." The dog barked and raced up the stairs beside them.

Lex held out her hands to Amanda. "My turn."

She kissed Eddie's head before she rested him against her shoulder. "You're getting big too, little man."

Amanda tucked her arm around Lex's waist as they followed at a more leisurely pace. "Are we going to survive their teen years?"

"Your guess is as good as mine."

Halfway up the stairs, Amanda stopped. "Do you think we should tell them tonight?"

"They're both old enough, especially Lorrie. But we might as well let them get a good night's sleep."

Amanda led them up to Eddie's room, which was across the hall from their own. She turned on the lamp beside his crib and adjusted the bedding. "We're going to have to convert this to a toddler bed pretty soon."

"Yeah. I'll try to get to it this week."

Lex put him on the changing table to give him a dry diaper. Eddie smacked his lips and stretched but didn't wake. "Think he'll be comfortable enough in this?" she asked her wife. The denim overalls were soft, as was the red undershirt covered in reindeer.

"I think so." Amanda tugged his matching red socks up as high as they would go. "Maybe these will actually last all night."

Lex snorted. "Yeah, right. He doesn't like socks any more than you do shoes. Good luck with that."

She carried Eddie to the crib and tucked him in. "Sleep well, buddy."

They stood at the crib and watched their son. Amanda leaned her head onto Lex's arm. "Grandpa was looking forward to teaching him how to build things." She rubbed her eyes. "I'm going to miss him so much."

"I know, love." Lex turned and held Amanda in her arms. "So will I."

They stood together quietly, each accepting the love and support the other offered.

Once she was able to get her emotions under control, Lex gently kissed her wife. "Let's go check on the girls."

"Good idea." Amanda kept close as they walked to the far end of the hall where the girls' rooms were located. "Too quiet."

Lex nodded and stopped at the first open door, which was to Melanie's room. "Aw, look at that."

Their youngest daughter had made it as far as her bed, but had fallen asleep dressed. She was stretched facedown across the foot of the twin bed, her most recent doll clutched in one hand.

"Plays until she drops," Amanda murmured, stepping into the room. "Do you want to check on Lorrie while I help her into her pajamas?"

"Sure." Lex stretched to lightly kissed Melanie's cheek. "Sleep well, Princess."

She passed through the bathroom the girls shared into Lorrie's room. Their oldest was sitting cross-legged on her full-sized bed, already in a pair of navy blue pajama pants and matching tank top. "I figured you'd be asleep, too."

Lorrie shrugged and lowered her eyes to the sports magazine in her lap. Her earbuds and MP3 player were beside her.

With a silent prayer to protect herself from her daughter's recently-arrived mood swings, Lex sat on the foot of the bed. "What's wrong, lil' bit?"

"Mom looks really sad." Lorrie closed the magazine and placed it on the floor beside her bed. "And you do, too."

Lex nodded. "That's true. It's been a pretty rough day."

"Are you..." Lorrie sat back against the wooden headboard and crossed her arms over her chest. "Are you and Mom getting a divorce?"

"What? No!" Lex held out her hand for Lorrie to take. "Whatever gave you that idea?"

Lorrie took her hand but kept her eyes on the gray and blue striped bedspread. "You were in town all day without us, and we didn't know why."

She started to cry.

"Mada and Pawpaw were talking secretly in the kitchen, and I heard them say something about telling us. My friend, Emily, said when her parent's started being all secretive, they were splitting up. She's hoping to live here with her mom, but her dad's being a butt about it."

Lex didn't bother calling Lorrie on her language. Instead, she tugged on their joined hands. "Come here."

Although their oldest swore she was too old to be babied, Lorrie quickly complied and crawled onto her lap. "I'm sorry we didn't tell you anything, sweetheart. But I promise you that your mom and I love one another more now than ever."

She made a quick decision. "Your mom got a call earlier today. It was about your Grandpa Jake. He, um, passed away this morning."

"What?" Lorrie looked up into Lex's sad eyes. "But he was fine on Christmas. Was he sick?"

"We don't really know, but we think it was his heart."

Lorrie rested her cheek on Lex's shoulder. "It's not fair." She began to cry anew.

Amanda came into the bedroom and sat beside them. With her arms around both Lex and Lorrie, she gave them what comfort she could.

HOURS LATER, WITH the house dark and quiet, Lex dozed on her back with Amanda snuggled against her side until a soft voice woke her. "Hmm?"

"Momma?" The voice was accompanied by a light touch to her cheek. "Are you awake?"

Lex opened her eyes. "Mel?"

She carefully moved Amanda and glanced at the clock. It was close to three in the morning. Always a heavy sleeper, her wife continued to sleep. "What's the matter?"

Melanie's eyes were large in the blue light from the alarm clock. "Lorrie's crying, but she won't let me come in."

"She's what?" Lex scooted to a sitting position. She swiped a hand across her face and rubbed her eyes.

"I had to go to the bathroom and I could hear her crying. But her door was closed and she told me to go away when I knocked." Melanie looked as if she was about to cry as well.

Lex opened her arms. "Come here, sweetheart." She pulled Melanie into her arms. "It's all right."

Amanda stirred and rolled over. "What's going on?"

"Mel heard Lorrie crying."

"Damn. I was afraid of that." Amanda rose and turned on the lamp beside her. "I'll go check on her." She put on her robe and finger-combed her hair. She gestured to Melanie. "Do you want to...explain?"

"Sure. Go ahead." Lex hugged Melanie as Amanda left the room. "Mel? Lorrie's sad, but she'll be okay, I promise."

Melanie looked up. "How come she's sad? Is she in trouble?"

"No, baby." Lex leaned against the headboard. "It's about your Grandpa Jake. He passed away today."

"He died?"

Unable to speak, Lex nodded.

"Then how come Lorrie's sad? Grandpa is in heaven, isn't he?"

"Umm, yeah. But she's sad because she'll miss him, honey. That makes you sad, doesn't it?"

Melanie thought for a moment. "Uh-huh. But it's good, too."

Now Lex was completely confused. "It is?"

"I remember when Grandpa Travis died, even if I was a little kid then." Melanie traced the scars on the back of Lex's hand. "I was worried that he'd be alone in heaven and wouldn't have anyone to play with."

The conversation made Lex's head spin. No matter how long she tried, she decided she'd never really quite understand the mind of a little girl. Especially this one. "And now he does, right?"

"Yeah. I know that Gramma will be sad, but we'll make her less sad. But now Grandpa Travis has his friend with him."

Lex hugged her daughter. "You're very smart, Melanie Leigh. I'm so proud of you."

AT THE END of the hall, Amanda knocked lightly on their eldest child's door. "Lorrie?" When she didn't get an answer, she opened the door and peeked inside. What she saw broke her heart.

Lorrie was curled beneath the covers of her bed. Her stuttering sobs were the only indication that she was awake.

Amanda walked to the bed and sat. She pulled the covers back far enough to see her daughter. "Oh, honey. Come here."

Lorrie placed her head onto her mother's lap and wrapped her arms around Amanda's waist. She cried so hard that she began to hyperventilate. "Wh...why did he...di...di...die?"

Trying to hold herself together, Amanda continued to stroke Lorrie's dark hair. "Sssh. It's going to be okay."

"B...b...but..."

"Honey, slow down and try to breathe."

Amanda tugged on Lorrie's arms and helped her sit up. She continued to hold her, but now Lorrie was against her chest. "That's it. Slow breaths, in and out."

Lorrie coughed, gasped and finally inhaled deeply. When she felt her mother wipe her face with a tissue, she took it and blew her nose. "T...th...thanks."

She was able to release a shaky breath and wipe her eyes. "Why does it hurt so much? I didn't feel like this with Grandpa Travis and he lived with us."

"We can't control how we feel, honey. There's no right way or wrong way to grieve." Amanda wiped her own cheeks free of moisture. It broke her heart to see Lorrie so upset. "But part of the hurt could be from you growing up. Remember that talk we had a few months ago?"

"Uh-huh. Is that why I cry at stupid things?"

"It's part of it. But don't worry, things will get better, I promise."

Lorrie didn't look too convinced. "If you say so."

"I do."

"Mom?"

"Yes?" Amanda brushed the hair away from Lorrie's face. "What is it?"

"Can I, umm," Lorrie looked down, unable to meet her mother's gaze. She wanted to be independent, but desperately needed comforting, too. "Can I sleep with you and Momma? Just for tonight?"

Amanda hugged her. "Of course you can. You never have to doubt that, honey." She slid off the bed. "Come on. I have a feeling we're going to have a full bed."

FOR ANNA LEIGH, it was the end of a very long day. She sighed and leaned against the closed door, relieved to have finally gotten rid of the solicitous Reverend Hampton. At the sound of the raised voices coming from the kitchen, she pushed away from the front door.

On her way to the kitchen, Anna Leigh felt torn. As much as she wanted privacy to grieve, another part of her was frightened of being alone after almost sixty years of marriage. She closed her eyes as she approached the doorway. She could hear Michael arguing with Jeannie.

"No, Jeannie. She's my responsibility."

Jeannie's voice quivered as she tried to keep from crying. "Daddy, stop. You can't just run roughshod over everyone. I think she'd be better off at our house."

Anna Leigh stepped into the kitchen, causing the conversation to come to a halt. "I don't suppose I have any say in what I do?"

Michael stood from the table and took his coffee cup to the sink. "Of course you do, Mom. We were just—"

"Making my decisions for me." Anna Leigh stopped at the table where Jeannie, Rodney and Lois sat. She rested her hand on her granddaughter's shoulder. "I appreciate everything you've done today, truly. But I would really like some time to myself."

Rodney moved away from the table and kissed Anna Leigh on the cheek. "That's the politest get-the-hell-out I've ever heard. Our offer stands, though. If you need or want company, give me a call."

"Thank you." She hugged him, then Jeannie. She touched her granddaughter's cheek after they pulled apart. "I'll be fine."

"Would it be all right if I came to see you in the morning?"

Anna Leigh nodded. "Of course. But only if the roads are clear. I don't want you to risk it, otherwise."

Rodney put his arm around Jeannie. "Don't worry. My SUV can wade through just about anything, and I can drop her off on my way to the office." He stopped. "If that's okay."

"Certainly."

Michael put his clean mug on the dish drainer beside the sink. "Mom, I really don't think you need to be alone at a time like this. Everyone in town now knows about Dad, and you have no way to protect—"

Lois had been quiet long enough. "Michael, stop."

She gave her mother-in-law an apologetic glance, before getting to her feet. "We're going home."

When Michael opened his mouth to argue, she held up her hand to silence him. "Now."

His face reddened. "Hold on, I'm—"

Anna Leigh cut him off. "Lois is right. It's time for you to go home, dearest." She softened her voice. "I appreciate your concern. But please give me this time."

Michael lowered his head. "Of course. I'm sorry." As the others left the kitchen, he stopped and put his arms around his mother. "I...I don't know what to say, Mom. I never thought this day would come so soon." His voice cracked on the last word.

"Nor did I, darling." Anna Leigh buried her face against his chest.

ONCE HER FAMILY left, Anna Leigh trudged up the stairs. The silence covered her like a heavy fog. She stopped at the door to the bedroom she had shared with Jacob. Someone had straightened the floral comforter and folded the quilt she had covered herself with earlier.

She stepped across the room to the adjoining bathroom. Stacked neatly on one side of the dual sinks were five mini-towers of pennies. They were next to a half-empty bottle of aftershave, a deodorant stick and a short, plastic black comb. Anna Leigh opened a drawer and removed a paper tube.

"He probably forgot to roll these, with all the excitement of Christmas," she muttered as she expertly placed the pennies in the tube. The bottom of the tube opened and pennies spilled across the counter.

"Damn it!" Anna Leigh threw the remaining pennies, along with the roll, against the wall. When the curse tumbled from her mouth, she immediately covered her lips with a shaking hand. "Oh, Jacob." She cried as she took a navy, cotton bathrobe from a nearby hook. "I don't think I can survive without you." She wrapped herself in the robe and stumbled from the room.

She went to his side of the bed, not bothering to turn down the blanket. Fully clothed and covered with his heavy robe, she curled against Jacob's pillow and sobbed.

Chapter Four

THE PRESSURE AGAINST her ribcage woke Amanda. For a long moment, she thought she was dreaming about being pregnant, until she realized the nudge came from outside her body. She slowly opened her eyes and had to cover her mouth to keep from giggling and waking everyone.

At some point during the night, Lex had brought Eddie to bed with them. He was lying with his face on Lex's chest, a puddle of drool making her blue T-shirt stick to her body. The overalls he had worn to bed were missing, as was one of his socks. His feet were tucked against Amanda and he had a handful of Lorrie's hair.

Lorrie was curled in a ball with her head against Lex's belly while Melanie lay on her stomach, draped on the lower part of Lex's legs.

Another nudge to her ribs made Amanda roll off the bed and hurry to the bathroom. When she returned, Melanie sat up. She opened her mouth, but Amanda softly shushed her and helped her from the bed. "Let's get your robe and slippers, okay?"

"'Kay." Half-asleep, Melanie took Amanda's hand.

In her room, Melanie found her bright pink robe at the foot of her bed. She pulled it on and looked around for her slippers, but didn't see them. "Mommy, I don't know where my slippers are."

Amanda had her back to her daughter. A handmade, wooden box on Melanie's art table caught her eye. She picked it up carefully, as a sad smile touched her lips at the elegantly carved initials on the lid. "Oh, Grandpa."

She felt a tug on her nightgown and turned to see Melanie looking up at her.

"Are you still sad about Grandpa?"

"Yes, I am." Amanda moved to the bed and sat at the foot.

"Are you always gonna be sad?" Melanie climbed up beside her mom. "I'm gonna miss Grandpa." She snuggled closer when Amanda's arm went around her shoulders.

"I know, sweetie. I will, too." Amanda kissed the top of her head. "And, yes, in a way I'll always be sad that he's gone. But he'll be in my heart forever."

Melanie looked up and saw the tears in her mother's eyes. "Will I be in your heart, too?"

The question was so innocent and sincere that Amanda's laugh came out as a half-sob. "Oh, honey. Of course you will."

She hugged Melanie and rocked her.

"MOMMA."

SMALL HANDS squeezed Lex's cheeks and caused her to open her eyes. The close proximity of Eddie's face startled her. "Huh?"

"Momma." Eddie giggled and lightly clapped her face. "Momma!"

Lex groaned and sat up. She and Eddie were the only ones left on the bed, and from the odor that emanated from him, they had been alone for quite some time. "Whoa, buddy. That can't be comfortable. Let's get you cleaned up."

"Uck."

"Come on." Lex stood and picked him up, frowning at the horrid smell. "What did Mada feed you yesterday?" she asked, as she crossed the hall to his room.

"Mada yum."

Lex placed him on the changing table, and went about taking care of his diaper. "You know, you're looking a lot like your Uncle Hubert."

He giggled and reached for her hands as she fastened his clean diaper.

"And don't tell anyone I said this, but I miss him."

During the past year, Lex and her brother, Hubert, had become very close, especially after he and Ramona were married and moved into a house in Somerville. Not long after Halloween, Ramona's father had suffered a stroke, and Hubert went to Oklahoma to help his wife take care of her father's business.

"I think I'll give him a call sometime today."

Although it was pretty much one-sided, Lex enjoyed the conversation with her son. Once Eddie was clean and covered, she raised him above her head. "One of these days, you're gonna be too big for me to do this, kiddo."

Eddie laughed and cheered as he was flown around the room. His cheers stopped when Lex lowered him to the floor. "No! More, Momma!"

"Sorry, but the airport is closed on account of it being old and out of breath." Lex coughed and cleared her throat. "Why don't we go see what we can scrounge up for breakfast? How does that sound?"

"Yum!" Eddie danced in place and clapped. "Momma, go!"

She groaned and lifted him up to her hip. "Yeah, yeah. I'm just your packhorse, aren't I?"

"Go!"

"All right, your highness." Lex carried him from the room and headed downstairs.

Halfway down, Eddie heard voices in the kitchen and began to wriggle in Lex's arms. "Mommy!" He pointed toward the kitchen.

Lex tightened her grip. "Settle down, son. We'll get there soon enough."

She grinned at Amanda, who met them at the doorway to the kitchen. "I think you've been summoned."

"Mommy, Mommy, Mommy!"

Amanda held out her hands and grunted as he lunged. "Whoa!" She smothered Eddie's face with kisses. "Did you have a good sleep, honey?"

She turned her attention to Lex. "I was just on my way to check on you."

"Your timing could use some work." Lex kissed her on the cheek. "I already changed his diaper."

She walked into the kitchen, which was empty. "Where are the girls?"

"Lorrie's in her room, as usual." Amanda sat at the table and watched her wife pour two cups of coffee as she settled Eddie in his high chair. "Mel's next door. They're making a big batch of breakfast burritos to take to town. Martha's afraid it's going to be a madhouse at Gramma's today."

Eddie slapped at the tray. "Mommy, Mommy, Mommy."

"What do you want for breakfast? Hmm?" Amanda asked, as Eddie smacked his lips. "Oatmeal and fruit?"

"Yum."

Lex took the requested items from the refrigerator.

"How are you holding up?" she asked her wife gently as she made their son's breakfast. Barred from the kitchen in her younger days, Lex had now gained enough skills to take care of the kids' needs.

"I think I'm still in shock. I mean, I know he wasn't going to be around forever, but to lose him like this is just..." Amanda took the bowl from Lex and placed it in front of Eddie. "Unreal."

"Yeah, I know." Lex stood beside her chair and rested her hand on Amanda's shoulder. "I wish there was more I could do for you."

She cringed as Eddie dug into the bowl with gusto. In only seconds, he was covered with the sticky substance and enjoying every minute of it.

Amanda leaned against her. "You're doing it. Would you mind keeping an eye on him, while I check on Lorrie?"

"Let me go upstairs. You're looking a bit ragged."

"I'd argue with you, but you're right. Thanks."

"Sure thing, sweetheart."

Eddie waved his spoon around. "Momma!"

Laughing, Lex carefully bent to kiss the only clean spot she could reach on him: the top of his head. "Be good for Mommy, kiddo."

"Ha! Yum."

AT THE KNOCK on her door, Lorrie turned around in her desk chair. "Go away, Mel. I mean it!"

"I'm not Mel." Lex's voice was quiet, but firm.

"Crap." Lorrie placed her spiral notebook in the top drawer of her desk and quickly slammed it closed. "Come in."

Lex stepped into the room and stood not far from Lorrie. "How are you doing, kiddo?"

Lorrie shrugged and turned around to stare out the window.

Another step and Lex stood directly behind her. She laid her hand on Lorrie's shoulder and waited quietly.

It took several minutes, but Lorrie was the first to break the silence. "This sucks."

"Yeah, it does."

"Everybody dies, though."

"Yep."

Turning around, Lorrie looked up at Lex. "I don't want you or Mom to die."

"Sweetheart." Lex dropped to one knee beside her chair. "We don't plan on dying anytime soon."

Lorrie frowned at her. "Neither did Grandpa." She released a heavy sigh. "Do I have to go to the funeral?"

"Um, well. No, I guess not. Why?"

"'Cause it's gonna take forever and be boring." Lorrie started to turn her chair back around, but was stopped by Lex. "What?"

"Get your boots and jacket on. We're going to check the horses."

"I don't want—"

Lex stood. "I didn't ask what you wanted." She walked toward the door. "Meet me downstairs in five minutes."

The callous attitude of her daughter made Lex so angry that she needed time to cool down. The barn had always been a place of comfort for her and the repetitive brushing of the horses had a soothing effect. She'd need something to do in order not to lose her temper.

Once her mother left, Lorrie stuck out her tongue at the closed door. "Stupid horses."

FIVE MINUTES LATER, Lex was dressed and waiting by the back door with Amanda as Eddie kept them entertained. One of his new favorite pastimes was to race down the hall and hit the front door with the palms of his hands. Then he'd laugh, turn around, and run the other direction.

Several heavy thumps from upstairs caused Lex to grind her teeth together. "I ought to go up there and—"

"Hold on." Amanda kept a firm grip on her wife's arm. "This is a rough time for her, honey."

"It's hard for everyone. But she seems to be the only one who's being a pain in the ass about everything."

"Lex—"

Lorrie charged down the stairs and almost ran down Eddie, who let out a loud wail. She caught him by his arm to keep him from falling. "Sorry, Eddie."

His cry quickly stopped. "Leelee!"

"Yeah, yeah." Although Lorrie tried to keep up her air of indifference, she couldn't resist the gleeful plea from her little brother. She picked him up and rested him against one hip before joining her parents. "I'm ready."

Lex put on her jacket and took Lorrie's from its hook. "Don't act like I'm throwing you in front of a firing squad, Lorrie. I just thought you'd like to get out of the house for a little while."

"Yeah, sure." Lorrie handed Eddie to Amanda. She slipped her jacket on and zipped it. "Bye." With her head down, she left the house before Lex.

Amanda whispered to her wife, so that she wouldn't be overheard. "Good luck."

Lex shook her head. "Thanks a lot. Next time, you get to do the heart-to-heart."

Amanda grinned and waved Eddie's hand at her. "Bye, Momma. Have fun."

Grumbling under her breath, Lex stepped onto the porch and closed the door behind her. "Smartass."

She watched Lorrie kick snow along the walk to the gate. The temperature was supposed to stay above freezing in the coming days, for which Lex was grateful. The snow was already melting on the roads, but the fields were still a mess and she didn't envy Roy's task of feeding the herd. She moved quickly to catch up. "Hold on."

Lorrie opened the gate. "Where's Freckles?"

"Probably with your sister at Martha's. They both enjoy the goodies there."

"I guess so." Lorrie moved ahead. She was in such a hurry to get away from Lex, she didn't notice an icy patch and started to fall.

Lex caught her by the back of her jacket and kept her upright. "Are you okay?"

"I'm fine." Red-faced, Lorrie straightened her coat and went into the barn. Once inside, she stopped at the stall of her horse, Mine. "Hey."

The mare nickered and stretched her nose across the top of the stall, receiving the expected scratch. She butted Lorrie's hand, bringing a smile to the girl's face.

Lex removed her jacket and dropped it on a bale of hay. "I think she's missed you."

Lorrie turned and bit off a smart aleck remark. "Yeah, school's been kinda tough, lately."

"A lot of things have, haven't they?" Lex stood beside Lorrie. She placed a cautious hand on Lorrie's arm, silently relieved when it wasn't brushed away. "You know you can always come to us when you have a problem, right?"

"Yeah."

Lex cleared her throat. "About earlier. Up in your room." She blew out a heavy breath. "Do you understand why I got upset?"

Lorrie shrugged. "I guess."

"Lorrie, look at me." Once she had her daughter's full attention, Lex moved her hand away. "What you said about the funeral was very disrespectful. If you don't want to go because it upsets you, fine. But not wanting to go because you think you'll be bored..." Lex stopped in order to get her anger under control. "That's not only rude, it's bullshit."

"But, I didn't mean—"

"No!" Lex lowered her voice. "Don't try that with me. Take responsibility for what you said."

Lorrie stepped away from the stall. With her hands in the pockets of her jacket, she looked like a frightened little girl, not the surly youth she had been earlier. "All right. I didn't really mean it. I'm sorry, Momma. I'll go."

Her face fell and her lower lip trembled. "I don't know why I said that. Do you hate me?"

Lex moved quickly, and soon held Lorrie in her arms. "No, sweetheart. I could never hate you. I may be upset at times, but only with your behavior. Never with you."

THE SMALL KITCHEN at Martha and Charlie's cottage was a beehive of activity. Charlie individually wrapped breakfast burritos in parchment as Martha supervised the filling being prepared by their granddaughter.

Martha praised the girl. "Perfect, Melanie. You're going to be a wonderful cook."

"I'm really good." Melanie accidentally dropped a spoonful of the egg and bacon mixture on the floor. "Oops."

She giggled when Freckles immediately lapped up the mess. "Good dog."

Charlie laughed at his wife's expression. "Sure beats using a broom, doesn't it?"

"Don't encourage them." Martha gestured toward the sheet cake carrier that her husband had filled with the food. "Do you think that will be enough?"

"Honey, we're not feeding the entire state. Just any folks that stop by Anna Leigh's."

Melanie stopped what she was doing. "We're going to Gramma's? Is she having a party?"

Martha took the bowl from her and placed it in the sink. "No, sweetie. It's not a party. But a lot of folks will probably stop by to see her today."

"Oh." Melanie hopped off the chair she had been standing on. "Because Grandpa died?"

"That's right." After she ran water into the bowl, Martha started washing the dishes in the sink as Melanie peeped around her.

"How come you don't have a dishwasher like we do? Mommy says it works better than Momma." Melanie dropped her serving spoon into the water.

Martha laughed. "Because Pawpaw and I don't dirty up enough dishes to make it worthwhile."

Melanie frowned as she noticed all the pots and bowls by the sink. "This is more than we have when Mommy makes breakfast."

"I'm betting she doesn't make as much as we did this morning, does she?" Martha handed a wet bowl to Charlie, who dried it with a dishtowel.

"No. But Momma can make a mess. Last week, she was busy with Eddie and my oatmeal bubbled over and got all in the microwave. We was trying to let Mommy sleep late 'cause she had a tummy ache." Melanie got a case of the giggles, remembering the mess. "But she heard Momma's cussin' and came downstairs anyhow."

Charlie almost dropped the bowl he was drying as he laughed. "Was your momma in trouble?"

"Uh huh. They was so busy talkin' about the mess that they didn't see Eddie smear his applesauce in his hair. It stuck straight up and looked like boogers."

"Good lord." Martha laughed so hard she had to hold onto the counter to keep from falling.

Chapter Five

"ARE YOU SURE you don't mind?" Amanda asked, for the third time in as many minutes.

Helen rested Eddie on her hip and kissed his cheek. "Are you kidding? I love any excuse to play with this guy."

He giggled as she gave him butterfly kisses. "Isn't that right?"

"Go!"

"Okay, okay." Amanda allowed Lex to help her into her coat. "I don't blame the kids for wanting to stay home." She turned and smiled at her wife. "Thanks."

"Anytime." Lex draped her own coat on her arm. "I guess I'll have to pay Shelby and Roy double for spending the day with the girls. Although why Mel has decided she wants to become a cowgirl is beyond me. Last week, she was going to be a princess."

"Why can't she be both?" Helen laughed at the look on Lex's face. "Oh, come on, Lex. She could be a rodeo queen."

"Lord, help me." Lex turned to Amanda. "We should pick up Charlie and Martha and head on into town, sweetheart."

Amanda opened the back door. "Thanks again, Helen. We'll call you if we're going to be too late."

"Don't worry about a thing, hon. You just take care of yourself, and your grandmother." She squeezed Amanda's arm. "And let me know if you need anything else."

Unable to answer due to the lump that had grown in her throat, Amanda could only nod before she headed down the steps. Lex watched her until she got into the passenger's side of the Expedition, then turned to Helen. "We really do appreciate your help."

She kissed Eddie's fingers as they came close to her face. "Be good for Aunt Helen."

"Good." Eddie waved his fingers and giggled.

"Why don't I believe you?" Lex asked as she tickled his belly. "His newest thing is trying to ride poor Freckles like a horse, which is why she's hiding upstairs. Anyway, give me a call on my cell if you need anything."

"We'll be fine. Give my best to Mrs. Cauble. I can't even begin to imagine what she's going through."

"I will, thanks."

WITH THE ROADS relatively clear, it didn't take long to make the trip into Somerville. The silence inside the large SUV was oppressive. Lex took her eyes from the road long enough to glance at her wife, who had a slight frown on her face. "Dollar for your thoughts?"

Amanda blinked and shook her head. She stared into her lap at the tissue she had shredded. "Not worth it."

"Of course they are." Lex checked the rear-view mirror, satisfied that Martha and Charlie were busy with their own conversation. She held out her hand until Amanda grasped it. "As the mother of my children and the head of our household, you're worth everything to me."

She brought their hands up and kissed Amanda's knuckles. "And as the love of my life, your worth is beyond value."

The small laugh she received caused her to smile.

"Head of the house, huh?"

"Yep." Pleased with herself, Lex returned her attention to the road, but kept her hold on Amanda's hand.

Amanda looked at the strong hand that held hers. It was covered in a sprinkling of scars, attesting to the hard work that Lex had done her entire life. But to Amanda, beauty laid in those nicks that dotted the tan surface. She rubbed her thumb across the back of Lex's hand. "You're something else, you know that?"

"So I've been told." Lex glanced in the mirror as Martha let out an unladylike snort. "No comments from the back."

"I wouldn't dream of it." Martha pointed her finger. "Don't you be giving me that look, Lexie."

"What look?"

Martha leaned forward and lightly thumped the back of her head. "You know exactly what look."

"Ow!"

Charlie wisely kept silent, except for the light snicker that escaped. When his wife glared at him, he shrugged and turned to look out the window.

There was little traffic on the streets as they drove through Somerville, as most people were enjoying sleeping in after the holiday. Lex parked behind Anna Leigh's Cadillac and turned off the engine. She released her grip on the steering wheel and flexed her fingers.

Charlie and Martha gathered their things and got out. They clung to one another as they navigated the cleared walk toward the house.

Lex made it around the SUV and stood at Amanda's door. Her wife hadn't moved, so she opened the door. "Amanda?"

Amanda shook her head and continued to stare directly ahead.

"Sweetheart." Lex removed her gloves and touched Amanda's arm. "We need to get inside."

Amanda jerked her arm away and hugged herself. "I can't."

At a loss, Lex stood by silently. She tucked her gloves into the pocket of her slacks. "All right. Would you like me to take you home?"

"I don't know." Amanda lowered her face and covered it with her hands.

"Lexie? Are y'all coming?" Martha asked from the front porch.

Not taking her eyes from Amanda, Lex waved. "Go on without us."

She didn't know if they heard her, and didn't care. All of her thoughts were on the woman inside the SUV. She gentled her voice. "Amanda."

When she didn't get an answer, she carefully closed the door and returned to the other side. She pulled out her gloves and tossed them on the dash. She watched her wife for a clue as to what to say.

Amanda turned when Lex sat inside and closed the door. "I'm sorry."

"Hey." Lex held out her hand and relaxed when Amanda gripped it. "Talk to me, sweetheart."

Holding their linked hands to her chest, Amanda closed her eyes. "I don't think I can go in there."

"All right. What would you like to do?"

Amanda raised her head and looked at her. "Just like that?"

"Yep."

They were quiet for a minute, until Amanda sighed. "I love Gramma."

Lex gave a small nod, but kept silent.

"But I don't think I can go into that house. It seems empty and sad, and I don't know if I can face that." She lowered her head again. "Or her."

Lex glared at the console between them before making her decision. She was soon out of the vehicle and around to Amanda's side, opening the door. She released her wife's seat belt and pulled her gently into her arms. "I'm sorry, sweetheart."

She lightly stroked her hair and continued to murmur simple words of love.

Amanda cried harder as she clung to Lex. The knowledge that she'd never see her grandfather again hit her all at once, pushing through the careful barriers she had constructed to make it through the previous day.

It took a while, but Amanda was finally able to get herself under control. She took the handkerchief Lex gave her and wiped her face. "Thanks."

Lex brushed her fingertips along Amanda's cheek. "Wish I could do more."

"You are." Amanda cleared her throat and kissed Lex's chin. "I think I can go in, now."

"Are you sure? Because I'll do whatever you want, take you wherever you want to go."

Amanda smiled and patted her on the chest. "I'll be okay. But I wouldn't complain if you stayed close today."

"You got it."

Lex held the door open for her and kept a firm grip on her hand.

BY NOON, AMANDA wanted to find a place to hide. The good intentions of the people of Somerville were making her nerves raw. She had tried to protect her grandmother from the onslaught by having Lex take her upstairs, only to be cornered in the kitchen by a bevy of women from the Ladies Auxiliary.

"Amanda, dear. We think it's wonderful, how you're here for Anna Leigh," one of the women prattled in a loud whisper. The seventy-eight year old's horribly dyed, coal-black hair looked comical against her pale, wrinkled face. "I was just telling Nena this morning how lucky Anna was, having such a good family."

The well-meaning women landed on Amanda's last nerve. "Thank you, Mrs. Russell. If you'll excuse me, I need to—"

"Maude said that you're pregnant again. Is that true?" Mrs. Russell asked.

"What? No!" Amanda couldn't understand where they got their ideas. "Do I look pregnant?"

She bit her tongue to keep from going off on them. "I need to go check on my grandmother, ladies. Excuse me. Thank you all for coming."

Amanda pushed by them.

As she rushed from the kitchen, she muttered, "Snow and ice on the roads, and yet they still come in droves." She was so intent on her escape that she almost bowled down her sister.

"Hey, watch out." Jeannie stopped Amanda in the hall. "Where are you headed in such a hurry?"

"Anywhere but in there. Nosy old biddies."

Jeannie made a face and tried not to laugh. "Ouch. Cornered you, did they?"

"Yeah." Amanda brushed her hair away from her eyes. "Do you think we'd get into too much trouble if we just started kicking people out?"

"It's tempting, isn't it?" Jeannie locked arms with her sister and turned away from the kitchen. "Have you seen Gramma?"

Amanda led her toward the stairs. "I asked Lex to take her upstairs about fifteen minutes ago. Let's go check on her."

"Good idea."

As they ascended the steps, Jeannie spoke. "When I saw you coming out of the kitchen alone, I wondered what could separate you two. You looked joined at the hip this morning."

Before her sister could say anything, she hurriedly continued. "That's not a bad thing, Mandy. I'm glad you have her to watch out for you."

"Thanks."

Jeannie sighed. "You're really lucky, you know. We hadn't been here half an hour, before Rodney took off to the clinic."

They stopped at the top of the landing. "It's so much quieter up here," she added.

"Yeah." Amanda took a deep breath and released it slowly. She turned to her sister. "Do I look pregnant to you?"

"What?"

Amanda shook her head. "Never mind."

"No, wait." Jeannie grabbed her arm. "What are you talking about? You aren't, are you?"

"Of course not! Good grief, do I look insane to you?"

Jeannie laughed. "No kidding. But seriously, why did you ask me that?"

"One of the women in the kitchen said something, that's all."

"Oh. Well, no. You don't look pregnant." Jeannie pulled at Amanda's blouse, which fit snugly against her slender form. "Where would you put a baby, anyway? In your shoe?"

Down the hall, Lex stepped out of one of the rooms and closed the door behind her. "What are y'all doing?"

The sisters looked at one another and then back to Lex. Jeannie was the first to find her voice. "We were just talking about you knocking up Mandy, again."

Lex stumbled as she walked toward them. She braced her hand against the wall and leaned into it. "Excuse me?"

When her wife hurried to her aid, Lex straightened and put her arm around Amanda's shoulder. "Is there something you forgot to tell me?"

"No, my sister is just being her usual, bratty self." Amanda lightly patted Lex's stomach. "How's Gramma?"

"Finally resting. I was able to talk her into taking one of the sedatives her doctor prescribed."

Jeannie joined them. "How did you manage to do that? Daddy fought with her for hours about it."

"I just asked her if she thought getting some rest would be a good idea."

Amanda shook her head. "That's it?"

"Well, I may have mentioned how stressed you were, and that if she were upstairs resting, I could probably talk you into doing the same."

"Very sneaky." Jeannie turned to Amanda. "Why don't y'all relax in the back guest room, and I'll get Martha and Lois help me clear this place out. These people are just sitting around gossiping, anyway."

Lex cleared her throat. "How 'bout it, sweetheart? Wanna stretch out with me for a bit?"

"That sounds great." Amanda tugged on Lex's belt loop and led her down the hall.

THE RANCH HOUSE was quiet that evening, as the tired family went to bed earlier than usual. The girls picked up on their parent's melancholy and were quiet throughout dinner. Once they were excused, they went upstairs and spent the rest of the evening in their rooms.

Not long after midnight, a high-pitched wail startled Lex out of a sound sleep. She quickly sat up and glanced at Amanda, who rolled and opened her eyes. "Did you hear—"

"Momma!" Melanie ran into their bedroom and darted onto the bed. She climbed into Lex's arms. "Lorrie screamed and scared me!"

Amanda quickly flipped the covers away and stood. "I'll go check on her."

"See? Lorrie's gonna be fine." Lex held the frightened little girl close and kissed the side of her head.

"Can I stay in here with you? Please?"

Lex turned and placed Melanie in the middle of the bed and covered her. "Yep."

She brushed the blonde curls away from her daughter's eyes. The older Melanie became, the more she looked like Amanda. And Lex had a hard time telling her no. "Close your eyes, sweetheart. Everything's all right." She continued to comb Melanie's hair with her fingers.

Down the hall, Amanda quietly opened the door to Lorrie's room. "Lorrie?"

Thanks to the glow from the night-light in the adjoining bathroom, she could make out Lorrie's thrashing form beneath her blankets. Amanda crossed the room and pulled the covers back. "Lorrie?"

Lorrie cried out, opening her eyes when she felt Amanda's touch on her shoulder. "No!"

"Shhh. It's okay, sweetie. You're all right." Amanda sat on the edge of the bed and continued to talk softly. "Wake up, honey. Everything's all right."

Lorrie blinked and rubbed her eyes before she sat up. "Mommy?"

"I'm right here. You were having a bad dream." Amanda rubbed Lorrie's back, which was damp from sweat. "Do you want to talk about it?"

Leaning into the touch, Lorrie took a trembling breath. "It was scary."

Amanda used her free hand to turn on the lamp beside the bed, bathing the room in light. "How's that?"

"Better." Lorrie's eyes closed and she started to sway.

"Why don't you lie back down, sweetie?" Amanda helped her get more comfortable. "That's it."

Lorrie opened her eyes. "You and Momma are okay, right?"

"We're both fine. Was that what your dream was about?"

"I kept looking for you, and everyone told me you were dead." Lorrie wiped her face with her hands. "It seemed so real."

"I'm sorry you had a bad dream, honey. But, I promise we're okay." Amanda leaned down and kissed her forehead. "Do you think you can sleep, now?"

"I think so." A yawn punctuated Lorrie's answer. "Love you, Mom."

Amanda lightly stroked her cheek. "I love you, too."

She adjusted the covers and sat quietly until she was certain Lorrie was asleep. Beneath the bed, she heard the sound of claws on the wood floor. Amanda dropped to her knees beside the bed and coaxed the frightened dog out.

"Come on, Freckles." She scratched the rat terrier's head and then patted the blanket. "Hop up and keep her company."

Freckles sprang onto the bed in one quick move. She circled twice beside Lorrie's hip before settling against her.

"That's a good girl." Amanda gave her one final head scratch and stood.

Usually Freckles slept in a cushy dog bed in the corner of the room, but Amanda decided that Lorrie's peace of mind was more important than worrying about a dog-scented quilt. She stopped at the doorway and turned, hoping that Lorrie would be able to sleep peacefully for the rest of the night.

Chapter Six

ONCE THE TEMPERATURE rose above freezing and melted the snow, it seemed as if the entire town of Somerville had come to pay their respects to Jacob Cauble. There were no seats available in the large Methodist Church, and many were left standing against the back wall. After the service was complete, they began to gather in small groups as a line formed to speak to the family.

Amanda stood beside her grandmother at the front of the church and greeted the well-wishers who passed and gave their quiet condolences. The funeral service was open to everyone but it had been decided that the interment would be for the immediate family only, hence the large crowd. She felt lost and wished she had accompanied Lex and the children outside. To keep grounded, she glanced to the other side of Anna Leigh for her father. He looked years older as he spoke with each person who came up to him.

"Thank you." Michael Cauble shook hands with yet another person he didn't know. He turned to his mother. "How are you holding up? Can I do anything for you?"

Anna Leigh kissed the cheek of a woman from the Ladies Auxiliary and accepted her commiseration before speaking. "I'm quite all right, Michael. Please don't worry about me."

At the sound of someone clearing their throat, Amanda turned around to see two familiar women in front of her. "Oh. Hi."

Shelby Fisher, dressed in black jeans and black shirt, held out her hand. "I'm truly sorry for your loss, Amanda."

"So am I," Rebecca added quietly. She was wearing a simple black skirt and gray blouse, and her red hair was pulled back into a bun. "If there's anything we can do for you, please let us know."

"Thank you." Amanda leaned closer. "Would you mind going outside and checking on Lex and the kids?"

"Sure." Rebecca kissed Amanda on the cheek. "If you need any quiet time, we'd be more than happy to watch the kids for you."

"I may take you up on that."

As the pair moved toward Anna Leigh, Amanda introduced them. "Gramma, these are friends of ours. Shelby Fisher and Rebecca Starrett."

Anna Leigh gave them a genuine smile. "Thank you both for coming. Lorrie and Melanie have told us..." She caught herself. "Told *me*, so much about you."

Shelby took her hand and squeezed it lightly. "Please accept our condolences, Mrs. Cauble. If there's anything that you need done around your house, have Amanda give me a call. I'll be honored to help."

"Thank you, dear. I'll do that." Anna Leigh studied Rebecca for a moment. "Forgive me, but have we met?"

"It's possible, Mrs. Cauble. I'm an assistant manager at Carson's Western Wear. Have you shopped there?"

"Of course. I'm sorry I didn't place you."

"No, that's all right. But if you need anything, please call either of us." Rebecca shook her hand before following Shelby down the line.

"You have lovely friends, Mandy. The dark-haired one reminds me somewhat of Lexington. Although smaller."

Amanda put her arm around her grandmother. "She's a lot like Lex. As a matter of fact, she works at the ranch. And Rebecca gives me another adult to talk to that's closer to my age. She comes for coffee and to spoil the kids."

"Speaking of the children, where are they?" Anna Leigh noticed an empty space on the other side of her granddaughter. "I didn't think Lexington would leave your side."

"Lorrie's been having some problems coping with everything. Lex took the kids outside to get away from the crowd." Amanda gave a small wave to her departing friends, who stepped through the side door of the church. "But I asked Shelby and Rebecca to check on them."

ALTHOUGH THE GROUND was no longer frozen, the wind was cold enough to bring a chill down Lex's spine. Not for the first time, she wished she had worn her duster instead of her suit jacket which matched her black slacks and complimented her dark gray shirt. She leaned against a tree in the church's playground, holding Eddie as her two girls played on the swings.

"Go, go!" Eddie bounced in her arms and pointed to his sisters. "Momma, go!"

"Sorry, son. You're not big enough to be on those swings. Besides, if I put you down, you'd find the first bit of mud you could. And then we'd both be in trouble."

"Need a hand?"

Lex turned and saw Rebecca and Shelby. "Hey."

She grimaced as Eddie's enthusiasm bubbled out as a screech when he saw the newcomers.

"Bibba!"

"Hello, handsome." Rebecca moved closer and held out her hands. "How about we give your poor momma a break?"

"Be my guest." Lex relinquished her son and chuckled at his excitement. She relaxed against the tree as Rebecca took Eddie to the slide and slowly guided him down the hard plastic surface.

Shelby tucked her hands into her coat pockets. "Kinda cold out here, ain't it?"

"Yeah. But the kids were getting antsy." Lex turned to her friend.

"Thanks for coming, Shelby."

"Sure. Um, I'm really sorry for your loss. We saw Amanda inside."

Lex blew out a heavy breath. "Is she all right?"

"Hard to say. I mean, she wasn't falling apart or nothin', but..." Shelby shrugged. "She didn't look great." She stared at her partner, who was laughing at Eddie's antics on the slide. "You're a damned lucky woman, Lex."

"Yeah, I know." Lex noticed where Shelby's attention lay. "Have you ever thought about kids?"

The ex-rodeo rider laughed harshly. "Oh, yeah. I'm the perfect mother type."

"Don't be so hard on yourself. Hell, look at me. I never thought I'd be in this position, but here I am."

Shelby lowered her voice so she wouldn't be overheard. "I know you were kinda pushed into it, weren't you?"

She spoke of how Lex and Amanda had taken Lorrie's care from Amanda's sister, Jeannie. She had suffered a stroke during Lorrie's birth, and her husband had been killed in an automobile accident shortly thereafter. "I mean, you didn't really have much of a choice, did you?"

"Not at first, maybe. But when we had the chance to adopt Lorrie, I couldn't sign the papers soon enough."

Once Jeannie had recovered, she realized that Lex and Amanda had been the only parents Lorrie knew for the first two and a half years of her life. As hard as it had been for her, Jeannie did the right thing for her daughter, and gave her up. "When Amanda told me she wanted another baby, it scared the hell out of me. But I'd do anything for her, and now I'm glad that I did. And then, with Eddie, well, I couldn't imagine my life without any of my kids."

"Huh." Shelby rubbed the back of her neck. "I don't think I'd make a very good parent. I never had much of a role model."

"You're a good person, Shelby. That's the most important thing."

Lex gestured toward Rebecca. "What does Rebecca think about it?"

Shelby snorted. "Hell if I know. It's not something that's ever come up. I mean, I see her with your kids and wonder if she wants one of her own. Not like I could do anything about it."

Lex laughed at her expression. "There's ways around that, you know." She patted her friend's back. "You might want to talk about it with her, sometime."

"Yeah." Shelby exhaled in relief when she saw Amanda leave the church and walk outside. "Here comes your better half—" her voice trailed off when she realized that Lex had stepped away the moment Amanda came out of the building.

Meeting her wife halfway, Lex embraced Amanda in the middle of the playground. She felt Amanda's body tremble, which caused her to strengthen her hold. "I'm here, sweetheart."

Amanda rested her face against Lex's chest and cried.

For her part, Lex continued slowly to rock Amanda from side to side in an attempt to soothe her. "Hang in there, love," she whispered.

"I...I...don't know if I can handle the cemetery." Amanda sniffled and wiped her face with a wadded tissue. "But I want to be there for Gramma."

She looked down as she felt arms around her hips.

Lorrie had seen Amanda come outside. Needing the comfort of both parents, she huddled close. She had heard her mother's comment. "I don't want to go either."

Lex kissed Amanda's forehead before holding her arm out to her oldest child. "Come here, lil' bit."

From a few feet away, Shelby cleared her throat. "Um, if you want, we can take the kids home with us."

"Mom? Can we?" Lorrie looked up at them with a tear-stained face.

Amanda glanced at Lex and caught her slight nod. "I wouldn't want to impose on Shelby and Rebecca like that."

Shelby put her hand on Lorrie's shoulder. "Actually, I could use Lorrie's help. Rebecca's birthday is coming up soon, and I was hoping for some ideas."

"Mommy! Momma! Look how high I can get," Melanie demanded from the swing. "I can almost kick the sky!"

Lorrie wiped the tears from her face with her hand. "She's crazy."

"Lorrie," Amanda warned.

"Sorry." Lorrie lowered her eyes and stared at the ground. "Can I—" she caught herself. "I mean, may I go with Miz Shelby and Miz Rebecca?" She raised her face and looked into Lex's eyes. "Please?"

Lex considered the question. "Go get your sister while we discuss it, all right?"

"Yes, ma'am." Lorrie hugged Lex before she ran to the swings.

Amanda waited until Lorrie was out of earshot. "Are you sure you're up to them, Shelby? Not that I don't appreciate the offer, but Lorrie's become a handful lately."

"Oh? What's wrong?"

Lex snorted. "Hormones."

On her way to join the trio, Rebecca overheard Lex's comment. "Turning into a teenager early, is she?"

"Mommy!" Eddie reached for Amanda.

"I see where I rate." Rebecca relinquished her little friend. "How are you doing, Amanda?"

"Okay." Amanda hefted the toddler into her arms and kissed his cheek. "Did you have fun with Ms. Rebecca?"

Eddie patted her face and chin. "Gink, pease."

Amanda smiled and kissed his fingers. "I can take a hint."

She turned to Lex. "Did we bring his sippy cup?"

"Yep. It's in his bag. Which of course, I left in the truck. Be right back." Lex jogged toward the gate that led to the parking lot.

Shelby put her arm around Rebecca. "Darlin', I offered to take the kids with us while Lex and Amanda go to the burial."

"That's a good idea." Rebecca turned to Amanda. "I noticed Lorrie was having an especially hard time."

"She's been having bad dreams all week. Poor thing is terrified of one or both of us dying." Amanda brushed a stray tear from her cheek. "Melanie, of course, takes everything in stride. I think she's handling it better than any of us."

Rebecca leaned against her partner. "Kids are so different. I don't know if I could be as good a parent as you or Lex."

"Mommy, Lorrie said we have to leave. Can't we swing some more?" Melanie asked, as she tugged on Amanda's black dress.

"No, honey. But, Ms. Shelby and Ms. Rebecca asked if you'd like to go home with them for now."

"But I wanna swing."

Lorrie stood a few steps away, with her arms crossed over her chest. She was wearing black jeans, matching turtleneck and a dark green barn coat. "Quit being such a baby, Mel."

Melanie turned and glared at her sister. "I'm not a baby."

She stomped her black patent leather shoe for emphasis. The navy-blue dress and matching overcoat had been a Christmas present from her Grandpa Michael and Grandma Lois. It was covered with tiny red birds, and she had begged to wear it to the funeral. "You're a grump."

"Are not," Lorrie argued.

"Are too!"

"Girls, please!" Amanda shifted Eddie in her arms. "If you don't behave, I'll take you back to the ranch and you can spend the rest of the day in your rooms."

She looked at Shelby and Rebecca. "Are you sure about this? We'll keep Eddie with us, so you'll at least have a fighting chance."

Rebecca held out her hand to Melanie. "We'll be fine. Come on, sweetie. You can help me beat Shelby at Monopoly Junior."

She had a few children's games for the girls, who often came to visit with their parents. "How about you, Lorrie? Would you like to come home with us?"

Lorrie nodded, until a sharp look from Amanda reminded her of her manners. "Yes, ma'am. Thank you."

"Well, come on, then." Shelby motioned for the sullen girl to come closer. "Remember," she whispered. "I'm going to need your help."

For the first time in several days, Lorrie smiled. "Okay."

"AMEN." REVEREND HAMPTON closed his Bible and raised his head. He crossed to Anna Leigh, who dabbed at her face with a handkerchief. "You don't have to be strong all the time, Anna Leigh. Let your family and your faith see you through."

"I will." The sun cut through the cloud cover and glinted off the silver casket. Anna Leigh stared at the reflection. "It was a lovely service, Reverend. Thank you."

"No thanks are necessary. Jacob was a good man, and an even better friend. He'll be missed by all who knew him."

The clergyman lightly touched her arm before addressing Michael, who stood beside her. "Michael. You're always welcome to services."

Michael clenched his jaw in an attempt to keep from breaking down. "Thanks. I may bring Mom in the next week or so."

"Very well."

Anna Leigh turned to her son. "I'm perfectly capable of taking myself where I want to go, Michael." His solicitous behavior was already more than she could stand. "I'm not feeble-minded or made out of porcelain."

"Mom, please. Let's not get into that here."

Lois tugged on the arm of his jacket. "Michael."

He jerked his arm from her and stomped away.

Lois gave her mother-in-law an apologetic shrug and followed him.

"He's going to blow," Jeannie whispered to her husband.

"Should I go after him?" Rodney asked.

"No. When he gets like that, it's best to leave him alone. He'll calm down, eventually." Jeannie kept a tight hold on Rodney's hand. "Can we pick up our kids? I want to spend the rest of the day with them."

Their seven-year old, Teddy, was recovering from a bad cold. He and Hunter were staying with Wanda and her husband.

"Sure. It's going to be a madhouse at your mother's, anyway."

On the other side of Anna Leigh, Amanda blew her nose and leaned into her wife's body. "Dad's been driving Gramma crazy all week."

She glanced at the stroller in front of her. Eddie was sound asleep beneath his favorite blanket.

Lex rested her chin on Amanda's shoulder and tightened her arms around her. "Yeah. He's trying to be helpful, but it's coming off as bossy. Maybe one of us should talk to him."

"I've already tried. He about bit my head off."

"He what? When?"

Amanda turned in Lex's arms so they were face-to-face. "Yesterday, on the phone. I called Gramma's house to see if she needed anything, and he answered. From what I could hear, he practically took the phone away from her."

"Not good." With her protective streak in full mode, Lex stared at the back of the retreating man. "Maybe I should see what I can do."

"No, I think—"

Anna Leigh's voice cut into their conversation. "Are you girls ready to go? I'm certain that Martha and Charlie are tired of waiting at the house for us."

With so many people planning to drop off food and flowers after the funeral, she was grateful to them for staying behind.

Lex loosened her hold on Amanda. "Only if you're ready, Gramma."

"Yes, I believe so." Anna Leigh stepped forward and placed her hand on the casket. "Would you give me a moment, though?"

As soon as they started toward the cars, she leaned closer. "My darling. This is not what we agreed on, was it? I wanted to fall asleep in your arms for the last time, not be here without you." She covered her mouth with one hand and lowered her head.

At their SUV, Michael stopped pacing and glared at his wife. "I don't appreciate you dressing me down in front of everyone, Lois. This is a family matter."

Lois stopped and tilted her head. "Wait a minute. Dressing you down? A family matter? We've been married for years, Michael. Do you not consider me part of your family?"

"Don't twist my words. That's not what I meant."

Amanda left the stroller beside Lex and stood next to Lois. "Daddy, this isn't doing anyone any good. Let's all calm down. You know as well as I do that Lois was only trying to help."

Michael's face turned red. "So, you're turning against me, too? That's just fine." He loosened his tie. "I have to take care of her now. My father would expect nothing less."

When Amanda began to move toward him, Lex stopped her with a hand on her shoulder. "Dad."

At his angry look, she softened her voice. "Michael, come on. I know you're hurting. We all are. But let's not say anything we might regret later, all right?"

"Excuse me? Don't you *dare* talk to me that way." He pointed a shaky finger at Lex. "You have no idea what I'm feeling."

"I lost my father a few years ago, D—Michael." Lex stepped around the car and lowered her voice. "So I think I do."

His laugh was bitter. "Oh, yes. A man you barely knew, who only came home when he was dying." He turned away from her. "You know nothing."

"That's quite enough, Michael." Anna Leigh tightly gripped the handkerchief she held. "I'll ride with the girls. Why don't you go home and get some rest?"

Michael spun around. "No. I—" He noticed the no-nonsense look in his mother's eyes. "You're right."

Turning to Lex, he shook his head. "I'm sorry, Lex. I didn't mean what I said."

She nodded. "I know. It's all right. We'll get through this," she promised softly.

"Yeah." Michael stepped away. "Mom, I'll call you later?"

"Of course, dearest." Anna Leigh climbed into Amanda's

Expedition and closed the door.

Jeannie exhaled heavily. "Are you okay, Slim? Daddy's upset, but you know he loves you."

"I know." Lex hugged her. "I guess we'll see you at the house."

Rodney awkwardly patted Lex on the back. "Actually, we've decided to pick up our kids and go home."

"I don't blame you. Hopefully we'll be able to do the same, soon."

TWO HOURS LATER, Lex thought the well-meaning crowd would never thin out. She wandered through the house, feeling out of sorts after telling Martha and Charlie goodbye. Her arm was caught by a claw-like hand that pulled her to a stop near the kitchen.

A wizened old woman peered up through thick, black-rimmed glasses. "Lexington Walters! It's so nice that you're here for Anna Leigh. She and Jacob have always said nice things about you."

"Um, thank you, ma'am." Although familiar, Lex couldn't remember the elderly lady's name. She tried gently to remove the woman's grip, to no avail. "There isn't anything I wouldn't do for Anna Leigh."

"Good, good." The old woman grinned, showing nothing but gums. "Have you seen Chester?"

Lex glanced around. "Chester?"

"My great-nephew. He was supposed to rinse my teeth and bring 'em back. I can't find the little turd anywhere."

She released Lex's arm and slapped her hard on the back. "Bet you wouldn't have runned off and left me hangin', would ya?"

"No, ma'am. Of course not. Would you like me to find him for you?"

The old lady laughed and tucked her arm around Lex's. "What I'd like is a nip from my purse, but Chester took that, too. But I'd be mighty beholden to you if you'd help me find a place to rest my weary old bones."

"Of course." Moving slow in deference to the smaller woman, Lex escorted her toward the living room. "There's an empty chair by the fireplace, ma'am. Would that be all right?"

"I suppose." The old woman groaned as she sat. "Thanks, honey. Now, if you see Chester, tell him to move his lazy arse. I may be ninety-two, but that doesn't mean I'm senile. I can't eat half the stuff here without my choppers."

Lex coughed to cover up her laugh. "Yes, ma'am. I sure will." She hurried out of the room and had to stop to keep from running down the slender woman in front of her. "Oh! Hi, Gramma."

"Lexington. Are you all right?"

"Yes, ma'am. I just..." Lex pointed to the room she had just vacated, "I mean, well, she—"

Anna Leigh peeked around Lex. "I saw you helping Nellie Fowler. She's something else, isn't she?"

"She sure is. Um, have you seen a fella by the name of Chester? She said he has her teeth."

Anna Leigh laughed. "I'm glad I caught you. That's one of her favorite things to do at a gathering." At Lex's confused expression, she explained. "Nellie doesn't have a great-nephew. As a matter of fact, she doesn't have any family left at all. I think one of the ladies from the auxiliary brought her today."

"What about her, umm, you know?" Lex pointed to her mouth.

"They're probably in her purse. She loves the attention."

Anna Leigh's face slowly lost the smile, replaced by a weary resignation. "How horrible would I be if I started chasing people out? All I want to do is spend some time alone."

Lex put her arm around her. "Why don't you let me help you upstairs, and I'll take care of everything."

"Oh, Lexington. I couldn't ask that of you. No, these people were kind enough to come over, the least I could do is be a better hostess."

"Pardon my language, Gramma. But...bullshit."

Anna Leigh's eyebrows rose, but she didn't argue as Lex led her toward the stairs.

"Most of these folks are just here to gossip and eat. They can do that anywhere."

"Well, I suppose. Where's Mandy and Eddie? I haven't seen them for a while."

Lex kept her arm around Anna Leigh as they ascended the staircase. "In the back guest room. Eddie's napping and Amanda's fighting off a migraine. I sent them up about an hour ago."

"Poor thing. You should take them both home."

Anna Leigh stood in front of her bedroom door and touched Lex's cheek with the palm of her hand. "I know I don't say this often enough, but you are a beautiful gift to our family, Lexington."

Her emotions getting the best of her, Lex felt tears burn her eyes. "This family has been the gift, Gramma." She had to clear her throat. "I'm so damned sorry about Grandpa Jake. If I can do anything for you—"

"Thank you, dearest. The best thing you can do for me is to take care of my granddaughter and my great-grandchildren. Which I know you will."

"Yes, ma'am. I surely will." Lex kissed her on the cheek. "Are you sure you don't want to come out to the ranch with us?"

"I'll be fine, here." Anna Leigh bit her lip. "I have to be. It's something I need to become accustomed to."

She stepped into her room and turned around. "I'll call you tomorrow."

"All right." As the door closed, the bleak expression on the older woman's face broke her heart. Unable to hold them back any longer, Lex finally allowed the tears to fall.

Chapter Seven

ONCE THEY PICKED up the girls at Shelby and Rebecca's, Lex talked Amanda into letting her drive them home. She knew Amanda's migraine was most likely caused by the stress of the past week. While the worst had abated, the hangover left Amanda feeling exhausted.

"And then, Miz Rebecca showed us a picture of Miz Shelby bull riding! It looked so scary," Melanie related, her eyes wide. "Momma, did you ever ride a bull?"

Lex glanced in the rear view mirror to make eye contact with her youngest daughter. "Uh, no. Can't say that I have."

"Your momma did face off against a bull once, though. Remember that, honey?" Amanda asked Lex.

"Faced off? Oh, crap. That wasn't a face off."

Not long after they had gotten together, Lex and Amanda had come across a large Brahman bull. Lex had tried to get their jeep out of the mud, and the bull walked up to her and bumped her with its nose. They found out later that it was their neighbor's pet, and had a good laugh about the situation — once they were safely home.

Amanda quickly related the story. "But I don't want you girls to ever think about getting that close to a bull, all right?"

She looked back at Lorrie, who was staring moodily out the side window. "Lorrie? Did you have a nice time this afternoon?"

Lorrie shrugged. "I guess."

"She sat on the couch and read magazines," Melanie said. "She wouldn't even play Monopoly with us."

"I didn't feel like playing a stupid old game. Miss Rebecca said I could read her horse magazines, so I did."

Melanie wrinkled her nose. "You're just an old grump."

"Am not."

"Are too."

Lex had heard enough. "Girls, stop arguing. Melanie, leave your sister alone. Lorrie, you should —" She slammed on the brakes and caused the vehicle to slide to a stop. "Damn it!"

Amanda released her grip on the dash and turned to the kids. "Is everyone all right?"

"Haaa!" Eddie shook a fist. "Go!"

Melanie held her nose. "Mommy, Eddie pooted."

"Melanie, you don't have to tell us every time he passes gas." Amanda squinted through the windshield. "What kind of idiot dumps a box that size on the road?"

Lex put the SUV in park. "I dunno. But I might as well put it in the back. We can get rid of it when we get home."

She removed her seat belt and opened the door. "Be right back."

She walked in front of the truck and knelt to get the box. She suddenly jumped back and almost fell.

Amanda rolled down her window and stuck her head out. "Lex? Are you all right?"

"Yeah. Hold on." Lex opened the box and looked inside. "What the hell?"

Amanda's curiosity got the best of her, so she turned to the girls. "Stay in here and keep an eye on your brother."

She hopped out of the Expedition and hurried to her wife's side. "What's going on?"

Lex straightened and pointed. "See for yourself."

"What?" Amanda cautiously lifted the edge of the box and peered inside. "Is it alive?"

"Yep."

Amanda put her hands on her hips. "Well?"

"Well, what?"

"We can't just leave it here."

Lex shook her head. "Oh, no. Uh-uh. There's no way in hell I'm taking that thing back to our ranch. Ain't happenin'."

"Lex."

"No."

Amanda cocked her head and frowned. "Pick up the box, Lexington."

Seriously considering her options, Lex paused. "Amanda—"

"Don't." Amanda held up her hand. "Get the box and put it in the back of the truck, Lex. We'll argue about it later."

Like a petulant child, Lex lifted the box and carried it to the Expedition.

Once they were both buckled in, Amanda noticed the look on her wife's face. "Don't say it."

"What was it, Momma?" Melanie asked. "That box looked heavy. Was it heavy? Why did you put it in the back?"

A sound emanated from the rear of the vehicle as they began moving forward.

"Maaaaaaa."

Melanie tried to twist in her seat to see behind her. "What is that?"

"The bane of every cattleman's existence," Lex muttered darkly.

"Maaaaa."

Lorrie, for the first time since they'd picked her up, appeared interested. "A lamb?"

"Almost as bad," Lex answered. "A freakin' kid."

Melanie's eyes almost popped out of her head. "A boy or a girl? And why is it in a box, and not buckled up like us?"

"A baby goat," Lorrie said. She laughed at her sister's lack of knowledge. "They're called kids."

"That's silly." Melanie leaned forward as far as she could and tapped Lex's headrest. "Momma, is she making that up?"

Lex shook her head. "Unfortunately, no."

"Maaaaaa."

LORRIE HELD THE back door open for Amanda. "Why does Momma hate goats? I think they're kind of cute."

Freckles raced down the hall, yipping. She bounced around Lorrie, who absentmindedly scratched the dog's head.

"Thanks, honey." Amanda carried Eddie inside and struggled to take off his puffy jacket. "Stay still, mister."

"Mommy, no!" Eddie twisted and fussed. "Noooo!"

Amanda laughed as she hung up his coat. "See? You survived."

He always threw a fit when she tried to put his coat on, or take it off. She removed hers and hung it beside Eddie's. "Lorrie, your poor, disillusioned momma seems to think that mixing cattle and goats are bad luck. Why, I don't know."

"Because the little devils ruin the grazing land," Lex grouched as she brought the box into the house. She raised the box higher as Freckles tried to see what was inside.

"Freckles, down! As for goats, they pull up the grass, roots and all, so nothing is left to grow back. I wish Ron wasn't sunning himself on a beach in Mexico. I'd take the damned thing to the vet's office."

Ron Bristol was their vet. He had been adopted by Martha and Charlie as a teen. While in college, he met his future wife, Nora Haden. They were married before Christmas and were on their honeymoon in Puerto Vallarta.

"Watch it, rancher," Amanda warned. "Lorrie, lock Freckles in the bathroom until we get the goat settled, please. Lex, honey, let's put the poor thing in the laundry room. Ron will be back in a few days, we can survive for that long."

Lex grumbled but did as she was told. "Where the hell would a baby goat come from, anyway? I don't know of any goat farms nearby."

"Me, either." Amanda handed Eddie to Lex before she opened a cabinet and took out a towel that was usually reserved for Freckles' bath. She folded the top of the box open. "It's so tiny."

She turned to her wife. "How old do you think it is?"

"I haven't a clue. Few weeks, I'd guess." The disgusted look never left Lex's face as she watched Amanda carefully wrap the small, white Nubian in the blue towel and cradle it close to her.

Melanie edged closer to her mother and pinched her nose with her fingers. "It smells."

"Well, duh." Lorrie stood beside her. "It's dirty. Once we clean it up—"

Lex shifted Eddie so he was on her hip. "Oh, no. I'm taking it to town first thing tomorrow. We aren't going to bathe it."

"Her," Amanda corrected.

"What?"

Amanda giggled as the kid nibbled on the collar of her dress. "It's a girl. And I think she's hungry."

"Momma, Momma, Momma," Eddie chanted as he rocked back and forth. "Down."

Lex turned to their oldest. "Lorrie, would you mind taking your brother to the living room? Mel, please go with them while your Mom and I figure out what to do with..." She pointed to the bundle in Amanda's arms. "That."

"Lex," Amanda warned.

Lorrie looked from one parent to the other. "Are you going to fight?"

"No, sweetheart, we're not," Lex assured her. She lowered Eddie until his feet touched the floor. "Your mother just has to remind me sometimes that I need help in making the right decisions."

She winked at her wife. "If you'll let your brother walk to the living room, I'll go out to the barn and see about getting something to feed the little critter."

Melanie held out her hands. "Can I walk Eddie? I'll go slow."

"All right." Lex chuckled as Melanie chattered to her little brother as they left the laundry room.

"We'll play with your trucks and my dolls, Eddie. If you're really nice, maybe we can have a tea party later. You like to play tea party, don't you?"

"Ha!"

Lorrie put her hands in her front pockets. "Since Mel's with Eddie, can I help you?"

She got as close to Amanda as she could, her eyes rarely leaving the little animal. "Please?"

"Sure, honey." Amanda's face took on a wicked grin. "Sit here beside me and you can hold her while your momma and I get some supplies."

"Cool." Lorrie sat cross-legged near the dryer, a genuine smile on her face as she was handed the kid. "It's a lot tinier than the calves I've seen."

She stroked the small, white head and giggled when the goat sucked on her fingers. "That tickles!"

Amanda stood and brushed off the back of her dress. She patted Lex on the rear as they stepped out of the laundry room. "I'll see if I can find an old baby bottle while you get some hay."

"Very sneaky, Amanda," Lex whispered. "But we're still not keeping that thing."

"Of course we're not." Amanda turned and pointed toward their daughter. "But it's good to see something pull Lorrie out of her depression, isn't it?"

Lex shook her head. "Amanda—"

"No, no. You're right. A cattle ranch is no place for a goat." Amanda kissed Lex on the cheek.

As her wife walked away, Lex knew that she had lost the battle. But the war had only begun.

AFTER AMANDA DID a quick Internet search, she sent Lex to the barn for a bucket of high-protein horse feed. While her wife was gone, she found one of Eddie's old bottles and cut a larger hole in the nipple. "This should do until we get a better bottle at the feed store."

She filled the bottle with milk and warmed it.

Lorrie looked up when Amanda brought in the baby bottle. "Do I do it just like a calf?"

"Try and see." Amanda squatted beside her.

The goat instinctively knew what to do when the bottle was presented to her and greedily attacked it.

"Mom, look!" Lorrie laughed, even as the warm milk dripped down the kid's chin and onto her shirt.

As she came in the back door, Lex heard her daughter's laugh. She quietly stood in the doorway of the laundry room and watched. Unable to stop herself, Lex smiled tenderly as the sullen girl transformed into the sunny child she remembered. She brought the bucket into the room. "We'll put a bit of this in the box, in case she gets hungry."

"Momma?" Lorrie raised her head. "Remember that project I'm supposed to start in February?"

She was a member of the Junior Farm Club at school. Their spring project was to take care of an animal and write reports on their progress.

One look at the hopeful face and Lex's reservation's vanished. She had lost the battle, and the war. "Decided against a calf, huh?"

"Is it okay?" Lorrie looked at the bundle in her lap. "I'll do all the research tonight, so I'll know exactly what to do. And you won't have to do a thing, I promise."

Although she was already agreeable to the idea, Lex knelt in front of Lorrie and Amanda. "What do you plan to do with her once she's grown and your project is done?"

"The same thing I was going to do with a calf. Sell her at the fall auction."

Lex rubbed the back of her neck and tried to appear thoughtful. "And you'll feed and clean up after her? We'll have to build her a pen inside the fence, to protect against predators. Will you help with that, too?"

"Yes, ma'am."

"I must be out of my mind," Lex muttered. "All right."

She stood. "She doesn't have a mother, like a calf would. So she's going to need a lot of extra attention for a while. That's going to cut into your spare time."

She put her hands on her hips. "If your grades go down, we find her a new home. No arguments."

"Yes, ma'am. Can I sleep down here with her tonight? I don't want her to be scared."

With a quickly mouthed 'thank you' to her wife, Amanda stood. "What do you think, Lex?"

"I don't think so. The laundry room will be too cold tonight."

As if in deep thought, Lex rubbed her chin. "But, since I don't think she can get out of the box, how about the two of you camp out in the living room?"

"Really?" Lorrie practically glowed. "Thanks, Momma!"

Lex held up one hand. "Only for tonight. Tomorrow, we'll get her a stall set up in the barn until it gets warmer."

"But—"

Amanda stopped Lorrie. "She's right, honey. The kid will be fine in the barn. Now, run upstairs and get in your pajamas while we find a good place in the living room for your little friend. Oh, and take Freckles with you and leave her upstairs. We'll introduce her to the goat tomorrow."

"Yes, ma'am." Lorrie gently placed the kid in the box. "Thank you, Mom." She hugged Amanda and turned to Lex. "Thanks, Momma." As she squeezed Lex she said, "I love you."

Lex put her hand on Lorrie's back. "I love you too, sweetheart."

After their daughter left, Amanda sidled up to Lex and put an arm around her waist. "Thank you for bending on this one. I believe this is just what Lorrie needed."

"Yeah." Lex kissed the side of Amanda's head. "Guess I'm getting soft in my old age."

Amanda laughed and patted her on the stomach. "You've always been soft."

"I noticed you didn't argue about me being old."

"True." Amanda squealed when she felt a light pinch on her rear. "Watch it."

Lex swatted the spot she had pinched. "Turn around and I'll be glad to watch it."

"I'm going to get you."

"And I'll let you." Lex jumped away. "As soon as we get our *kids* settled."

Amanda rolled her eyes. "That was baaaaad." She laughed at the look on her wife's face. "Gotcha."

"You'll think gotcha when I get through with you." Lex lifted the box and settled it in her arms. "Lead on, Mo...o...o...me...e...e."

When Amanda threatened to swat her, she raised the box. "Careful.

Don't want to make me drop this little critter."

"Any more of your goat jokes or imitations and I'm going to have to think of something wicked to do to you."

"Promises, promises."

When they walked into the living room, the first thing Lex noticed was the silence.

"Should we be worried?" she whispered to Amanda.

"I don't think so." Amanda pointed to the quilt spread on the floor in front of the dark television.

Lying amongst toy cars, wooden blocks and dolls, were their two youngest. Eddie was on his stomach, drooling on his fist. Melanie, who was stretched out on her side across from him, had a naked doll clutched firmly in one hand.

Lex left the box near the fireplace before she moved to stand beside her wife. "That's too cute."

She picked up their son and handed him to Amanda. "I'll give you the lighter one, this time."

"Ugh." Amanda adjusted her hold on Eddie, who was dead weight. "He won't be the lighter one for long, at this rate."

"Yeah." Lex dropped to one knee so she could lift Melanie without too much effort. "But at least by that time, this one will be too big to lift." She groaned as she stood. "What have we been feeding them?"

Amanda snickered. "Fertilizer, I think."

She took the lead and they trailed upstairs. "All three are growing like weeds. It won't be much longer before Lorrie's taller than me."

"Well, sweetheart—"

"Don't say it."

"Say what?"

"You know damned good and well, what." Amanda led the way to Melanie's room. As Eddie slept against her shoulder, she took a pair of pajamas out of Melanie's dresser and handed them to Lex. "No short jokes."

Lex expertly traded Melanie's clothes for the pajamas and tucked her under the covers. "Sleep well, baby girl."

After kissing Mel goodnight, Amanda followed Lex to Eddie's room. She picked out his sleepwear as Lex undressed him and changed his diaper.

"Whoa!" Lex coughed and discarded the diaper. "Toxic waste has nothing on him. How can such a sweet little guy leave such a nasty mess?" she muttered, as she cleaned him up.

"Sometimes I wonder the same thing."

Amanda rested her cheek against Lex's upper arm and watched as her wife got him ready for bed. They took turns placing kisses upon his soft, dark hair after settling him in his crib. "He's really starting to look like his momma."

"Poor little tyke. Hopefully he'll take after his mommy." Lex gave him a final rub on the back and followed Amanda to their bedroom.

"Why would you say that?" Amanda asked as she took off her dress and changed into her nightgown.

Lex switched into her flannel boxer shorts and T-shirt then joined Amanda in bed. "Do you seriously have to ask that?" She rolled so that they were face to face. "The Walters' side of the family is not known for their mild temperament." She touched the tip of Amanda's nose with her finger. "You, on the other hand, could give saint lessons in patience."

"You obviously don't spend much time around me when I have to take care of the kids, because our two girls could drive a saint to drink."

Her face sobered as the day's events caught up with her.

"Yeah, there is that." Lex cupped Amanda's face and brushed her thumb along the dark shadow beneath her eye. "Long day."

Amanda turned her head and kissed Lex's palm. "Yeah. My heart aches for Gramma. They were together for sixty years. Just the thought of losing you kills me."

"I'm not going anywhere for a long time, love. I promise."

"You can't promise that, Lex. Things happen."

Lex tugged on Amanda until she was safely in her arms. "I'm planning on at least seventy years with you. We'll be surrounded by our great-grandkids, and I'll still be trying to chase you around the house. Of course, by then you hopefully won't make me run too far, since I'll be so damned bowlegged from horseback riding."

The mental image of an ancient, bowlegged woman chasing after her changed Amanda's tears into giggles. "Will you have spurs?"

"If you want me to." Lex took a breath and began to sing, "I've got spurs...that jingle, jangle...wheeze."

Amanda totally lost it and laughed as hard as she had been crying. "You're completely warped, you know that?"

"Yep." Lex kissed her on the forehead. "Get some sleep, buckaroo. We'll be goat herders tomorrow. And those critters are more ornery than cattle."

Chapter Eight

THE DUPLEX'S FRONT window rattled as the door slammed behind the two women. The slammer, slight of frame with streaked, brown hair, dropped a navy blue backpack on the floor. "That's the last time I let you pick our vacation spot."

She removed her heavy coat and haphazardly hung it in the entry closet. "I still can't feel my toes."

"It wasn't that bad," the muscular blonde argued.

Kyle Lind placed her dark green backpack beside the other one, took off her coat and handed it to her partner.

"Not that bad?"

Eleanor Gordon placed the coat next to her own and shut the closet door with more force than was necessary. "Our tent collapsed from snow." She poked her lover in the chest with her index finger. "*Snow*, Kyle. I'm from southern California. The only snow I was familiar with was from television and movies."

The two had left Somerville before Christmas for two weeks of hiking in Big Bend National Park. Kyle had always been an avid hiker and, during the year that they had been together, she had shown her partner how much fun it could be. Kyle brushed her hand across her crew cut.

"It never snows there. How was I supposed to know? Besides, it wasn't that much snow. At least we were prepared for the cold, right?"

The double sleeping bag had kept both of them warm, also giving opportunities for more than simple sleeping.

Ellie sighed. No matter how hard she tried, it was impossible to stay mad at Kyle. The mischievous gleam in those sparkling, hazel eyes always made her smile. "That's true."

"Let's not worry about unpacking right now. I could use a hot shower." Kyle put her hands on Ellie's hips. "And maybe some beautiful woman to scrub my back?"

Heat filled Ellie's face. Although they had been living together for more than three months, she still couldn't figure out what Kyle saw in her. She considered herself plain—brown hair, brown eyes and no figure to speak of. There had to be other women that should have caught the mechanic's eye. But for some reason, Kyle only had eyes for her.

"Let me check my voicemail for anything important, then I'll be right there." She kissed Kyle lightly on the lips.

"The messages can wait." Kyle tugged on Ellie's belt. "That reminds me. Tomorrow, we need to get you a new cell phone. Who knew they didn't bounce?"

Ellie hugged her. "I doubt anything would bounce from that height.

It was my fault, anyway. You told me to leave it in my backpack. I was just curious if there'd be a signal that high up."

She unbuckled Kyle's belt. "Maybe I'll be like you, and not carry a cell."

"No way." Kyle unbuttoned Ellie's shirt as she was backed into the bedroom. "I worry about you enough as it is, driving that old clunker. I don't want you stranded somewhere without a way to call for help."

Ellie's flannel shirt hit the floor, quickly followed by Kyle's denim top. Ellie playfully shoved her lover onto the bed and straddled her hips. "Enough about phones. So." She opened Kyle's shorts and popped the elastic on her red satin bikinis. "How dirty are you?"

Kyle raised her hips as her cargo shorts were pulled down. "Guess you'll just have to find out."

She laughed when the shorts became tangled in her hiking boots. "Need some help?"

"No." Ellie wrestled with the shorts. With a final, powerful tug, she jerked them free of Kyle's boots with a victorious yell. "Ha!"

Her grin faded as she toppled backward off the bed. "Aaaah!" A heavy thump came from the wooden floor.

"Ellie?" Kyle sat up. "El?"

"Ugh." Elle blinked rapidly at the ceiling, which seemed to be spinning. "Huh."

Kyle rolled and peeked over the edge of the bed. Her lover was lying flat on her back, still holding the shorts. "Baby? Are you all right?"

"Ow." Ellie blinked and tried to focus her eyes. "Not tonight, I've got a headache." She tried to get up, but decided against it. "Kyle?"

"What, baby?"

"I don't feel so good." Ellie put one hand on her head and closed her eyes.

KYLE HUDDLED IN the chilly waiting room and anxiously rubbed her bare legs. "I should have changed into jeans. This place is an icebox."

She stood and walked to the window, peering at the night and the brightly-lit parking lot. "Stupid."

Her denim shirt was buttoned crookedly and as she hugged herself, she wished she had remembered her jacket. She turned in time to see the disgusted look from the only other occupant in the area, a middle-aged woman wrapped in a heavy overcoat. "What?"

The woman lowered her gaze and ignored her.

"Whatever." Kyle turned away from the windows and paced across the room. She looked up as a nurse came into the waiting area, but deflated as she stopped and spoke quietly to the other woman. "Damn."

It had been more than an hour since she had brought Ellie into the emergency room. Her lover had feebly argued as she bundled her up, but gave in when Kyle had to hold her as she threw up in the hedges by their garage. Now Kyle was left waiting for word about Ellie's condition. She had considered calling Ellie's cousin, Lex, but decided to wait until she had something definitive to tell her. Besides, the rancher intimidated the hell out of her. It wasn't only her height, but her demeanor. Although Lex was always friendly toward her, her quiet stare seemed to look completely through Kyle.

"Uh, ma'am?" A young nurse came through the emergency doors and stopped a few feet away from Kyle. "Are you here for Miss Gordon?"

"Yes. Is she all right?"

"Are you family?"

Kyle answered without pause. "Yes."

The nurse cocked her head and stared at her for a moment. "Follow me, please."

She led Kyle through the emergency doors and down a quiet hallway, before stopping by a partially-closed door. "Exam room four."

"Thank you." Kyle tapped lightly on the door and entered. Two women stood by the bed, one on each side. One wore green scrubs and a lab coat while the other wore a pair of navy scrub pants and a brightly decorated top.

"Excuse me? I was told—" Kyle paused when her eyes met those of her lover. "El?"

Ellie was propped up in bed, her eyes partially closed in pain. She did her best to glare at the physician. "I'm fine."

"Now, Ellie," the doctor admonished. "As a nurse yourself, you know how cautious we have to be with head injuries. A concussion is a serious matter."

"I know, doctor. But I think I could rest just as well at home."

Ellie held her hand out to Kyle, who moved quickly to the side of the bed. "Kyle, this is Dr. Borden. She's covered at Rodney's office in the past. Just my luck she was the doctor working the emergency room tonight."

Kyle shook hands with the middle-aged woman. "Nice to meet you, Doctor. What's the verdict?"

"As I was just telling Ellie, we'd like to keep her overnight for observation. It's standard procedure for a concussion."

Ellie's expression darkened. "And as I was telling the good doctor, I'll be fine at home."

Kyle put her hand on Ellie's shoulder. "I know you want to go home, but maybe you should listen to her. That's a pretty good-sized knot on the back of your head."

"Whose side are you on?"

"Yours, of course." Kyle leaned closer and lowered her voice. "Baby, please do as the doc says. You scared the crap out of me tonight." She took Ellie's hand in both of hers. "Do this for me, please?"

Ellie sighed. "You don't play fair."

"Never have." Kyle lightly rubbed her lover's hand. "Do you want me to run home and get you anything?"

"No, that's okay. I think I can survive one night here." Ellie yawned. "Sorry."

Dr. Borden turned to Kyle. "If you don't mind returning to the waiting area, I'll have a nurse come get you once we have her settled in a room."

"Sure, Doctor. Thank you." Kyle shook the doctor's hand again and nodded to the nurse. "Thanks for taking care of her."

Kyle walked into the waiting room and stared at the bank of pay phones on the far wall. It was after midnight and she warred with herself about calling her lover's family.

"Damn it." She dug in her pockets for change and headed for the phones. Right now, the idea of owning a cell phone sounded pretty good.

AMANDA SPOONED AGAINST her wife and buried her head deeper into Lex's back when she heard the phone ring. "It's on your side."

Lex groaned and picked up the receiver. "Walters. What?" She sat up and flicked on the bedside light. "Slow down, Kyle."

"What is it?" Amanda sat up and rubbed her eyes.

"It's Kyle. Something about Ellie being in the hospital."

Lex climbed out of bed and reached for her jeans. "Where? All right. I'll be there as soon as I—what?"

She stood in the middle of the bedroom with the phone up to her ear and her jeans dangling from her other hand. "Are you sure? Okay. I'll see you tomorrow. Thanks for letting us know."

Amanda adjusted her nightgown, which had somehow ended up twisted beneath her arms. "Honey?"

Lex put the phone back on its base and dropped onto the bed. "After they got home this evening, Ellie fell. Kyle took her to the emergency room."

"Oh, no. Is she okay?"

"She has a concussion, so they're keeping her overnight." Lex braced her elbows on her knees and rested her face in her hands. "Damn."

Amanda put her arms around her. "But she's going to be all right, isn't she?"

"Yeah, Kyle seems to think so. I'll go tomorrow and see them."

"*We* will go and see them."

"Right." Lex leaned into her and closed her eyes. "Never a dull moment, is there?"

"Not since I've met you," Amanda rolled onto her back and

brought Lex with her. "Maybe I should explain the family curse to Kyle."

"Curse?" Lex leaned closer. "What curse?"

Amanda ran her finger across the small scar that bisected Lex's right eyebrow. "The one where you always seem to have a bruise, cut, broken bone or some other injury. And from what Martha tells me, it's been a lifelong thing with you."

Lex snorted. "Martha exaggerates."

"Right." Amanda poked a bruise on Lex's forearm, where she had accidentally rammed it into a gate.

"Ow!"

"Exaggerates, huh?" Amanda's victorious grin disappeared when Lex pinned her hands above her head. "Umm, honey?"

"Yeeees?"

Amanda squirmed as Lex took her time unbuttoning the front of her nightgown. "Umm...the door's open."

"Then you'll have to be extra quiet, won't you?"

"You know damned good and well how loud I—" Amanda's mouth slammed shut as she felt Lex's gentle lips work their way down her throat, and stop in a very sensitive place. "Mmm."

THE NEXT MORNING, Ellie was grateful for her lover's arm hooked around her waist, as they moved from the car to the duplex. Her head was killing her. The nausea was a little better, but the dizziness made it hard for her to walk. She leaned heavily against Kyle.

Kyle unlocked their door. "Almost there, baby."

"Thanks." Ellie stumbled against the door frame. "Damn it." Her head spun for another reason when she was scooped into Kyle's arms. "Put me down before you hurt yourself."

"Give me a break. I've carried heavier car parts than you."

Kyle kicked the door closed and took her precious cargo to the bedroom, gently placing Ellie on the bed. "See? Nothing to it."

She removed her lover's shoes and tugged on the sweatpants she had dressed Ellie in the previous evening. "What about these?"

Ellie struggled to open her eyes. "Leave 'em. I can't seem to get warm." She couldn't help but smile as Kyle slowly took off her coat and tucked her under the covers. "Thanks."

"What's that smile for?"

"You're really sweet." Ellie closed her eyes. "I love you."

Kyle sat on the bed beside her and stroked Ellie's face. "I love you too, El. Get some rest, okay?"

"Mmm." Ellie leaned into the touch as she drifted to sleep.

WITH HER HAND tucked around Lex's arm, Amanda snuggled

close as they walked toward the duplex. "How exactly did Ellie hurt her head?"

"Kyle didn't say." Lex stopped at the front door. "I'd also like to know why Ellie never returned any of my calls. It's not like her."

"I'm sure she has a perfectly good explanation." Amanda knocked on the door. "You did call and tell them we were coming, didn't you?"

Lex shook her head. "I thought you did."

"No, I didn't. I was busy getting Eddie to Martha's, remember? Maybe we should come back later."

"Hell, it's almost noon. I'm sure—"

The door opened and a bleary-eyed Kyle poked her head out.

"Hey." Her shirt was wrinkled and her shorts were zipped, but not fastened. She rubbed the top of her head. "What time is it?"

"We're sorry about just dropping in, but I thought Lex called, and she thought I had. Go back to bed and we'll come back later."

"No, no. That's all right." Kyle opened the door wider. "Come on in. I must have dozed off as I was keeping an eye on El." She led them into the living room. "Can I get y'all anything?"

Lex sat beside her wife on the sofa. "We're fine, right?"

"Yes." Amanda leaned against Lex, who stretched her arm across her shoulders. "How's Ellie?"

Kyle played with a button that was coming off one of the pockets of her cargo shorts. "The doctor said she'd be fine. She's been resting since we got home from the hospital this morning. She was able to eat some toast, but threatened to throw the scrambled eggs at me."

Amanda laughed. "Don't feel bad, it's hereditary." She prodded Lex. "Right?"

"I don't know what you're talking about." Lex held Amanda's hand. "So, what time did y'all get in?"

"Just before nine, last night." Kyle scooted forward in her chair until she was on the edge. "We would have called to let you know, but I was afraid the kids were already asleep."

Amanda squeezed Lex's hand before pulling hers away. "Would it be okay if I checked on Ellie? I won't bother her."

"Sure. She's in the bedroom." Kyle noticed the time on the cable receiver. "As a matter of fact, could you wake her so she can take her meds? She's a little overdue."

"Of course." After standing, Amanda patted Lex's arm. "Be back in a few."

Once Amanda was out of the room, Lex turned to the mechanic. "Did Ellie not check her messages on her phone while you were gone? Or were you not able to get a signal down there?"

"Yeah, well, that's kind of a funny story," Kyle began, with a chuckle. At the serious stare she received, her smile faded. "What? You act like someone died."

Lex's face looked stricken.

"What?" Kyle leaned toward Lex who sat silently on the sofa. "What's going on?"

"I'm sorry." Lex slowly rubbed her hands on her jeans before answering. She gazed sadly at Kyle. "The day after Christmas, Jacob passed away." She took a deep breath and released it slowly. "It's been a little rough since then."

"Oh, my God. I'm so sorry, Lex. Ellie's going to be devastated. She considered Jacob another grandfather." Kyle joined Lex on the sofa and put her hand on Lex's knee. "I had no idea. We were climbing on Christmas morning, and Ellie's phone fell about two hundred feet."

When she realized where her hand was, she quickly moved it away. "Uh, anyway, it's my fault. I should have gone to the park office and checked in every day, but I honestly didn't think about it. I'm sorry."

Lex shook her head. "No, I'm the one who's sorry. I should have contacted the park and had a message delivered, but it never dawned on me. It's done. Not much we can do about it now."

Kyle still felt bad. "How about I make some coffee? I think we could all use it."

"Sounds like a good idea."

AMANDA PUSHED THE bedroom door open and stepped inside. There was enough light coming in through the window blinds to see, but not enough to disturb the woman huddled in bed. She stepped lightly on the wood floor and was surprised when Ellie turned toward her.

"Hi," she whispered. "How are you feeling?"

"Ugh." Ellie struggled to sit up. "Amanda? What are you doing here?"

"We came by to check on you." Amanda sat on the edge of the bed. "If I hadn't thought you were related to Lex before, getting a concussion at home is a sure way to prove it."

Ellie chuckled and winced. "Ow. Don't make me laugh, it hurts."

"How did you manage to hurt yourself, anyway? Did you slip in the shower?"

"Um, no."

Amanda watched as Ellie's face turned a deep red. "What?"

Ellie covered her face. "Oh, God."

"Oh, come on, it can't be that bad. It's not like you and Kyle were..." Amanda stopped. "You're kidding me! How can you get a concussion doing that?"

"I wanna die," Ellie muttered.

Unable to help herself, Amanda began to giggle. "Really? What happened? Come on, you've got to tell me, or I'll be thinking of all sorts of kinky things."

"Geez." Ellie picked up a pillow and put it over her head. "I'm not here."

Amanda tugged at the pillow until she got it away from her. "Let's hear it, sunshine. How did you hurt yourself?"

"You're going to laugh."

"Probably," Amanda agreed. "Tell."

"IwashelpingKylewithhershortsandIfellbackwardsoffthebed," Ellie rushed out in a single breath.

Although she only caught about every third word, Amanda understood. "Ouch." She reached for Ellie's head. "I'm glad you weren't more seriously hurt."

"You're not going to tell Lex, are you? She'll never let me live it down."

Amanda got off the bed. "Like I can keep a secret from her? I'm sorry, Ellie. But I'll tell her not to pick on you...too much."

She picked up a pill bottle from the nightstand. "I'm supposed to get you to take your medication."

Ellie took the pill and drank deeply from the glass of water that had been left on her side of the bed. "Thanks." She sat back against the headboard and closed her eyes. "So, did you and Lex survive the kids during Christmas break? Or were you ready to kill them?"

"Uh." Amanda covered her mouth with her hand. "Something happened the day after Christmas, Ellie."

When she saw the tears in Amanda's eyes, Ellie leaned forward. "Oh, no. Are the kids—"

Amanda shook her head. "No, the children are all right. But, my grandfather," her voice broke. "Grandpa Jake passed away."

"What? No. How is that possible?"

"Gramma found him in his shop." Amanda stopped. "He, uh—"

Ellie forgot about her headache and her embarrassment. She took Amanda's hands in her own. "I'm so sorry. He was such a great guy." She blinked the tears away and concentrated on Amanda.

"Thanks. It's still hard to believe."

"How are the kids taking it?"

Amanda took a moment to compose herself. "Melanie thinks he's in Heaven, playing with Travis."

She squeezed Ellie's hands to soften her pain on losing her own grandfather. "Lorrie is trying our patience, but we're hoping she'll outgrow it, soon, she said. "She's also terrified that something is going to happen to Lex or me."

"And, knowing my cousin, she's still going full-steam ahead, damn the consequences."

"Pretty much."

Before Ellie could say anything else, she frowned as two Amandas appeared in front of her. "I'm sorry, but I'm not feeling so well."

"It's okay. Lie back and get some rest."

Ellie did as she was told, but didn't release her grip on Amanda. "I'm really going to miss your grandfather," she whispered.

"Me, too," Amanda agreed softly, as Ellie's eyes closed.

ON THE OTHER side of town, another woman was thinking about Jacob. Anna Leigh removed a shirt from the closet she had shared with her husband. She brought the soft fabric to her nose, unable to detect even the slightest scent of him. She carefully folded the shirt and placed it on top of the others on her bed.

"I may never forgive you, Jacob." She shook her head. "No, that's not true. I could never stay angry with you, love."

She removed a pair of slacks from the closet. "Perhaps I should have allowed Lois to help, after all. This is so much more difficult than I had imagined."

The sound of footsteps coming up the stairs caused her to turn and face the doorway. For a moment, she allowed herself the fantasy of Jacob returning from his shop. A smile crept onto her face as she anxiously watched the doorway.

"Mom? Are you up here?" Michael poked his head around the doorway. "Oh. There you are. I knocked on the door for five minutes when you didn't answer the doorbell."

Anna Leigh's face fell, but she covered up her disappointment by folding the slacks and adding them to the stack.

"Your father was supposed to fix that." She turned away from him so that he wouldn't see the tears in her eyes. "What brings you by today?"

"I was on my way to lunch and thought I'd see how you're doing." He stopped when he saw the stack of clothes on the bed. "What's going on?"

"I'm gathering Jacob's clothes to donate." She placed another folded pair of pants on the bed. "Reverend Hampton is sending someone to pick them up, later today."

Michael grabbed her arm. "Mom, wait. You don't have to do this now."

"Of course I do. There are needy families right here in Somerville who could use these things."

She pulled her arm away and turned toward the closet. "Since you're here, would you mind clearing out his shop? I promised the high school that I would donate his woodworking tools and inventory."

"Have you lost your mind? Do you have any idea how much that stuff is worth?"

Anna Leigh glared at him. "I'm not a feeble old woman, Michael. Of course I know."

"Then how can you do that?" He gestured to the clothes stacked neatly on the bed. "How can you do this? It's like you're trying to get rid of anything that reminds you of Dad. Next thing you'll be telling me is that you want to sell the house."

"Well, not immediately, but—"

He tossed his hands into the air. "What the hell?"

At her look, he held out his hands. "Mom, please. Think about this. You don't have to clear everything out this very minute. When it's time, I can help you."

"I believe I just asked you to help." She crossed her arms. "Michael, I'm perfectly capable of making these decisions. Hanging onto Jacob's things won't bring him back. But I can help other people by donating what I don't need. Don't you understand?"

"No, not really." He brushed his fingers through his hair in frustration. "I can't, Mom. Don't ask me to go through his shop. I don't think he would agree to what you're doing."

She spun away from the closet and pinned him with a vicious glare. The look was so unlike her, he took two steps back. "How dare you!"

"What?"

"How dare you stand there and tell me what my own husband would say, or do. I believe I know Jacob better than you ever will."

She stepped closer and poked him in the chest. "For your information, he told me years ago that he wanted his workshop donated to the high school. But you didn't bother to ask. You just assumed I was doing it out of some misplaced grief."

She glanced at the neat piles of clothing on the bed. "As a matter of fact, it's all spelled out in his will."

Michael leaned against the door frame and sighed. "He had a will? Who's the executor?"

"We both have wills. And our lawyer is the executor. I thought you knew that."

"No, Dad never said anything to me." He pushed off the door frame and flipped through the stacks of clothes. "Are you getting rid of all of his things?"

Anna Leigh's anger dissipated and left a bone-deep weariness in its stead. "Of course not. Only the excess. Why? Is there anything you would like to have?"

He shrugged, looking much like the little boy she and her husband had raised. "I dunno."

"Michael." When he didn't respond, she softened her voice. "Dearest, please. This is a horrible time for us all." Anna Leigh touched his forearm, grasping it when he didn't pull away. "As much as I love you, I cannot tolerate you trying to take control for me. I'm a grown woman who is fully in control of her faculties. Just because I'm grieving the loss of your father, doesn't mean I need you to guide my every moment."

"I know, Mom." Michael rubbed his eyes. "But I'm trying to help you."

She put her arm around his waist and hugged him. "If I ask, it's help. If you bulldoze in and take over, it's annoying and unnecessary."

Michael laughed. "Yeah, I know. Lois tells me the same thing."

He kissed the side of her head. "As much as I want to, I don't know if I can go into his shop. The memories are just too strong."

"As are mine, dearest. But don't worry, I'll see if Lexington can help me. She never spent much time in the shop, so perhaps it won't be as bad for her. But I'd really like to get the tools and things to the high school before they let out for summer."

"I understand." Michael put both arms around her and held her close. "I love you, Mom. Don't worry, we'll get through this."

She rested her cheek against his chest and held back a sob. As much as she wanted to believe him, Anna Leigh knew deep in her heart that she'd never get passed her loss.

Chapter Nine

A STRONG, COLD wind rattled the barn door, which caused two of the horses to whinny and snort. Lorrie looked up from the halter she was working on.

"Ugh. I hate winter."

Although it was the beginning of February, the ranch had been barraged by sleet and cold rain for the past week. On one hand, the precipitation was welcome, due to the drought of the previous year. On the other, softball practices had been postponed indefinitely.

Lorrie spent a lot of time alone, either in her room or the barns. Everything made her mad lately, and she got tired of getting into trouble for her attitude. Melanie seemed to look for ways to aggravate her, at least in her mind. She kicked her heels against the bale of hay she sat on. "Stupid Mel."

She tightened a strap on the halter. "Come here, Snow."

"Maaaa." The goat stood in the middle of the barn.

"Snow, I mean it. Come here." Lorrie stood and held out her empty hand. "Come on."

The goat trotted close and sniffed her fingers.

Lorrie carefully put the red halter on Snow's head. Snow began to back up. "Stop it." She checked the fit and scratched the goat behind the ear. "See? That's not so bad."

The barn door opened, blowing a chill inside. Shelby stopped just inside and took off her cowboy hat. "Hey, Lorrie."

"Hi, Miz Shelby." Lorrie led Snow to the stall that was hers and put her inside. "Behave yourself, Snow. I'll be back in the morning, okay?"

She rubbed the kid's nose before she closed the stall door. When she turned around, she saw Shelby take off her coat. "Whatcha doing?"

"I'm going to check all the horse's hooves to see how many need new shoes. Would you like to help? The farrier is due next week."

Lorrie brightened. "Can I? What do I have to do?"

Shelby tugged her leather gloves from her rear pocket. "Would you mind writing the name of the horse and the condition of the shoes?" She took a small notebook out of her shirt pocket and tossed it to Lorrie. "It would sure save me a mess of time. And my handwritin's so bad I can't read it."

"Okay."

"Thanks." Shelby opened the first stall. "Hello there, Stormy."

She slowly ran her hand down the horse's front left leg and leaned into her. "Come on, you stubborn old thing."

Once she realized what Shelby was doing, Stormy patiently allowed her to check all four hooves.

Shelby patted her on the shoulder before leaving the stall. "Looks like her right rear hoof could use a new shoe."

Lorrie wrote the information in the notebook. "Can I ask you something, Miz Shelby?"

Shelby entered Mine's stall. "Sure. What's up?" She checked the mare's hooves carefully.

"Umm, well. Do you like doing this?"

"This?" Shelby's hand ran across the bottom of a shoe. "Counting horseshoes?"

"No, not that." Lorrie leaned against the stall and rested her chin on a board. "Working on a ranch."

Shelby never stopped what she was doing, but gave the question careful thought. "It's a living. Why?"

"I dunno. Just wonderin'." Lorrie turned away and leaned her back against the stall. "Did you always want to be a cowgirl?"

After she put Mine's foot down, Shelby tipped her hat back from her face as she stepped out of the stall. "To tell you the truth, I never thought about it, one way or the other. I was born into the rodeo life and it was all I knew. I'm pretty good around animals, so it's a decent job."

She followed Lorrie across the barn, where they both sat on bales of hay. "Do you like it here?"

Lorrie looked at her scuffed boots. "I love my parents. And Mada and Pawpaw." She picked at the hay. "But I don't know if I want to live here all my life."

"Well," Shelby drawled slowly. "You ain't about to graduate or anything, are you?"

The comment made Lorrie laugh. "No."

"Then I reckon you don't have to worry about it right now." Shelby stretched her legs and crossed her ankles. "What do you want to do when you grow up?"

"Not this. But Momma will probably want me to take over the ranch." Lorrie mimicked Shelby's posture and crossed her feet the same way. "I want to be a professional softball player. I think I could be good enough."

"From the way your Mom talks, I think you could, too. Anything else?"

Lorrie took a piece of hay and chewed on the end. "I thought about being a vet, like Uncle Ron. But I don't know if I want to go to school for that long."

She turned and looked at Shelby. "Did you like school?"

"I'm ashamed to say I didn't get a chance to like it. If it weren't for Rebecca, I wouldn't even have my GED. I didn't like school, so I never bothered to finish."

"Oh." Lorrie considered that for a moment. "How come? Did your parents not make you?"

Shelby took off her gloves and placed them on the hay beside her.

"My parents were rodeo bums. My mom left when I was a kid, and when I was about your age, my dad was killed riding a bull. I got sent to live with my aunt, and gave her a load of hell. I ran off as soon as I could and rejoined the rodeo, 'cause I didn't have enough sense to do anything else."

"Wow. That's bad. Are you sorry you did?"

"Yeah." Shelby removed her hat and twisted the battered felt around in her hands. "Listen, kid. You can do whatever you put your mind to. But do your parents a favor, and talk to them. Don't let all these bad feelings fester up inside until it ruins you."

She stood and put her hat on. "But if you ever need to try it out on someone first, I'll be glad to listen."

Lorrie threw the hay stalk down and got up. "Thanks, Miz Shelby."

"How about you just call me Shelby? I reckon you're old enough."

"Really?" Lorrie walked to her and held out her hand, like she'd seen Lex do to seal a deal. "Thanks, Shelby."

For the first time in several months, everything felt right in Lorrie's world.

THE SLEET STUCK to the windshield of the Jeep and the condensation gathered inside, which made it hard to see the muddy road. Lex used the sleeve of her coat to wipe the glass in front of her. "What's up with this damned weather?"

Roy wiped the window on his side. "Your guess is as good as mine, Lex. All I know is that the trees are so heavily iced that the branches break off and destroy the fence. I brought in four extra guys to help with repairs."

"And yet, we're still out here." She put both hands on the wheel as the vehicle started to slide off the road. "Damn it."

Once it was under control she glanced at Roy. "Are you in as much trouble as I am for going out in this?"

"More." He pointed to a break in the trees ahead. "There's the marker that Jack Graham left. He's on the west perimeter with Chet, repairing the fence by the highway. I thought it was more important than this location."

Lex nodded and cut through the trees. "So we get to play around near the creek, instead."

"Yup."

As the Jeep cleared the trees, Lex groaned at the sight that greeted them. At least fifteen feet of fence was crushed beneath fallen branches. She parked as close to the fence as possible. "This is gonna take all day."

Before getting out of the Jeep, she blew her nose. "Damned allergies."

She stepped out of the jeep and adjusted her hat so that her face was as protected as possible.

Roy followed suit and was soon standing beside her, surveying the damage. "You know, we'll probably be able to salvage most of the fencing."

"I was thinking the same thing. All we have to do is set new posts and attach the fence to them. But clearing the damn limbs away will take a while."

"You want the chainsaw or the ax?" Roy asked, as he opened the back hatch of the jeep.

Lex joined him. "Your choice. We can switch off later."

He handed her the chainsaw. "I'll check the other side and make sure we don't have any cattle around the creek."

"Chicken." Lex followed him to the downed fence. "Watch your step, Roy. I don't want to be fishing you out of the creek. It's too damn cold to be swimming."

Roy waved at her and carefully navigated over the fallen fence. He headed down the slope toward the creek.

Lex shook her head and pulled on the chainsaw's cord three times before it started. She meticulously cut the first fallen branch into manageable pieces, using well-placed kicks to move the debris out of her way. Once the first tree was cleared, she exhaled and stopped. She shut off the chainsaw and looked around, not seeing her foreman.

"Roy? Where are you?" With her ears still ringing from the loud saw, she set it on the tree stump. "Hey, Roy! I'm not going to do this all by myself," she yelled.

She sniffled and cleared her throat.

Her only answer was the sound of sleet hitting her hat and the ground around her.

"Damn it. I'd like to get this finished before nightfall," she grumbled, as she followed his footprints toward the creek. "Roy?"

"Over here!"

Lex stopped just short of the swiftly running creek. "Where?" She squinted against the sleet and rain as she scanned along the creek bank. "Roy?"

"Down here," he yelled.

She looked toward the sound of his voice, finally spotting him about twenty yards downstream from her position.

Waist-deep in the cold creek, Roy had his arms around the neck of a calf, trying to keep its head up. Roy's back was against a pile of debris that consisted of trash and brush. He looked as if he was losing the battle with the water.

Lex cursed under her breath and ran toward him, sliding as her boots hit patches of slick mud. "Get out of there, you idiot!"

"I'm already drenched," he argued. "Are you gonna stand up there and yell at me, or help?"

"Can you hang on long enough for me to get a rope?" Lex wasted no time racing up the rise. She stumbled several times, but kept her feet under her and continued as quickly as possible.

At the Jeep, she removed her hat and duster and left them on the seat, then gathered both of their ropes. She steeled herself against the cold rain and hurried back to the creek.

Roy slipped beneath the water as the calf struggled to break free. The calf kicked its legs as it thrashed around. Roy felt a sharp pain in his right leg as he broke the surface of the freezing water. "Stay still, you stupid thing. I'm trying to help you!"

The calf reared and squalled, taking Roy under the water again. He felt a strong grip beneath his arms and his head was pulled above the swirling water. Gasping for breath, he coughed. "Thanks."

Lex held him against her chest. When she saw Roy go beneath the water, she had tossed the ropes on the creek bank and jumped in, heedless of the cold. "Have you lost your damned mind? No calf is worth you drowning," she yelled above the sound of the sleet and water.

"I know that. But I don't have a lot of choice at the moment. My damned leg is hung on something. Probably the same thing the calf is caught on."

"Crap. All right, let me see if I can pull you loose." Lex took a deep breath and dropped to her knees. Her head dipped beneath the water.

She kept her eyes closed and ran her gloved hands down Roy's legs. Near the bottom of the creek, she felt his boot wedged in a tangle of tree branches. She tugged on the branches as hard as she could, but couldn't pull them away. As her lungs began to burn, she popped her head above the water. "Damn it!"

"Boss?"

Lex coughed and shook her head. "Hang in there. I'll get it next time."

She inhaled and exhaled several times then ducked beneath the water again. She followed the same path and began to tug on his boot. The calf continued to struggle and suddenly Lex felt Roy's hand grab her shirt and pull her up. She broke the surface and gagged on the muddy water. "What the hell did you do that for? I almost had it."

Roy had his face buried against the neck of the calf. He raised his head. "S...s...sorry," he gasped. "I felt it," he swallowed hard, "grind together."

"What?"

"I think my leg's broken," he finally choked out. "Hurts something fierce."

"Where?"

"Right below my knee."

"Fuck!" Lex wiped the hair out of her eyes. "Let go of the calf, Roy. It's not worth it." She clenched her jaw to keep her teeth from chattering.

He shook his head. "I c...c...can't. The blasted thing's the only r...r...reason I'm still upright."

"All right. I'm going to try and get it loose first. Maybe it'll help pull you free." She put her hand on his shoulder. "It's gonna hurt like hell."

"I know." He tightened his grip on the calf and lowered his head. "Go ahead."

Lex patted his back and ducked beneath the water again. With renewed energy, she found where the calf's front leg was caught in a small length of barbed wire. Even with the protection of her work gloves, her hands were numb from the cold water as she worked to pull the animal free.

With a final, painful tug, the calf's leg slipped from the wire. In its haste to get away, it kicked out and knocked Lex away.

In shock, Lex inhaled a mouthful of muddy water. She stood on shaky legs to surface and held her right arm as she tried to catch her breath.

Roy released his hold on the calf and watched as it swam toward the shore. "Crazy thing."

He grimaced as he saw Lex's arm hanging limply. "What happened?"

"I think..." Lex coughed and spit into the water. "The damned thing kicked a nerve, or something. I can't feel much or move it." With her good hand shaking from the cold, she removed her knife from the leather holster on her belt. "I'll try not to get you, but I'm afraid I'm going to have to cut your boot off."

His eyes widened before he nodded. "Better than staying here all day." He watched as she tried to open the knife with one hand. "Let me help."

Lex handed him the knife. "Th...than...thanks." She took it back after it was opened. "Good thing I'm left-handed, huh?"

"Yeah." Roy clenched his jaw against the cold. "At this point, I wouldn't care if you cut my foot off."

"I'll try not to do that." Lex took a deep breath and disappeared underwater.

As he felt his leg being pulled, Roy bit his lip to keep from screaming. The grinding of the bones made him nauseous and he saw dark spots swim across his vision. Another powerful tug on his lower leg and he felt it come free.

Lex popped up out of the water, her open knife in her teeth. She put her good arm around Roy to keep him from falling.

"Thanks." With a shaky hand, he took the knife out of her mouth. "Thank God the water's not that deep."

"Yeah." She spit off to the side. "Think you'll be okay if I drag you to shore?"

"Don't have much choice."

Lex put her good arm under his and across his chest. "Try to let your leg just float, if you can." She slowly walked backward toward the creek bank. Roy's pained groans got louder the closer they got to shore. "Sorry."

"S'all right," he gasped.

The rushing water against his leg and the continued pain was too much for Roy to bear. He was unconscious before they arrived on the bank of the creek.

Once they were clear of the water, Lex fell back against the muddy bank. She panted and raised her face to the sky. With her mouth open, she caught as much of the icy rain as she could and spit several times. "God, that creek water's nasty. How're you doing, Roy?"

When he didn't answer, she turned his head so that she could see his face. Blood ran down his chin from where he had bitten his lip to keep from crying out. "Damn."

Now shivering violently from the cold, Lex wriggled until she was out from underneath Roy. She tried to use her right arm to pull herself away, but the sharp pain was too much. The only warmth came from her right hand. She looked down and saw blood seeping from the palm of her shredded glove, where she had fought with the barbed wire. "We're a mess."

It took her more than a minute to take the folded bandana from her back left pocket, since her soaked jeans were skintight. Lex grabbed her right wrist and brought her hand closer. The pain in her arm made her sick, but she quickly wrapped the bandana around her bloody palm. "Fuck! Damned barbed wire. I can't believe anyone uses it these days."

She knelt beside Roy and shook him by the shoulder. "Come on, Roy. I can't carry you up to the Jeep."

Roy groaned and blinked his eyes open. "What—"

"We've got a problem." Lex tried to lean over him and block the worst of the sleet.

"Yeah?"

"You can't walk like that, and there's no way I can get you up to the Jeep."

He closed his eyes. "Leave me here and go get some help, then."

"That's another part of the problem. I can't drive the Jeep with this arm." The stick-shift was hard enough to handle on a good day. Without her right arm, there was no way Lex could drive.

"Damn."

Lex struggled to her feet. "Let me run get my phone out of my coat." Her face paled as her injured arm swung away from her body. "Maybe I'll walk."

Roy carefully rose to a sitting position. "You're not looking too good there."

"No, I'm okay." Lex swallowed the bile that rose in her throat and tried to keep from passing out. "Hang in there, and I'll be back as soon as I can."

She slowly headed for the Jeep, silently praying that she wouldn't collapse before she called for help.

It seemed like forever, but Lex reached the Jeep within ten minutes. She opened the door and tried to pick up her duster with her right hand. "Fuck!" Her head spun and she thought she was going to pass out. Instead, she turned away from the Jeep and threw up, which brought more pain to her injured arm. She rested her forehead against the top of the vehicle and struggled to take deep, calming breaths.

When she was certain that she would remain standing, Lex put on her hat, grabbed her coat and the blanket they kept in the back for emergencies. On her way to where she left Roy, she took her phone from the coat pocket and flipped it open. Her hand shook so badly from the cold she hoped she wouldn't drop it.

The familiar voice was like a balm to her nerves. "Rocking W Ranch, Martha speaking."

"M...Martha? W...where's Am...manda?" Lex asked, as she tried very hard not to slip down the bank of the creek.

"Hello, Lexie. Nice to talk to you, too," Martha quipped.

Lex stumbled but kept on her feet. "S...s...sorry. Do you know if any of the g...guys have m...made it back, yet?"

"Not that I'm aware of, honey. Do you really need to speak to Amanda? She's giving Eddie a bath."

"Uh, I g...g...guess n...not. D...damn it!" Lex stumbled over an ice-covered clump of weeds and fell to one knee. She dropped her coat, the blanket and her phone, and grasped her injured arm. "Fuck!"

"Lexington Marie!" Martha scolded. She paused, but didn't get the expected apology. "What's going on? Where are you?"

Lex picked up the phone and stretched out on her back in the mud. She closed her eyes against the sleet that continued to fall. "C...could you p...please send someone to the n...n...orth trail that heads to the c...c...creek? Roy and I need s...s...ome help getting back to the h...h...house."

"Lordy, girl. What have you done now?"

"Can I explain l...later? It's f...f...freezing out here and I'd really like to get R...R...Roy back where it's warm."

Lex climbed to her knees, then to her feet. She adjusted her hat and put the blanket and coat over her shoulder. "Jack knows our ex...act l...l...location. He's the one that f...found the ruined fence."

She trekked slowly to where she had left her foreman.

Martha could be heard on the radio. "Base to Jack, do you read?"

As she listened to Martha handle things, Lex knelt beside Roy, who had his eyes closed. "Hey, take off your coat and put mine on."

Roy opened his eyes. "I can't take your coat." But even as he argued, he struggled to unbutton his soaked barn jacket.

"I sure as hell can't put it on. Not with this damned arm."

"Yeah, I didn't think of that." He gratefully accepted her heavy coat. "Thanks."

Lex sat next to him and held her phone closer to her ear. "I'm sorry, Martha. W...w...hat?"

"I couldn't reach Jack or Chet, but Charlie said he'd be glad to come."

"R...Roy's got a broken leg, and we're down by the creek." Lex braced herself for the explosion, and Martha didn't disappoint.

"A broken leg? I swear, you can find trouble in a church, Lexie."

Lex bit off a vulgar reply. Martha had no way of knowing how cold and miserable she and Roy were. "Yeah, I know. But Charlie w...won't be enough. And my d...d...danged arm is numb."

"All right. I'll see who else I can scrounge up. You hang in there, honey."

After she closed her phone, Lex shoved it into the breast pocket of her denim shirt. "M...Martha's gathering the c...cavalry, R...roy."

With his help, she was able to get the wet blanket around her shoulders. The sleet continued to fall and drench everything in sight so the blanket wasn't doing much good. "T...thanks."

He patted the ground beside him. His chattering teeth were almost as bad as hers. "D...don't be shy, Boss. Maybe we can share your m...m...onster of a coat."

Lex edged closer. "B...best offer I've h...had all afternoon."

She put her good arm around his shoulder and leaned into him.

LESS THAN HALF an hour had passed since Martha had informed her of Lex's call. Amanda couldn't keep still in the front passenger seat of the Expedition. She jiggled her foot, tapped her fingers on the center console and sighed for the fourth time since they'd left the house.

From behind the steering wheel, Charlie used his right hand to cover her fingers. Amanda had given him the keys, stating she was too nervous to drive. "We're almost there. Settle down."

"Easier said than done." Amanda pulled her hand away and crossed her arms. "Are you sure the three of us will be enough?"

Helen, sitting behind Amanda, leaned over the seat. "Both Martha and I tried to reach the hired hands via radio right up until Charlie got all the supplies together. We're all there is. And I don't know how he managed to break his leg, but I'm going to kill Roy when I get my hands on him."

Charlie squeezed Amanda's hand and released it. "You can't go blaming Roy. I'm sure he just got in the way."

"Don't listen to him, Helen." Amanda lightly swatted him on the arm. "Charlie's just picking on you."

"Now, Amanda, you know darned good and well that if there was trouble to get into, Lex is usually the first one to find it," Charlie said. "I reckon poor Roy just got in front of her."

Shaking her head, Amanda knew he was right. Her wife did tend to find the craziest things to get into. "That's so true."

She leaned forward and strained to see through the fog and rain. "Is that the Jeep?"

Charlie turned off the road and parked behind the vehicle. "Good eye, Amanda." He released his seatbelt. "Are you ladies ready?"

"The sooner we leave, the sooner we get out of the weather." Helen flipped the hood up on her coat.

Charlie followed behind Amanda. He carried a light-weight, aluminum stretcher while Helen brought the specially-packed first aid kit. Lex had purchased the double-folding, emergency stretcher a few years ago. It had come in handy more than once.

Charlie slipped in the mud. "Amanda, slow down. Some of us aren't as spry as we once were."

"Sorry." Amanda stopped and waited for the pair to catch up to her. She kept looking toward the creek, then back at them.

Helen's pace was similar to Charlie's. "Go on, we'll catch up."

With a nod, Amanda turned and jogged down the other side of the bank. As she reached the edge of the creek, she stopped and looked around. "Lex? Can you hear me?"

She listened carefully as she continued to try and see through the sleet and haze. "Lex!"

HALF-ASLEEP, LEX RAISED her head and blinked. "D...did you h...hear that?"

Roy shook his head. "J...just you snoring."

"I d...don't snore."

"Yeah, r...right." Roy shifted and cried out as another sharp pain went through his leg. "Damn. I've g...got to quit d...doing that."

Lex gave his shoulder a squeeze and slowly got to her feet. "I'm g...going to w...alk a ways and see if the troops have arrived."

The sodden blanket on her shoulders wasn't any help against the cold, so she tossed it to the ground. "I don't think I'll ever get w...w...warm again."

"I t...told you to g...go sit in the J...Jeep."

She held her arm against her body. "Oh, yeah. L...like I was going to l...leave you here alone. R... Right."

The sound of her name being called brought a smile to Lex's face. "S...speaking of the cavalry." She headed toward the voice, the smile never leaving her face. "Over here!"

"Lex?" Amanda called.

"We're over here," Lex yelled, as she walked toward her wife.

A FIGURE MATERIALIZED out of the gloom and Amanda's breath caught in her throat. Soaking wet, her clothes stained, Lex was still a welcome sight. Amanda broke into a run, disregarding the freezing rain and mud. She was solely focused on reaching Lex. Amanda stumbled forward and reached out for her. She noticed Lex's posture.

"What happened?"

"You p...probably wouldn't believe me if I t...told you." Lex grimaced as Amanda's arms went around her. "Ugh. Sweetheart, hold on." She gently pushed Amanda away. "Sorry, it's just—"

"What's wrong with your arm?" Unable to be completely free from Lex, Amanda had one hand resting on her wife's hip. Lex's right arm was against her side, and her left hand held it still at the elbow. The gray bandana wrapped around her hand was dark with blood. "Honey?"

Lex opened her mouth, but was saved from answering by Charlie.

"Good to see you in one piece." Charlie patted Lex roughly on the back. "Where's Roy?"

"I'll s...show you." Lex noticed the third rescuer. "Helen?"

The older woman tipped her head back and peered at Lex from beneath the hood on her coat. "Lex. Am I going to have to ground my husband from playing with you?"

Lex laughed and shook her head. "I hope n...not. Come on, he's right t...t...there." She led the group to where Roy lay wrapped up in her duster. "Hey, Roy. I told you t...the cav...alry was on the w...way."

He raised his head. "I sure am g...glad to see that."

Amanda could see Lex shivering. "Why don't you go on up and get in the truck? You're going to catch cold out here."

"Little l...late to be worrying about that," Lex muttered. "I'll stay."

Helen knelt beside her husband. "I don't know whether to kiss you or pinch you. Just what were you doing that caused you to hurt yourself?"

She held his hand as Charlie and Amanda put a splint on his injured leg. When Roy groaned and flinched, Helen brought their linked hands to her chest. "Sssh. It'll be over in a minute, honey."

UNABLE TO DO anything but stand in the rain, Lex watched silently as they tended to Roy. As she listened to Helen lovingly chastise her husband, Lex tried to stave off the bone-deep chill that had settled in her body. Her entire right arm was numb and she feared that it had sustained more damage that she originally thought. "M...m...maybe it's just the c...cold."

Amanda stood and wiped her hands on her jeans. "Did you say something, honey?"

"Nah. J...just thinking out l...loud."

Charlie stood and rubbed his hands together for warmth. "Lex, do you feel up to helping us get Roy out of here?"

"S...sure. I can take this side." She bent and took a firm grip on the stretcher near Roy's leg. She only hoped she could hold up her side with one hand. "Well? Are we gonna sit out h...here all d...day?"

"Don't get your knickers in a bunch," Charlie teased. "We're not the ones who thought it would be fun to go out in this nasty weather."

A light poke to her back kept Lex from mouthing off. She turned to Amanda and glared at her. "W...what?"

"Your arm."

Lex tried to appear as if she misunderstood. "I only n...need one for t...this."

Amanda lifted her end of the stretcher at the same time as everyone else. "We're going to have a nice, long chat when we get back to the house."

Knowing it was useless to argue, Lex nodded. She learned long ago that it was easier to go along with Amanda than to try and sneak anything past her.

"Yes, m...ma'am."

Her wink was received with an answering grin, as they carefully carried Roy's stretcher up the creek bank.

Chapter Ten

ALONG WITH THE slam of the back door, Lorrie's excited voice echoed in the hallway. "Then Kim pushed him right into the mud puddle! It was so funny."

"Well," Shelby drawled as she removed her coat, "I reckon that boy will think twice before he picks on her again."

"He told Mr. Nicks that he tripped. I think Jesse was embarrassed being knocked down by a girl."

Lorrie hung her coat next to Shelby's and followed her into the kitchen. She stopped short when she saw Martha at the stove. Rebecca was at the table, watching Eddie eat. "What are y'all doing here?"

Martha turned and put a hand on her hip. "Lorrie! That's not very nice."

"Um, sorry?" Lorrie hugged Martha and went to the refrigerator. "What's for dinner?"

"Lorraine Marie Walters. I know you were raised better than that," Martha scolded. "Sit at the table and think about what you said."

Eddie waved a grubby hand in the air. "Leelee!"

Lorrie grumbled under her breath, but did as she was told. She glared at the placemat in front of her. "I said I was sorry."

Shelby covered her mouth with her hand to hide her grin. She nodded to Rebecca and sat in the chair next to her. "Hey, darlin'. How's Mister Eddie doin' today?"

"Ha! Yum." Eddie crammed a bite of soggy graham cracker into his mouth. He pointed his grimy fist at Shelby, who used a napkin to wipe it clean.

"Thanks, buddy. I think I'll pass." She laughed at the look on his face.

"Yum." Eddie picked up a new cracker and proceeded to gnaw on it. "Mmm."

Martha brought Shelby a cup of coffee. "Here. You look a bit chilled."

"Thank you, ma'am." Shelby sipped the coffee and peered at her lover. "Not that I'm complainin', but what brings you out here today?"

Rebecca glanced at Lorrie, then back to Shelby. "Umm, well. Martha was sharing her stew recipe with me, and I wanted to make sure I got it right. I think I can cook it without poisoning you. I told Martha that I'd taken a cooking course one summer at the high school, but I'm not very creative. She's been very helpful."

"May I be excused?" Lorrie asked softly.

Martha put a tray in front of her. "Why don't you take this hot chocolate and cookies to the den, and share with your sister? Dinner won't be for a while, yet."

Lorrie's frown disappeared. "Yes, ma'am." She got up from the table. "I'm really sorry for how I acted."

Martha's smile of forgiveness lightened her step as she carried the tray out of the kitchen.

With a heavy sigh, Martha sat in the vacated chair. "I swear, that girl gets more like Lexie every day."

"Aw, she's a good kid," Shelby said.

"Oh, I know. But she's as temperamental as an old brood mare in the spring. Hormones are a terrible thing for young girls to go through." She lowered her voice. "I'm guessing you don't know what's going on."

Shelby cocked her head. "Uh, no. Lorrie and I just got back from the barn up at the bunkhouse. She was helping me check the shoes on the horses."

"Are the boys back?"

"No, ma'am. But with the weather being like it is, they're all out in trucks. Why?"

Martha turned to Rebecca. "I know he probably doesn't understand much, but would you mind taking Eddie to the den to play with his sisters?"

"Sure." Rebecca unfastened the belt that held Eddie in the chair. "Come on, handsome. Let's get you cleaned up so you can play."

"Pway!" Eddie cheered as he wrapped his grubby arms around Rebecca's neck. "Go!"

Shelby stood the moment her partner did. "You sure you don't want one of these?"

"I think I'll stick with spoiling everyone else's kids." Rebecca winked at Shelby before leaving.

"All right." Shelby sat beside Martha. "What's with all the secrecy?"

Martha patted her hand. "It's a bit of a long story. I'm hoping to hear some news from Amanda at any time. She, Helen and Charlie took Lexie and Roy to the hospital earlier today."

"What?"

"The last I heard, Roy's leg is broken, and Lexie," Martha shook her head and closed her eyes. "Lexie hurt her arm. She didn't think it was too serious, but Amanda put her foot down and made her get it checked out."

Shelby chuckled. "I can just imagine how well that went over. Bet Lex is chompin' at the bit, by now."

LORRIE SAT IN front of the fire and sipped her hot chocolate. She tried to keep her surly attitude going, but when Melanie directed Eddie during their tea party, she couldn't help but smile.

"No, Eddie. You have to hold the cup like this." Melanie held out her pinkie finger as she lifted the plastic teacup.

"Mine!" Eddie pounded his cup on the small table. "Yum!"

Melanie dramatically sighed. "Eddie, that's not right. Do you want to play tea party, or not?"

"Ha! Potty!" Eddie waved the teacup over his head. When he heard the pretty lady on the couch laugh, he did it again. "Potty!"

"It's par-tee, not potty," Melanie corrected.

"Potty, potty, potty," Eddie chanted. "Meemee potty!" His version of Melanie's name was amusing to everyone except Melanie.

Rebecca turned around and winked at Lorrie. "I think she has her hands full."

"Yep." Lorrie got off the hearth and walked around the sofa to sit next to Rebecca. "Do you know where my mom is?"

"Um, yes. I do." Rebecca lowered her voice. "She and Charlie went to help your momma and Roy. They had some trouble while repairing the fence by the creek."

Lorrie stuck her lip out and frowned. "How come they didn't come and get me? I coulda helped."

Rebecca put her arm around Lorrie's shoulder. "Well, honey, it was kind of a spur-of-the-moment thing. Since the weather's so rotten, they really wanted to get out there in a hurry."

"How come they're not back yet?"

Lowering her head so that she could speak quietly into Lorrie's ear, Rebecca said, "All I know is they had to take Roy to the hospital for a broken leg. Your mom is supposed to call when they have some news."

"They treat me like a little kid. I'm old enough to know stuff, too." With her arms crossed, Lorrie unintentionally belied her comment. "Miz, I mean, Shelby said I could call her just Shelby. That proves I'm older, right?"

"It sure does. But, you know that even grownups have to do things we'd rather not do." Rebecca playfully poked her in the ribs.

Lorrie giggled and squirmed away. "Like babysit them?" She pointed to her siblings. Another poke caused her to laugh. "Hey, stop!" Her laughter wound down and she turned serious again. "Was Momma really okay?"

"Leelee!" Eddie seemed tired of playing with Melanie. He tossed his teacup on the floor and toddled to the couch. With another happy scream, he tried to climb next to her. "Leelee!"

Rebecca caught him and pulled him up between them. "Careful there."

"Eddie! Our tea party isn't over." Melanie stood and stomped her foot. "Come back here."

"Potty," Eddie chirped. He grinned up at Rebecca when she laughed. "Potty."

Rolling her eyes at her little brother's charming smile, Lorrie shook her head. "It's par-tee. Can you say par-tee?"

Eddie waggled his head back and forth comically. "Parrrrrrteeeeee," he sang.

IN THE HOSPITAL waiting room, Amanda handed Charlie a steaming paper cup. "I'm not guaranteeing how good their coffee is, but it's all I could find."

She handed Helen a can. "This was the only diet drink they had. I hope it's okay."

"It's fine, thank you." Helen rested the chilled can on her thigh and stared at the closed doors to the emergency room.

Amanda sat next to Charlie. "Still no word?"

Charlie stared at the door. "Not a damned thing."

They had been waiting more than an hour and no one had come out to speak to them. "I realize they're busy, but still."

He sipped from the cup and made a disgusted face. "Good God. This is nasty."

Amanda patted his leg. "Bet you didn't have to wait like this when you were sheriff, did you?"

"Never." He set the coffee cup on the table beside him. "I think that coffee is how they keep business going. Stuff would kill a normal human."

They all turned toward the gray-haired doctor who stepped through the emergency door. "Is there someone here for Roy Wilson?"

Helen stood. "I'm Mrs. Wilson. How is my husband?"

The doctor was slight of frame, with a pressed lab coat that covered his faded blue scrubs. He glanced at the tablet in his hand. "We can step into the other room, if you'd like."

"We're all family. Please, how is he?"

"We'll prep him for surgery first thing in the morning."

He went on to explain how they would repair the damage to Roy's lower leg, and that the healing time varied from twelve to sixteen weeks. After answering several questions, he led Helen through the door to see her husband.

Amanda turned to Charlie. "Poor Roy. It sounds like he's in for a long recovery."

"Poor Helen," Charlie contradicted. "She's the one who's going to have to put up with him for that amount of time. If he's half as bad as some others I know, but refuse to name, she's in for a rough few months."

"I didn't even think about that." Amanda chuckled, but soon sobered as she thought about her wife. She understood how it would take a lengthy amount of time to run tests, but not being able to be with Lex was driving her mad. She had been sent to the waiting room when they took Lex to radiology. "I wonder how she's doing?"

Charlie rubbed her back. "She's probably giving the nurses fits.

You know how she can be. Why don't we call the house and see how the kids are doing? You promised Martha that you'd check in from time to time."

Amanda continued to stare at the door, as if willing it to open. "I know. But I'd hate to call with nothing to say. That would only upset her more." She frowned and started walking toward the door at the same time it opened.

An exhausted and disheveled Lex moved slowly into the room. Her right arm was in a sling, and her muddy clothes had been exchanged for a pair of faded green scrubs. She held a plastic bag full of clothes in her good hand, and her hair had dried in wild disarray.

Amanda met her halfway and carefully embraced Lex in the middle of the waiting room. "I'm so glad to see you."

She took the bag from her, but kept one arm around Lex's back. "You look like you're about to collapse."

"Thanks. I think I did that an hour ago. Has there been any word about Roy?" Lex followed Amanda to the chairs.

"The doctor just took Helen back to see him. They're supposed to do surgery on his leg in the morning."

Lex leaned her head against the wall and closed her eyes. "Damn. Bad break?"

"Bad enough." Amanda used her fingers to try to comb Lex's hair. "What did the doctor say about your arm?"

When Lex didn't answer, she caressed her cheek. "Honey?"

"Huh? Oh, yeah. Sorry." Lex yawned and opened her eyes wide, as if that would help her stay awake. "The bone in my upper arm is fractured. They put a plastic splint on and told me to come back in a couple of weeks for a regular brace. And I'm supposed to use this blasted sling until then, too." She glared at the contraption. "How the hell am I supposed to run the ranch, wearing this stupid thing? With Roy laid up, we're going to be short-handed enough as it is."

Amanda's hand traced along Lex's good arm until she was able to grip her hand. "We'll figure it out," she assured her wife with a squeeze. She looked at the heavy bandage on Lex's right hand. "What did they say about your hand?" She remembered all too well the mangled mess that had been hastily wrapped with a bandana.

"Not much. Gave me a tetanus shot and some stitches."

"Lex."

"What? Seriously, that was it. They cleaned it up, asked how it happened, and then gave me a damned shot."

Amanda leaned against her wife. "I'm sorry. I was hoping they'd tell you if there was any permanent damage."

Lex rested her head on Amanda's. "No, I'm sorry. I shouldn't have snapped at you. But the doctor seemed more worried about his canceled golf game. All I want now is a hot shower and a bed."

She sniffled and rubbed at her forehead. "Damned headache. Do you have any idea how long Helen will be?"

"Why don't you two go on home, and I'll stay here for Helen," Charlie offered.

Amanda wanted to be available for their friend but her first concern was for Lex's welfare. "Thanks, Charlie. We'll send someone back to get you." She slowly stood and held out her hand to Lex. "Come on, honey."

"I feel bad, leaving Helen like this. And I was hoping to see Roy." But as she spoke, Lex allowed herself to be pulled to her feet.

Amanda's arm immediately went around Lex's waist. "I'm sure Helen will understand. And from the way the doctor spoke, Roy isn't up to visitors. We'll come see him after his surgery."

Lex grumbled under her breath, but her exhaustion soon won out. "Not like I have a lot of choice, is there?"

"Nope." Amanda winked at Charlie. "See you later."

IT WAS AFTER eight o'clock that night by the time Amanda had Lex clean and settled in bed. She knew she needed to go downstairs and reassure their children, but all she wanted to do was sit beside her wife and watch her sleep.

Between her exhaustion and the pain medication, Lex barely made it through the shower before she fell asleep. Her face still showed signs of tension, even in deep slumber. Amanda lightly rubbed her wrinkled brow in an attempt to soothe her.

A soft knock at the door turned her attention away from Lex. She smiled at their oldest, who stood in the hall. "Come in, honey."

Lorrie frowned and looked uncertain. "I just wanted to see how Momma's doing. Is she okay?"

"She's sleeping," Amanda said softly. "But she'll be fine." She held out her hand. "Come here."

Taking her time, Lorrie cautiously edged into the room. She stopped a couple of feet from her parents. "She doesn't look very good."

Amanda turned and glanced at Lex. Dark circles were under her eyes, along with a few small scratches on her face. Her right arm sling was above the covers, and her hand was heavily bandaged.

"It was a long day." She patted the bed beside her. "Hop up."

"Are you sure?" Lorrie asked, even as she sat beside her. She lightly placed her hand on Lex's knee. "It's just her arm and hand, right?"

"Yes."

Lorrie traced the quilt pattern with her finger. "Mada said that we'll probably all have to pitch in now, since Momma and Roy can't work. Does that mean I have to help check fences and stuff?" She appeared panicked at the words that came out of her mouth. "I mean, I don't mind helping, really. But riding the fences is really boring."

"No, honey. That's not what Mada meant. Most of the fences can be checked from a truck nowadays. Since Helen will be busy taking care of Roy, Martha will most likely take over cooking at the bunkhouse. But you and your sister can be a big help, too."

"How?"

Amanda put her arm around Lorrie and kissed the top of her head. "I'm going to need someone to help with your little brother while I try to keep your Momma from going crazy."

Lorrie giggled. "Momma does like to work."

"I don't think she likes it as much as she knows someone has to do it. And she's going to get pretty cranky when she can't do as much as she wants."

An indignant squall from downstairs caused her to shake her head. "Do you think you can keep an eye on your Momma while I go see what Eddie's so upset about?"

"Sure." Lorrie looked around the room. "Can I get a book out of my room? I've got to finish two chapters before tomorrow."

Amanda stood and gave a final glance to her resting wife. "Of course. Why don't you get your pajamas on and get comfy on my side of the bed? I'll be back in a little while."

She kissed Lex on the forehead. She waited until Lorrie returned before she stepped from the room.

At the sound of footsteps, Amanda stood by the open baby gate at the top of the stairs and waited. She shook her head at Melanie, who was trying to outrun Freckles. "Mel, you know better than to run on the staircase."

"But, Mommy, Mada wanted—"

Amanda held up a finger, which immediately silenced Melanie. Even Freckles slowed down and slinked past her. "Now, what were you saying?"

"Mada needs clean pajamas for Eddie. He had an accident." Melanie stood on the step below her mother. "Is Momma feeling better?"

"She's asleep. But if you're quiet, you can go in and see her for a little while." Amanda ruffled Melanie's hair. "I'll take care of Mada and Eddie."

Melanie gave her a quick hug. "Thanks, Mommy."

She skipped down the hall toward her room, with Freckles bouncing along beside her. "Come on, Freckles. Let's get my markers and go see Momma."

Amanda started to call out to her to slow down, but decided against it. She knew that Lorrie would take her job as Lex's protector seriously, and wouldn't allow her sister to be a disturbance. With a heavy sigh, she slowly descended the stairs.

By the time she was at the last step, Amanda could hear Martha in the kitchen.

"I ought to put your little rear in the kitchen sink, mister," Martha scolded good-naturedly.

"Ha!" Eddie countered.

Amanda peeked around the kitchen door and had to cover her mouth with her hand.

Eddie sat on the counter, wearing only a diaper and a very satisfied look on his face. His hair was plastered to his head by what appeared to be oatmeal, which also liberally coated his chest and belly. He patted his stomach and giggled. "Pbbbbttt."

"Don't talk back to me, young man." Martha wiped at the mess on his head with a wet paper towel.

"No, no, no!" Eddie shook his head. He tried to wriggle away from her, but Martha had a firm grip on his diaper. He swatted at her hand. "No!"

Martha stopped what she was doing and pointed a finger at him. "I know you didn't just hit me, did you?"

Eddie gave her his most charming grin. He patted the congealed mess on his stomach. "Uck."

"That's right, young'un. Uck. Now stay still and let me get you cleaned up."

Amanda stepped into the kitchen. "Need a hand?"

"I could use more than two, I think."

"Mommy! Uck!" As Amanda stepped closer, Eddie tried to jump toward her. "Mada, no!"

Martha put both hands around him. "You're not going anywhere until we get some of this goop off you. Maybe next time you'll think twice before playing in your food."

"No!"

Amanda grimaced. "How about I take him upstairs for a bath? I think you're fighting a losing battle."

"Are you sure you're up to it? I can always bathe him down here and take him home with me for the night."

"No, that's okay." Amanda took a clean dishtowel and put it between her shirt and her son, who she picked up and held close. "Are you ready for a bath?"

"Yay!" Eddie started wriggling. "Go!"

Martha laughed as she wiped down the counter. "Looks like his majesty has spoken." She turned and kissed Eddie on his cheek. "Be good for your mommy."

"Muwah." Eddie blew her a kiss and giggled. "Mada, Mada, Mada," he sang. "Go!"

Amanda tightened her grip. "Thanks for everything today. I don't know what we'd do without you."

She blew out a shaky breath and leaned her head against Eddie's, not caring if the oatmeal transferred to her own hair. "I have a feeling it's going to get worse before it gets better."

"Don't you worry about a thing." Martha removed her apron and draped it across a chair. "There's enough folks around here to handle just about anything. I'm going to do the cooking for the hands, and Charlie's going to help Shelby get a handle on what Roy does."

She hugged Amanda with one arm as they walked from the kitchen. "You take care of Lexie and the kids, and we'll keep an eye on everything else."

Amanda's laugh came out as a half-sob. Martha's matter-of-fact attitude reassured her more than any words ever could. "You've got it all figured out, haven't you?"

"Darn right. I've been on this ranch for a lot of years, honey. Ain't nothing we can't fix if we put our minds to it." She stopped at the back door. "If you need anything before morning, just give me a holler."

She bundled a heavy scarf over her head and buttoned her coat. "I've left a breakfast casserole in the fridge for tomorrow, so you won't have to cook."

"Thanks, Martha. You're a lifesaver. Have a good night."

"Mada, Mada!" Eddie added gleefully.

"I'll see y'all tomorrow." Martha headed out into the cold and wet evening, leaving a bemused and grateful Amanda behind.

ONCE EDDIE WAS clean and in warm pajamas, Amanda kissed his head and tried to put him in his recently converted toddler bed.

"No," he argued weakly. His eyes wouldn't stay open, but he refused to go to sleep. "Momma."

"Honey, Momma is asleep. You'll see her tomorrow, I promise." Amanda tucked a blanket around him, which he promptly kicked away.

"Momma, Momma, Momma." He pulled himself up and stood, rubbing his eyes with one hand. "Momma."

The battle had been lost. Amanda gathered his blanket and picked him up.

"I can't really blame you." She carried him across the hall to the master bedroom. "We might as well..." Her voice trailed off as she stopped inside the door. "What I wouldn't do for a camera."

The king-sized bed that had been lovingly built by her grandfather was covered with sleeping bodies. Lex was peacefully resting as she had left her, with a couple of additions. Melanie had snuggled against her side while Lorrie was near the foot of the bed, her head pillowed on Lex's shin. Both were covered with the quilt that belonged to Lex's grandmother.

Amanda tucked Eddie near her wife's left shoulder. He immediately rolled and tangled his fingers in Lex's sleep shirt, his eyes closing instantly.

"At least they left me some room." Amanda removed Melanie's coloring book, markers and Lorrie's book from the bed.

After brushing her teeth and changing into her nightgown, Amanda crawled beneath the covers and turned to watch Lex and the children. The long day finally caught up with her and she felt tears burn her eyes. She brushed Lex's hair out of her face and wasn't surprised to feel overly-warm skin. "I knew you'd catch a cold out there."

Lex opened her mouth and inhaled, releasing the breath in a deep snore.

Amanda chuckled and pulled the blanket over Eddie. "I wonder if I can get Rodney to make a house call tomorrow."

She kissed her fingertips and then touched Lex's lips. "Goodnight, love."

Chapter Eleven

THE FOLLOWING MORNING was a whirlwind of activity. In the kitchen, Amanda made breakfast while Eddie watched from his high chair. Since their son was easily occupied by the scrambled eggs on his plate, Amanda considered her part of the morning ritual the easier of the parental tasks. Lex's job was to get both girls up and moving for school after she returned from the barn. If they didn't get up in a timely manner, the following school day she'd wake them before her barn excursion, which was almost a full hour earlier. At any rate, she would usually end up having to make more than one trip to the girl's bedrooms to urge them along.

"Mommy, yum," Eddie said, as he smacked his lips. He had tidbits of egg on his face. He seemed to be enjoying his breakfast.

Amanda laughed as she checked the clock. "So glad you like it. Your sisters had better get down here soon or they won't have time for their yum."

"Leelee mm Meemee?"

"That's right. Lorrie and Melanie."

Amanda moved to the doorway. "Girls," she yelled, "you're going to be late!"

Soon, frantic footsteps were heard racing down the stairs. Melanie was the first to enter the kitchen. "Sorry, Mommy. I couldn't find my shoe." She climbed into a chair and reached for a glass of orange juice.

"You have more than one pair of shoes, honey."

Amanda placed a plate with Martha's breakfast casserole in front of Melanie. It consisted of scrambled eggs, hash browns, sausage and cheese.

"Do you want an apple or an orange with your lunch?"

Melanie chewed a forkful of food before answering. "Orange, please. Like my socks." She wriggled her right foot, showing a bright orange sock.

"All right." Amanda added an orange to Melanie's insulated, purple lunch bag and placed it on the table next to her.

Lorrie skidded into the kitchen, sneakers in hand. "Can I have mine in a tortilla, so I can eat it on the way to the bus?" she asked as she sat and hurriedly put on her shoes.

Amanda placed the wrap on Lorrie's plate. "I figured as much. Where's your—"

Lex came into the room and dropped into her chair. "You girls about ready?" she asked quietly.

After she placed an insulated lunch bag beside Lorrie's plate, Amanda took a closer look at her wife. Lex always got up before the rest of them to take care of the horses, so this was the first time she had seen her since the previous evening. She was pale and still wore her barn jacket, but her sling was missing. "Honey? Are you feeling all right?"

Lex cleared her throat. "Yeah, just a blasted cold." She slowly rose to her feet. "Okay, girls. Get your stuff together and we'll head for the bus stop."

The girls scurried about and they each got a kiss from Amanda as they left the kitchen to get their coats.

Amanda stopped Lex before she had a chance to follow. "Do you need me to take them?"

"Nah." The tickle in her throat couldn't be ignored any longer and Lex coughed so hard that she had to grab the back of a chair for balance. She took a couple of slow breaths. "Whoa."

When Lex coughed, Amanda immediately put her arm around her waist to keep her from falling. "I think you'd better stay here. I'll take the girls."

Lex straightened and shook her head. "I'm fine." She wasn't fast enough to avoid the hand that touched her face. "Stop it."

"Honey, you're burning up. Please stay here."

When Lex opened her mouth to argue, she was seized by another cough. This time, she found herself guided to the chair. While she caught her breath, Amanda unbuttoned her coat.

"You and Eddie keep one another company while I take the girls," Amanda gently ordered. She carefully slid the coat from Lex's shoulders. "Where's your sling?"

"Upstairs."

Amanda caressed her wife's cheek. "Do me a favor?"

"What?"

"Don't try to lift Eddie out of the high chair. I think he gained five pounds last night."

Lex leaned into Amanda's hand and kissed her palm. "No problem."

WHEN AMANDA RETURNED from the bus stop, she found the kitchen empty. And clean. "I'm going to kill her," she muttered.

She heard Eddie laughing and followed the sound to the living room, cursing her wife's stubbornness. "Dammit, Lex, your arm won't heal—" Her voice trailed off when she saw Charlie and Eddie on the living room floor. "Where did you come from?"

Charlie looked up from the building blocks that Eddie had gleefully knocked over. "I was born in Bastrop, but I don't guess that's what you're asking."

Eddie carefully stacked one block on top of another. "Boom!" he slapped at them, causing the top one to skitter across to Charlie. "Mommy!"

Amanda sat on the footstool and brushed Eddie's dark hair back. "That's good, honey. Can you stack them higher?"

Eddie gathered several blocks and began to put one on top of another.

Charlie gestured toward the ceiling. "She's upstairs."

"Did she ask you to come over?"

"No. I called to see if y'all needed anything from the store, and she could barely talk. I figured she needed some help. I sent her upstairs as soon as I got here. She looked like he—" He stopped and glanced at Eddie. "I mean, like she had been wrung out. When she tried to argue with me, I threatened to call my wife."

"Ha! That'll teach her. Thanks, Charlie. If you're okay here, I'll run up and check on her."

"Sure, no problem. I've got this young 'un to keep me company. Right?" he asked Eddie.

Eddie picked up a block and tried to bite it. "Ugh." He stuck his tongue out and made a funny face. "Uck." He handed the slobbery wood to Charlie. "Pawpaw?"

Charlie took the block and wiped it off with a tissue. "Thanks, buddy. Why don't you show Pawpaw how to build a fence?" He winked at Amanda, who used the opportunity to sneak from the room undetected.

As she navigated the stairs, Amanda tried to think of some way to get her wife to take it easy for a day or so. She had a good idea of the arguments that Lex would use. Unfortunately, many of the points Lex would make would be perfectly reasonable. With Roy incapacitated, someone had to take charge. Shelby didn't know all the ins and outs of the ranch just yet, but Amanda hoped she was a fast learner.

At the top of the stairs, Amanda could hear Lex cough in their bedroom. She grumbled under her breath and walked into the room, ready for a battle. She froze when she saw Lex kneeling beside the bed. "Lex!"

Lex ignored her and used the bed to pull herself up with her good hand. She took a shallow breath, then another. "I'm okay," she wheezed as she rubbed her chest with her good hand.

"That didn't look okay to me." Amanda put her arm around Lex's back and forced her to sit on the bed. "I'm calling Rodney."

"No." Lex tried to get up, but Amanda had a firm grip on her. "It's just a cold."

"Like hell it is. You've had colds before, and none of them have taken you to your knees." Amanda reached for the phone on the nightstand. "He might have time to see you this morning."

Lex caught her hand. "Wait. Maybe it's not just a cold. I swallowed some creek water and it made my throat sore. Between that and the allergies I've been fighting the past week, I've got a little bit of a cough."

She cleared her throat. "There's a ton of stuff to do since Roy's laid up. But I'll try to make it a short day, all right?"

Amanda squeezed her hand. "Damn. Why didn't you tell me before now? And, no, it's not all right. Going out in the cold air will make you feel worse. You hired Shelby for a reason. Let her and the guys handle things. How about a compromise? Take some heavy duty cold meds and sleep until lunch." She looked into Lex's eyes and added softly, "Please?"

"You know, one of these days that look isn't gonna work on me," Lex whispered. "All right. I'll call Shelby and let her know she's on her own."

"Save your voice, and let me give her a call. I saw her drive up while we were waiting for the bus. Right now she's probably fending off Martha's offer of breakfast."

Amanda stood. "Need help with your clothes?"

Lex tried to give her a sexy grin, but ended up coughing. Once she was able to breathe again, she lowered her head and watched as Amanda carefully removed her shirt.

"This would be a lot more fun...if I could catch my breath." She stifled another cough.

"Sssh." Amanda bent and helped with her boots then slid the well-worn jeans down Lex's legs. "We can have fun another time."

Once she had Lex dressed in her pajamas and tucked under the covers, Amanda went to the bathroom and returned with the cold medicine. The water in the paper cup fizzed as she handed it to Lex. "Bottoms up."

Lex made a face at her but did as she was told. "Thanks."

She grinned when Amanda took the cup away and motioned for her to lie back. "Are you gonna read me a story, too?"

"I can, if that's what it takes to keep you in bed."

"There's several ways to—" Lex broke into another coughing fit. By the time she was finished, Amanda had tucked another pillow beneath her head to keep her from lying flat. "Damn."

Amanda sat beside her and touched Lex's cheek. "Did you take anything for your fever when you came up?"

Lex closed her eyes at the cool touch. "Nah. That cold stuff should help," she answered hoarsely. "Mind leaving your hands? They feel good."

"Sure." Amanda continued her gentle caress until Lex fell asleep. "Sleep well, love."

AMANDA CONSIDERED IT a major victory when Lex didn't come downstairs for lunch. After Charlie took Eddie home with him, she cleaned up their dishes and decided it was time to wake Lex and get her to eat. She heated a bowl of chicken noodle soup and placed it on a tray with a slice of homemade bread and a glass of iced tea.

Upstairs, she stopped at their door. Part of her wanted to let Lex continue to rest. It wasn't often she would take time off, no matter what the reason. Amanda put a smile on her face and stepped into the room.

Lex hadn't moved since that morning. Her mouth was slightly open and a rattling wheeze came out with each labored breath.

"Honey?" Amanda placed the tray on their dresser before she crossed the room. "I've brought you some lunch." She sat next to her wife's hip and touched her cheek. "Come on, love. Time to wake up."

Lex continued to wheeze, but didn't wake.

Amanda was alarmed by the heat coming from Lex's face. She lightly swatted Lex's face. "Lex, wake up."

Her labored breathing continued, but slowly Lex opened her eyes. "Wha—" a rattling cough cut her short. She found herself raised into Amanda's arms with her forehead resting on her wife's shoulder. "God."

"Sshh. I've got you," Amanda whispered, as she held Lex close. Once Lex's breathing slowed, Amanda leaned back so she could look into her eyes. "Now can I call Rodney?"

Lex struggled to keep her eyes open. "Yeah." She closed them and rested against Amanda again.

Keeping one arm around her wife, Amanda grabbed the cordless phone from the nightstand and used her thumb to hit the speed dial. The medical office's receptionist answered on the second ring.

"Hi, Ellen. This is Amanda. Does Rodney have a moment to talk? Sure, I can hold. Thanks."

Another cough came from Lex, this time ending with a strangled gasp. She accepted a tissue from Amanda and spit into it. "Ugh."

The slight action had worn her out. Lex closed her eyes and leaned against the headboard.

"Honey, I...oh. Hi, Rodney. I'm sorry to bother you, but Lex seems to have come down with something, and I was wondering," Amanda paused as Rodney spoke. "Fever, horrible cough and she just recently started having trouble breathing."

Amanda listened as her eyes never left Lex's face. "We thought she might have gotten a cold from the swim in the creek. What? Yes, she's burning up, but I'm not sure what her temperature is."

Amanda kept the phone in place by resting it between her head and her shoulder, as she used her hand to touch Lex's face. "Honey?"

Lex stifled a cough and opened her eyes. "Yeah?"

"Rodney wants to know if your chest hurts."

"Like a horse sittin' on me."

"Did you hear what she said? Uh huh. Are you sure? Well, yes. She'd been fighting her allergies for the past week, so we thought..."

Amanda stood. "Yes, all right. Thanks, Rodney. We'll leave here in a few minutes. Bye." She put the phone back on its cradle and exhaled.

"Honey, Rodney wants us to head into town."

"Probably to give me a damned shot." Lex slowly rose into a seated position on the bed and watched Amanda take a pair of sweatpants from the bottom drawer of the dresser. "I can wear what I had on earlier."

She tried to stand, but a sudden cough kept her seated.

Amanda rolled her eyes as she brought the sweatpants to Lex. "Humor me. It's easier to get you into these than to try and put your boots and jeans on."

"I can dress myself," Lex muttered, even as she allowed Amanda to slip the sweats on her legs. "This seems like a lot of work for a damned cold."

"Maybe. But he thinks it could be more serious than that." Amanda tied the laces on Lex's tennis shoes and patted her knee. "Let me call Charlie and see if he can watch Eddie while we're gone, and maybe pick the girls up from the bus stop, in case we don't make it back in time."

Lex shakily got to her feet then ran a hand through her hair. "I should have taken a shower."

"I don't think so. You'll just get more chilled."

Amanda noticed the tray of food that she'd abandoned earlier. "Damn it. Your soup is probably cold by now."

"That's okay, I'm not hungry."

Another hard coughing fit struck, and Lex had to lean into Amanda to keep her balance. Once she caught her breath, Lex slowly straightened. "Right now, a shot's not soundin' so bad."

THE WALLS OF the tiny examination room seemed to close in on Amanda as she watched her brother-in-law move his stethoscope from one side of Lex's chest to the other. To stay out of his way, she stood behind the head of the table with one hand on her wife's arm. On the opposite wall, a poster of the respiratory system taunted her, and she closed her eyes momentarily to settle her nerves.

Lex was partially reclined and appeared asleep. The trip from the ranch had drained her of any energy she had left. Amanda had to help her into the clinic and Lex didn't even fuss when Rodney asked her to change from her sweat shirt to a paper gown. Now she rested quietly on the exam table, without her usual bravado.

Rodney straightened and removed the stethoscope from his ears. He shook his head and patted Lex on the leg, but looked directly into Amanda's eyes. "It's definitely not a cold, but I'd like to get a few chest x-rays before I make a diagnosis."

Amanda looked from Lex to Rodney. She frowned and cocked her head. "Why? What do you think it is?"

"Yeah. Come on, Rodney. I don't think—" Lex coughed so hard that she ended up gasping for air.

Rodney opened the door and called for his nurse, Laura. They conferred quietly before she scurried away.

In less than five minutes, Laura wheeled a portable oxygen tank into the room and hooked it up to a mask. She brought the mask close to Lex, who turned her head.

Lex weakly pushed it away. "I don't need that."

Amanda grabbed her hand. "Shut up and let Laura do her job."

Her worry continued to grow when Lex surrendered without another word and rested her head against the pillow.

When Lex closed her eyes, Rodney removed his stethoscope and tucked it into his coat pocket. "Lex, let the oxygen give you a break while I get the radiology room set up, okay? Amanda, let's go outside to talk so she can rest."

"All right." Amanda kissed Lex on the forehead. "Behave for Laura, or I'll send Ellie in here."

Lex opened her eyes and gave her a weak smile. Her eyes drooped and closed. "'Kay."

Amanda followed Rodney into the hallway. "What is it?" she asked.

"I think the best thing for Lex is to be admitted to the hospital."

"What?"

He held up his hands in an attempt to calm her. "I'll need to see x-rays to be sure, but I'm fairly convinced that she has Streptococcus pneumonia. And if that's the case, it'll continue to escalate."

"Pneumonia? Can't you just prescribe her some stuff and let me take her home? Going to the hospital sounds rather drastic. She bounces back pretty quickly when she gets sick. The last time she had the flu, she only needed a day or two to get better." Amanda's worry caused her to babble. "And you know we're going to have one hell of a fight on our hands about this. She'd rest much better at home."

Rodney gently grasped her forearm. "I wouldn't suggest it if I didn't think it was necessary." He squeezed her arm to get Amanda to focus on him. "I don't want to alarm you, but if Lex isn't treated properly, and quickly, she could get much worse. People die of pneumonia all the time. Do you understand?"

Amanda was quiet for a moment as she considered his words. "You mean like the elderly and children, right?"

The negative shake of his head scared her. She never considered losing Lex to something as innocuous as a bacteria. She fought down a surge of panic and took a deep breath. "All right. Let me go in and talk to her."

When he began to follow, she stopped him. "Alone, okay?"

"Of course. I'll make certain we can rush her through x-ray."

"Thanks." Amanda slowly opened the door. "Laura, do you mind if I spend a few minutes alone with Lex?"

Laura checked the meter on the tank and patted Lex on the leg.

"Not a problem. You just lie there and relax. Amanda, holler if you need anything."

After the nurse left, Amanda moved to stand next to her wife. She brushed her fingers through Lex's hair. "How are you doing, honey?"

"Mmm." Lex opened her eyes and struggled to focus. She tried to slip the mask from her face, but Amanda stopped her.

"Sssh. You don't have to talk. Listen, I spoke with Rodney, and he thinks you may have pneumonia."

Lex frowned.

"Yeah, I know." Amanda touched Lex's cheek. "And, it's not going to get better without some serious medication."

Lex's voice was barely a whisper. "Shots?"

"No, worse than shots." Amanda fussed with the thin blanket that covered Lex. "Even though he wants to x-ray your chest to be certain, Rodney thinks that you need to go into the hospital to be treated."

Lex sat up and tugged the mask off her face. "No. Hand me my shirt."

"Stop it." Amanda took the mask from Lex's lap and slipped it over her head. "You'll do what you need to do to get better. And if going to the hospital for a night or two is what it takes, then I'll personally drive you there and sign you in."

Although muffled through the mask, Lex continued to argue. "I can—"

"No, Lex. You can't." Amanda stepped away from the table and walked across the room to stare at the lung poster. She turned to look at her wife, gesturing at the poster behind her. "You can't even take a breath without coughing your head off. This is a lot more serious than a cold, Lex. Breathing is kind of a big deal. So." She moved to stand by the bed. "Do this for me, please?"

Her laugh was forced as she pushed her hair away from her eyes. "Don't you dare leave me alone with three kids, you hear me?"

There was a quiet knock on the door before Laura peeked inside. "X-ray time."

Amanda squeezed Lex's hand. "Are we good?"

Lex pulled the mask away. "You cheated."

"How did I cheat?"

"Kids."

"I'll use whatever I have to, when it comes to you. Even our children." Amanda kissed Lex's forehead. "I love you."

"Love you, too." Lex coughed and glared at the oxygen tank. "Hate this."

Her frown deepened when Laura brought in a wheelchair. "No."

Laura grinned and whipped the blanket from Lex. "Yes. Be good, or we won't do wheelies down the hall."

She winked at Amanda as she helped Lex into the chair. "If you want to wait in Dr. Crews' office, we'll be done in a few."

She turned off the oxygen and disconnected the mask. "Quick reprieve, then back on the good air when we're done."

"Thanks, Laura." Amanda followed them and watched the nurse push Lex down the hall. "I'd better call the ranch and let them know. Martha's going to throw a fit," she told herself. She turned and almost ran into Ellie, who stepped from another room.

Ellie laughed and embraced her. "I'm sorry, I didn't mean to startle you. I just found out y'all were here. Where's Lex?"

"Laura took her to get some x-rays." Amanda leaned against the wall. "Rodney thinks she may have pneumonia."

"Oh, no." Ellie glanced toward the radiology room. "Why don't you grab some coffee from the break room and I'll keep an eye on her? I can come get you as soon as she's done."

Amanda shook her head and hugged herself. "No, that's okay. I'll just go back to her room and wait."

Ellie gently took her by the elbow. "No, that won't do at all."

She guided Amanda to the staff break room, which consisted of a small, round table and four plastic chairs, a microwave and a refrigerator. One wall had a row of cabinets. Below them was a steel countertop, which had a sink in the middle, with a coffee pot on one side of the sink. The opposite wall had a worn, gray microfiber sofa.

Ellie lightly pushed Amanda toward the sofa. "Have a seat."

"Are you this bossy at home?"

"Maybe." Ellie opened the cabinet above the coffee maker and searched for a clean mug. "And if I am, Kyle doesn't seem to mind. Ah ha!" She rinsed her find at the sink before she poured the coffee. "Do you want anything in it?"

"That's not—" Amanda rolled her eyes at Ellie's glare. "Okay. One sugar, please."

Ellie brought the doctored cup to her. "Can I get you anything else?"

"No, this is good, thanks." Amanda stared into the dark liquid. "I guess I'd better start making some calls, if Lex is going into the hospital."

Ellie sat beside her. "Why don't you wait for the results of the x-rays? Nothing against Dr. Crews, but he tends to be overly careful. And if Lex does have to be admitted, I'll be glad to help you with whatever I can. And so will Kyle."

"Thanks, Ellie. That means a lot to me."

"No thanks are necessary. That's what I'm here for." Ellie stood and adjusted her purple scrub top. "I'm going to run and check on Lex's progress. Be back soon."

Amanda removed her cell phone from the back pocket of her jeans. She hit the speed dial number and glanced around the room while she waited.

On the fourth ring, Martha answered. "Rocking W Ranch,

Martha speaking."

"Hi, Martha, it's Amanda."

"Hello, sweetie. Are y'all already back from the doctor? Charlie said you might be a while."

Amanda shook her head, then realized Martha couldn't see her. "No, we're still at Rodney's. He thinks—" She paused as she tried to think of the best way to phrase the news.

"What's wrong?"

"Um, Rodney thinks Lex needs to go to the hospital."

Martha snorted. "For a cold? That's nonsense. He does tend to jump the gun. Why, just last month, he told Charlie that he needed to go to a specialist for his ingrown toenail. Can you believe that? Old Doc Anderson used to just deaden the toe and take care of it. I mean, really. A specialist? Horse puckey."

"It's not like that. By the time we got here, Lex could barely breathe. He was so concerned that he put her on oxygen."

"What? And Lexie went along with that?"

Amanda sighed. "It's not like she had much choice, Martha. We're waiting on the x-rays to be sure, but Rodney believes she has pneumonia."

"Pneumonia? But Lexie hasn't been sick enough for that." Martha spoke to someone on her end of the call. "No, they don't know for sure. Hush up, Chet."

She returned her attention to the call. "Amanda? If you need anything at all, give me a call. I can be there in no time."

"All right, thanks." Amanda got up from the couch and began to pace around the small room. "I'll call you back as soon as we know something for certain. They should be finished with the x-rays anytime, now."

"Of course, honey. You do what you need to do. I'll have Charlie meet the girls at the bus stop this afternoon. Don't you worry about a thing."

"Thanks. I'm going to go see about Lex. Talk to you later." Amanda disconnected the call and returned the phone to her pocket. She heard a commotion in the hall and went to investigate.

Two EMT's moved quickly down the hall with a wheeled stretcher. Their rubber-soled shoes squeaked loudly on the shiny linoleum tile.

Amanda saw Laura at the end of the hall, motioning for the paramedics. She was stopped from rushing past them by Ellie, who had eased by the stretcher. "What's going on?"

Ellie guided Amanda out of the hallway and into the break room. "Rodney called them. He wants Lex taken to the hospital in Parkdale."

"I need to be with Lex." Amanda tried to step by her, but Ellie blocked the doorway. "Move."

"Give them a minute to get her settled. Then we'll follow them over, okay?"

Amanda grabbed her arm and pulled her away from the door. "No, it's not okay. That's my wife!" Amanda stumbled into the hall in time for the loaded stretcher to head toward her. Lex was strapped to it but in an upright position.

The paramedic in front stopped. "Excuse us, ma'am. We need to get by."

Lex pulled the oxygen mask away from her face. "Good luck with that," she gasped, before the paramedic behind her put it back in place.

"Ma'am, you need to keep quiet," the second paramedic ordered.

She tried to glare at him, but her eyes wouldn't stay open as she struggled through another ragged cough.

Amanda pushed by the paramedic and met Rodney at the head of the stretcher. She rested her hand on Lex's shoulder. "What the hell is going on?"

Rodney tried to move her aside, but Amanda stood firm. "Amanda, please let them do their job."

"Not until you tell me why."

"Lex started choking during the x-rays and couldn't get her breath. Her pulse/ox level dropped dangerously low, and I didn't want to take any chances. So I thought it would be best to err on the side of caution and transport her immediately."

Amanda stared at him for a moment, before she turned her back on him and looked down at Lex. "Looks like you get the fun ride." She played with Lex's hair. "Behave yourself until I get there, all right?"

Lex tried to remove the mask, but her hand was caught by Amanda.

"No. Just keep quiet." Amanda leaned closer and kissed her forehead. "I love you."

Unable to talk, Lex mouthed the words back to her. Their hands remained linked until the stretcher moved away.

Chapter Twelve

THE EMERGENCY ROOM for Parkdale Memorial Hospital was crowded, since it was the largest hospital in the county. Amanda stepped through the entrance and was inundated with an overwhelming cacophony of crying children, multiple conversations, and the constant blare of the overhead speaker. She turned to Ellie, who had ridden from Rodney's office with her. "Is it always like this?"

"Pretty much. A lot of folks don't have insurance, so they have to come here for everything."

Ellie gestured to the far side of the room. "The line's not too long. Come on."

Ten minutes later, Amanda was ready to slap the woman in front of them. The woman was trying to get the nurse working the counter to let her call her son, long distance, from the hospital phone. After a particularly loud whine from the woman, Amanda tapped her on the back. "Excuse me."

The woman turned around and wrinkled her nose at the pair. "What?"

"There are several pay phones on that wall," Amanda said as she pointed to their right. "If I give you a dollar, will you leave this poor woman alone and make your damned call?"

"What gives you the right to butt into my business?" the woman sneered.

Ellie cringed when Amanda stiffened, but wisely kept quiet.

In a deadly calm voice, Amanda whispered, "You just lost the dollar. Get out of my way before you have to be admitted."

"Are you threatening me?"

Ellie grabbed Amanda's arm and stepped in front of her. "No, of course she's not. But, please. We need to find out about my cousin, who was recently brought in. I'll loan you my cell phone if you need to make a call that badly."

"No, that's all right." The woman gave Amanda another dirty look. "But I'd advise you to keep her on a leash."

She pushed by them and headed for the pay phones.

"A leash? I'll show her who needs a damned leash." Amanda tried to brush off Ellie's grip.

Ellie stepped to the counter and smiled at the harried, gray-haired woman across from her. "Hi. Could you please tell us if my cousin, Lexington Walters, is still in the emergency room? She was brought in around fifteen minutes ago by ambulance."

The triage nurse, whose badge read Margerie, asked, "Do you have some identification?"

Amanda joined her and handed her driver's license across the counter. "I'm her next of kin."

"Ah." Margerie's fingers flew across her computer keyboard. "I'm sorry, but this shows that she's on her way to intensive care." She glanced up from her screen. "Take the elevator to the second floor and turn left, and show your identification to someone at the nurse's station."

"Thank you." Ellie tugged on Amanda's arm and led her away. "Let's try to keep out of trouble, all right? You won't do Lex any good if you're in jail."

"I wasn't going to do anything." Amanda pushed the up button for the elevator. "That woman just got on my nerves."

"Mine, too." When the elevator door opened, Ellie motioned for Amanda to precede her. "But I think my cousin's temperament is rubbing off on you."

Amanda pushed the button for the second floor. "Lex would be the first to disagree with you. But if you want, you can ask her yourself." The smile disappeared from her face. "If she's able to."

"Hey, she's going to be fine, Amanda. I'm sure of it." Ellie tried to keep upbeat for Amanda's sake. As a nurse, she knew how unpredictable pneumonia could be, especially since it had escalated so quickly. When the door opened, she patted Amanda on the back. "Come on. Let's see how she's doing."

TWO HOURS LATER, Amanda was beside herself. They had been relegated to the critical care waiting area, and not even Ellie could get any information. Amanda paced the small room, pausing only long enough to glare at the door that led to Intensive Care.

Ellie sat sideways on a chair, with her feet stretched out on another one. She had tried more than once to get Amanda to settle down, with no luck. She lowered her chin and closed her eyes so she wouldn't have to watch Amanda pace.

"How can you just sit there?" Amanda asked as she dropped into the chair beside Ellie. "And why won't they tell us anything?"

Ellie turned so that she could put her feet on the floor. "One of us going crazy is enough, don't you think?" She took Amanda's hand in hers." It takes a while to get someone settled in ICU. I'm sure we'll hear something soon."

They both turned as the elevator door opened, and Jeannie stepped out. She hurried to join them in the otherwise empty room, and embraced her sister when she stood to greet her.

Jeannie's eyes were full of tears as she hugged Amanda. "I came as soon as I heard. How's Lex?"

Ellie stood up and stretched. "We haven't heard anything, yet. I was just about to make a coffee run. Would either of you like anything?"

Amanda sat and pulled Jeannie down beside her, but kept their hands linked. "Instead of coffee, do you think you could bring back a bottle of water? My stomach already hates me."

"Sure, no problem. How about you, Jeannie? Coffee, water, candy bar?"

"No, I'm good. Thanks, Ellie."

Once they were alone, she squeezed Amanda's hand. "How are you holding up?"

Amanda kept her eyes glued to the entrance to the ICU. "We thought she had a cold."

"Mandy, it's going to be all right. You know how stubborn Lex can be. She's not going to let a little thing like this keep her down for long. Rodney told me that you caught it in time."

"Did we?" Amanda turned and focused on her sister. "She wasn't that sick. How did it get so bad, so fast?"

A slender, middle-aged man in dark blue scrubs came through the ICU door and made a beeline for the two women. "Walters?"

Amanda stood so quickly that Jeannie had to follow, or tumble from her chair. "I'm Amanda Walters. How is she?"

He glanced at Jeannie before returning his attention to Amanda. "You're her...sister?"

"Wife," Amanda succinctly answered. The look that accompanied her comment dared him to dispute her claim.

"Oh. Uh, well." He straightened and regained his composure. "We ran several tests and have concluded that Ms. Walters has a particularly virulent strain of streptococcus pneumonia. She's already quite weak, but we still had to sedate her in order to keep her from fighting the BiPAP."

At the distressed look that appeared on her sister's face, Jeannie gently put her arm around her waist. "What's BiPAP?"

He cocked his head at her and looked at Amanda.

"This is my sister, Jeannie Crews. Her husband is Dr. Rodney Crews," Amanda explained.

"I see. I'm afraid I don't know Dr. Crews." He spoke to Jeannie as if she were a child. "BiPAP is bilevel positive airway pressure. It's a noninvasive ventilation to help the patient breathe. As the wife of a physician, you should already know this."

Jeannie wrinkled her nose and was about to go off on him, when Ellie returned with a box filled with drinks and snacks.

"Dr. Robens, hello." Ellie placed the box on a chair and joined the others.

He blinked and took a moment to place the newcomer. He nodded when he made the connection. "Are you still in the ER, nurse?"

"No, I'm working for Dr. Crews, in Somerville. Lexington Walters is my cousin. When can we see her?"

"I'm afraid that's out of the question for the time being. As I told them," he gestured to Amanda and Jeannie. "Ms. Walters has been sedated and put on non-invasive ventilation. She should be out until sometime tomorrow morning."

Amanda wouldn't be dissuaded. "I'd still like to see her."

Dr. Robens glanced at his clipboard. "She won't even know you're there. I'd suggest you go home and get some rest. The next few days will be difficult."

Amanda gritted her teeth and took a step forward. She was quickly stopped by Jeannie, who moved in front of her. "Doctor, would it be possible for my sister to see Lex for just a moment? She has to go home to their three children, and it would be nice if she had something to report back to them."

"Three children?" His gaze went from Jeannie, to Amanda and back again. "Very well. Come with me, Ms. Walters."

Jeannie's smile was meant to reassure. "We'll call the family and let them know. Right, Ellie?"

"Yeah, sure." Ellie watched Amanda and the doctor disappear through the door before she sank to the nearest chair. "Damn it. This is not good."

ONCE THEY PASSED through the doors, Amanda stopped to take in the ICU. It wasn't much wider than a hallway, with glass-partitioned rooms along one side and a long desk opposite. Two women were at the desk, one typing on a computer while the other looked up from her paperwork to acknowledge the doctor.

Dr. Robens gestured to the room directly across from the desk. "Ms. Walters is in room four. Please don't touch anything, and if you have any questions, I'll be at the nurse's station."

"Thank you." Amanda walked as quietly as possible to the room. She stood in the doorway for a moment to get her bearings and composure.

Lex lay deathly still with her upper body raised to a near forty-five degree angle. A clear, plastic mask covered her nose and mouth. The beeping of the monitors and the clicking and forced air from the BiPAP mask were fighting for dominance in the small room. Her injured arm was once again secured across her abdomen, and an IV was attached to the inside of the uninjured arm that rested outside the thin covers.

Amanda moved slowly into the room and stood next to her wife. She raised a shaky hand to touch Lex's face. "You really did it this time."

She stroked Lex's cheek. "They won't let me stay with you, but I'll be here as much as I'm allowed. I promise."

She glanced through the glass wall before she leaned and kissed Lex's forehead. "I love you."

Although she hadn't expected an answer, it was still hard for

Amanda not to hear Lex return the sentiment. She touched her wife's face once more before she backed out of the room.

AMANDA DROVE HOME after a long and heated argument with Jeannie and Ellie, who both wanted to accompany her. While she appreciated their concern, she needed the time by herself to come to grips with Lex's illness and its consequences. Before she left the hospital, Rodney had arrived to explain in better detail what was happening. She now understood that the next day or two would be critical, which didn't make it easier to leave and return home without her wife.

She drove along the familiar route as if on automatic pilot, and it wasn't until she pulled up to the house that the weight of the day landed on her shoulders. She turned off the engine and mentally prepared herself for what was to come.

The children would be in the kitchen, enjoying an after-school snack.

Amanda picked up her purse from the passenger seat and opened it. She removed the small bag of personal items they had taken from Lex. Her watch, wallet, cellphone and a small handful of change rattled in the plastic bag. She returned the bag to her purse and played with the ring that was on her left thumb. The nurse had suggested that Amanda keep Lex's wedding ring, at least until she was out of ICU. She told her that while they didn't expect any problems, it was always better to take the valuables home instead of leaving them in the hospital.

Amanda closed her eyes and kissed the ring. She knew she needed to be with their children, but the largest part of her heart was in Parkdale.

Freckles greeted her at the gate, prancing circles around Amanda's legs when she stepped into the yard. "Why aren't you inside, begging for goodies?" Freckles barked and followed her to the house. When she stopped on the porch, the dog reared up on her hind legs and danced. "Goofy dog."

Amanda took a deep breath before she opened the back door. She stepped inside and was not surprised to hear Melanie chattering happily about her day.

"And then Heather laughed until she had to run to the bathroom! It was so funny!"

Lorrie giggled. "Did Rose get into trouble for making fart noises?"

"No, but Mr. Sandlin looked mad. He didn't know who did it, and we wasn't tellin'."

"All right, girls," Martha gently scolded. "That's enough of that kind of talk at the table."

Eddie blew a raspberry that caused both girls to laugh harder. He was the first to notice Amanda standing in the hall. "Mommy!"

Amanda hung up her coat and walked into the kitchen. "Hi, everyone." She kissed all three children on their heads and sunk into Martha's motherly embrace.

Martha rocked them in place for a moment. "How are you holdin' up, honey?"

"I've been better."

Martha lightly pushed her toward an empty seat at the table. "You're just in time for some sliced fruit and cheese. Lorrie, would you mind getting your mom a glass of milk?"

"Yes, ma'am." Lorrie was eager to help and quickly did as she was asked. She set the glass in front of Amanda and rejoined them at the table.

"Mada told us that you took Momma to the hospital. Is she really that sick?"

Amanda gave Martha a grateful smile for preparing the children. "Yes, she's sick, and Uncle Rodney decided that it would be better if she stayed in the hospital so that they can help her get better."

Eddie looked around. "Momma?"

"How come she didn't just stay with Uncle Rodney? He's a doctor," Melanie asked.

Lorrie rolled her eyes. "'Cause hospitals are for sick people, silly." When she got a look from Martha, she added quickly, "Sorry. I meant that hospitals are made for sick people to stay at, and Uncle Rodney's house isn't."

"Oh." Melanie shrugged and bit into an apple slice.

Eddie looked at Martha, then at Amanda. He swatted his high chair tray to get their attention. "Momma?"

Amanda got up and took him out of the high chair. "I'm sorry, honey. But Momma's not here." She kissed his cheek and rested him against her hip.

"Can we go visit her?" Melanie asked.

Martha answered for Amanda, who looked to be at a loss for words. "I'm sure you'll see her soon, sweetie. But your momma needs to rest so she can get better. But I bet she'd love some of your pretty artwork for her room."

"I can do that!" Melanie took her plate to the sink and practically ran from the room.

Lorrie looked at her plate. There was a lone cube of cheddar cheese, which she picked up and began to break into tiny pieces. "Momma's too sick to see us, isn't she?"

Amanda sat beside her. She shifted Eddie to the opposite side of her lap so that she could put her arm around Lorrie. "You're old enough that I don't have to keep things from you, so you know I'll tell you the truth, right?"

Lorrie didn't look up.

"Momma's very sick, and they've got her in a part of the hospital so they can take the best care of her. But she's not allowed many visitors, and you have to be at least thirteen years old to be allowed in."

"Is she gonna die?" Lorrie looked up into Amanda's face. "I don't want her to die."

"Oh, sweetie." Amanda pulled Lorrie closer and kissed the top of her head. "She's not going to die. She just needs a little more care than we could give her here at home."

Lorrie sniffled and rested her face against Amanda's shoulder. She started to laugh when Eddie sweetly patted her cheek.

"Leelee," he cooed. "Mommy, love Leelee."

Amanda laughed and nuzzled his soft, fuzzy hair. "Yes, baby. We love Leelee."

She pulled both children as close as possible. "We're going to get through this, I promise."

JEANNIE WAITED UNTIL the rest of the family left the hospital. It took some patience, because Rodney had seemed determined to stay and keep her company. She finally got him to leave by telling him that she needed some time by herself. She easily talked her way past the nurse's station in ICU, but paused before she stepped into the space that Lex occupied.

She took a deep breath and moved through the doorway. "Oh, Lex. No wonder my sister was such a mess."

Jeannie slowly inched closer until she was beside the bed. She trailed her fingertips along Lex's unencumbered hand. It was overly warm and she fought off the tears that threatened to fall. "You listen to me, Slim. This is completely unacceptable. I don't want to have to try and pick up the pieces if anything happens to you."

Jeannie pulled up a chair and sat next to the bed. "I hope you can hear me." She reached beneath the bed rail and covered Lex's hand with hers. "Don't you dare leave us. I've had to struggle every day with losing Frank. Even after all these years, there's still a huge hole in my heart. Don't do that to Mandy. Please."

She squeezed Lex's hand and released it before she stood. "You're stronger than this, Slim. Don't give up." She straightened the covers on the bed before she slipped from the room.

EDDIE CRIED AND rubbed his eyes as Amanda carried him upstairs. "Momma," he sobbed.

"I know, sweetie." Amanda closed the child gate at the top of the stairs and headed toward Melanie's room. "Do you want to help me tuck your sisters into bed?"

She had bathed and dressed him in his pajamas earlier, but he had been too restless to go to sleep.

"No." He put his face on her shoulder and wiped it back and forth. "Momma."

Amanda grimaced but continued down the hall. Her blouse was properly covered in tears and snot, Eddie's new thing to do. She tapped on Melanie's partially opened door and stepped inside.

"Mel, are you ready?" She stopped and looked around at the total destruction of the room. Even Eddie stopped crying and was enthralled with the mess.

Sheets of construction paper were scattered from Melanie's easel to her bed. She had at least half a dozen watercolor paintings laid out as well, all in various states of drying. Melanie was stretched out on the floor by the easel. Her face had splotches of paint on it, and she had a handful of crayons in her left hand as she drew with her right. She looked up at Amanda and grinned. "Hi, Mommy. I'm almost finished."

"Uh." Amanda blew out a breath. "I'm going to check on your sister. Get this straightened up before I come back, okay?"

"But, Mommy," Melanie whined. "I'm not done."

Amanda gave her the patented mom stare.

"I was gonna—" Melanie started, but when her mother didn't say anything, she put her crayons in a box and jumped up. "Yes, ma'am."

Eddie pointed to the floor. "Ugh. Bad."

"Your room isn't much better, mister," Amanda reminded him.

His favorite pastime was seeing how many toys were in his toy box, by removing them all and scattering them across the floor. She laughed when he gave her his cute face, which usually got him out of trouble. "Uh huh. Come on, let's see about Lorrie."

"Leelee?"

Amanda walked through the bathroom and tapped on the door to Lorrie's room.

"Leave me alone, Mel," Lorrie yelled.

"It's us," Amanda announced as she opened the door and stepped through.

Lorrie was lying on her bed in her pajamas, navy blue cotton pants with a light-blue tank top. She sat up when they came into the room. "Sorry, Mom. But Mel's been coming in and showing me her drawings all night."

Eddie struggled in Amanda's arms. "Leelee." The moment she put him down, he toddled to the bed and tried to climb. "Leelee."

"Okay, hold on." Lorrie pulled him up beside her. Before he could grab her earphones and MP3 player, she snatched them off the bed and placed them on her nightstand. "Sorry, Eddie. You're too little for those."

Amanda sat on the foot of the bed. "Other than your sister bothering you, how are you doing, honey?"

Lorrie shrugged. "Okay, I guess."

"I know it's going to be tough, but while Momma is gone, I'm going to need your help."

"Like with the horses and stuff?"

Amanda shook her head. "No, the guys can take care of the horses. You're still responsible for your usual chores, but I need you to help me keep an eye on Eddie and Melanie."

"Babysitting?" Lorrie sounded as if it were a life sentence.

"Something like that, yes." Amanda grabbed one of Lorrie's sock-covered feet and gently shook it. "Pawpaw will probably be here more, but if you could help him, that would be great."

"Okay. But do I have to play with her all the time? She does silly things."

Amanda laughed. "Honey, it wasn't that long ago that you did some of those silly things, too. Try to have a little more patience with her."

"All right." Lorrie held out her hand to Eddie, who giggled and attacked her wriggling fingers. "I'd rather be with Eddie. At least he doesn't want to play with dolls all the time."

"Just be more tolerant with her. She's worried about Momma, too."

Lorrie looked into Amanda's face. "Are you? Worried, I mean?"

"Of course. Any time you're in the hospital, it's serious. But..." Amanda smiled and touched the tip of Lorrie's nose. "I have complete faith that she will get well soon, and come home."

"You're not just saying that to keep me from being upset, are you?"

Amanda stood. "Have I ever lied to you? Come on, kiddo. Bedtime."

She held out her hands to Eddie, who gave Lorrie a slobbery kiss and then crawled across the bed.

He used Amanda's body to climb off the bed. "Nigh nigh!"

Amanda laughed and kissed Lorrie on the forehead. "I love you, sweetie."

"Love you, too." Lorrie hugged her close. "Are you going to see Momma tomorrow?"

"Yes, as soon as visiting hours start. Why?"

Lorrie appeared embarrassed. She suddenly found the end of her blanket fascinating and wouldn't look up at her mom. "Just wondering."

"Is that all?"

Lorrie nodded.

"All right, then. Get some sleep." Amanda took Eddie by the hand. "Goodnight, honey."

"'Night, Mom."

Amanda and Eddie bypassed the adjoined bathroom and headed down the hall. "Bedtime for big boys." She led the way into his bedroom.

"Big boy." He let go of her hand and climbed into his toddler bed. "Big."

"You sure are." Amanda knelt by his bed and helped him cover up. She handed him his favorite stuffed toy, a gray armadillo that Lex had found and given to him as a joke. Now it was the only thing he'd sleep with. Much to everyone's amusement. "What book do you want to read tonight?" she asked, picking three from a nearby shelf.

Eddie cuddled the armadillo. "Momma."

"I know, honey. Momma usually reads to you, but she's sick. How about this one?" She held up a book with a cow on the cover.

"Moo." Eddie stuck his thumb in his mouth and blinked away tears.

IT TOOK LONGER than usual, but Amanda got Eddie to sleep and Melanie tucked into bed. Afterward, she called Hubert in Oklahoma, to tell him of Lex's condition. Although his father-in-law wasn't expected to live much longer, Hubert had offered to drive down immediately. Amanda had promised to keep him updated so he could stay there with Ramona.

To relax after the emotional call, Amanda spent a leisurely twenty minutes soaking in the tub—with the door open, just in case one of the children needed her. Once she was dry and dressed in her nightgown, she brushed her teeth and left the bathroom.

Amanda stared at the empty bed for a long moment before she crawled in on Lex's side and buried her face in the pillow. She inhaled the familiar scent of Lex's shampoo and felt the weight of the day crash around her. Only now, alone, did she allow herself to release the stress by crying into the pillow.

She cried for Lex, who was lying helpless in a hospital bed so many miles away, for their children who really didn't understand the implications, and for the fear of losing someone who meant everything to her.

Hours later, Amanda was awakened by the sound of crying. She hadn't even remembered falling asleep. As she listened, she quickly sat up and flung the covers off her legs. She made it to Eddie's room in record time, but he was still fast asleep.

Now that she was more awake, Amanda could tell it was Melanie's cries that she heard. She went into her youngest daughter's room, which was well-lit with a bright night light. "Mel? Honey, it's all right."

Melanie sat up with tears streaming down her face. "Mommy, Momma's dead!" she cried. "She's dead!"

"No, no, sweetie." Though chilled by her daughter's words, Amanda sat close to her and pulled Melanie into her arms. "Momma's not dead, honey. She's sick, but she's going to be okay."

Melanie shook her head and continued to cry. "We had to go to her funeral, it was raining and you was sad."

"Ssssh." Amanda slowly rocked back and forth. "Momma's okay."

"How do you know?"

Amanda closed her eyes and rested her cheek against Melanie's hair. "I just know, baby. But, if you want, we can go to my room and call the hospital to check on her."

"We can?"

"Yes, we can."

There was a shuffling sound from the bathroom doorway. "Can I go, too?" Lorrie asked.

"Sure." Amanda stood. "Why don't you bring your pillows, and we'll all sleep in the big bed?"

Melanie kept a death-grip on Amanda's hand as they walked down the hall. Her pillow was tucked under her other arm. "Like a slumber party?"

"A little bit."

When they stepped into the bedroom, Amanda pointed to her side of the bed. "Get comfortable, and I'll call the hospital." She sat next to the nightstand and dialed from the cordless handset.

The girls were silent as Amanda was transferred to the nurse's desk in ICU.

She smiled with as much confidence as she could muster and was about to say something to them when the line was answered.

"ICU."

"Hi, I'm Amanda Walters. I'm sorry to bother you, but I wanted to check on my wife, Lex. She was brought in earlier today."

"Um, yes. Let me get the doctor for you, ma'am. Please hold for a moment."

Amanda frowned as a recording of a piano and flute duet played on the line. She shrugged and winked to the girls.

"I'm waiting for the doctor. I'm sure the nurse wasn't allowed to give out any—" She stopped when there was as click, and a woman's authoritative voice spoke up.

"This is Doctor Stevens. Who am I speaking to?"

"My name is Amanda Walters. My wife, Lexington Walters was admitted around noon today. You should have my name listed there as the next of kin."

The doctor cleared her throat. "Yes, of course. Were you not contacted earlier this evening?"

A cold chill raced down Amanda's spine and made the back of her skull tingle with fear. She stood and stepped away from the bed.

"No, I wasn't." She lowered her voice to keep from being overheard. "Is there a problem?"

"The nurse on duty was supposed to call you and inform you. I'm sorry, Ms. Walters."

Amanda's heartbeat speed doubled. "What?"

"There were complications this evening. Ms. Walters' oxygen saturation dropped below eighty-five percent, and her blood pressure bottomed out."

As the doctor continued to explain, the only thing Amanda could hear was the blood rushing through her ears. She stepped into the bathroom and closed the door, so Melanie and Lorrie wouldn't be able to hear her conversation.

"Doctor, please." She leaned against the door and closed her eyes. "What does this mean, exactly?"

"After two hours on BiPAP, Ms. Walters was non-responsive. In fact, her condition worsened. We made the decision to place her on mechanical ventilation."

"Oh, God." Amanda slid down the door until she was on the floor. "How..." she struggled to get the words out. "How is she now?"

"Her condition has stabilized. We're hoping the antibiotic treatment will help so that we can remove the tracheal tube by tomorrow evening."

For a moment, Amanda couldn't breathe. She swallowed hard. "So, she's going to be all right?"

"We are doing everything in our power for her. The next twelve to twenty-four hours will be critical, though. If she responds to treatment, then yes. She should be fine. I'm sorry, Ms. Walters, I wish I could tell you more."

"Thank you, Dr. Stevens. I appreciate everything you're doing for her."

Amanda disconnected the call. She rested her arm against her knee and held the phone to her forehead. "What do I tell the kids?" she whispered.

There was a light tap on the bathroom door. "Mom, are you okay?" Lorrie asked.

Amanda took a deep breath and released it slowly. "I'll be right out, honey." She got off the floor and went to the sink to splash water on her face.

When she stepped from the bathroom, Amanda almost ran into both girls.

Melanie shifted from one foot to the other. "Is Momma better? Can we go see her?"

Amanda put her hand on Melanie's shoulder. "Let's go get comfy, and I'll tell you about the call."

Once the girls were settled in bed, Amanda adjusted the covers but didn't lie down. Instead, she sat on the opposite side closest to them. "First, I want to start by telling you that Momma's okay, and she's getting the best care possible."

Lorrie frowned. "What does that mean?"

"It means that she's had a little bit of a setback. They had to put her on a machine to help her breathe, so her body can rest and get better. And, while that means you won't be able to see her for a few days because she'll still be in ICU, I'll still take any cards or drawings to her that you want to send."

"So, she's worse," Lorrie muttered.

Melanie began to cry. "Does that mean Momma's gonna die? I knew it! I told you, Mommy!" She dove into Amanda's arms.

Amanda brushed her hand across Melanie's hair and gave Lorrie a scolding look. "She's going to be fine. And we're not going to have any more negativity. Right, Lorrie?"

"I was just—"

"I know, sweetie. But remember what Mada always says. Prayers and good thoughts work, while bad thoughts just make us feel worse. I believe that, and so does Momma."

Lorrie blinked tears from her eyes and looked at the comforter. "I know, Mom. I'm sorry."

"Come here." Amanda held out her free arm, which she put around Lorrie when she snuggled close. "I know you're scared for Momma. I am, too. But we're going to get through this, I promise you."

She closed her eyes as she kissed the top of their heads as she silently hoped that she'd not be proven wrong.

ON THE FOURTH day of Lex's hospitalization, Amanda stepped off the elevator and greeted the nurse at the station. "Good morning, Jennifer."

The nurse, who was close to Amanda's age, looked up. "Good morning, Amanda. How are you?"

"Tired, but okay." Amanda stopped and noticed the door to Lex's room was closed. "What's going on?"

"Oh, Dr. Stevens is in there. She should be out before long. Trust me, everything's good."

Amanda wanted to ask what she meant by the remark, but was instantly diverted when the doctor came out of Lex's room.

"Ms. Walters, hello," Dr. Stevens greeted her warmly. She wasn't much older than Lex, but was closer to Amanda's size. Her light, brown hair was streaked with gray, and her brown eyes twinkled behind the gold-framed glasses she wore. "How are you this morning?"

"I'm all right, Doctor." Amanda gestured to the room. "How's Lex?"

Dr. Stevens exchanged glances with Jennifer before she gestured toward the door. "Why don't you see for yourself?"

It took great restraint not to run, though Amanda's pace was just below a jog. As she broke through the threshold, she couldn't stop the sob that escaped. "Oh, God."

Lex was upright with her eyes open. The monitors attached to her were muted, and only an oxygen tube ran from her nose. She gave Amanda a tired grin. "Hey." Her rough voice was barely above a whisper.

Amanda rushed to her side and took Lex's hand in hers, but was careful not to dislodge the IV. "Thank God." She held their hands to her chest as tears of happiness tracked down her cheeks. "How are you feeling?"

"Tired," Lex rasped. "Weird, huh?"

Amanda shook her head. "No, not at all."

She kissed Lex's knuckles and then rubbed them against her face. "God, you scared the hell out of me."

"Sorry." Lex coughed and winced.

"Sssh. It's okay, love. I just—" Amanda's voice broke. Unable to speak, she kissed Lex's hand again and again.

Lex squeezed her hand with what little strength she had. She closed her eyes and slowly drifted off, but not before whispering, "Love you."

"I love you too, honey."

Amanda stood there for several minutes, just to watch her sleep. She finally kissed Lex's hand one final time before leaving the room to talk to the doctor.

She met Dr. Stevens at the nurses' station.

"That was a wonderful surprise." Amanda wiped her eyes with a tissue. "How much longer will she be here?"

"If there are no setbacks, we should be transferring her to a regular room this afternoon. Let's just take things one step at a time."

A giddy laugh escaped from Amanda as she looked back toward the room. "I understand. But, it's just so nice to see her doing better."

"I know. Now, if you'll excuse me, I have a meeting I'm late for." The doctor gathered folders from the counter and headed for the elevator.

Amanda glanced at her watch. "I think I'll go to the waiting area and make some phone calls. Jennifer, thank you for everything."

"You're welcome, Amanda. I'm glad she's doing better."

THE FOLLOWING AFTERNOON, Amanda picked the girls up after school and took them to Parkdale to visit Lex. Along the way, Melanie kept up her usual non-stop chatter as Lorrie stared gloomily out the window.

Melanie bounced in her seat as much as the seat belt would allow. "Mommy, I don't have any of my pictures for Momma. Can we go home first?"

Amanda glanced in the rear view mirror. "No, honey. That's too long a drive. But you can bring them tomorrow, okay?"

"Okay." Melanie chewed on her thumbnail for a moment. "Oh. Can we get her a card, instead?"

"We'll see. Lorrie, are you all right?"

Lorrie sighed and looked away from her window. "Do we have to go?"

"What?" Amanda stopped at a light and turned to look at her. "I thought you wanted to see Momma. Why the change?" The light turned green before she could get an answer. "Damn it."

Melanie giggled. "Mommy said a bad word," she sang.

"Big deal," Lorrie grumbled.

"Lorrie, what's wrong with you today? Did something happen at school?"

"No. I just don't feel like going all the way out to the hospital." Lorrie crossed her arms and looked at the passing scenery.

Amanda bit her lip to keep from going off on her. She gripped the steering wheel tighter and kept her eyes on the road. When she had time, and more patience, she'd talk to their oldest about her attitude.

Once in the hospital elevator, Lorrie stood at the back, as Melanie held Amanda's hand. Melanie swung a small, stuffed bear in her other hand and couldn't contain her excitement. "Mommy, do you think this is big enough? I want Momma to be able to sleep with it, so she's not lonely."

"It's perfect, Mel. Momma's going to love it, because you picked it out," Amanda assured her.

When the elevator doors opened, Amanda stepped out first. "She's going to be thrilled to see you both. Now, remember. You have to be quiet, because there are a lot of people who need their rest, okay?"

Melanie practically skipped beside her. "Okay!" She turned to Lorrie, who trudged behind them. "Come on, Lorrie. Momma's waiting!"

They came to the door to Lex's room. Amanda stopped and knelt beside Melanie and touched the tip of her nose. "Remember, Momma still gets tired really easily, so we won't be staying very long."

Lorrie finally voiced what was worrying her. "Are you sure we won't make her sicker, again? I want her to come home."

"She's doing a lot better." Amanda stood and gave her a quick hug. "Come on." She opened the door and peeked inside.

Lex was upright and awake, with the television remote in her good hand. By the look on her face, she hadn't found anything worth watching. She dropped it in her lap when she noticed her visitor.

"Hey." Her voice was soft and raspy.

Amanda opened the door wider. "Hi, love. Brought you a present." She let both girls go in front of her.

"Momma!" Melanie ran across the room and skidded to a halt beside the bed. She noticed the oxygen tube under Lex's nose, as well as the IV attached to her good arm. "Wow. What's that?"

Lorrie stood on the other side of the bed. "Hi, Momma." She stuck her hands in her coat pockets, as if she was afraid to touch anything.

"Hi, sweetheart." Lex's smile was tired and there were large, dark circles beneath her eyes.

"We brought you a bear," Melanie said, putting the stuffed animal on Lex's stomach, which was covered by a tan blanket. "I made you lots of pictures, but they're at home. Mommy picked us up at school, and we didn't have to ride the bus. I like riding the bus, because we're almost the last ones to get off, and we get to ride on the back seats. They bounce when we hit bumps."

Amanda put her hand on Melanie's head and leaned to kiss Lex lightly on the forehead. "How are you feeling?"

"Better." Lex fought through a rattling cough and grimaced at the pain in her chest and throat. "Sorry."

"Sssh, it's okay." Amanda brushed Lex's limp hair back with her hand. "Try not to talk too much. I just thought you'd like to see the rug rats."

"Thanks," Lex mouthed. What small amount of energy she had seemed to be ebbing away.

Amanda noticed. She helped Melanie stand on the chair beside the bed. "Give Momma a kiss so we can go. It's time for her nap."

"Momma has to take naps?" Melanie asked. She kissed Lex on the cheek. "Have a good sleep, Momma."

"I will," Lex whispered. "Love you."

Melanie giggled when Lex poked her stomach. "Love you, Momma."

She climbed down and pointed to the bear. "Don't forget to sleep with Mr. Bear."

Lex nodded. She turned to Lorrie, who appeared embarrassed. "You okay, lil' bit?"

"Yeah." Lorrie awkwardly patted her on the arm. "Hope you feel better."

Lex looked at Amanda, who shrugged. Lex started to say something, but another painful cough wracked her body. She held her good arm to her chest and closed her eyes until the sharp pain lessened then fell back against the pillows.

Lorrie and Melanie both looked scared to death. Amanda put her arm around Mel and held out her other arm to Lorrie. "It's okay, girls. Momma's going to cough like that for a while, but she's going to be all right."

"Yeah," Lex wheezed. "Sorry."

Amanda hugged the girls and released them. "See?"

She stepped around them and touched Lex on the cheek. "Behave yourself, so you can come home soon. All right?"

Lex opened her mouth, but Amanda covered it before she could say anything.

"I love you, too." Amanda replaced her hand with her lips for a brief moment. "Get some rest."

"Yes, ma'am," Lex mouthed.

She raised one hand and waved to the girls, who waved back. "Be good," she whispered, getting a grin from each of them. She looked at her family for as long as her eyes would stay open, keeping her eyes on Amanda's until she drifted off to sleep.

Chapter Thirteen

ELLIE PARKED HER old Corolla in the driveway and turned to her partner, who sat in the passenger seat. "Have I thanked you for taking today off?"

"Several times. I'll have to admit, when you first asked me to take Valentine's Day off, I thought your plans would be a little more romantic." Kyle rubbed her hands together. "At least it's warmer today."

In deference to the warmer temperatures, she was wearing a tight, black T-shirt with her faded jeans instead of a denim shirt.

"Yeah." Ellie turned off the car. "I'm not sure how long this will take, but I'll be glad to take you out to dinner afterward."

Kyle put her hand on Ellie's thigh. "Babe, don't worry about it. I was kidding." She squeezed her lover's leg. "Neither one of us is the candlelight dinner and flowers type. And I'd rather show you every day how much I love you, instead of making it once a year."

"You're a lot more romantic than you let people think." Ellie leaned across the car and kissed her lightly on the lips. "Come on, hot stuff. Let's get this over with."

They got out of the car at the same time and walked toward the house side by side. Before they reached the front porch, the door opened.

Anna Leigh waved as they drew closer. "Come in, girls. I have some coffee and iced tea prepared, whichever you prefer." She gave each of them a hug as they crossed the threshold.

"Mrs. Cauble, you didn't have to go to any trouble," Ellie said.

"Please, call me Anna Leigh. I thought we've talked about that before. It was so nice of you and Kylie to come clean out the workshop. Michael won't step foot out there and poor Jeannie's too busy with the children."

As she did with Lex, Anna Leigh used Kyle's proper name, much to the younger woman's embarrassment. She led them to the kitchen and directed them to a chair. "Now. Coffee or iced tea?"

Kyle waited until Ellie was seated before taking the chair beside her. "Iced tea would be nice, ma'am."

Anna Leigh poured them each a glass. "Do you have any special plans for this evening?"

They looked at one another and laughed. Ellie said, "We were just talking about that in the car. But no, we don't."

"I see."

"Neither one of us thinks it's right, to celebrate on just one day," Kyle explained. "That's like saying I only love you when I'm told to.

And I don't like that at all."

Anna Leigh patted her hand. "You sound a lot like my Jacob. He used to grumble that all the holidays were invented by card companies." Her smile faded. "I have an entire drawer full of little notes he'd write to me, just because he felt like it."

She cleared her throat and straightened in her chair. "Well, you're not here to listen to the musings of an old woman. Let me show you to the workshop."

Ellie shot a panicked glance at Kyle, who nodded.

Kyle covered Anna Leigh's hand with her own. "Mrs... I mean, Anna Leigh, we're here for you, however you need us. I can only hope to have that kind of long-lasting love."

"Thank you, dear. I would have to say that you both are off to a very good start."

She stood and brushed off her slacks, as if to brush away painful memories. "I've already had someone from the high school come by and gather all the projects and leftover wood, so all that is left is to go through the tools and pack them up."

Ellie stood and gave the older woman a hug. She didn't say anything, content to just hold Anna Leigh and give her whatever comfort she could.

AMANDA HUMMED TO herself as she swept the small pile of dirt and dog hair into the dustpan. She glanced around the kitchen, satisfied that the floor was as clean as it was going to get. With the girls in school, and Eddie spending the morning with his Pawpaw Charlie, it was the only time she had to get housework done. She turned to take the broom and dustpan to the hall utility closet and screamed when she saw someone in the doorway.

"You scared the crap out of me," Amanda scolded. "What are you doing down here?"

Lex leaned against the door frame. Her face was pale and her pajamas hung loosely on her. "It's too quiet upstairs, so I thought I'd come down and see what you were doing." Her voice was soft, as if every breath was difficult.

"Honey, you should have called. I would have helped you." Amanda leaned the broom against one of the kitchen chairs and walked to her wife.

"I've been out of the hospital..." Lex coughed and held onto the door frame to keep from falling. She took a moment to catch her breath. When she spoke again, her voice was just above a whisper. "I've been home for almost a week."

Today was the first time she had even felt like getting out of bed. Now she wanted to get her strength back and forget about the past couple of weeks.

Amanda put her arm around Lex's waist. "And you spent a full week in the hospital with pneumonia. Forgive me if I worry about you."

"Nothing to forgive." Lex leaned against her and kissed the top of Amanda's head. "But if I don't start moving around some, I'll never get my strength back." She held back another cough, pressing her left hand against the pain in her chest. "Damn."

"Come on, tough stuff. If you want to stay downstairs, let's get you comfortable in the den."

"Tough stuff, huh?" Lex moved slowly as she was led to the front of the house. "I could probably walk by myself, you know."

Amanda poked her in the ribs. "Don't ruin my fun."

"Yes, ma'am." Lex shuffled along beside Amanda. By the time they reached the den, she was breathing heavily. "This is ridiculous," she panted, as she dropped onto the sofa. When Amanda sat beside her, she put her left arm across the back of the sofa.

"I'd ask if you'd like to fool around, but I don't think I'm up to it."

"You're not?" Amanda scooted to the opposite end of the sofa and patted her lap. "How about you stretch out and catch your breath?"

When Lex didn't move, she gave the stubborn woman a glare. "Let me rephrase that. Lie down and put your head in my lap."

"Is that an order?"

"Let's just say it's a forceful request. Come on. If you don't, I'll have to get up and do more housework."

"Well, we can't have that, can we?"

Amanda kicked off her shoes and turned so that her legs were on the couch. "I forgot that you're not supposed to lie flat. Come here and lean against my chest."

"The things I have to endure," Lex sighed dramatically, but did as she was told. As she rested against Amanda, she felt the security and comfort of her wife's arms around her. "This is nice."

"Sure is." Amanda kissed the back of Lex's ear. "How's your arm?"

After she'd returned from the hospital, Lex had removed the sling, since the most strenuous thing she did was go from the bed to the bathroom.

"A little achy, but not bad."

In the hospital, Lex had been fitted with a smaller brace for her upper arm. She slowly clenched her right hand into a loose fist. The stitches had been removed before she left the hospital, and she was determined to get the full use of her hand as soon as possible. She began to cough and Amanda's arms tightened around her. After she was able to breathe again, she closed her eyes and relaxed. "Thanks."

"You don't have to thank me, love. But I hate to see you suffer like this."

Lex turned her head so she could see Amanda's face. "What? No I told you so because I was out in the rain and sleet for hours?"

"Not this time. It's not like you did it out of spite. You had work to do. That's different. Besides, the doctor said you were already coming down with pneumonia before you were out in the elements."

"Ah." Lex kissed Amanda's arm. "Maybe you could talk to Martha, then. She gives me grief at least once a day."

Amanda giggled and squeezed her. "Poor baby. Is big, bad Mada picking on you?"

"Uh-huh."

"Aww." Amanda kissed the top of her head. "Bless your heart."

Lex nodded pitifully, then realized what Amanda had said. "Hey!" When Amanda nuzzled her hair, Lex closed her eyes. "Feels nice," she mumbled.

"Sssssh." Amanda rested her head against Lex's. "Rest."

"Yes'm."

THEY HAD BEEN working for hours without a break. Ellie glanced at her lover, who was clearing out a lower cabinet. Kyle was covered with sawdust, but seemed completely at ease with the task before them. Unlike Ellie, who had almost immediately broken out into a sweat and was slower because she didn't want to get dirty.

"Hey, cool!" Kyle crawled from beneath the cabinet and raised a wooden item. "Check it out, Ellie."

Ellie wiped her hands on a paper towel and stepped over a pile of rags. "What is it?"

"An old toolbox." Kyle held the box with the reverence usually reserved for a priceless artifact. "Isn't it awesome? My great-grandfather had one."

Wrinkling her nose, Ellie cocked her head and studied it. "Uh, I guess."

The lower part of the wooden box was rectangular, with a piece of wood across the top for a handle. It was empty, but she could tell that it had been used for many years before being retired. "Wouldn't the tools fall out?"

"Nah. It's deep enough to hold them, but not so deep that you can't find anything. I wonder if Mrs. Cauble would let me buy it."

"Absolutely not," a voice echoed from the door. Anna Leigh carefully stepped through the shop.

Kyle set the box down. "Hey, no problem. I was just—"

Anna Leigh held up her hand. "What I meant was that you won't pay me a cent, Kylie. I want you to have the tool box."

She picked up the box and turned it around slowly in her hands. "This was one of the first things Jacob made, you know. I think he'd be thrilled that it would go to someone who would enjoy it." She handed it to Kyle.

"Thank you, ma'am. I'll treasure it. Maybe one of your great-grandchildren will like it, when they're older. I'll take good care of it for them."

"I know you will, dear. I'm happy to keep it in the family." Anna Leigh made a show of looking around. "It appears as though you girls are almost finished. Why don't you come in for lunch?"

Both women looked at one another. Kyle was the first to speak. "I'm going to have to do some serious washing up before I'd even think of joining you inside. I think I have years of sawdust on me."

"There's a washroom in that corner." Anna Leigh pointed to their left. "I'm sure there are enough clean towels. Jacob was always afraid of bringing in half his work with him, so he had it built years ago. Come inside as soon as you're ready. I have a huge pot of chili on the stove."

She smiled at them and turned to walk away.

On her way to the door, Anna Leigh paused and looked at a bare spot on the floor. No longer surrounded by pieces of furniture, the surface was eerily clean. Unaware of her audience, she said something softly under her breath and slowly moved away. Her shoulders were slumped, and she shuffled along as if she felt every one of her years.

Once they were alone, Kyle walked to where Anna Leigh had stood. "I wonder what that was all about?"

Ellie stepped next to Kyle. "She came out to get Jacob, and found him on the floor. I guess this must be the spot." She felt a cold chill and hugged herself. "How horrible, to come in and find him like that."

Kyle put her arms around her lover. "Yeah. I don't know how she's survived."

She lowered her voice. "How could you function, after losing the person you'd spent sixty years loving? God."

She rested her head on Ellie's shoulder and closed her eyes. She had only known Ellie for a year. Just the thought of losing her made her weak. "I couldn't handle it."

WHEN LEX AWAKENED, she was alone and the house was silent. She sat up and realized she had been resting on a large pillow that Amanda had sneaked behind her. She blinked and checked the clock above the fireplace. "Almost four? Damn, I didn't realize I was that tired."

She stood with a yawn and a stretch. She quietly walked past the dog bed where Freckles slept.

Lex cautiously inhaled, pleased when she didn't go into a coughing fit. When her stomach growled to remind her that she had missed lunch, she headed for the kitchen. Halfway down the hall, she saw the back door fly open.

"I win!" Melanie yelled. She charged through the door and tossed her backpack near the bench it belonged on. "Ha! I kicked your hiney, Lorrie." She skidded to a halt when she saw Lex. "Momma! You're all better!"

"Yep."

Melanie raced toward her. She pressed her cheek against Lex's stomach and hugged her with all her might. "I'm so glad."

"Me too, kiddo." Lex stroked the mop of blonde curls.

A happy bark came from the den and Freckles sprinted down the hall. She danced around Melanie, before she raced toward the back door.

Lorrie came into the house much quieter than her sister. "Hey, Momma."

She laid her backpack on the bench and hung her denim jacket on one of the hooks above. "I guess you're feeling better?" She absently scratched Freckles behind one ear as the dog kept up with her.

Lex walked forward with Melanie hanging onto her. "I decided I goofed off long enough."

"Mel, quit hanging on Momma. She's been sick," Lorrie ordered.

"Hey, I'm fine." Lex held her hand out to Lorrie. "Come here."

Lorrie shrugged. "No, that's okay." She leaned against the wall and stuffed her hands into the front pockets of her jeans. Freckles obediently sat next to her, staring up with an adoring look.

Lex just barely refrained from rolling her eyes at Lorrie's attempt at being cool. "Where's your mom?"

"She went to get Eddie at Pawpaw's," Melanie answered. "I got to sit in the back seat of the bus today."

"That's great, sweetheart." Lex patted her back. "Why don't you run see if your mom needs any help?"

"Okey-dokey." Once her back was turned toward Lex, Melanie stuck her tongue out at Lorrie. "See ya."

Lorrie glared at her, but didn't say anything. She pushed away from the wall, intent on leaving.

"Hold up, lil' bit. What's going on?" Lex moved closer and put her hand on Lorrie's shoulder.

"Nothin'."

Lex touched Lorrie's chin so that she'd raise her head. "It's got to be something, to make you so surly." A tickle in her chest couldn't be ignored and she began to cough.

Worried, Lorrie stepped forward and held her mother until the cough subsided. "Maybe you should go back to bed."

"No," Lex wheezed. She used her good arm against the wall to hold herself upright. Truth be told, she didn't think she could walk that far. "Let's go to the kitchen and wait for your mom."

"Are you sure? If Mom comes in and sees you, she's gonna be mad."

"Nah. She'll be fine."

Once they were seated with a glass of milk for Lorrie and juice for Lex and a plate of Martha's brown sugar cookies between them, Lex tapped the table. "Now, it's just you and me. Want to tell me what's got your britches in a bunch?"

"I dunno." Lorrie nibbled on a cookie. She ignored the plaintive whine from beneath the table and stared at the cookie plate for a long moment. "Momma?"

"Hmm?"

Unable to look Lex in the eye, Lorrie stacked the cookies in a neat pile then changed it to a circle. When her mother covered her hand, she finally looked up. "Before you met Mom, did you have a best friend?"

"No, not really. I didn't have time to make many friends, because I had to help my dad with the ranch. Why?"

Lorrie turned away. "Allison's been my best friend forever. We've always done everything together, you know?"

Not sure where the conversation was headed, Lex scooted her chair closer. She put her hand on the back of Lorrie's chair. "Yep."

"Since Jerry's come back, we've all been hanging out together. And that's cool. But now they're doing stuff without me." Lorrie looked up at Lex and there were tears in her eyes. "When I ask Al why, she just makes excuses."

She blinked the tears away, impatiently wiping them off her cheeks. "How come she doesn't like me anymore? What's wrong with me?"

Lex sighed. She didn't think she was ready for this particular talk. She rubbed the back of her neck, praying for a relapse. "Well, it sounds like Ally and Jerry like one another in a different way from being just friends. That's probably why you're not included."

"Different way?"

"Yeah. You know, as boyfriend and girlfriend. That doesn't mean they don't like you anymore, but they want to spend time together as a couple."

Lorrie put her elbow on the table and propped her chin on her upraised hand. "You think Al likes Jerry *that* way? Eww."

Lex laughed. "I know, kiddo. But you can't choose who to love. It just happens."

"Love? Momma, that's *really* gross. I liked it better when I thought they didn't like me."

The back door opened and Melanie raced into the kitchen. "We're back!" She got into the chair on the other side of Lex and stood on her knees. "Mada was there, and she said you'd better behave, or she'll take a spoon to you, Momma."

Amanda came in with Eddie, who struggled out of her grasp. "Melanie, go put your backpack where it belongs."

She kissed Lex on the cheek. "I see you two are enjoying a snack."

"Momma! Up!" Eddie demanded of Lex.

Lex looked down at him. "What was that?"

"Pease?" he asked, adding his most charming grin.

"I thought so." Lex raised him to her lap. She caught Lorrie's eye. "Okay?"

Lorrie nodded and finished her milk. "May I be excused? I need to go check on Snow."

"Leelee." Eddie reached for his sister when she stood. He swatted Lex's shoulder in an attempt to get Lorrie's attention. "Leelee!"

After rinsing her glass and placing it in the dishwasher, Lorrie stopped long enough to ruffle Eddie's hair. "I'll be back in a bit."

She patted her leg, and Freckles vacated her post beneath the table to prance behind her as they left the kitchen.

"Can I have cookies, too?" Melanie asked. When Amanda gave her a no-nonsense look, she amended her words. "May I? Please?"

"Mmm." Eddie reached for the plate that Lex had passed toward Melanie. "Mine."

Amanda filled two glasses with milk, and Eddie's sippy cup with the same. She took Eddie from Lex and put him in his high chair, along with a toddler cookie and his cup. "Enjoy." She gave Melanie her milk and sat in the chair Lorrie had vacated. "How are you holding up, Lex?"

"Great." Lex frowned as Eddie tipped his cup enough to get milk on the tray, then smeared his cookie across it. "Ugh."

Eddie picked up the cookie and chewed on the soggy end. "Yum, yum, yum."

Melanie laughed at his antics and dipped her cookie in the top of her milk. She bit off the end. "Eddie's right. It's good."

"Don't encourage him." Lex touched the tip of Melanie's nose. "Like he needs the encouragement."

Amanda nibbled on her own cookie. "We won't mention who taught everyone how to dip their cookies in milk."

"Kids have to learn skills." Lex covered her mouth with a paper napkin and coughed. Once she was able to breathe again, she wadded up the napkin and held it in her fist. "This is driving me nuts."

"Honey, Rodney explained that the cough would take the longest to get over. I'm surprised you're even well enough to come downstairs."

Lex didn't want to tell her that halfway down the stairs, she had thought about turning around and going back. Amanda had spent enough time worrying as it was. "Nothing to it."

Amanda shook her head and glanced at Melanie. "Do you have any homework tonight?"

"I have spelling words to practice." Melanie turned to Lex. "Will you help me with them, Momma?"

"Sure. We'll work on them after dinner."

Melanie shoved a full cookie into her mouth. She chewed as fast as she dared, wanting to go upstairs and play. She tried to drink the last of her milk, only to have it spill from her lips and go down the front of her shirt. After she swallowed, she looked at her parents. "Can, I mean, may I be excused?"

Lex covered her mouth to keep from laughing as Amanda tried to appear stern. "You have to go upstairs and rinse the milk off that shirt, before it dries. Maybe next time you won't be in such a hurry."

Amanda pointed to her wife. "Not one word."

"Thank you!" Melanie moved quickly. She rinsed her glass and placed it in the dishwasher before she hustled out of the kitchen.

Amanda sighed but couldn't help laughing at Melanie, who seemed to have a never-ending supply of energy. "I wish I could understand Lorrie as well as I do Mel."

"Melanie's an open book," Lex agreed. "And I'm sure we'll figure Lorrie out by the time she's twenty."

"Good lord, I hope it's sooner than that. She was so quiet on the drive home today. I just don't know what to do with her."

Amanda reached across and cupped Lex's cheek. "You look exhausted. I think we need to get you upstairs. We can talk more about this later."

Lex stood and pushed her chair toward the table. She put an arm around Amanda's waist and kissed her temple. "Lorrie's feeling the age old third-wheel syndrome. Her two closest friends have hooked up and she's feeling left behind."

"Her two?" Amanda stopped at the foot of the stairs. "Allison and Jerry? You're kidding me."

"Nope. We discussed it before you came in. She thought something was wrong with her, since they were leaving her out of their plans." Lex began the slow ascent toward their room, glad to have Amanda's arm to keep her steady. "I explained to her that they weren't mad at her, but needed some time for just the two of them."

Amanda tightened her grip as she felt Lex tremble. "How'd she take that?"

Lex's laugh turned into a cough. She paused at the door to their bedroom and leaned against the frame. "She thought it was gross, and liked it better when she thought they hated her."

Trying not to pant as she crossed to the bed, Lex sat on the edge to catch her breath. "Damn."

"Honey, it's just going to take time."

Amanda sat beside Lex and carefully leaned against her. "I know it's rough on you, but I'm kind of enjoying spending all this extra time together."

"Yeah, that is a bonus." Lex turned and kissed her lightly on the lips. "Thanks for taking such good care of me, even when I'm a grump."

Amanda put her arms around Lex's neck and looked into her eyes. "You're cute, even grumpy."

She kissed her on the nose, giggling when Lex countered by nibbling on her chin. "Better get your strength back soon, Slim. I've got plans for you."

Lex leaned back, bringing Amanda with her. "Lucky me."

Chapter Fourteen

THE SMALL HOUSE'S illumination was a beacon in the night to Shelby, who parked her truck close to the front steps. She shut off the engine and took a deep breath, trying to get up the energy for the short walk inside.

She was met at the door by Rebecca, who wore a pale green robe atop her nightgown.

"It's after ten," Rebecca mentioned unnecessarily. She removed Shelby's hat and hung it on the coat tree by the door. "Are you all right?"

"Darlin', I honestly don't know." Following her partner the few feet to the sofa, she dropped onto her usual spot. "I don't know how Lex has done this all her life."

Rebecca ran her fingers through Shelby's hair. "That's probably how. She's had plenty of practice at it." She kissed Shelby on the cheek. "You were just kind of thrown into the deep end all at once. I'm so proud of you."

Shelby leaned into the touch and closed her eyes. "Thanks. But I feel like I'm chasin' my tail most of the time, with no chance to catch it."

"Sssh. You're doing fine. Did you get dinner?"

Shelby laughed at the question. "Dinner, dessert, and two big glasses of iced tea. Martha wouldn't let me go back to work until I finished everything on my plate." She patted her flat stomach. "No wonder Lex runs non-stop. Eatin' like that every day would turn a body heavy in no time."

"I think you're safe." Snuggled up against Shelby, Rebecca sighed. "Unlike me."

Her voluptuous figure was quite different from Shelby's thin form.

"Hey, now, darlin'. Don't be talkin' smack about my girl. I think you're perfect."

Shelby turned her head and kissed Rebecca on the forehead, then met Rebecca halfway and kissed her lips.

After a leisurely few minutes of getting reacquainted, Rebecca pulled away. "Would you like to take this to the bedroom?"

"That's the best offer I've had all day." Shelby grinned as she was hoisted off the sofa. "I need to get cleaned up. I think I have half the barn on me."

Rebecca lightly swatted her on the rear. "How about I help you? I can always get those hard to reach places."

Shelby tugged on the bow that held her lover's robe closed. "This night just gets better and better."

AFTER SHE STARED at the clock for more than an hour, Lex gave up trying to sleep. It was close to midnight, but her brain wouldn't shut off. She stifled a cough with her hand and headed downstairs.

The office light burned her eyes for a moment, but soon Lex was able to blink away the discomfort. She settled behind her desk and booted up her laptop, a recent Valentine's Day present from her wife. Although she was becoming stronger every day, she tired far too easily. The laptop was Amanda's way of helping Lex pass the time while she was ill.

She checked her email and then pulled up a favorite game. The squalling birds that destroyed whatever she aimed at had hooked her from the beginning. Lex lost herself in the game for an hour before she closed it and logged on to the program she had come downstairs to check.

With both she and Roy incapacitated, Lex had to lean heavily on Shelby's assistance. The ex-rodeo rider worked hard and never complained but Lex realized she had become overwhelmed trying to keep everything running smoothly. She wrote a few lines on a notepad. "I'll call Roy in the morning and see if he's up to a visit. Maybe the three of us can figure out some way to keep Shelby from working herself into the ground," she muttered to herself.

"What are you doing up?" Amanda asked from the doorway.

Lex looked up and couldn't help but smile. Her wife was adorably tousled with her short hair sticking up in every direction. She wore a long T-shirt, and, from the way the lamp from the living room backlit her body, nothing else. "Uh."

"Well?" Amanda put her hands on her hips, causing the shirt to rise to a near X-rated level.

Unable to speak, Lex shook her head. She started to cough, which brought Amanda into the office.

"Honey, are you getting sick again?" Amanda rubbed Lex's back until she was able to breathe.

"No," Lex gasped. "I'm fine." She spun the chair around and pulled Amanda into her lap. "I'm feeling a lot better."

Amanda linked her hands behind Lex's head. "You are, huh?"

"Yep."

Leaning in close, until they were breathing the same air, Amanda whispered to her. "Then maybe we should go back to bed." She gave her wife a light peck on the lips.

"Yeah," Lex agreed, breathlessly.

"And," Amanda nipped her chin. "Get some sleep."

Lex blinked and pulled back. "What?"

"Honey, you're still weak from your illness."

Amanda turned and pointed to the laptop, which still had an accounting program open. "And I know you're driving yourself nuts, not being able to do much right now. Don't think you've fooled me, rancher. I notice when the program has been updated."

"Damn."

Amanda laughed. "Good try, though." She caressed Lex's cheek. "Is there anything that I can help you with?"

"I was just trying to find a better way to run things, until Roy and I are back on our feet. Shelby's doing a great job, but there's only one of her."

"What about the other guys? Some of them have been here forever. Surely they can handle more responsibility."

Lex closed her eyes and leaned her head against Amanda. "Chet has been here the longest. He's a great guy and does okay at handling instructions."

"But he's not the best at thinking things through," Amanda finished for her. "How about Jack? He seems pretty sharp."

"He's not interested. Says he enjoys being stress-free."

"That's kind of selfish of him."

Lex shook her head. "He's a recovering alcoholic, sweetheart. He really doesn't want the added stress."

"Oh."

"Tomorrow, I'm going to take Shelby with me to see Roy. Maybe we can come up with some solutions."

Amanda opened her mouth to argue, but stopped when Lex's finger touched her lips.

"I'll ask Shelby to drive, and we won't stay long. I promise." Lex replaced her finger with her lips, leaving a soft kiss behind. "But I can't just sit around the house forever, Amanda. And I can't leave poor Shelby hanging in the breeze, either."

"All right." Amanda slid off Lex's lap and adjusted her nightshirt. "In that case, shut down your laptop and let's go to bed."

Lex quickly exited the program. "I thought you'd never ask."

"To sleep," Amanda stressed, as they left the office.

"I'm sure we'll get to sleep sometime." Lex patted her on the rear.

THE SUN WAS barely above the horizon when Rebecca left the barn. She grinned as the back door to their home opened and her lover appeared. "Good morning, sleepy head."

Shelby tipped her hat back on her head. "You cheated."

"No, I made an executive decision." Rebecca kissed Shelby and patted her side. "I turned off the alarm clock because you needed the sleep. I'm perfectly capable of taking care of our horses before work."

"Executive decision, eh?" Shelby put her arms on Rebecca's hips and pulled her closer. "And I have no say in the matter?"

Rebecca melded her body into her partner's. "Nope."

They stood together silently, no words needed, as the rest of the world woke around them. Finally, Shelby kissed Rebecca one more time. "I need to get goin', darlin'."

"I know." Rebecca squeezed then released her. "I'm off today, so as soon as I get things finished around here, I thought I'd run and see how Amanda's doing."

"She'll like that, I imagine." Shelby adjusted her hat and backed away, slowly. "Maybe I'll see you for lunch."

"Maybe so." Rebecca blew her a kiss and watched as the old truck lumbered out of the drive.

AMANDA CLOSED THE back door and hung up her coat. Although she enjoyed the time with her children, she felt a guilty pleasure at seeing them off to school. At the sound of voices, she stepped into the kitchen. She touched Lex's shoulder and waved to their guest on her way to the coffee pot. "Good morning, Shelby."

"Good mornin', Amanda. Rebecca said she'd be here in a little while, if that's all right with you."

"Mommy!" Eddie wailed from his high chair. He swatted the tray, which was covered with oatmeal.

"Sounds wonderful. Hello, handsome." Amanda poured herself a mug and kissed her son on the head, quickly sidestepping his grimy hand. She sat beside her wife, who stopped feeding Eddie. "What are your plans today, besides talking to Roy?"

Lex placed Eddie's spoon in the bowl in front of her. "Not much." She gave Shelby a look, which Amanda caught.

"Uh huh." Amanda stared at Shelby, until the other woman decided her coffee cup was very interesting. "Lex?"

"Mmm?"

Amanda turned in her chair. "What's going on?"

"What makes you—" Lex stopped at the serious glare she received. She rubbed the back of her neck, a nervous gesture that showed up any time she was caught doing something she shouldn't. "I'm going to ride with Shelby for a while today. In the truck," she added hurriedly.

"Tuck," Eddie parroted. He grinned at the adults, who were all too busy to look at him.

"I see." Amanda got up and walked to the sink. She stared out the window.

"Tuck!"

Shelby quickly swallowed the last of her coffee. "I'll run check the horses in the barn," she announced, leaving the kitchen as quickly as possible.

Shelby made her exit and Lex wiped Eddie's face. He fussed until she gave him his spoon, which he immediately stuffed into his mouth. "That's right, buddy. Truck."

She moved to stand behind Amanda and rested her hands on her wife's hips. "I was going to tell you as soon as you got back from the bus stop."

Amanda turned and leaned against the counter. She did a slow perusal of Lex's face. The dark circles from her illness were gone, although she was still too pale as far as Amanda was concerned. She held out her hands and waited until Lex held them. "Will you promise me something?"

"Anything."

"I mean it, Lex. You have to promise not to wear yourself out."

Her lips twitched, but Lex was able to keep a serious look on her face. "I promise."

Amanda brushed her hands along Lex's arms. "Don't get out in the cool air too much, please?"

"I won't."

"I really don't like this. You were so sick."

Lex kissed her on the forehead. "I don't want you to worry. If we run across anything that needs handling, we'll radio the boys and have them take care of it." She lowered her voice and looked directly into Amanda's eyes. "Sweetheart, being in the hospital scared me, too. I don't plan on going back."

"It was more than a little stay. You were in intensive care, fighting for every breath. I don't want that to happen again."

"It won't. I swear I'll be extra careful."

Amanda rested her cheek against Lex's chest. She could hear the strong heartbeat, almost feeling it in her own body. "I love you."

"I love you, too."

"Momma!" Eddie cried, whacking his spoon on the tray. "Momma!"

Lex laughed and unbuckled him from the chair. "I love you, too, Eddie. C'mere, piggy."

REBECCA WAS ON her way out the door when her cell phone rang. She fished it out of her purse as she walked toward her car. "Hello? Oh. Hi, Mr. Carson. I wasn't scheduled to work today, was I?"

"No, Rebecca. But I do need to talk to you."

She got into the car and lowered the driver's window. "Okay. Do you need me to come in?"

"Not exactly, no." The store owner sounded tired and defeated. "Rebecca, I hope you understand that this is no reflection on you. But, as I'm sure you're aware, business has been very slow lately. And—"

"Oh, my God. Are you firing me, Mr. Carson?"

He was quiet for a moment. "Uh, well."

"You are!" Rebecca accused.

"No!" Mr. Carson softened his voice. "I'm cutting everyone's hours, Rebecca. It's either that, or layoffs."

She considered her co-workers. They had slowly lost employees during the past few years until only a few were left. Mark, a part-time student who lived with his parents, showed up late most of his scheduled days. Susan, a retired schoolteacher who covered during holidays, didn't need the money. A couple of high school students who giggled more than they worked filled out the list. The other manager, Regina, was a single mother of two small children, who lived more paycheck-to-paycheck than Rebecca. "Even Regina?"

"Of course." He sounded insulted that she asked. "I don't play favorites."

Rebecca closed her eyes and rested back against the seat. She hoped Shelby would forgive her. "Give her my hours, Mr. Carson. I'll try to find something else."

"Are you sure? I mean, that's a kind sentiment and all, but what about, um, your friend? Will she mind?"

"What's that supposed to mean?"

"Well, she's the um, you know, uh," he stammered.

"She's the what?"

He quickly changed the subject. "I'll be more than happy to write you a glowing letter of recommendation, Rebecca. And if more hours become available before you find something else, I'd be thrilled to have you back."

"Thank you, Mr. Carson. I'll drop by soon for the letter. Goodbye."

Rebecca disconnected the call and tossed the phone toward her purse, which was open on the passenger seat. She pounded her fists on the steering wheel in frustration. "Damn it! Shelby's gonna freak."

She sat in the driveway for half an hour, trying to figure out the best way to break the news to her lover. They had a small savings built, but certainly not enough to sustain them for any length of time. Shelby's work at the Rocking W had been a godsend, allowing them to think about their future. "And now I've screwed that up," she told herself.

THE ENTICING AROMA of fresh-baked bread wafted through the house. Lex took a deep breath, but stopped when she heard Helen laugh. "What?"

"It should be out in another five minutes, Lex. Don't worry, you'll get a piece."

Shelby snickered into her coffee cup, but didn't offer anything verbal.

Roy gazed fondly at his wife. "Now you understand how I'm gaining weight."

Helen looked around the table. "Would anyone like more coffee?"

"Stay put. I'll get it." Lex was up and into the kitchen before Helen could argue with her.

Roy leaned across the table toward Shelby, so he couldn't be overheard. "She's doing better, isn't she?"

"Yeah. Although Amanda threatened to skin me if she overdoes it today. And I know better than to cross her."

"No one ever does." Roy sat back in his wheelchair as Lex returned. "Ain't that right, Boss?"

Lex refilled all the mugs before placing the coffee pot on a wooden trivet in the center of the table. "What's right?"

"Shelby was just tellin' us about your boss," Roy teased. "I think Amanda has put the fear of God into your new foreman."

"She has a tendency to do that." Lex dropped into her chair and stretched out her legs. "While we're on the subject of foremen, we need to figure out a few things around here."

Roy set his coffee cup down. "I'm supposed to be whittled down to a walking cast in the next couple of weeks, so at least I'll be more mobile. But the doc has already warned me against riding until I'm fully healed."

Helen poked his arm and cleared her throat.

With a roll of his eyes, Roy added, "The doc also told me I needed to start taking it a little easier. Said I'm not getting any younger. I told the old—" he glanced at his wife, "so-and-so that none of us are."

"He also said that you have high blood pressure." Helen looked smug. "No more fried foods for you, hon."

"Welcome to the club." Lex turned to Shelby. "How about you? Does Rebecca keep you on the straight and narrow, too?"

Shelby snorted. "Nope. We pretty much eat healthy all the time, though. Don't bother me none."

"Just wait," Roy warned. "One of these days, you're gonna wake up and find out that too many years have passed without warning."

"Yeah, you're such an old fart," Lex joked. But then she took a moment and looked at him. Somewhere along the way, Roy's blond hair and mustache had turned silver, and the creases in his bronzed face had deepened. With a start, she realized he was more than sixty years old. "Damn."

He frowned. "What?"

"Nothing." She tapped the table. "So, once you're more mobile, do you want to ride along with Shelby and give her some pointers?"

"Sure. Sound okay to you, Shelby?"

Shelby swallowed the mouthful of coffee she had taken and sat back in her chair. "Yeah. Rebecca will be glad, too. Between her work and mine here, we don't see one another as much. It'll be nice to get home before dark-thirty."

The oven timer buzzed, causing Helen to get up and heed its call. "No one go anywhere," she warned. "I'll bring some fresh bread and butter right out."

Roy leaned closer to Lex and Shelby. "Once I'm on my feet again, we'll pack up."

"Why?"

"I'm sure you'd want Shelby here on the property, since she's going to be doing my job. Even with therapy and all, my days as foreman are over."

Shelby cut Lex's reply off. "Like hell I will. Look, I've got a nice little spread of my own, Roy. I enjoy working here, but you can keep the title of foreman and the house. I ain't got enough schoolin' to be in charge."

"I sure as hell can't do it anymore. And all I have is a high school diploma. You've got what matters, which is common sense. This job isn't that complicated, just busy. Right, Boss?"

Lex crossed her arms and watched the two argue back and forth. "Oh, so now you want my opinion?"

When Roy blushed and Shelby lowered her gaze, Lex laughed.

"Damn it, Roy, I don't want you to go anywhere. There's more than enough work around here for all of us. As a matter of fact, I thought it would be nice if we set you up with the accounting program that I use to keep track of the cattle. That would free me up to do other things while Shelby handles what you can't."

"Sounds good to me," Shelby agreed. "Roy?"

"Yeah." He blinked and cleared his throat in an attempt to cover up his emotions. "I'm happy here."

AMANDA HANDED REBECCA another tissue, as the redhead continued to cry. Rebecca had shown up on her back doorstep not long after Lex and Shelby left, her face splotchy and her eyes swollen from crying. It took more than fifteen minutes to calm her down enough to find out what was wrong. "I don't think Shelby is the type to get angry about something that was out of your control, Rebecca."

"No, she's not. But I don't know how she's going to take me giving up my job completely."

Rebecca blew her nose then added the used tissue to the large pile on the coffee table. She watched Eddie quietly play with his wooden blocks on the floor nearby. He seemed unaffected by her emotional display. "Even a few hours would have been better than none."

"Not necessarily. You would have spent all your check on gas. Why don't you think of this as an opportunity? I was devastated when we had to shut down the real estate office. But now I wouldn't have traded all this time with my kids for anything in the world." Amanda patted her hand. "Is there something else you've always wanted to do?"

Rebecca took a cleansing breath and leaned back against the sofa. "I've never really thought about it. Work was just a way to bring home money. It wasn't something that I really enjoyed."

"And now you have a chance for something new." Amanda took a drink of her iced tea. "I know you love horses and competing. What else?"

"You'll probably laugh."

Amanda handed her another tissue. "I doubt that. Here."

"Thanks." After wiping her face, Rebecca stared at the coffee table. "Being with your kids, made me realize something."

"It has?" Amanda looked at Eddie. "You want to have a baby?"

Rebecca's head snapped up. "Oh, no! I mean, I love kids, but not for myself. I love being just a couple with Shelby. She's the only one I need."

Amanda finally laughed. "Don't look so panicked. Luckily, I don't think you have to worry about becoming pregnant by accident. Although you can have fun trying."

"Oh, my God." Rebecca buried her flushed face in her hands. It took her a minute or two to get her embarrassment under control. She pointed a finger at Amanda. "You're evil."

"I've lived with Lex for too many years. She can still make me blush. So, what is it you realized?"

Rebecca laughed. "You also have a one-track mind."

Amanda tapped impatiently on Rebecca's thigh.

"Okay, okay. I realized that while I don't want children of my own, I love being around them. I know I don't have the business sense or the money to start my own daycare but I'd love to work in one. Maybe teach the little ones things they need to know before they start school."

"What a wonderful idea! You're a natural teacher. Have you ever thought of going to college to get your teaching certificate?"

Rebecca shook her head. "I didn't make very good grades in school. And I couldn't afford to go, even if I wanted to. Trust me, I hated school almost as much as I love horses. It drove both my parents crazy for me to refuse college after I graduated."

"Not everyone needs college to be successful. You should do what you feel is best."

"Thanks. Would you mind talking to my father? He still bitches at me, all these years later." Rebecca blew her nose and wadded the tissue. "But in all seriousness, I would take a few child education classes if I had to."

Amanda gave her a hug. "If there's anything we can do to help, let us know. I think you'll be great. Now, do you want to run to Martha's with me? She's got a couple of pies that are due to come out of the oven anytime."

"You are such a bad influence on me, Amanda Walters." Rebecca stood and picked up Eddie. "Lead the way."

SHELBY STOPPED THE truck and pointed to the west. "Is that what y'all were talkin' about, Lex?"

"Yep. See how those damned vines totally cover that part of the fence? We've tried just about everything. It'll die off for a while, then come back again with a vengeance."

"Damn. And it grows too thick for the animals to see?"

Lex nodded. "Stupid cows can really hurt themselves trying to barrel through it. For some reason, the guys have to be told to check this fence at least once a month, especially in the spring." She rubbed her chest and frowned.

"You okay?"

"Pretty much." Lex checked her watch. "It's close to lunchtime. Why don't we head back to the house? I promised Amanda to take it easy today."

"Sure." Shelby turned the truck around and started down the dirt road. "You and Amanda have been together for quite a while, haven't you?"

"Yep. Close to thirteen years." Lex turned to her. "And she's everything to me. Why?"

Shelby tapped her thumbs on the steering wheel. "Well, I know she took your name. And y'all had a ceremony—"

"Uh-huh."

"Have you ever thought about going someplace and doing it, legal-like? You know, get a license and all?"

Lex thought about the question for a moment. "Nah. I don't need a damned piece of paper to tell me what's already in my heart." She shrugged. "Who knows? Maybe someday we can do it in Somerville."

Shelby laughed. "Oh, yeah. I can see that happenin'. Probably 'bout the same time it snows in July around here."

"Stranger things have happened. So, you and Rebecca ever going to have a ceremony, or anything?"

The truck lurched to one side. "What?"

"You heard me." Lex laughed at her panicked look. "It's not that bad, Shelby. Hell, y'all have been together for a few years, right?"

"Uh-huh."

"So? Why not take that extra step? Show her what she means to you." Lex paused. "Um, unless you don't think—"

"No, you're right. I'd love to do that. But her family barely tolerates me now. I don't even want to think about how they'd act if I asked her to marry me." Shelby frowned. "Her brother still threatens to hire someone to get rid of me, just about every time I see the little piss ant. And her folks are nice enough, but I know they still give her grief about us."

Lex tipped her hat back. "That sucks. I guess family gatherings are uncomfortable, huh?"

"Oh, yeah. We don't even sit near one another anymore. Her brother would get his knickers in a bunch and start making a scene, and all it did was cause trouble."

"Damn." Lex could see that Shelby was upset by the conversation. "Well, if you ever want to have a ceremony, you're welcome to do it here at the ranch. I can take the little brother out behind the barn and teach him some manners."

"I'd pay good money to see that." Shelby parked the truck by the barn and turned off the motor. "Thanks, Lex. I may take you up on your offer, someday."

Lex got out of the truck and walked to Shelby's side. "Anytime, my friend. Now, let's go see what Martha has for lunch. I bet you five bucks that Amanda and Rebecca are already there."

"What makes you say that?" Shelby asked, as they headed toward Martha's.

"Pecan pie. Martha was gonna make a couple of them today, and they're Amanda's favorites."

"Martha might end up being a referee, then. 'Cause Rebecca loves 'em, too."

"We'd better hurry, then, before they're all gone." Lex sped up her pace, laughing along with Shelby.

Before they made the steps to the porch, Martha opened the front door. "What on earth are you two up to?"

Lex walked by her and swatted her on the rear. "Not a damned thing," she teased.

"Lexington Marie!" Martha squawked. "I'm gonna tan your hide with a spoon," she threatened.

Shelby paused and removed her hat. "Afternoon, Martha."

Martha tipped her head in acknowledgment. "Good afternoon, Shelby. I hope you kept Lexie out of trouble today."

"I did my best, ma'am." Shelby held the door for Martha before following her inside. "It's a tough job, though."

Lex ignored them and headed for the kitchen. She found Amanda and Rebecca at the table, talking quietly. "Hey. I hope y'all saved some pie for us."

Rebecca looked up and saw Shelby standing behind Lex. Her eyes filled with tears and she popped up from her chair.

"Shelby!" She rushed across the room and fell into her lover's arms. "I'm so sorry."

"Um, darlin'?" Shelby automatically embraced her and looked to Amanda for clues to Rebecca's behavior. "What's wrong?"

Amanda stood and put her arm around Lex's waist. "You look worn out."

"Nah. I'm fine. Ow!" Lex rubbed her ribs where Amanda poked her. "Bully."

"Have a seat at the table, and I'll get you something to eat. Then we're going home so you can get some rest before the girls get home."

Martha pushed Lex into a chair. "Shelby, why don't you and Rebecca go into the living room? Since Charlie and Eddie are napping in the bedroom, you should have plenty of privacy."

"I appreciate that. Thank you." Shelby turned to lead Rebecca away. "C'mon, darlin'."

Lex turned to Amanda. "What was that all about?"

"Rebecca lost her job. Carson's business is so slow right now that they had to cut everyone's hours."

"Damn. That's rotten." Lex brightened when Martha placed a piece of pecan pie and a cup of coffee in front of her. "Thanks."

Martha patted her shoulder. "You're too blasted skinny, girl. And pale, too."

"It's winter. I'm always pale this time of year."

Amanda choked on the sip of iced tea she had taken. "Martha, how have you let her live this long?"

The older woman handed her a napkin. "It hasn't been easy." She pointed a finger at Lex, who appeared to be considering a snarky retort. "Not one word, Lexie."

Lex grinned and stuck a forkful of pie into her mouth.

SHELBY LED REBECCA to the sofa and sat beside her. She kept a grip on her lover's hand. "Okay, darlin'. What's got you so upset?"

"I feel so stupid." Rebecca wiped her eyes with a crumpled tissue. "I mean, I know it's not the end of the world, and I'm sure I can do something about it soon, but—"

"Slow down. You're not makin' a whole lotta sense."

Rebecca took a deep breath and looked into Shelby's eyes. "I think I've really screwed up."

"You ain't pregnant, are ya?" Shelby asked with a chuckle. When she didn't get an answer, her eyes grew bigger. "Rebecca?"

"No! Of course not!"

Shelby blew out her breath. "All right, good. I didn't think so. We haven't really ever discussed it, and I know you like Lex and Amanda's kids."

"I lost my job," Rebecca whispered.

"What? How did that happen? I thought being a manager was more or less a secure spot."

Rebecca shook her head and squeezed Shelby's hand. "Mr. Carson called me this morning and said he was going to cut everyone's hours. Even Regina's."

"That's a hell of a lot different than firin' someone."

"Mr. Carson didn't fire me. I quit."

Shelby pulled her hand away and stood. She tucked her hands in the back pockets of her jeans and walked to the fireplace. "You quit your job?"

"I thought it was the best thing to do." Rebecca got off the couch and stood behind her lover. "Could you turn around, please?"

Shelby lowered her head and slowly turned. She closed her eyes and stayed silent, with her clinched fists by her sides.

"Shelby, I know I should have probably at least talked to you before I—"

In a low voice, Shelby cut her off. "Remember when I thought about going back on the circuit?"

"Of course. But—"

"And do you remember that big fight we had?" Shelby opened her eyes and stared into Rebecca's. "All because you told me we were partners, and partners discussed things before any big decisions were made."

"I know. And I remember how mad you got, because you said that you were a grown woman, and could make up your own mind."

Shelby opened and closed her hands several times in an effort to calm down. She kept her voice soft. "You read me the fucking riot act for even thinking about going back to the rodeo. But you can quit your damned job without even mentioning it to me?"

"Shelby, wait. It's not like that."

"Six years, Rebecca. Don't you think I deserved a little consideration after six years together?" Shelby held up her hands and backed away. "I need to take a walk before I say something I shouldn't."

She left the living room and closed the front door quietly behind her.

Chapter Fifteen

TWO DAYS LATER, Lex looked out the kitchen window and saw Shelby go into the horse barn. She placed her coffee mug in the sink and turned to her wife, who was feeding Eddie his lunch. "I'm going to the barn."

"Hossie!" Eddie kicked his feet. "Hossie!"

Amanda wiped his face. "We'll go see the hossies later," she promised.

"What's wrong?" she asked Lex.

"Shelby."

"Honey, maybe we should stay out of it."

Lex ignored her and stepped into the hall to get her hat. "I won't be long."

"Momma, hossie!" Eddie pounded his fists on his high chair tray. "Momma."

Amanda gave her the *see what you did* look when Lex returned to the kitchen. "You're the one who started taking him to the barn with you."

"I know. But I really want to check on Shelby." Lex kissed them each on the head. "Be good for Mommy, and we'll see the hossies later," she promised Eddie.

"Momma." He reached for her with spaghetti-covered fingers.

Amanda caught him before he could grab Lex. "Are you sure you want to get in the middle of this?"

"We're already in the middle," Lex said. "Or don't you remember Martha's house guest for the past couple of days?"

After Shelby left Martha's, Rebecca had become inconsolable. Only Martha's gentle mothering and offer of their guest room could calm her down.

"And no offense to Rebecca, but I can only handle a woman crying her eyes out for so long, before I feel the need to step in."

"She's not crying her eyes out. She's just upset. Wouldn't you be if I walked out on you?"

"I'd follow you, sweetheart. Then we'd get into a *discussion* in the yard, and Martha would have to hose us down."

"Sounds about right." Amanda stood and kissed her on the cheek. "Don't be out too long, okay? The wind is still chilly."

"Yes, ma'am." Lex tipped her hat, causing Eddie to giggle and clap. "Be good."

"Good." Eddie used his fingers to wipe up the spaghetti sauce. He stuck them in his mouth. "Mmm."

Lex laughed and waved before she stepped out onto the back porch. A gust of wind ruffled her long-sleeved, denim shirt. "I should have worn a jacket. Why is she always right?"

As she approached the barn, she could hear Shelby inside. Lex slowly opened the door.

"Damned mess, I tell ya," Shelby griped, as she cleared out a stall. "Was I askin' too much? Hell, no. Sometimes she still acts like a damned kid." She shoveled out more dirty straw.

Lex leaned against the opposite stall. "You're both acting like kids, if you ask me."

Shelby yelped and dropped the shovel. "You scared the shit out of me!"

"Good thing you've got a shovel, then."

"Funny." Shelby stepped out of the stall. "Amanda let you off your leash?"

The smile left Lex's face. She pushed away from the stall and got in Shelby's face. "Let me make something perfectly clear."

Her voice lowered as she leaned above the smaller woman. "You can yell at me, tease me, even cuss me out. But don't *ever* say anything about my wife, you got me?"

"Yeah, I got ya." Shelby picked up her shovel and started back into the stall. "You come in here to bust my balls?"

"Nope." Lex relaxed against the stall gate. "I came in here to see how you were doing."

Shelby stopped her shovel. "You think I can't do this job?"

"What?" Lex fought the urge to shake her. For someone with a lot of common sense, Shelby could certainly be stupid. "I'm talking about how you're doing since Rebecca's been at Martha's, you pig-headed idiot."

"Oh." Shelby leaned on the shovel and scratched beneath the band on her hat. "I'm okay."

Lex snorted. "Right."

"Hey, I am. I can do just fine until she comes to her senses."

"Really?"

Shelby glared at her. "Yeah, really. I took care of myself for a lot of years before she came along, you know."

"Did you wear your shirts inside out very often?" Lex asked as she tried to keep from laughing.

"What?" Shelby looked down at the gray shirt she wore. "Hell, no wonder I couldn't get the damned thing buttoned right." She peeled off her shirt just as the barn door opened.

"Lex, Martha asked me to—" Rebecca paused when she saw her partner standing in the stall, clad only in her sports bra. "What's going on in here?"

Shelby hurriedly put her shirt back on, correctly this time. "Not what you're probably thinkin', that's for damned sure."

"I believe my wife is calling me." Lex tipped her head to Rebecca as she left the barn.

Rebecca stared at her lover until Shelby couldn't stand it anymore. "What?"

"I've missed you," Rebecca admitted softly.

Shelby noticed the tears in her eyes and moved quickly across the barn. She stopped in front of Rebecca. "You've ignored my calls."

"What? No, I haven't. My phone's been silent for two days." Rebecca crossed her arms. "I've kept it with me this entire time."

"Where is it?"

Rebecca dug it out of her back pocket. "Right here. See?"

When Shelby held out her hand, she passed the phone to her.

"Rebecca," Shelby asked gently, looking at the display. "When was the last time you charged your phone?"

"Just the other—" Rebecca stopped. "It's dead, isn't it?"

"Yeah." Shelby handed it back to her. "I'm sorry, darlin'. I shouldn't have gone off on you like that."

Rebecca frowned as she tucked the phone back into her pocket. "Did Lex tell you to say that?"

"No, she did not." Shelby removed her work gloves and tossed them on the floor. "I know the wonderful Lex Walters is fuckin' perfect, but I can make up my own mind on things without her help!"

"Hey, no. I didn't mean it like that." Rebecca held out her hands and smiled when Shelby accepted them. "And I don't think she's perfect."

Shelby snorted. "Yeah, right."

"She's too tall, for starters. I'd get a crick in my neck if I had to be around her all the time. I feel sorry for Amanda." She pulled Shelby closer.

"Uh-huh."

Rebecca let go of Shelby's hands so she could grab her hips. "And her eyes? They're so dark blue you can't tell what she's thinking. Spooky. I like my women more my height, with simmering brown eyes."

Shelby laughed at that. "Simmering? Have you been reading your mother's books again?"

"Good God, no." Rebecca ran her hands up Shelby's sides until they were locked behind her neck. "Are we okay?"

"Yeah, we're good." Shelby closed the distance between them and kissed her. "Wanna go check out the hay barn?"

Rebecca giggled. "Sure, as long as you don't think your boss will catch us."

"Nah. I have a feelin' we won't be seeing her for a while." Shelby took her hand and led her through the back door of the barn.

LEX HUNG HER hat by the back door and peeked into the kitchen, which was empty. She stood quietly for a moment and listened. The sound of laughter from upstairs told her where her wife and son were, so she followed the sounds.

She found them in the master bathroom, both soaking in a tub full of bubbles. "Well, what do we have here?"

Amanda waved as Eddie squealed and splashed. "I gave up trying to get us both clean with a washcloth."

"Momma!"

"I see." Lex rested against the sink and smiled fondly. "I guess that explains the spaghetti in your hair, then."

"What?" Amanda reached for her head until Lex started laughing. "You are such a brat."

"Bwat," Eddie parroted.

Lex laughed and moved to kneel beside the tub. "You think so, little guy?" She flinched as she was splashed. "Oh, yeah?" Using only her fingers, she splashed him back, causing a fit of giggles from the toddler.

"You proved my point." Amanda leaned back and relaxed as Lex bathed Eddie. "How did things go in the barn?"

"Before or after I threatened to kick her ass?" Lex asked quietly. "Good grief, Eddie. How did you get sauce on the back of your neck?"

Her sneaky grin was hidden from Amanda. "Or maybe after Rebecca came in and saw Shelby topless?"

Eddie fought the washcloth. "No!"

"Wait a minute, what?" Amanda grabbed Lex's hand. "Shelby was topless?"

"Well, yeah. That's what usually happens when someone takes off their shirt." Amanda's splash hit Lex in the face. "Thanks."

"Serves you right. Would you mind taking him? I don't want him to get pruny." She wiped the water from Lex's face. "And don't think this gets you out of explaining yourself."

"Yes, dear." Lex lifted Eddie and wrapped him in a towel. "Let's get a diaper on you before you give me another surprise."

"Momma, go!"

Lex held him close and kissed his forehead. "Yes, sir. Right away, sir."

"I'll be out in a minute," Amanda called after them.

"Take your time," Lex answered as she carried him through their room and across the hall. "It's more fun to make your mommy squirm, right?"

"Mommy," he sang, rocking in her arms. He laughed when he was put on the dressing table. "Ha! Momma, go!"

Rolling her eyes, Lex quickly diapered him and dressed him in a white shirt and green overalls. "I need to talk to your Aunt Jeannie about color choices, don't I?"

"Pbbbbsstt. Go, Momma."

"Almost done." The socks she added wouldn't last long, but Lex knew better than to not put them on him. "All right, buddy. Ready to check on Mommy?"

"Go!"

"I thought so."

When they entered the bedroom, they met Amanda, clad only in a towel. Lex playfully covered Eddie's eyes. "Oops. Howdy."

Amanda allowed the towel to drop to the floor. "Howdy? That's the best you can do?"

"If we didn't have little eyes and ears nearby, I'd do a heck of a lot better." Lex let Eddie down carefully.

He made a beeline for Amanda. "Mommy." Eddie wrapped his arms around her bare leg. "Uck!" He patted her damp skin.

Lex took mercy on her and carried him to the bed. She stretched out beside Eddie and used her fingers to comb his fluffy, dark hair. "How about you help me take a nap?"

"No!"

Soon Amanda was dressed and on the other side of Eddie. "Okay, I think I've been pretty patient with you, Lexington."

"You usually are," Lex agreed, being purposely dense.

"Lex."

Laughing, Lex rolled onto her side and faced Amanda. "What do you want to know?"

Amanda mirrored her posture and lightly rubbed Eddie's stomach, causing his eyes to close. "You said you and Shelby got into a fight?"

"No, not exactly a fight. She just said something that pis..., ah, made me mad." Lex lowered her voice when she realized their son was lightly dozing. "But everything's okay now."

"How did she lose her shirt?"

Lex kept her face neutral. "She took it off."

Amanda looked toward the ceiling and growled. "And why did she take it off?"

"Cause it was inside out."

Carefully reaching across Eddie, Amanda grabbed her wife's ear. "Spill it, woman."

"Ow. Okay, okay." Once her ear was released, Lex continued. "She told me she could take care of herself just fine, and I asked if she was used to wearing her shirt wrong." She tapped Amanda on the nose. "That's why she took her shirt off. Unfortunately, Rebecca came in right after that."

"Oops."

"Yeah, oops. I'm just glad there wasn't a pitchfork nearby, or I might have gotten my butt kicked."

Amanda giggled. "I would have loved to have seen your face."

"I'm sure it was hilarious. Anyway, when I left, they were at least speaking to one another."

"You're such a chicken!"

"No, I'm not."

Amanda laughed at her. "Yes, you are." She lifted herself above Eddie and kissed Lex. "But that's okay. You're my chicken."

"Geez." Lex rolled off the bed and picked up Eddie. "Just for that, he's going to nap in his room, so we can *nap* in here."

"Oooh."

AMANDA CLOSED THE door on her SUV and watched the girls race for the back door. She gave up a long time ago asking them not to run. Instead, she followed at a more sedate pace. She heard Freckles' welcoming bark before the door closed behind her children. As she reached the porch, she met Rebecca and Shelby coming up the walk.

Rebecca released Shelby's hand and embraced Amanda. "Thanks for everything," she whispered in her ear. She stepped back and added, "Do your girls ever slow down?"

"Not often. Lorrie promised to show Mel something on the computer, so I'm sure they're already upstairs in her room." Amanda turned to Shelby. "How are you doing?"

"A lot better, thanks." Shelby put her arm around Rebecca. "Sorry for any problems I might have caused."

Holding the door open, Amanda gestured for them to precede her. "As long as you two are okay, we're okay." She stepped into the kitchen, surprised to see Lex at the table alone. "Where's Eddie?"

Lex looked up from the newspaper in her hands. "Isn't he with you?"

Amanda dropped her keys on the table. "No. He was here playing with his truck, when I left."

"Are you sure?" Lex folded the newspaper and set it on the table. "I don't remember that."

Before her wife could totally fall apart, she tugged her onto her lap. "Calm down, sweetheart. I was just messing with you. Charlie showed up right after you left and stole him." She grunted as she was elbowed in the stomach. "Ow."

"I swear, one of these days." Amanda didn't finish, since both Shelby and Rebecca were standing in the doorway, laughing. "Come in and make yourselves comfortable."

Rebecca sat across from them, but her partner remained standing. Shelby removed her hat and held it in her hands. "Lex, can I have a word with you?" She tipped her head toward the door. "Outside?"

"Sure." Once Amanda was in her own chair, Lex stood. "This gonna take long?"

Shelby shrugged. "Most likely not." She led the way out of the kitchen.

Once they left, Amanda asked Rebecca, "What's going on?"

"Did Lex tell you what happened today?"

"Yes. She told me that Shelby had said something to make her mad, but they worked it out. Why? Is Shelby still angry?" She started out of her chair, but Rebecca stopped her. "If she asked her outside so they could fight, I'll—"

"No, I don't think so. Shelby's not a fighter. Although I know she'll probably think twice before making Lex mad again." Rebecca released her grip on Amanda's arm. "She's a lot of things, but stupid isn't one of them. Lex could probably take her out with one swing."

"Lex has mellowed a lot during the years. But she's just now getting past that bout of pneumonia and isn't at full strength. Maybe I should go out there and make sure they're okay."

"We could always peek out the window."

LEX FOLLOWED SHELBY to the swing set and leaned against the slide. "I think we're far enough from the house. What's up?"

"You know, I didn't much appreciate the way you talked to me in the barn today." Shelby kicked a pebble away from the swing. "And I sure as hell didn't like how you threatened me."

"Yeah?" Lex put her hands in the front pockets of her jeans. "Trust me, it wasn't a threat."

Shelby stared at her for a moment then burst into laughter. "You're a tough son-of-a-bitch, you know that?"

"So I've been told. Look, you hit a nerve when you mentioned Amanda. I probably shouldn't have snapped like that."

"Nah, I don't blame you a bit." Shelby walked forward and held out her hand. "I was an asshole. It's a bad habit I have. Truce?"

"Hell, that makes two of us." Lex shook her head and slapped her on the back. "Truce. Now let's get back in the house so our better halves can step away from the window."

Shelby laughed. "Nosey, ain't they?"

"Yep." Lex walked beside her toward the house. "We could always get into a wrestling match to freak them out."

"Damn, you're evil. I like that."

Chapter Sixteen

THE SMALL, WOODEN table was covered with several days' worth of newspapers. Rebecca circled another ad with her marker and wrote the information on the notepad beside her coffee cup. She had searched for a job for two weeks with little luck. Since her only experiences were retail and horses, it was hard to get into any other field.

Shelby came into the kitchen. Her dark hair was wet and combed against her skull. She passed Rebecca and poured herself a travel mug of coffee. "Mornin', darlin'."

"Good morning." Rebecca pushed the newspaper aside.

"Still can't find anything?" Shelby took her usual place at the table, the chair to the left of her partner.

"Most of the jobs out there want experience, and I can't get the experience without the job. It's driving me nuts."

"Yeah, I know what you mean. When I'd be healin' up from the rodeo, I'd try to find a job until I could go back. I'd usually end up digging post holes or washin' dishes. Not a whole lotta stuff out there for someone like me."

"At least you have a good job, now." Rebecca moved away from the table and opened the refrigerator. "Do you want me to fix you some breakfast?"

"Nah. I'm sure either Martha or Helen will have something ready." Shelby cringed when her lover slammed the door closed. "Is that call from your Dad last night still botherin' you?"

Rebecca spun around and leaned against the counter, crossing her arms. "He practically called me lazy! Then he ranted about me not going to college, and how he was sure I'd be past this *fling* by now." She just barely restrained from stomping her foot. "I told him that after all this time, he needed to get over it. I'm in this relationship with you for as long as you'll have me." She looked at the floor. "I thought I was doing the right thing by giving my hours to someone who needed them more."

"Well, things are a mite rough everywhere, right now. He's just worried about you." Shelby stood and stretched. "We'll get through this." She moved closer to Rebecca and put her hands on the younger woman's hips. "Besides, I kinda like being the major breadwinner right now. It's my turn to take care of you."

Resting her forehead on Shelby's shoulder, Rebecca sighed. "I don't want to be taken care of. I like being equal partners." She put her arms around Shelby's neck. "I love you."

"Love you, too," Shelby whispered. "It's gonna be all right."

LEX STEPPED OUT of the barn and blinked to adjust her eyes to the mid-morning sun. Not far from the house, one of the doors to the garage was open. "Which one of those dumbasses forgot to close it, this time?"

As she neared the open door, she found the interior light on as well. "Damn it. Those idiots need to be more careful."

She stood inside the doorway of the garage and glanced around. The protective cover for Amanda's Mustang was in the floor. The sixty-seven, powder blue car had been a gift from Amanda's grandfather, and was rarely driven.

"What the hell?" Lex moved close and saw a familiar form slumped against the steering wheel. "Amanda?" She half stumbled, half ran the rest of the way to the car, to squat beside the open driver's door. "Hey."

Amanda raised her head and looked mournfully into her wife's face. Her eyes were puffy and red and she had tear tracks down her cheeks.

"Aw, sweetheart. Come here." Lex pulled Amanda from the seat and onto one her knee. "I'm so sorry."

"He loved this old car," Amanda whispered.

Lex kissed her hair as she continued to stroke Amanda's back. "He loved how much *you* loved this old car." Her voice was as gentle as her touch.

"I think you're right." Amanda rested her cheek against Lex's chest. "I just can't seem to get past him being gone. I think I'm doing fine, then something just hits me and I realize I'll never see him again."

"Yeah. I find myself picking up the phone to call and tell him a joke. He always loved the ones I'd get from the guys at the bunkhouse."

Amanda brushed her hand down Lex's smooth, cotton shirt. "Then Gramma would catch him relaying it to a friend and chew him out. He enjoyed that most of all, I think."

Lex laughed softly. "Good thing I'd only pass along the tamer ones then, huh?"

"Definitely. I think they both loved the game. God, I don't know how she's survived this. But when I call her, she tells me she's fine. And I know she's lying, but we both pretend it's okay."

"I try to stop by any time I'm in town. But she runs me off pretty quick." Lex blew out a heavy breath. "Maybe we should see about bringing her out here, at least for a while. I worry about her being alone in that big, old house."

"Good luck. She wouldn't even let me bring the subject up. Stubborn woman."

"Family trait." Lex didn't get the expected poke or slap. "Sweetheart, I think we're going to have to realize that she's a grown woman who knows what she wants, and she's not about to take any crap from us about it."

"I know. But it's so damned frustrating." When her seat wavered,

Amanda said, "I must be killing you." She climbed off and helped Lex to her feet. "Thanks."

"I'm glad I found you. I don't want you going through this alone." Lex put her arm around Amanda's waist. "What caused you to come in here?"

Amanda leaned into her wife and fell into her embrace. "I don't know. After I saw the girls off on the bus, I just needed to feel closer to him. I sound like an idiot, don't I?"

"Not a bit. You both put a lot into this old car, it's only natural you'd feel closer here."

They spent a few minutes staring into one another's face. "You have very expressive eyes."

"Yeah?" Lex grinned to lighten the mood. "Know what they're saying right now?"

Amanda smiled as well. "I have a pretty good idea." She kissed Lex's chin and squeezed her. "And for the record, I agree. I think a nap is exactly what we need."

Lex gave her the lead as they left the garage. "I was actually thinking more of a morning ride."

"Uh huh. What I think is that we can't be too careful with your health."

"Really?" In one quick motion, Lex kept one arm around Amanda's shoulders and the other behind her knees to scoop her off her feet.

"Lex! Stop it!" Amanda squealed. "You're going to hurt yourself."

"Open the gate."

Amanda opened the gate and put her arms around Lex's neck. "You're not planning on carrying me all the way upstairs, are you?"

"Nah." Lex slowly navigated the sidewalk and steps. "Door, please."

"Yes, dear." Amanda pushed the door open. "Who did you pawn our son off on?"

Lex snorted. "I did no such thing. Helen needed a babysitter for Roy, and who better than a real baby?" She started breathing heavy before they reached the stairway. "I think this is the end of the ride, ma'am."

Amanda landed nimbly on her feet. "Are you all right?"

"Yep." Lex inhaled then slowly released the breath. "See? No cough." She leaned closer and kissed Amanda. "Wanna race upstairs?"

"Nope." Amanda loosely put her arms around Lex's waist. "Thanks for coming to get me, love. Sometimes I get so bogged down in everything, I forget what's really important."

Lex cupped her cheeks and stared into her eyes. "You're the most important thing in the world to me, Amanda. I hope you realize that."

"I do. It goes both ways, you know."

"Yep." After a soft kiss, she ran her fingers through Amanda's hair. "I love you."

"I love you, too. Come on. Nap time for cowgirls."

THE MID-AFTERNOON TRAFFIC made downtown parking difficult, but not impossible. Rebecca found a space less than a block from the diner. She checked her hair in the rear view mirror before she got out of her car.

As she walked toward her destination, she brushed her hands down her black, knee-length skirt. Along with the white, silk blouse she had borrowed from her mother, she felt completely overdressed and uncomfortable. She couldn't wait to get back to her parents' house and change into her jeans.

When she reached the entrance of the diner, an elderly man held the door open for her as he was leaving. "Thank you."

He tipped his gray western hat, dusty and stained with age. "Miss."

Rebecca stood inside the door and took a deep breath, then let it out slowly. It was well past lunchtime, yet several booths and many of the counter stools were in use.

"Well, don't just stand there, honey. Come on in," a well-bosomed blonde chided from behind the counter. Her platinum hair was too bright to be natural, and her lined face covered in makeup didn't hide her age.

"Um, thanks." Rebecca took the nearest vacant stool. "I saw your ad in the paper and would like to apply for the part-time waitress job."

The nametag on the blonde's chest was faded and chipped. Francine stopped in front of Rebecca and scratched her head with the eraser of her pencil. "Why would you want to do that, hon? This old place ain't for someone as young and pretty as you."

"I need a job," Rebecca whispered. She shifted on the stool and leaned closer to Francine. "Please. I'll do whatever you need. Wash dishes, mop, anything."

Francine glanced toward the window to the kitchen to make sure they wouldn't be overheard. "Trust me, you don't want to work here. The money's shit, the hours are worse and the boss," she gestured over her shoulder, "is a sorry bastard." She took a coffee cup from beneath the counter and placed it in front of Rebecca. "You ever done this before?"

Rebecca shook her head. "But I'm a fast learner."

"Your husband leave you?"

"No, nothing like that. I worked at Carson's, but business was slow." She wrapped both hands around the empty mug. "I really need the work."

Francine cocked her head and nodded. "I understand, sugar. But you won't get much here, I'm afraid. Rusty just wants some young thing with a nice ass and tits. Not that yours aren't nice, 'cause they are. But you can do better."

Rebecca blushed and barely kept from covering her chest with her hands. "Um, I don't...I mean—"

"Oh, hon. You're too cute," Francine teased after she stopped laughing. "Carson's?"

"Yes." Rebecca kept her eyes on the coffee cup. "I was an assistant manager, up until recently."

The middle-aged man at the other end of the counter tapped his empty cup on the counter. "Francine, I could use a refill."

"Hold your horses. Why don't you go get rid of the first four cups, Earl? I'll be there in a sec." Francine turned to Rebecca. "I've heard they need some counter help at the feed store. Don't you think that might be a bit more your speed, sweetie?"

"Really?" Rebecca placed her purse on her lap and opened it. "Let me pay for the coffee, then I'll go by and see."

Francine covered her hand. "No need. You just tell 'em Francine sent you, all right? And if that don't pan out, I think the Rocking W may be looking for help."

"My partner already works there," Rebecca answered then blushed. She hadn't meant to share such personal information with a complete stranger, no matter how friendly that stranger seemed to be. "Uh."

With a saucy wink, Francine laughed. "Well, next time you see Lex, you tell her Francine said hello. Go on, now."

She turned away and took the glass coffee pot off its burner.

THE TREES ALONG the residential street dropped their buds on Michael's windshield, which left a powdery, yellow mess. He grumbled and used his wipers to clear the debris away, only to be hit again as the brisk March breeze knocked more free. He was on his way to his mother's before work. A daily ritual since his father passed away, he would often try to discuss her bills or expenses, although Anna Leigh didn't always seem to appreciate his input.

He frowned as he pulled into her driveway. Jeannie's SUV was taking up two spaces, and he had to park behind a rusty, beat-up truck that he'd never seen before. He slammed his car door and stomped up the walk.

As he ascended the steps to the porch, the front door opened. Two people were carrying a large, oak dresser. "What's going on here?"

The person closest to Michael backed into him. The man stopped and was shoved when his partner kept moving. "Hey, watch it."

"Oh, hey, Mr. Cauble," Kyle greeted him. "Could we squeeze by you? This thing is heavy."

He stepped off the porch and stared at them as they carried the piece to the truck.

"Michael, hello," Anna Leigh called from the door.

"What are they doing?" he asked as he followed her inside.

Anna Leigh continued to the kitchen as if she hadn't heard his question. "I believe there's enough coffee left for one more cup, but I can always start another pot."

"Don't bother, Mom." Michael stood beside the table with one hand on the back of a chair. "I've got an early appointment this morning, anyway. Where are they taking the dresser?"

"To the VFW pavilion." She turned from the coffee pot and brushed her hair away from her eyes. She hadn't been to her hairdresser since before her husband died, and her usually short style had grown out. There were more lines in her face than before, and dark shadows beneath her eyes that not even a week's sleep could erase.

He heard a thump from upstairs. "What's going on?"

"The high school needs new band uniforms, and they're having their annual rummage sale this weekend. Jacob always donated a few pieces for them." Another thump caused Anna Leigh to look up at the ceiling before taking a seat at the table. "Jeannie is cleaning out two of the rooms for me."

Michael shook his head as if to clear it. "Excuse me? Why haven't I heard about this? And just how much stuff are you giving to them?"

"I don't care for your tone, Michael. Please sit so we can discuss this rationally."

He angrily shoved the chair away from the table. It tipped and landed on the tile floor with a loud crack. "My tone? I've done everything I could for you since Dad passed away! How dare you keep me out of the loop!"

"Um, excuse me. Is everything all right?" Kyle stood in the doorway, her friend right behind her.

Anna Leigh nodded. "We're fine. Michael was just leaving."

"We'll get the bed from the back bedroom, if that's okay." Kyle waited for the older woman's nod, before giving Michael a pointed look. "If you need anything else, just holler."

"Thank you, Kylie."

Once they were alone, Michael picked up the chair and resettled it. "I'm sorry, Mom. I just want to help you."

"Yes, but taking control of my life is not helpful. I'm fully capable of making my own decisions." She rested one hand on the other atop the table and stared at them. "And one of those decisions has to do with this house. I can't stay here any longer."

Michael dropped into the chair he had righted. "You're selling it?"

"No, dearest. I'd like to give it to Jeannie and Rodney."

"I see." He rubbed his face and stood. "If you're sure about this, I'd better let Lois know. We'll need to clean out and paint the guest room, maybe install a new sink in the hall bath."

It took a moment, but Anna Leigh finally understood. "I'm not moving in with you and Lois, Michael."

"Of course you are. Where else would you go? To the ranch? Nothing against Lex and Amanda, but you'd never get any peace if you stayed there. Our place is perfect."

Anna Leigh had heard enough. She slapped the table with the flat of one hand. "I've made my plans, Michael. And that does not include becoming a burden to my family."

"A burden? What are you talking about?" He sat next to her and put his hands over hers. "Mom, please. You've obviously distraught. Now isn't the time to be making these sorts of decisions. It's only been three months."

"I know exactly how long it's been." She gentled her tone. "Darling, you must understand. I'm not feeble, nor overwrought. But this house is far too big for me to stay in alone."

"But, where will you go?"

She patted his hands before she sat back. "I've found a lovely little duplex not far from here. It's perfect for my needs and has recently been renovated."

"All right. Then I'll—" Michael was stopped by her steely glare. "Uh, is there anything I can do to help, Mom?"

"Not yet. But thank you." Anna Leigh graced him with a real smile for the first time in months.

THE RINGING PHONE brought Amanda out of her pleasant dream and she fought her way from beneath the covers. She glanced at the clock, relieved she still had more than an hour before the school bus dropped off the girls. As she stretched across Lex, her wife opened her eyes.

"Hey." Lex's arms automatically circled Amanda. "Aren't you tired?"

The phone rang again.

"Oh." She laughed and quickly kissed her wife and reached for the phone. "I'll get it. Walters."

"Lex? This is Michael. Is Amanda nearby?"

Lex sat up and grinned at her equally naked partner. "Uh, yeah. She's right here. Hold on." She handed the phone to Amanda. "Your dad," she whispered.

Amanda covered herself with the sheet and accepted the handset. "Hi, Daddy."

"You need to talk to your grandmother. The more I think about it, the madder I get."

"Gramma? What do you mean? I talked to her yesterday. She seemed okay to me." Amanda met Lex's questioning look with a shrug. "Is she all right?"

"I think she's finally lost her senses," he snapped. "Did you know she wants to move?"

Amanda dropped the sheet and slid out of bed. "What? Since when?" She held the phone to her ear with one shoulder as she reached for her robe.

Lex gave a low whistle as Amanda bent to pick her robe up off the floor. She waggled her eyebrows at the look she received, then sighed as Amanda covered up.

"How the hell should I know? I went there this morning, like I always do, and she was donating furniture to some rummage sale. Furniture that my father spent a lot of time building. Can you believe that?"

"Daddy, they've always—" Amanda trailed off as Lex got out of bed and slowly stretched. She covered the mouthpiece of the phone. "Stop that!"

Lex gave an exaggerated yawn and stretched again. She staggered backward as a pillow hit her in the chest. "Brat."

"Are you listening to me?" Michael asked.

"What? Oh, um, yeah. Sorry." Amanda shook her finger at Lex, who waved and disappeared into the bathroom. She replayed the conversation in her mind. "Wait. Gramma actually told you she wants to move?"

"She's already got a place picked out, and said she's going to give the house to your sister. Haven't you been paying attention?"

"I'm sorry. But when did she decide this?"

"This morning was the first I've heard of it. And I'm the one that should take care of everything. She didn't even bother to consult me first."

Amanda rolled her eyes. "Okay. I'll give her a call and see what's going on. But, if she's made up her mind, there's not much anyone can do about it. And I can't say that I blame her. That house is far too big for her to stay in alone."

Hearing the sound of the shower starting, she removed her robe. "I have to go, Daddy. Lex is..." she blushed. "Lex needs my help with something."

"Fine. Could you call me, later?"

"Uh huh. Love you, bye." Amanda turned off the handset and tossed it on the bed. She hurried into the bathroom and opened the glass shower door. "Starting without me?"

Lex tugged her inside. "Never."

Chapter Seventeen

IT WAS MID-AFTERNOON when Shelby received a call to return to Roy's. As she drove toward the house, she tried to figure out why. Going through the past few days of work in her mind, she couldn't come up with anything she did wrong, but the summons still worried her. She enjoyed her job at the ranch, and now with Roy able to move around more, she feared he had changed his mind about working less.

To Shelby, the few short months she had been here were the most rewarding of her professional life. She'd found a place that felt right, and a job that seemed to have been tailor-made for her. She respected her boss, and had even made a good friend in the process. "Damn. I didn't want to lose this job."

She parked between the house and the corral, so she could spend a few minutes with the horses on what she assumed was her final day of work.

Unable to put it off any longer, Shelby trudged up the steps to the house. She was met at the door by Roy, who shook her hand.

"Come on in, Shelby. Hope you weren't too busy when I radioed you."

Shelby wiped her boots on the mat and removed her western hat before following him inside. "Nah, not really. Just checkin' the south pasture for strays. The guys seem to be taking care of their responsibilities just fine."

"That's great. Let's go into the office." Roy led the way, his walking cast making a loud thump on the wooden floors with every step. He waited until she sat in the visitor's chair before he closed the door and took his own seat. "The boss and I had a pretty long talk about you this morning, Shelby."

Her face flushed, but she didn't look away. "I figured as much."

"Yeah? Well, we've both noticed you coming in before dawn, and leaving after sundown just about every day." He straightened up and looked her in the eyes. "Is there really that much work to do around here? 'Cause, while I know this ain't no nine-to-five job, I wasn't aware of enough things going on to warrant you working yourself to death."

"I don't log any overtime. You can double-check my book, if you need to." Shelby carried around a small, spiral notebook in her shirt pocket, where she posted her work times as well as any notes or questions for Roy.

"I'm well-aware of the time you clock. If anything, we owe you a lot of back pay, for the hours you haven't logged."

Roy rested his elbows on the desk and sat forward in his chair. "Damn it, Shelby. Lex is just now getting back on her feet. I don't want to see you end up in the hospital, too."

"What?"

"Listen, I admire your dedication to the job. But you're going to run yourself into the ground at this rate, and then where will you be?"

Shelby's anger flared, but quickly died when she realized she wasn't losing her job. "Wait. You're not firing me?"

Roy's laughter echoed off the paneled walls of the small room. "Are you shittin' me? Good lord, no. Where on earth did you get that idea?"

"Well, you've been gettin' around better, and with Lex feelin' up to snuff again, I figured." She shrugged. "I reckon I figured all wrong, huh?"

He slapped the desk before he stood. "Hell, yeah. You figured totally wrong. I love this ranch as if it were my own. But I'm getting too damned old to ride all over the place. No, I'll leave that to you young-uns."

Shelby stood. "I don't know about the young'un's part, but I appreciate it, Roy. Some days I feel older than the hills."

"And that's why you're going to start coming in after the rooster crows. As a matter of fact, why not take the rest of the day off? I'm sure Rebecca would like to see you before the moon comes out."

"Thanks, I think I will." She shifted her hat to her left hand and extended her right. "I'll see you tomorrow, Boss."

Roy shook her hand and slapped her on the shoulder. "Not too early, though. I don't want Lex chewing me out for overworking you."

"Right." She laughed and settled her hat on her head. "I'll try to keep you out of trouble."

"IT FEELS GREAT to be behind the wheel again." Lex navigated her truck through the residential streets of Somerville with ease.

Amanda laughed at her. "Let's see how you feel about it around July. By then, you'll be begging for another break."

"Probably. But for now, I'm going to enjoy it." As they rounded the corner, Lex slowed the truck. "What the hell is going on?"

The long driveway of the Cauble house was overrun with vehicles. Two old pickup trucks, Anna Leigh's Cadillac, Jacob's Suburban, Jeannie's SUV and Michael's SUV crowded the drive. A flat-bed tow truck was on the street, but the driver was nowhere in sight.

"Good lord. I bet poor Gramma is about ready to pull her hair out."

Lex parked behind one of the pickups. "Are you sure you don't want me to stay? I can run interference."

Amanda patted her thigh. "No, go on and get the girls from school. You deserve a fun afternoon."

"I already had that." Lex took Amanda's hand and brought it to her lips. "But ice cream does sound like a nice way to top off the day."

"You," Amanda declared, touching Lex's nose with the tip of her finger, "are dangerous." She stretched across the seat and kissed her. "Try to stay out of trouble." She hopped out of the truck and headed up the sidewalk, turning around once to wave.

Lex returned the wave. "Stay out of trouble. Ha. She's the one who's walking into a war zone," she muttered. Once Amanda went inside, she backed the truck into the street. "It's not like I go out looking for stuff. It just happens."

It wasn't long before she parked near the elementary school. Lex checked her watch before she left the truck. "Ten minutes early. Perfect." She needed to check in with the school office before getting the girls, so their teachers wouldn't try to put them on the bus.

The single-story, putty-colored, brick building was the same elementary school that Lex had attended. Once inside, she tapped on the door frame to the office. "Good afternoon, Mrs. Clevens."

At the main desk, an older woman raised her head from the paperwork in front of her. She was Martha's age, and kept her gray hair cut short and stylish. "Lexington, come in. To what do I owe this pleasure?"

"I had to be in town today, and thought I'd pick up the girls." Lex scribbled her signature on the clipboard placed on the counter for that reason.

Mrs. Clevens removed her reading glasses, but let them hang on the beaded chain around her neck. "It's good to see you up and around again, dear. You had more than a few people worried, that's for sure."

"Thanks. I'll admit to being a little worried, myself." Lex tucked her hands in the front pockets of her jeans and tried to ignore the blush that covered her face. "And thank you again for the cornbread and chili you brought to the house. Everyone loved it."

"My pleasure. I know Amanda had more than enough on her plate while you were sick, without having to worry about cooking all the time."

Lex laughed. "We've still got a freezer full of food that Martha put up for us. I doubt she'll have to cook for at least another month." And that didn't include the meals that Martha had disposed of, including one woman's sardine meatballs, which Martha had threatened to bury in the adjoining county.

"That's wonderful." Mrs. Clevens turned her chair and quickly entered something on the computer. "I've messaged the teachers that you're here, so Melanie and Lorrie won't get on the bus."

"I appreciate that." The school bell cut off any other comment Lex might have made. "Guess I'd better get outside, before the stampede starts."

The older woman left her desk and stepped around the counter. "Take good care of yourself, Lexington. Those little girls need you." She took Lex's hand and squeezed it. "Be good."

Fighting off a blush, Lex nodded. "Yes, ma'am, I sure will.

Thanks." She escaped outside, moments before a dozen little bodies descended from the first grade classroom.

Lex ignored the looks of disdain she received from two women standing nearby. Her jeans and long-sleeved western shirt were clean, as were her boots. When one of the women kept staring, Lex winked, which caused her to turn away quickly. "Heh."

"Momma!" Melanie dodged two boys who were playfully shoving one another.

"Hey there, kiddo." Lex took the backpack from her daughter. "How was school?"

Melanie latched onto Lex's hand and swung it back and forth. "Good! Are you not sick no more?"

"Nope. I'm fine."

"Yay! How come you're here? Is something wrong?"

Lex noticed Lorrie walking slowly through the doors and waved to her. "No, nothing's wrong. I just thought I'd take you girls for some ice cream. How does that sound?"

Melanie cheered again. "Hey, Lorrie! We're going for ice cream!"

"Big whoop." Lorrie headed for the truck.

"She's an old grump," Melanie observed.

"Be nice," Lex warned, although she secretly agreed. "Come on. Let's go get that ice cream."

FOR THE FIRST time in several weeks, Shelby drove down her driveway in broad daylight. She parked beside Rebecca's car and stretched after she got out of her truck. Her lower vertebrae popped which sent a muscle spasm along her spine. "Ugh. I hope Rebecca doesn't want to do anything tonight, I'm beat."

She trudged up the steps and barely got the door open, before she was embraced by her lover. "Hey, darlin'."

"I called the ranch and they told me you were already on your way home." Rebecca stepped back and gave her a long look. "Are you feeling okay?"

"I'm fine." With her arm around Rebecca, Shelby led the way to the sofa and dropped gracelessly onto the worn cushions. "Just tired." She couldn't help but notice the sparkle in her lover's eyes. "What?"

Rebecca jumped up. "Wait right here." She raced to the bedroom and returned quickly with a dark green polo shirt. She held it up to her torso. "Well? What do you think?"

"It's a good color for you, but," Shelby paused and noticed the print above the right breast. "McAlister's Feed Store? Really?"

"Yes!" Rebecca tossed the shirt on the end of the sofa and sat beside Shelby. "I had gone to the diner to apply for the part-time waitress position, and the woman there told me about the feed store. Tom, the manager, recognized me from Carson's. I start work Monday.

And it's full-time!"

Shelby laughed as Rebecca crawled onto her lap facing her. "That's great, darlin'. Do you think you're gonna like it there?"

Rebecca rested her arms on Shelby's shoulders and looked into her eyes. "Yes. And, I get a ten percent discount on everything. Isn't that great?"

"It sure is."

"How tired are you?" Rebecca softly traced the edge of her lover's ear.

Shelby grinned and released the top button of Rebecca's blouse. "Funny you should ask. I don't feel a bit tired, at all."

At her lover's gentle touch, a renewed energy had surged through Shelby. She continued to work the buttons, until the shirt was completely open. Her hands gently cupped the white, lacy bra. "Nice."

"Oh." Rebecca leaned into the touch and closed her eyes. "M...maybe we should move into the bedroom." The clasp on her bra was unfastened and those same hands now covered her breasts. "Shelby, please."

"I'm pretty comfortable where I am." Shelby lowered her head and placed a few tender kisses on her lover's skin. "Mmm."

Rebecca moaned as she suddenly felt herself lowered to the couch. She tangled her fingers in Shelby's hair as the older woman kissed a trail down her stomach.

LEX SAT ACROSS from the girls at the ice cream shop. She tried to feign interest in the rambling story being told by Melanie as she kept a covert eye on her oldest child.

Lorrie used her plastic spoon to stir the strawberry topping around her half-eaten sundae. She ignored her sister's chatter, until Melanie tapped her on the arm. "What?"

"Don't you like your ice cream? I thought strawberry was your favorite? How come you're not eating it?"

"I'm full." Lorrie pushed the red plastic bowl away. She looked up at Lex. "Is Mom home with Eddie?"

Lex rattled the ice in her cup to see if it was truly empty. "No, she's at Gramma's. Aunt Helen and Uncle Roy are watching Eddie."

Lorrie perked up at the mention of Anna Leigh. "Can we go see Gramma, too?"

"Uh, sure. Do you have any homework?" Lex gathered the assorted used napkins they had tossed on the table.

"I don't." Melanie wriggled in her seat. "Mrs. Cooke said she wants to watch us do our work. I think it's 'cause she thinks Robbie's mom does his."

Lex tried to keep from smiling. "Why don't you go wash up before we go, sweetheart? You have chocolate on your face."

Melanie licked around her lips. "Did I get it?"

"No, dummy. On your face," Lorrie snapped.

"That's enough, Lorrie." Lex lightened her tone. "Go on, Mel. We'll wait for you."

"Okey-doke!" Melanie scrambled from her chair and skipped to the back of the shop, where the rest rooms were located.

Lex stretched across the table and lowered her voice. "That was uncalled for. When she gets back, you owe your sister an apology."

"She's not my real sister, and you're not my real mother!" Lorrie jumped up and stomped out of the shop.

Ignoring the stares from the others in the room, Lex took their trash and dumped it. When Melanie came out of the rest room, Lex held out her hand. "Are you ready to go?"

"Yep! Are we going to Gramma's?"

"Sure." When they got outside, Lex noticed that Lorrie had lowered the tailgate and swung her legs from where she sat. She silently counted to twenty then Lex unlocked the doors. "Get buckled up, Mel."

Melanie looked at her sister, who was staring at the ground. "Is Lorrie in trouble?"

"Not yet. Go on, now." After Melanie was inside, Lex leaned against the truck. "Is there something you'd like to talk about, Lorrie?"

Lorrie continued to swing her legs, but didn't answer.

Lex's silent count continued to fifty. She moved to the back of the truck until she stood directly in front of her daughter. "Look, I don't know what burr got under your saddle blanket, but we're not going anywhere until you talk to me."

Lorrie raised her head and wiped the tears from her face. "Can I talk to Mom, instead?"

Although it broke her heart, Lex nodded. "Sure. Get in the truck and we'll head over." She squeezed the edge of the tailgate before she slammed it closed.

THE MOMENT AMANDA stepped into her grandmother's home, she could hear her father's angry voice in the living room. She closed the door behind her and followed the noise.

"Jeannie, I realize you're getting the deal of a lifetime, but have you really thought this through?"

"Daddy, if you'd just listen to me for a second, you'd—"

Michael threw his hands in the air and spun away. "Damn it!" He spun into his other daughter. "Oh. Amanda, hi."

"Hi. I could hear you from outside. What's going on?" Amanda exchanged looks with her sister as she sat on the loveseat. "Where's Gramma?"

Jeannie perched on the arm beside her. "She's upstairs, showing them the stuff to take."

"How much stuff?" Amanda looked at Jeannie, whose red-rimmed eyes belied her flippant attitude. She put her hand on her sister's knee. "Daddy told me a little about it, but—"

"If you wouldn't have brushed me off when I called, I'd have told you more," Michael muttered. "Amanda, you need to talk to Mother. Maybe she'll listen to you."

Amanda turned to him. "I didn't brush you off. But you were ranting and not making much sense."

He lurched to his feet. "I was not ranting! I was asking for your help but you had more important things to do. And now, my mother is upstairs, giving away everything that's not nailed down! The woman has totally lost her mind."

"That's enough, Michael." Anna Leigh stood in the doorway. Her hands were on her hips and her tired eyes sparked with anger. The navy blue track suit she wore had spots of dust on the knees and belly, but she still held herself with grace. "I thought we finished this discussion this morning. If you have nothing useful to say, you're welcome to leave. I'll need you to move your vehicle so that the tow driver can get to the Suburban."

"Now, look. I'm just trying—"

"To run my life," Anna Leigh finished for him. "Which I don't need you to do. We've talked about this too many times already. I'm tired of discussing it." She smiled at her granddaughters. "Girls, would you like to join me in the kitchen? I made a fresh pitcher of tea, earlier."

Michael sputtered and shook his head. "All right."

He stopped in front of his mother. "I only want what's best for you, you know."

Her anger faded. "I know, dearest." She held out her hands, which he took. "It's quite all right. As long as you remember, I am a fully functional adult. Your father's truck is worth more as a donation than anything else. It will help the church in so many ways." She kissed his cheek and whispered into his ear. "It's going to be fine, Michael."

"Uh, yeah." He held her tightly to him for a moment. "I love you, Mom. Call me if you need anything, okay?"

"I will."

Michael murmured his apologies to both daughters before leaving. Once the front door closed, Jeannie exhaled heavily. "Thank God."

She looked at Amanda, then to Anna Leigh. "Gramma, are you sure you won't stay here with us? There's plenty of room."

Anna Leigh put her arm around Jeannie's shoulders. "I truly appreciate the offer, but no. As much as I love this house, I cannot live here without Jacob. It's too difficult."

Amanda moved to her other side. "I understand, Gramma. I couldn't stay at the ranch without Lex."

The front door opened and closed, followed by two sets of feet.

"Mommy!" Melanie called.

"In here," Amanda answered.

Melanie came into the room and hugged each woman. "Mommy, we had ice cream! Guess what I had?"

Amanda wiped at a smudge on her daughter's cheek. "Chocolate?"

"How did you know?"

Jeannie laughed at the earnest question. "Moms have secret powers, Mel."

From the doorway, Lorrie scoffed. "Yeah, right." She walked into the room. "If you'd learn to wash your face better, no one would have known."

She stared at Jeannie before turning to Amanda. "Can I talk to you?"

"Lorrie! You're being very rude." Amanda put her hand on her daughter's shoulder. "You owe everyone an apology."

Looking as if she'd argue, Lorrie took a deep breath. "Sorry." She raised her head and tried to keep her voice from cracking. There were tears in her eyes. "Please, can we go somewhere and talk?"

Amanda nodded. "Sure. Let's go upstairs." On her way out of the room, she stopped beside Melanie. "Where's Momma? Didn't she bring you?"

"Momma said she had to pick up some stuff, but would be back later," Melanie answered. "I was supposed to tell you."

"Okay, thanks, sweetie." Amanda followed Lorrie into the hallway, but stopped as two people carried a queen-sized oak headboard down the stairs. She waited until they had fully descended before speaking. "Hi, guys. I see Gramma's kept you busy today."

Kyle took a handkerchief from her back pocket and wiped her face. "All for a good cause." To Anna Leigh she said, "I heard from Ellie a few minutes ago. She'd like to come after work and help you with the sorting of the linen closets, if that's okay."

"That would be wonderful, thank you." Anna Leigh stepped around them. "I'll pour you some fresh tea. Please join us in the kitchen when you two come back."

Tony, a friend of Kyle's who had been enlisted to help, exhaled heavily. "Thank you, Mrs. Cauble. Kyle seems to forget I'm a chef, not a moving man. An iced tea sounds fantastic."

"I'm saving you a trip to the gym. Come on, muscles. Let's get this thing out to the truck." Kyle ruffled Lorrie's hair before she picked up her end of the headboard. "Good to see ya, kid."

Lorrie scowled and brushed her hand through her hair to straighten it. She started up the stairs, not bothering to answer Kyle.

"Aunt Jeannie, where's Hunter?" asked Melanie. Hunter Laurence Crews, her cousin, was eleven months old and Melanie was totally enamored with him.

"He's at the church daycare. I was afraid of bringing him today, with all the commotion." Jeannie returned Mel's hug. "Let's go see if

Gramma has anything good to drink. I think I saw some grape juice in her refrigerator."

"Yum, grape juice!"

"Good luck," Jeannie mouthed to Amanda and followed Melanie into the kitchen.

With the gait of a doomed woman, Amanda walked up the stairs. She found Lorrie in the nearest guest room, which had been completely emptied of furniture except for a queen-sized mattress and box springs.

Lorrie stood at the window and stared at the cars below. "Why are they taking Gramma's furniture?"

Amanda sat on the bed. "She's decided to give the house to Jeannie and Rodney, and buy a smaller place for herself. Since she doesn't need the extra furniture, Gramma has decided to donate it to the high school band for their rummage sale."

"But why does she want to move? I like visiting her here."

Amanda patted the spot beside her. She put her arm on Lorrie's shoulders once she sat down. "I don't think she feels she can take care of the house all by herself. And you can still visit, since your Aunt Jeannie and Uncle Rodney will be here."

"Not really," Lorrie mumbled.

"What's that, honey?"

Lorrie stood and moved away from Amanda. "They're not my aunt and uncle. You're my aunt! And Rodney's my—" Her face scrunched up as her mind worked. "Step-dad. We're studying genealogy in class this week. Do you know how hard it is to figure everything out?"

"I know it's a little more complicated than only having a mother and father, like a lot of kids in school. But we've discussed this. A lot."

"Taylor's dad was a baseball star in college. She has a lot of pictures of him playing ball. And Jessie's dad was in the Army, and she brought his uniform shirt to show." Tears formed in Lorrie's eyes. "I don't have anything from my dad! I don't know that much about him, and I don't have any memories of him. It's not fair!"

Amanda got up and stepped toward her. "I know it's not, honey. Believe me, if we could change things, we would." Just seeing Lorrie's tears caused Amanda's eyes to well up. "Your father was a wonderful man that we all loved very much. We've shown you pictures and told you about him."

"But I don't know him, M—" Lorrie stopped. "I don't know if he had a deep voice or an accent, or what his favorite color was. Or if he liked the things that I like." Her hands clenched and she slammed her fists on her thighs. "This sucks!"

"Sweetie, it's all right." Amanda tried to embrace Lorrie, only to be pushed away. "I'm sure Jeannie has some things that you could show at school. We could ask her."

Lorrie swung her arms and kicked at the air, totally out of control. "Why don't I have a dad? Damn it!"

Having stood outside listening as long as she could, Lex hurried in and wrapped her arms around Lorrie. "Calm down, sweetheart."

"No! I won't!" Lorrie struggled to break free. She continued to kick, some of her shots landing against Lex's legs. She was openly crying, her words coming between huge sobs. "You...can't...make...me."

Lex refused to let go, holding on tighter. "It's going to be okay."

"Noooo!" Lorrie collapsed to the floor, bringing Lex down with her. Amanda dropped beside them and held on as well. "Every...thing is...chang...ging," Lorrie sobbed. "P...pl...please," she begged. "M...make it stop."

Amanda looked over Lorrie's head, to see a similar sadness in her wife's eyes. "We'll get through this together. I promise you." Her words were directed toward their daughter, but her eyes never left Lex's.

After Lorrie stopped crying, she wiped her eyes with the handkerchief Lex handed her. She looked into the sad eyes of the woman whom she had adored forever. "I'm sorry about what I said at the ice cream place."

"I know, sweetheart." Lex touched her cheek. "Did someone give you a hard time at school? About your family?"

Lorrie nodded.

Amanda rubbed her back. "Who was it? I'd like to have a talk with them."

"Just some of the kids. Mrs. Moore took care of it."

Lorrie sat cross-legged between them and rested her chin on her upraised hand. "I want to know more about my dad." She lowered her voice. "And my real mom."

At the pained look on Lex's face, Amanda touched her wife's back. "Honey, you're always welcome to learn about the rest of your family."

"I am?"

"Of—" Lex had to clear her throat. "Of course." She pasted a grin on her face. "We've got a very unusual family, but a good one."

Lorrie looked up. "But, you're not related to me, right? Not really my mom." She seemed very sad about the prospect.

"Excuse me for saying this," Amanda growled, "but that's bullshit."

Lex was startled by the venom in her wife's voice. "Amanda."

Amanda put her hand under Lorrie's chin and forced the girl to look into her eyes. "To begin with, when we adopted you, we both signed enough paperwork and legal forms to fill this room. That means that as far as the law is concerned we *are* your parents. Period."

She gentled her tone. "And we're your parents by choice, Lorraine Marie Walters. And we're not going anywhere."

Shaking her head, Lorrie said, "You can't promise that. Things happen and people die."

Lex finally found her voice. "That's true. But while we're here, we'll always love you." She put an arm around Lorrie and hugged her close. "And that's a promise we *can* keep."

Chapter Eighteen

THE CHILDREN HAD been in bed for hours, yet Lex couldn't bring herself to go back upstairs. She had tossed and turned, unable to sleep. Although they had resolved Lorrie's issues before bedtime, Lex couldn't get the scene from the ice cream shop out of her head. She sat at her desk, and stared at the card game on the computer screen. Lorrie's angry words kept echoing through her mind.

"You're not my real mother!"

Disgusted by the path her thoughts continued to take, she closed the program and stared at the picture on the desktop. It was one of her favorites. Amanda was on a hay bale in front of the corral, holding Eddie. Standing on the fence behind her were Lorrie and Melanie. All smiled big for the camera. The portrait had been a birthday present from her family, and Lex treasured it. But Lorrie's words continued to haunt her.

"You're not my real mother!"

"Damn it!" Lex shut down the computer. Her eyes burned and her heart ached. She rubbed her face as if to wipe the words from her mind.

Light footsteps alerted her and she looked up to see her wife standing at the door.

"It's late."

"Yeah, I know." Lex stood and moved around the desk. "Did I do something to wake you?"

Amanda held out her hand. "I missed you when I rolled over."

"Sorry. I couldn't sleep." Lex took her hand and kissed it. "I was trying to keep from disturbing you."

"Honey," Amanda led her into the living room. "Don't you know by now that when you're upset, it disturbs me?"

She tugged Lex toward the couch and pushed her to sit. She settled beside her and rested her head against Lex's shoulder as their hands stayed linked.

"Lorrie's going to be fine. And I'm going to have a talk with her teacher tomorrow at lunch." Amanda looked into Lex's face. "When are you going to tell me what she said today? All I know is that you were so upset you dropped the girls off, instead of coming into Gramma's."

Lex put her arm around her and kissed the top of Amanda's head. "It's not important now. Lorrie's all settled, that's what matters."

Amanda tugged on Lex's hair. "No, what matters is you." She shifted until they were nose to nose. "And, as much as I love our daughter, she said something that upset you."

Her hand touched Lex's clenched jaw. "Please."

In a soft, pained voice, Lex told Amanda what happened at the ice cream shop. When she was finished, she released a heavy breath. "Poor kid. She was so freaked out."

"Poor kid? My God, Lex. I would have been tempted to smack her for yelling like that."

"Yeah. But we've never raised a hand to one of our kids, and I wasn't about to start in a damned ice cream parlor." Lex rubbed her face. "Good God, I'm beat. Let's go to bed."

She got up and pulled Amanda up with her, embracing her. "Thanks for coming downstairs, sweetheart. I'd have probably brooded in the office all night."

Amanda patted her on the stomach as they left the living room. "Like I would have let you."

SATURDAY MORNING, ONCE everyone was fed breakfast, Amanda took Lorrie into town. They were going to meet Jeannie at Anna Leigh's, since that's where most of Jeannie's things from her first marriage were stored.

Lorrie was silent until they reached the city limits. "Momma hates me."

Amanda fought the urge to slam on the brakes. Instead, she pulled into the nearest parking lot. She took a moment to get her emotions under control before she shifted in her seat to give Lorrie her full attention. "You know that's not true."

"She's not here, is she?" Lorrie crossed her arms and stared through the windshield. "At least she's related to Eddie. He's probably her favorite."

Although she wanted to grab Lorrie by the shoulders and shake some sense into her, Amanda kept her hands on the steering wheel. "Do you think she loves me?"

Lorrie's head snapped around. "Of course. She says it all the time."

"And what did she say to you this morning, before we left the house?"

Caught in the trap, Lorrie lowered her face and stared at her knees. She mumbled something unintelligible.

"What was that?"

"She said to have a good time, and that she loved me."

Amanda took one of her daughter's hands. "Have you ever heard her say something she didn't mean?"

Lorrie shook her head, but refused to look at her.

"I learned a long time ago that whenever I asked your Momma a question, I'd get an honest answer. Even if it wasn't the answer I wanted."

Amanda leaned closer and softened her voice. "If you want to watch her panic, take her clothes shopping and ask her opinion on a hideous outfit. She'll stumble all over herself trying not to hurt your feelings."

Unable to help it, Lorrie laughed. She soon sobered when she considered the conversation. "Why didn't she come with us, then?"

Why, indeed? Amanda remembered asking Lex that very question before they headed downstairs for the day. Her wife, who had a thoughtful streak that not many knew about, had a very good reason. Lex told her that while she would love to be there for support, she believed that it would be extremely hard for Jeannie, and wanted to give them the time and space needed. "She knew it's going to be difficult for your Aunt Jeannie, and thought that the less people that were there, the better."

"Oh." Lorrie turned her head when she heard the pain in her mother's voice. "It's going to be hard for you too, isn't it?"

Amanda didn't bother to hide the tears in her eyes. "In a way, yes. Your father was my best friend and I loved him."

"You did? How come you didn't get married, then?"

When Amanda laughed, Lorrie blushed.

"Oh. 'Cause you're gay, right?"

"Right. And because, the minute I introduced him to Jeannie, he was hopelessly in love with her. Why, I don't know," Amanda joked.

She squeezed Lorrie's hand. "Are we good?"

Lorrie nodded. "Yep. We don't have to do this, if it's going to make you and Aunt Jeannie cry. You've always been good about answering my questions about my dad. I guess with all that stuff we're learning at school, it made me want to know more."

"We'll be okay, sweetie. But thank you. We should have done this years ago. Just wait until you see the wedding pictures. Momma laughed for days after seeing my hair back then."

REBECCA CAME OUT of the barn with her saddle, blanket and bridle and almost dropped them all when she saw two new horses on the other side of the corral. She slowed her pace toward the corral, where Patches, Duchess and Morgan watched her with interest.

"Who're your new friends?"

She placed the saddle and blanket on a lower rung of the corral before climbing inside. Shelby hadn't told her of any new boarders at lunchtime.

"Hey, guys." She kept the bridle draped on one shoulder. "Where did y'all come from? Hmm?"

The nearest horse snorted at her and looked at her with distrust. Its reddish-brown coat was tangled with dirt and twigs, and its matching tail and mane were matted with burrs. Its ribs showed through the scruffy winter coat and it stomped one foot when Rebecca got too close.

"Easy," she whispered. She peeked beneath the animal and could see that the mare had recently nursed. "Where's your baby?"

She kept her distance as she studied the other horse. Its muddy coat may have once been white, but for now it was in as bad of shape as its companion. Also a mare, it trotted a wide circle behind the other.

Rebecca moved closer. She knew she was safe as long as she was not on their side of the fence. Patches followed behind while her other two horses stood near the water trough and watched. Before she could get much closer, she heard Shelby on the front porch.

"Rebecca, don't even think about it!" Shelby jogged down the steps. The closer she got to the corral and fence, the slower she moved. "Where did they come from?"

"I thought you could tell me. They look half-starved, Shelby."

Shelby joined her in the corral. "Yeah. I don't recognize the brand on them, either." The marks on their hips were partially obscured by their coats, but a general outline could still be seen. It appeared to be a capital letter T, resting on its side, enclosed in a circle. "Circle Lazy T, I think. I wonder if Lex has ever seen it?"

"Do you think she'd recognize the horses? I mean, she knows just about everyone around Somerville, doesn't she?"

"Maybe." Shelby held out her hand for Rebecca. "Let's go back to the house and give her a call."

Rebecca put her bridle in the outstretched hand and laughed at the look she received. "Shouldn't we feed them, or something? They look pitiful."

"Maybe a little, until we can have a vet check 'em out. I'd hate to make one of them sick, or worse."

LEX FASTENED EDDIE'S diaper and slid his tiny jeans up his legs. "Okay, buddy. Let's see if we can keep you clean at least until dinner time."

"Momma, no." Eddie kicked as Lex put socks and shoes on his feet. "No!"

"Yes," Lex argued lightly. She swung him off the table and set him feet first on the floor. "Maybe you'll think twice before smearing grape jam in your hair."

Eddie stomped and giggled. "Ha." He grabbed her jeans at the knee and tugged. "Up."

"I just put you down." Lex walked carefully to the bathroom and washed her hands. "We need to start working on potty training with you."

When he heard the word potty, Eddie went to the toilet and tried to open the lid. The safety latch foiled his attempt and he slapped at it and screeched. "No!"

Lex dried her hands and laughed. "I think you're gonna have to start a little smaller, kiddo." She tapped him lightly on the head. "Do you want to go see what Melanie is up to?"

"Meemee?" Eddie turned and giggled. "Go!"

"That's what I thought." Lex held out her hand for him. When his little fist tightened around her index finger, a lump settled in her throat. It didn't matter which child she was with, the pure trust they gave her swelled her heart with pride. She never thought she'd feel this, the love of a child or the warmth of a loving home. But now that she had it, she'd fight to the death to keep it.

They walked down the hall and stopped by Melanie's partially open door. Eddie started to push inside, but Lex stopped him.

"Hold your horses. Gotta knock knock first." Lex made a fist and tapped the door frame.

Eddie laughed and mimicked her, beating on the wall. "Meemee!"

"Come in," Melanie sang.

Eddie looked up at Lex.

"Well, go on."

"Naw naw." Eddie shoved the door open. "Meemee, naw naw."

Melanie looked up from the doll house she was playing with on the floor. "Good boy, Eddie. You knock knocked." She held out a male doll. "Wanna play with me?"

"Pway." Eddie took the doll and sat beside his sister.

Lex's cell phone buzzed from her hip. She leaned against the door and watched the kids play.

"Walters. Oh, hey, Shelby." She frowned as Shelby told her about the two horses that showed up at their place. "Lazy Circle T? No, there's not anything even close to that around here. What? Uh, yeah, I guess I could. Y'all mind if I bring Mel and Eddie?" Lex laughed. "Great. I'll see you in a bit."

She clipped her phone onto her belt. "Hey, kids. Want to go see Ms. Shelby and Ms. Rebecca?"

JEANNIE TURNED THE page of the photo album and laughed. "Oh, my God. I'd totally forgotten about this." She tapped the picture lightly. "Amanda?"

"Oh." From Jeannie's left, Amanda giggled and shook her head. "Lorrie, this is your Dad and your Momma attempting to hang Christmas lights on Gramma's house."

Lorrie, who sat to the right of Jeannie, leaned closer to the album. "Why is she holding his legs like that?"

"Because they thought it would be easier to hang the lights from above, instead of having to move the ladder. They took turns reaching over the edge of the house while the other held their legs to keep them from falling off the roof."

"That's dumb."

Amanda snorted. "Funny, that's the same thing Grandpa told them, right before your Momma sneezed and let go of your Dad."

Lorrie's eyes went wide. "Did he fall?"

"Not exactly," Amanda explained. "When he started to slide down toward the edge, Momma fell forward to catch his feet, stumbled and dove off the roof."

"No way!"

Jeannie ran her finger across the photo. "Luckily, she fell into the very tall hedges by the living room windows."

Lorrie cocked her head and squinted at Jeannie. "There aren't any hedges there."

"Not anymore," Amanda added with a giggle. "Although she was very happy that Momma didn't hurt herself, Gramma was ready to kill both of them for ruining her hedges."

She tapped the page. "We should have taken pictures of them having to dig out all the plants. It took them two weekends to get it done."

"Wow. Momma's never said anything about falling off a house."

"Probably because it wasn't the first time," Amanda muttered.

Jeannie stopped giggling and turned to her. "It wasn't?"

"Unfortunately, no." Amanda realized they were waiting for more. "Um, maybe I shouldn't be telling—"

"Oh, no. You can't leave us hanging like that. Right, Lorrie?"

Lorrie giggled. "Right."

"Okay, but don't you dare tell Momma I said anything." Amanda pointed to her sister. "Promise?"

Jeannie put her finger and thumb to her lips and pantomimed locking them.

Amanda swatted her. "Smartass." She took a deep breath and let it out slowly. "Let's see. The first time—"

"First time?" Jeannie came close to dropping the album. "There was more than once?"

"First, second," Amanda shook her head. "Martha told me that she fell out of the top of the hay barn when she was twenty."

Lorrie gasped. "That's a long ways down."

"It is. And it would have been worse had she not landed on the trailer of hay. But her boot got caught and she broke her ankle."

"Ow. Poor Momma. Mine hurt bad enough when I jammed it into second base that time."

Jeannie patted her leg. "You're a lot like your father, in that way. Frank would have sprains and bruises from playing football, but he healed pretty quickly. I, on the other hand, have to spend a week in bed for a cold."

"That's okay, Aunt Jeannie. I don't like being sick, either." She leaned into the hug she received. After her talk with her mom, she was more secure in her familial relationships. "Mom, what else has Momma done?"

Amanda threw her head back and laughed again. "We don't have that much time, sweetie. Let's just say she's always been an accident looking for a place to happen, and leave it at that, okay? Jeannie, let's go to the next page. Don't you have pictures of Frank playing football?"

"Pictures? I have video." Jeannie closed the photo album. "Come on, ladies. There's another box in storage that's full of scrapbooks and DVD's converted from video tapes, and Gramma has a DVD player in the den."

Lorrie stood. "How come Gramma's not here?"

Jeannie got up and put her hand on Lorrie's shoulder. "She's at the home improvement store with Lois, looking at wall paper swatches and paint samples. We might not see them until dark."

"Oh, cool." In a move reminiscent of Lex, Lorrie held out her hand for Amanda and tugged her off the sofa.

Amanda saw the recognition in her sister's eyes. Jeannie may have given birth to Lorrie but the girl had become a carbon copy of Lex.

"Thanks, sweetie," she said.

LEX DROVE HER truck around the small frame house toward the barn. She cringed at Eddie's excited yelp from the back seat.

"Hossies! Momma, hossies!"

"Ooh, Momma, what's Ms. Rebecca doing?" Melanie asked as she pressed her nose against her window.

A large practice arena was fenced separately from the corral and open grazing field. Three barrels were set out in a triangular pattern, and Rebecca zipped around them on her paint pony, Patches. Horse and rider moved in tandem as they gracefully took the final turn and raced for the finish.

Lex stopped the truck and turned off the engine, but waited until Rebecca had pulled Patches to a stop before she stepped out and unfastened Eddie from his car seat. She kept him in her arms as Melanie jumped from her side of the truck and hurried around to catch up.

"Momma, what was she doing? That was so cool." Melanie stayed close to Lex as she had been taught. "Can I go see Ms. Rebecca? I wanna ask her why she was riding so fast. Momma, how come you don't ride that fast? Why was they going in little circles?"

Shelby had turned away from the arena and walked to meet them halfway. She laughed as she overheard the questions. "Hey, squirt! I'm glad you talked your momma into bringing you."

"Ms. Shelby! Did you see how fast they was going?" Melanie giggled as she was scooped up and swung around by Shelby. "Wheeee!"

Eddie didn't want to be left out of the fun. He outstretched his arms toward Shelby and grunted. "Me!"

Lex was barely able to hold onto him. "Settle down, Eddie."

She waited until Shelby returned Melanie to the ground. "I think my kids like you more than they do me."

Shelby grinned at her. "Can't blame 'em much. I'm such a ray of sunshine, ain't I?" She shook Lex's hand then held it out to Eddie.

"Well, c'mon, range rat. I ain't got all day."

Eddie squealed and dove toward her. He laughed as she swung him around in the same manner as Melanie. "Ha!"

"Hang on, young'un," Shelby told him, as she raised Eddie to her shoulders. "How's that?"

"Go, go!" Eddie ordered. His feet kicked her chest as his hands gripped Shelby's shirt collar. He bounced and kicked as they headed for the corral. "Ha!"

Melanie skipped beside Shelby and hung onto one of her belt loops. "Ms. Rebecca was going so fast. Was she scared?"

"You'll have to ask her yourself." Shelby's grin softened as Rebecca left Patches by the barn and walked toward them. "Hey, darlin'. I think you have a new fan."

"I do?" Rebecca winked at Melanie. "Did you like it, Melanie?"

Melanie moved away from Shelby to take Rebecca's hand. "It was so cool. You was going so fast and I was afraid you'd fall off, but you didn't and you kept riding, and then you went whoosh around that thing, and—"

Lex stopped her by a light touch to her head. "Slow down, kiddo. Take a breath." She nodded and tipped her hat to Rebecca. "That was quite a ride."

"Thanks, Lex. Where's Amanda and Lorrie?"

"They had some business in town." They followed behind Shelby, who led the way to the other side of the corral. "Picked up a couple of strays, I hear."

Rebecca swung hands with Melanie. "I'm sorry we dragged you out here on a Saturday. I'm sure you had better things to do. But we have no idea where they could have come from, and was hoping you could tell us."

"I'll try. And you didn't hurt a thing, calling. It's nice to get the kids out."

"You don't have to have a reason to bring them over. We love having them." Rebecca let go of Melanie, who quickened her pace to rejoin Shelby. "As much as she pretends differently, Shelby really enjoys being around the kids."

Lex nodded. "They do grow on a person, that's for sure." She stopped so that they were out of earshot of the others. "Y'all thinking about having one or two of your own?"

"Oh, my God, no," Rebecca hurriedly answered. "I mean, we love your kids, but I don't think either one of us are the parenting type. I'm very happy being just the two of us, and I know Shelby is, too. Maybe a dog someday, but that's about as close to a little one as we want."

"Yeah, that's just about exactly what Shelby has said about it. I'm glad y'all are on the same page about it, though. She seems really happy with the way things are."

REBECCA WATCHED AS her lover interacted with the children. Shelby had confided that she loved feeling like an aunt to the Walters' kids, but it didn't make her want any of her own. She was perfectly content to spend her life with just Rebecca as her family, although the circle had grown to include Lex, Amanda and their offspring.

"Shelby's very happy, and so am I. But you've always got free babysitting, anytime you need it."

"I'll surely keep that in mind, thanks."

Lex looked ahead to the horses that were nosing their way through some hay that had been given to them. "Damn, they look bad." She softened her voice as they moved closer. "That mare has a little one somewhere."

Shelby stood beside her, holding onto Eddie's legs. "That's what I thought, too. She's filled up since this morning."

Lex nodded. She took her cell phone from the holster on her belt. "Hi, Helen. Could you have Roy send a couple of guys to Shelby's? Yeah. Have them bring my horse and their own, please? Thanks. We've got a stray to find."

She put the phone back and winked at Rebecca. "Speaking of free babysitting, do you think I could talk you into watching my kids? Eddie's not real good on horseback just yet."

AS IT TURNED out, Helen drove the truck while Roy and Jack rode along. Chet stayed behind to keep an eye on things at the Rocking W.

Once the big rig stopped, Lex and Shelby unloaded the two horses, Mac and Coco. Roy limped to the back of the trailer. "Sure wish I could go with you."

"You'll be back in the saddle in no time," Lex assured him, as she checked Mac's cinch. "I'm glad you're here, though. Maybe you could make some calls and see where our strays may have come from."

"I'll be glad to. Bice's property backs up to this one, doesn't it?"

Helen joined them as Jack silently adjusted the saddle on Coco. "I'll head on to the house and relieve Rebecca, so she can join you." She kissed her husband's cheek. "Don't be too long."

Lex continued to check her gear. "I called him before y'all got here. He said his fence is secure, and he isn't missing any horses."

"All right. I reckon I can check with the feed store and see if they've heard of any missing animals. Then I'll contact the sheriff." Roy shifted his weight off the walking cast and leaned against the trailer. "Did you try the vet's office? Maybe Ron knows the brand, if he's not still in his honeymoon phase."

"Nope. Didn't think about it. I'd forgotten he was back, since we haven't heard from them yet." Lex ran her hands down Mac's legs and checked his shoes.

Shelby brought Patches and Duchess close when she saw Rebecca jog from the house. "We've only got about ten acres, so it shouldn't take too long to search. And I'm ashamed to admit I haven't checked our fence for a while. Didn't see much need, since we keep ours close to the house this time of year."

"Not like you've had much time, since you started working with us," Roy told her. "But things are settled down a bit, so you'll have more time for your own place."

She handed Rebecca the reins to Patches. "We're not complainin', are we, darlin'?"

Rebecca settled into the saddle and patted her horse's shoulder. "Not at all. Thank you all for coming out to help."

"It's a nice day for a ride." Lex nodded to Roy. "We'll keep in touch through our phones."

"Right." He started toward the house as the four riders left. When he reached the back steps, he stopped.

Melanie held the door open for him. "Ms. Rebecca is gonna show me how to race barrels when they come back."

"Really? That sounds like a lot of fun." Roy ruffled her hair as he passed her. He removed his western hat and hung it on the coat tree beside the door. "What do you think, Helen? Reckon Mel has a chance of being a barrel racer?"

Helen bounced Eddie on her knee, where he sat gnawing on a toddler cookie. "If she works hard at it, I'm sure Melanie can do whatever she puts her mind to."

"That's what Mada always tells us."

Melanie sat next to Helen at the table. "I use ta think horses were stinky, but they're fun, too." She dunked her graham cracker into a coffee mug of milk. "Ms. Rebecca said she's taught girls my age to race and they even get to win ribbons and trophies."

Roy sat beside her and propped his injured leg on an empty chair. "There's a lot of work involved before you can do that, though. We'd have to find you a barrel horse, since your little pony isn't trained."

Melanie shrugged her shoulders. "I guess, but Ms. Rebecca said I could start with Patches. She's a big horse, though."

"Hossie!" Eddie grinned at Helen and waved the soggy cookie. "Mmm." He aimed it for her mouth, but she gracefully moved it away.

"Thank you, sweetie. But you eat it." Helen glared at her husband, who couldn't hold in his laughter. "Watch it."

He held up his hands in defense. "Sorry." But he didn't sound contrite in the least.

Eddie laughed and swung his gooey hands. "Ha! Yum." He looked at his sister. "Yum!"

Melanie rolled her eyes. "Boys are so gross."

ANNA LEIGH STEPPED into her living room and saw her coffee

table covered with scrapbooks and photo albums. She smiled at the trio on the sofa. "My goodness, girls. You've certainly been busy."

"Hi, Gramma. Lorrie wanted to learn more about Frank, and all of this was in your storage shed. We've already watched his football highlights," Jeannie said.

Lorrie hopped off the couch and crossed the room to hug Anna Leigh. "We were just about to look at the wedding album, Gramma. Would you like to see it, too?"

"Thank you, dearest, but no. Lois is waiting in the car for me. I only dropped by to get a fabric sample from my bedroom." She kissed Lorrie's forehead. "I should be home in another hour or so."

Amanda noticed the room for the first time. "We'll be sure and have it all cleaned up, Gramma. I'm sorry about the mess."

Anna Leigh waved off the apology. "Please. Enjoy yourselves." A faraway look settled onto her face. "This old house has been far too quiet and still. It's nice to have you here."

"Maybe we should—" Jeannie stopped when Amanda poked her in the leg. "What?"

"What?" Amanda asked.

Their antics took away Anna Leigh's sad face. "You girls," she laughed. "Lorrie, would you make sure they don't fight?"

"We don't—"

"We wouldn't—" Amanda cut her sister off. "We'll behave, I promise. Right, Jeannie?"

Jeannie grinned at her. "Speak for yourself." A well-placed pinch stopped her. "Ow!"

"And with that, I will be on my way. Lorrie, don't let them get you into any trouble."

"Yes, ma'am." Lorrie said as Anna Leigh went upstairs.

Amanda laughed as her sister glared at her. "Teach you to pop off like that, brat."

"Turd." Jeannie patted the empty cushion beside her. "Come on, Lorrie. Let me show you how silly your mom looked at my wedding."

"It wasn't that bad."

Lorrie plopped down next to Jeannie. Her eyes tracked to the cover of the album, which Jeannie absentmindedly caressed. If things had been different, the woman who she knew as an aunt would be her mother. For a moment, she tried to imagine the changes in her life. A life in California would be without horses, and she would go to school far away from Somerville. She wouldn't know any of her friends, have her dog, Freckles, Eddie or even her annoying sister. As much as she complained about Melanie, she loved her. No, as sad as it was, she knew this was where she was meant to be. She was brought out of her thoughts as Jeannie opened to the first page. "You looked pretty, Aunt Jeannie."

The eight-by-ten photo was of the bride and groom, looking at one another lovingly. Frank Rivers was tall and handsome in his dark gray tuxedo and he had his hands on his bride's hips while her arms were loosely clasped around his neck.

"Thanks, sweetie."

Amanda put her arm around her sister and leaned her head on her shoulder. "Are you okay?" she asked in a whisper.

Jeannie nodded and turned the page. The next pictures were of the wedding party that included her maid-of-honor, Amanda, who sported a particularly atrocious hairstyle.

"Oh, wow. Mom, what's wrong with your hair?" Lorrie asked, between giggles.

"It's not that bad." Amanda sighed as her sister's laughter joined Lorrie's, then looked closely at the photo in question. She wore a deep purple, knee-length dress with short, puffed sleeves. Her hair was bleached almost white, permed in tight ringlets that somehow rose four inches on top of her head while also cascading along her shoulders. "Okay, so it was hideous," she agreed at last.

Lorrie rolled off the sofa and onto the floor, holding her stomach as she continued to laugh. "You looked like a cartoon cat that got scared!"

"Hey." Amanda tried to be stern before she too broke into laughter. "Behave, Lorrie. Or you'll get the same hairdo."

"That's a vicious threat," Jeannie scolded as she wiped her eyes. "Don't worry, Lorrie. I'll protect you from your mom."

After she said it, she realized that it was true. She hadn't thought of Lorrie as her daughter in quite some time. The girl's uncanny resemblance to Lex had helped, especially as Lorrie had gotten older.

Lorrie got up and returned to her spot on the couch. "Thanks, Aunt Jeannie. But I don't think she'd really be that mean to me."

She giggled at the mock glare she received from Amanda. "Hopefully."

Chapter Nineteen

SHELBY AND JACK rode in one direction as Rebecca rode with Lex the opposite way. Although they spent time together often, Rebecca was still a little uncomfortable around the taciturn woman. She struggled to find something to talk about, but everything she thought of seemed ridiculous to her. The only sounds were the singing of a nearby blue jay and the steady clomp of their horse's hooves along the dirt path.

"Nice little spread y'all have here."

"Um, thanks. It's nothing like yours, but it's plenty big for us."

Lex turned to look at her. "Are you all right?"

Rebecca nodded, but played with the reins in her hand. "Honestly, you scare the hell out of me."

"I do? Why? Have I done something to you?"

"Okay, maybe scared isn't the right word," Rebecca said. "I mean, I know that Amanda thinks the sun rises and sets with you, so you can't be all that bad."

Lex snorted when she tried to hold back her laughter.

"But, geez. When I was trying to figure out why boys weren't as interesting as girls, you were running that huge ranch all by yourself. Even now, you seem to have it all together while I just muddle along. I can't even hold down a decent job."

"Whoa." Lex pulled Mac to a stop. "I only run the ranch because I didn't have a choice. Hell, if it had been up to me, I wouldn't even be here." She took off her hat and wiped her forehead against her shoulder. "And that would have been the worst thing in the world for me, because I would have never met Amanda."

Rebecca raised her head and met Lex's gaze. "She means a lot to you, doesn't she?"

"She means everything to me." Lex brushed the dust from her hat. "Don't sell yourself short. We all do what we need to do and there isn't any shame in that."

She grinned and put the hat back on her head. "Besides, anyone who could live with Shelby, day in and day out, is pretty damned special."

Lex's cell rang and she took it off her belt. "Walters. What? All right. We'll try to send it toward the house." She put her phone back. "That was Shelby. Jack tried to lasso the filly, but lost his grip on his rope. We need to head west to either cut it off, or guide it back to its momma."

"All right." Rebecca adjusted her boots in the stirrups. "Thanks, Lex. I'm sorry about all of that. I'm not real sure where it came from."

Lex shrugged. "We all have doubts, just don't let 'em eat you up inside." She set Mac out in a trot. "Not like Amanda would let me."

"DAMN IT, JACK. That was a stupid-assed thing to do," Shelby snapped, as they followed the terrified filly. Its coppery-red coat shone in the sunlight as it galloped away.

"You said you wanted to catch it. I never miss with my rope."

She pointed to a group of trees ahead. "Maybe next time you'll have the end tied off, instead of thinking you could hold on. Circle up there so it'll keep going toward the house. We don't want it hung up in that cedar."

He slapped Coco's hip with his gloved hand. "Heeyah!"

Shelby saw two riders ahead and raised her hand. She received acknowledging waves and then her cell rang. "Yeah. Jack's going around to keep her out of the cedar, maybe y'all could run up ahead."

Lex waved her hat in the air before she took off at an angle.

Shelby kept her horse behind the sorrel filly. She spotted the rope trailing behind and urged her horse into a canter. As she came closer, she put all her weight on her left leg while lifting her right one across the saddle. When her horse was close to the rope, Shelby jumped to the ground and grabbed the end. She stumbled to her feet and pulled the rope taut.

The filly panicked as the rope tightened around her neck, and took off at a run.

"Fuck!" Shelby tried to keep up but soon fell and the filly easily dragged her. She grimaced as clumps of grass and rocks assailed her body.

Rebecca looked on in horror. "Shelby! Let go of the rope!" She kicked Patches into a gallop.

Instead of releasing the rope, Shelby wrapped it around her wrist. As she slid behind the filly, she twisted her body so that she was moving feet first, doing whatever she could to slow the animal's pace. "Whoa!"

"Shelby, damn it! Let go!" Rebecca rode close to her lover. "Shelby!"

Shelby spit out mouthfuls of dirt, but refused to release her grip. She gritted her teeth and, with renewed energy, dug her boot heels into the ground. "Goddamn it, horse. Whoa!"

Twenty yards ahead, Lex and Jack held their horses in the filly's path, blocking the entrance to the thick stand of cedar.

The filly started to slow at the sight. The heavy weight that pulled on her finally brought her to a halt.

Rebecca brought Patches up beside Shelby and dropped from the saddle before the dust cleared. "Shelby?"

Shelby spit then shakily held out her arm. "Take the rope."

"To hell with the damned rope, Shelby. You could have been killed!"

"Rope."

Rebecca gently unwrapped the rope from her lover's arm. She tied it to her saddle horn just as Lex rode up. The filly continued to struggle, but Patches held firm.

"Is she all right?" Lex asked.

"I think so." Rebecca returned to Shelby, who was still on the ground. "Have you totally lost your damned mind?"

Shelby spit again and wiped her mouth on her shirtsleeve. "Nope." She rested her arms on her upraised knees. "Strong little thing, ain't she?"

Lex looked down at her and shook her head. "You're insane. Why did you feel the need to hang on to that damned rope?"

"I was afraid she'd get hung up on something and hurt herself."

Rebecca slapped her shoulder. "So, instead, you try to get yourself killed? That's the stupidest damned thing I've ever heard of!"

She stomped away, muttering under her breath.

Jack joined them. "Nice catch," he told Shelby. Then he turned to Lex. "It was my fault, Boss. I thought I could rope her and bring her in easy. The filly had other ideas."

"Yeah. Do you think you can get her back to the corral without any problems?"

He nodded and stretched from his horse to untie the rope from Rebecca's saddle horn. "I'll take care of it. Sorry about that, Shelby."

"No harm done." Shelby slowly climbed to her feet. She brushed the dirt from her jeans and nodded toward her lover. "Looks like I've got some fence patchin' to do."

Lex leaned on her saddle horn. "Better you than me. If you're all right, I'll follow Jack and help get the new horses settled in the corral."

"Sure. Just put ours in the barn, if you don't mind. I'll be up shortly."

"Take your time. I think you scared a few years off Rebecca." Lex saluted her and turned Mac to follow Jack and the filly.

Shelby trailed Rebecca, who seemed intent on walking the entire length of field where she had been dragged. "Rebecca?" When her lover continued on as if she didn't hear her, Shelby picked up her pace. "Hey."

Rebecca stopped and picked up Shelby's hat. She shook it to get the worst of the dirt from it.

When Rebecca turned around and held out the hat, Shelby saw the tears that coursed down her cheeks.

"Aw, darlin'." Shelby took the hat and tossed it to the ground. "Come here."

She pulled Rebecca close and held her. "I'm sorry. But I figured she wasn't strong enough to do any serious damage to me, and I didn't want her getting hung up and hurt herself."

"It was still a stupid thing to do." Rebecca rested her cheek against

Shelby's shoulder.

"I know. But if I thought I had been in any real danger, I would have let go of the rope." Shelby chuckled. "Good thing there wasn't any cactus around, huh? I'd look like a porcupine."

Rebecca giggled and slapped her on the chest. "You're impossible."

"And you chose to put up with me. What does that say about you?"

Rebecca looked up into her face. "That I'm very lucky to have you," she answered softly. She drew Shelby's face down and kissed her, then pulled away and swatted her. "Don't scare me like that again, Shelby Fisher."

"Yes, ma'am." Shelby kissed her again.

AS SHE WAITED for Shelby and Rebecca to return, Lex climbed through the corral slats to give the mares a closer look. She took slow, cautious steps to keep from spooking them. It hadn't been very hard to get them into the corral, as they found the bucket of feed she lured them with quite fascinating. Now that they had eaten, the two mares eyed her warily as the filly stayed close to its mother's side.

Jack leaned against the side of the four-horse trailer. "You need any help, Boss?" His voice was just loud enough for her to hear. He worked a length of rope in his hand as he watched.

Lex shook her head. She stepped toward the gray mare and cautiously extended her hand toward its head. "Easy, girl." She grinned as she began to scratch beneath the mare's jaw. "Like that, do you?"

The chestnut on the other side snorted and slung her head to the side, but didn't move away from her foal. She also kept a very watchful eye on the human who gave her companion attention.

"Yeah, you're nervous, aren't you?" Lex ran her hand along the neck of the gray, grimacing at the tangles in its mane. As she scratched with one hand, she used the other to stroke the ragged coat. "I think we'd better get you into town and have Ron check you out. Some of these sores look infected."

A sideways glance at the chestnut verified that it was in as bad of shape, including a particularly nasty looking spot below its left front knee. The wound was swollen and crusted with blood and puss.

Jack brought her the three halters he had fashioned out of rope. "I figured we'd be making a trip to the vet today." He held one halter out to Lex.

"Good idea, thanks." She had no trouble placing the halter on the gray. Lex accepted another halter and moved closer to the chestnut. The animal snorted, bobbed its head and backed away, the foal following her. "Come on, this won't hurt."

Lex stopped trying to catch the animal and turned when she heard new voices.

Shelby and Rebecca arrived on the back of Patches. Shelby swung down from behind her partner. "Thanks for the lift, darlin'."

"Let's not make a habit of it, though. I'm going to put Patches away if you don't need me."

"Sure." Shelby patted the paint's shoulder. "'preciate the ride, Patches."

Lex stepped out of the corral and joined Shelby. "I was wondering if you had to walk back. Your horse beat us to the barn."

"Figures. And I didn't want to strain Patches." When Lex laughed at her, Shelby gave her a dirty look. "Shut up."

"Heh." Lex cleared her throat. "If it's all right with you, I think we ought to take the horses to the vet."

Shelby put her hands on her hips. "Why are you askin' me?"

"Well, they're on your property. Your place, your rules."

"Oh. Uh, sure. I was thinkin' of doin' that anyhow. Be okay to use your trailer?"

Lex nodded. "We could ask Roy and Helen to take the kids home in my truck. Then you and I could haul the strays into town, and I could pick up my horses when I drop you off."

"Yeah. No problem." Shelby turned to Jack, who had stood quietly by Lex. "Would you mind runnin' up to the house so Roy will know what we're gonna do?"

"Sure." He turned and ambled away.

Shelby took off her hat and wiped her forehead against her shoulder. "Heck of a way to spend a day off, ain't it?"

"What's a day off?"

Rebecca came from the barn. "What's the plan?" She stood beside her lover.

Shelby gestured to the horses. "We're gonna load up the strays and take 'em into town. Shouldn't take too long."

"I can handle taking them to town, Shelby. No sense in ruining your weekend," Lex said.

Shelby turned to Rebecca, who gave a slight nod. "Nah. They were on our property, so the least I can do is help. Right, darlin'?"

"Right." Rebecca patted her on the side before taking a step back. "I'll let you two handle it while I take care of the horses. Lex, do you care if I give yours a little feed?"

"No, that would be great. Do you need any help?"

Rebecca laughed at her. "I think I can handle two extra horses. But thanks for the offer." She gathered the reins of Mac and Coco and led them to the barn.

Lex moved closer to Shelby and lowered her voice. "Did I offend her?"

"Nah. I think you made extra points for askin'."

"Yeah? Cool." Lex tipped her head toward the house. "I'm going to run tell the kids goodbye." Lex ignored Shelby's laugh as she walked away. She was miffed at the other woman's teasing, until she realized how little it mattered. "Gotta quit being so damned sensitive about these things." She removed her gloves and tucked them into her back pocket. When she hit the top step, the back door opened and Melanie greeted her.

"Momma! Aunt Helen said we're gonna go home with her and Uncle Roy. Can't I go with you? I'm a big girl, you know."

Lex lifted Melanie into her arms. "You sure are, princess. But all we're going to do is take the stray horses to the vet's office. I'll be home before you know it."

Melanie's pout was reminiscent of Amanda's. "I won't get in the way, I promise."

"I know, sweetheart." Lex kissed her cheek. "I need someone to help Aunt Helen with Eddie while Uncle Roy gets some rest. Do you think you can do that?"

The pout disappeared. "I can, Momma. I promise."

"That's my girl!" Lex kissed her again and set her down. "Have you been good?"

"Yes'm. I drew a picture for the 'frigerator. Do you wanna see?"

"Sure. Then I'd better get back out there, so I can get home faster."

SHELBY CLOSED THE trailer just as a pained yelp came from the corral. She latched the door and jogged toward the sound. She saw the chestnut mare staring from the middle of the corral and the filly trotting around her. Rebecca stood with her back to the railing. "Rebecca? What happened?"

"I'm okay." Rebecca held one arm close to her body and crawled through the slats on the corral.

"What happened?" Shelby asked again. She reached for Rebecca's arm. "Lemme see."

Rebecca shook her head. "I was just being stupid." She had tears in her eyes and bit her lip as Shelby gently held her arm.

The skin on Rebecca's forearm was torn and bleeding. Shelby led her toward the house and didn't release her grip. "Let's get this cleaned up and see what we have."

"It's just a bite. The mare looked half-asleep, so I thought it would be easy to put a halter on her." Rebecca stumbled but Shelby's hold kept her from falling. "Damned thing snapped at me before I knew what was happening."

Shelby helped her up the steps and opened the back door. "It happens, darlin'." She led her to the kitchen sink.

Lex met them at the sink. "What happened? I was just on my way out there."

"Chestnut took exception to a halter." Shelby started a slow stream of water over the injury, and winced when Rebecca hissed at the pain. "Sorry."

Lex stood behind them, anxious to help. "Where are your first aid supplies?"

"Bathroom cabinet," Shelby answered.

Rebecca closed her eyes at the continued rush of the cold water. She was unable to stop a pained moan from escaping.

"Hang in there, baby. I'm almost done." Shelby turned off the water and accepted a clean towel from Lex, who had brought the supplies from the bathroom.

"What can I do to help?" Lex asked.

Shelby led Rebecca to a chair. "I'm not sure. This doesn't look real deep. But still, it's an ugly gash."

"I've been nipped before," Rebecca countered. "You're making a bigger deal out of it than necessary."

"Hush." Shelby's hands shook too badly to open the first aid kit, so she handed it to Lex. She watched as Lex cleaned the wound and covered it in antibiotic ointment. "I think you ought to go to town and see a doctor."

Rebecca sniffled and blinked tears from her eyes. She remained quiet until Lex wrapped a gauze bandage around her arm. "Don't be ridiculous. It's not that serious."

Shelby tried another tactic. "Well, I don't want you staying here by yourself. Why don't you come to town with us?"

When Rebecca's face darkened, Lex washed her hands at the sink, then gathered the leftover supplies. "Holler when you're ready." She left the room to give them privacy.

"I'm capable of being here alone, even with a horse bite." Rebecca took a deep breath and held it for several seconds, before releasing it slowly. "You're not usually this overprotective. What's going on with you?"

Shelby opened her mouth to disagree with her, but stopped. She sighed and removed her western hat. Her short hair was matted against her head with sweat and she ran her fingers through the strands before replacing the hat. "I've always cared about what happens to you, Rebecca." She looked at the floor. "Hell, my life wouldn't be worth livin' without you, you know that."

She took a breath to gather her courage and raised her head. "I love you, darlin'. And just thinkin' about somethin' happenin' to you scares the shit out of me." She smiled when Rebecca blinked in surprise. "Yeah. So, please let a doctor check out your arm, okay? Save me from makin' a fool outta myself in front of everyone?"

Rebecca laughed and put her good arm behind Shelby's neck and kissed her. "All right. You win, this time."

LEX RETURNED TO the kitchen and smiled at the couple who sat so close together they were almost one. "I'm going to put the gray back in the corral with the others. I called Ron. He said he'd come out here to look them over."

Rebecca tried to stand, but Shelby's firm grip on her hand kept her seated. "That's not necessary, Lex. I'm sure she only bit me because I spooked her."

"Maybe. But something doesn't look quite right about her, and I'd feel better if we had a vet's opinion."

"Sounds good to me." Shelby gave Rebecca's hand a squeeze before she got up from the table. "I'll help you."

Lex was about to brush off the offer, when she considered the look on her friend's face. Shelby obviously needed to talk. "All right, thanks. Rebecca, is there anything I can do for you?"

"Yes. Please drag Shelby out of here. I'm going to go change my shirt, since this one is trashed."

Shelby laughed. "I'm goin'. Holler if you need anything."

Rebecca swatted her on the rear. "I *need* to change my shirt. Now go on."

"Yes'm." Shelby tipped her head and followed Lex out of the house. Once they were halfway between the house and the corral she asked, "Do you think I overreacted?"

Lex slowed her pace. "No, not really. I've seen lesser bites than that get infected. Probably wouldn't hurt to have a doctor look it over."

"Yeah. That's what I thought, too."

They stopped at the corral and watched the three horses all acting differently. The gray relaxed in one corner. The sorrel filly stayed close to its mother as the chestnut mare continuously stomped its left front hoof.

Shelby propped her arms on the rail and rested her chin on them. "Wonder what she did to her leg?"

"Hard to tell, since she won't let us get close." Lex joined her and draped her arms on the top rail. "The filly seems to be the only one in decent shape."

"Too skinny, though. How long will it take the vet to get here?"

"Not sure. Why? You got something else to do?" Lex laughed at her friend's heavy sigh. She knew exactly what was bothering Shelby, but she didn't know if the other woman would have the nerve to say it aloud. "What?"

Shelby turned and glared at her. "You're a right smartass sometimes, ain't ya?" When Lex remained silent, she shook her head. "All right. I want to take Rebecca into town and get her arm looked at. Is there anythin' wrong with that?"

"Nope." Lex turned and leaned against the corral with her elbows braced along the top rail. "I was just wondering when you'd get around to saying it." She laughed as Shelby muttered and pushed away from the corral. "Go on. I'll keep an eye on things for you."

"Thanks." Shelby headed for the house. She turned and walked backward. "Sorry for snappin' at you."

Lex waved one hand at her. "Don't worry about it. I shouldn't have teased you. Take care of Rebecca."

"I sure will. See you later." Shelby spun and jogged toward the house.

Chapter Twenty

TWO AND A half hours after they arrived at the emergency room, Rebecca still had not seen a doctor. Her arm throbbed and she felt dizzy from her empty stomach. She rested her head against Shelby's shoulder and closed her eyes.

"Can I get you anything, darlin'?" Shelby asked quietly.

Rebecca shook her head.

Shelby glanced around the waiting room. "This is crazy. You could be bleedin' to death and no one seems to give a damn."

"I told you it wasn't that serious. Even the nurse thought so. Can we just go home?"

"I'd feel better if a doctor said it was okay. Who knows if that nurse even knew what she was talking about?"

"Shelby!" Rebecca looked around to see if anyone had overheard her. "She told us we'd be seen in order of importance. I'm sure they're just very busy."

"It's bullshit." Shelby stood and paced in front of her lover. The emergency bay doors swung open and a man was wheeled in on a stretcher. His hair was bright green and the matching paint on his face was smeared.

"Jus' slow down, guys. I ain't inna hurry." He began to sing an off-key, R-rated version of Danny Boy.

Rebecca covered her mouth with her hand to keep from laughing out loud. "I'd forgotten today was Saint Patrick's Day. We used to have to dress up in green tops and jeans at Carson's."

"He's obviously celebrated enough for all of us. There's got to be someone who can look at your arm. Hold on, I'll be right back." Shelby walked to the nurse's station and held a quiet conversation with the woman behind the counter.

RON BRISTOL SNAPPED off his rubber gloves and took a wide berth around the blindfolded mare. He stepped through the corral slats and ended up beside Lex. "The gray is malnourished, but otherwise in decent shape."

"And the chestnut?" Lex walked beside him to the open tailgate of his truck, which held a large bucket of antiseptic water.

"I'm not sure." Ron stuck his hands in the bucket and vigorously scrubbed up to his elbows. "I'd like to have Dr. Hernandez look at her before I say anything."

Lex handed him a towel. "Come on, Ron. This is me you're talking to, not some clueless city kid. That spot on her leg is an infected bite, isn't it?"

He dried his hands and arms then tossed the towel into the bed of the truck. "It might be, yes."

Lex nodded and thought about the implications. "Rabies?" The horse showed signs of the disease, especially the slight foam at its mouth.

"Possibly."

"Damn it, Ron!"

He held up his hands. "Honestly, Lex. I don't know for sure. We have no way of knowing without a test, and you know what that entails."

She knew all too well. The suspected animal had to be euthanized and its entire head sent to the Texas Department of State Health Services laboratory in Austin, where they could run the test. Anyone who had unprotected contact would have to start treatment. "Damn!"

"Hey, I swear I told you all I know."

"No, it's not that." Lex took out her cell phone and thumbed through her contact list. She put the phone to her ear and tapped her foot. "Come on, answer the damned phone. Hey, Shelby. This is...damned voice mail."

She listened to the prerecorded message and waited for the beep. "Shelby, this is Lex. Call me as soon as you get this message, it's urgent. Uh, bye."

She placed the phone in its holster. "The chestnut took a pretty good bite out of Rebecca's arm earlier today. Shelby took her into town to get it checked out."

"Lex, she needs to start treatment, just in case," Ron emphasized.

"No shit!" Lex stopped to take a deep breath then released it slowly. "I'm sorry. It's just that—"

He put his hand on her arm. "You're worried about her. For good reason. You wore your gloves when you handled the horse, right?"

"Yeah. Uh, Ron?"

"What?"

"It can't be transmitted through blood, can it?"

Ron shook his head. "No, just saliva. Why?"

"I bandaged Rebecca's arm. Had her blood on my hands." Lex looked at her hands, as if to see the blood still there. "Poor thing tried to be brave, but I could tell it hurt like hell."

He rubbed the back of his neck, a nervous gesture he had picked up from Lex. "If you were close, it's theoretically possible that you took in her breath, which could pass along the saliva. Dang it, Lex. I can't be one hundred-percent certain you're safe, providing the horse has been infected."

"Yeah, I figured that much. Let me call Rodney and see if he has time to start the injections. I need to reach Rebecca and Shelby, too. Maybe they can run by his office before they come home."

She took out her phone and stared at it. "Damn it, Shelby. Call me!"

WHEN HER NAME was called, Rebecca almost knocked Shelby out of her chair when she jumped up. "Sorry."

"That's all right." Shelby stood and began to follow her.

The nurse at the door gave Shelby a dirty look. "Are you family?"

"I am. Problem?" Shelby put her hand on the door. "After you."

With a disgusted snort, the nurse stepped in front of Rebecca. "Follow me, please." She walked purposefully down the hall and stopped in front of an open door. "Miss Starrett, if you'd take a seat on the table, we'll get your vitals."

Shelby followed them in and stood in the far corner of the tiny room. She leaned against the wall and crossed her arms. It took a lot of self-control for her not to drag the nurse away from her partner when she accidentally bumped Rebecca's injured arm and caused her to cry out at the sharp pain.

The nurse murmured an apology before she wrote on the chart. She patted Rebecca once on the knee. "The doctor should be in shortly."

Once they were alone, Shelby pushed off from the wall to stand beside Rebecca.

"Hang in there, darlin'." She put her arm around Rebecca's shoulder and held her the best she could. It broke her heart to feel the warm tears on her shirt and the silent sobs that came from the woman she loved. "Sssh. It's gonna be okay." She kissed the top of Rebecca's head and rested her cheek against her hair.

The door opened. A middle-aged woman, dressed in faded green scrubs and a wrinkled lab coat stepped in. Her short, salt-and-pepper hair curled behind her ears and was in disarray. She adjusted her black-framed glasses and looked at the chart. "Miss Starrett?"

Rebecca raised her head away from Shelby and wiped her face with her good hand. "Yes, that's me."

"I'm Dr. Kale." She held out her hand to Shelby, who gave it a firm shake.

"Shelby Fisher. I'm Rebecca's partner."

Dr. Kale set the chart on a rolling cart. She moved to the sink and washed her hands, dried them and then pulled on a pair of disposable gloves. She stepped close to Rebecca and held out her hands. "May I?"

Rebecca held out her injured arm and bit her lip in anticipation.

"So, horse bite, huh?" Dr. Kale gently unwrapped the gauze from the injury. Once it was exposed, she nodded. "Nicely cleaned. I don't believe stitches are necessary, but we'll need to start you on antibiotics, just to be safe."

"Okay." Rebecca looked up at Shelby, who rubbed gentle circles on her back. "See? I told you it wasn't that bad."

Dr. Kale laughed. "I didn't say that. It's good that you came in, if only for the antibiotics. Animal bites are the world's worst at getting infected."

Shelby gave her lover a wink. "That's what I said, doc. Thanks for backing me up."

Fifteen minutes later, Shelby escorted Rebecca from the hospital, with two prescriptions in hand. "I liked that doctor. She was all right."

"That's because she couldn't take her eyes off you."

Shelby stumbled. "What?" She stopped and looked at her lover. "You're crazy."

"Maybe. But it's true. Dr. Kale spent more time looking at you than at my arm." Rebecca giggled before Shelby opened her door. "Not that I can blame her. You are cute."

"Hush." Shelby swatted her on the rear. She was uncomfortable with the thought of the doctor being attracted to her, but was grateful for the painkilling shot Dr. Kale had given Rebecca before they left the exam room. She hurried around the truck and climbed in behind the wheel. On the seat between them was her cell phone, which had a rapidly blinking red light in one corner.

Rebecca rested her head against the back of the seat and closed her eyes. "Could we drive through somewhere and get a burger, or something? I'm starving."

"Sure. We need to call and let Lex know we're on the way, though. She's probably bored to death out at our place." She picked up her phone and looked at the screen. "Missed a call from her."

"Maybe it's about the horses."

Shelby listened to her voice mail. "Huh." She hit the speed dial for Lex. "Hey, Boss. Sorry about missing your call, but..." her voice trailed off as she listened. "Damn it. Is he sure?" She looked at Rebecca and felt an ache in her chest. "Yeah. Thanks. Um, what's the address?"

Rebecca opened her eyes and turned her head toward Shelby. "What's up?"

"Okay, I appreciate it, Lex. We'll see you in a bit." Shelby tossed her phone onto the seat. "The vet checked out the horses."

"Are they going to be okay?"

"The gray and the filly are all right, but the chestnut might not be." Shelby turned in her seat to face her. "That bad spot on her leg might be an infected animal bite, and she's showing possible signs of rabies."

"Oh, my God." Rebecca looked at her arm. "Does that mean that I—" she choked on the words. "I could have rabies?"

Shelby scooted across the bench seat and put her arm around her. "You may have been exposed, yeah. And since we don't know for sure, it's a good idea to go ahead and start the treatments. Just in case."

Rebecca started to cry. "I'm scared, Shelby. I don't know if I can handle this."

"You're not alone, darlin'. I'll be with you every step of the way." Shelby kissed the side of her head. "You're gonna be just fine, I promise."

We're heading to Amanda's brother-in-law, Dr. Crews. He's expecting us."

AMANDA PARKED IN her usual spot beside the house. Lex's truck was gone, which normally wouldn't surprise her, but her wife had planned to spend a quiet day at home with Eddie and Mel. "I wonder where she is?"

"Hmm?" Lorrie looked up from the scrapbook in her lap. "Where's Momma's truck?"

"Your guess is as good as mine. Let's see if Mada knows."

Lorrie tucked the book into her backpack. "Cool. I want to show her these albums." She climbed out and was on her way down the walk before Amanda could open her own door.

Amanda rolled her eyes and followed at a more leisurely pace. The cottage door opened when Lorrie hit the bottom step and Martha waved to Amanda. "Hi."

"Hello, there." Martha accepted a one-armed hug from Lorrie. "Did you have a nice time, sweetie?"

"Yes, ma'am. Aunt Jeannie had all sorts of cool things, and I even got to see a football game that my father played in. It was really awesome." Lorrie turned to Amanda, who had joined them on the porch. "And their wedding pictures were funny, too," she added with a giggle.

Amanda touched the tip of her nose. "Watch it. Remember what I said."

The threat of having a similar haircut was a good one, and Lorrie bit her lip, although her eyes still twinkled with mischief.

"Do you have any idea where Lex and the kids are? I thought they were staying home today."

Martha ushered them into her home. "Eddie and Mel are helping their Pawpaw with a jigsaw puzzle in the kitchen, and Lexie is at Shelby and Rebecca's." She patted Lorrie on the back. "There's fresh chocolate chip cookies, if you'd care to join them."

"Thanks, Mada." Lorrie headed that direction, and left the two women alone in the living room.

Amanda pursed her lips. "Did Lex pawn off the kids on you? She made such a big deal out of spending time with them today."

"No. She took them with her, but sent them back with Helen and Roy when she found out she'd be there a while. And you know we love having them here, so hush."

"Oh." Amanda followed her to the sofa and sat on the opposite end from Martha. "Helen and Roy were there, too? What on earth was going on? Is everyone all right?"

Martha sat back. "Something about some stray horses, according to Helen. One of the horses nipped a chunk out of Rebecca's arm, so

Shelby took her to town while Lexie stayed to keep an eye on the critters. Why she stayed, I don't know."

"You know how she is. I'm surprised she hasn't brought them home with her. I should call and check on Rebecca. I hope she's okay." Amanda tapped the arm of the sofa.

"Hon, why don't you run on and keep Lexie company? The kids are fine with us."

Amanda hopped off the couch. "Are you sure? I feel like we take advantage of you." At Martha's laugh, she shrugged. "Well, I do."

"That's just plain silly. You know we love the kids. They're already growing so fast, we don't get to see them as much as we used to. Before we know it, Lorrie and Melanie will be off to college and little Eddie will be chasing girls."

"Good grief, don't say that! The girls are too independent already." Amanda ducked and kissed the older woman's cheek. "Thanks. I'll call and let you know how late we'll be."

Martha waved her away. "Nonsense. We'll make up the guest bed for the girls, and Eddie can sleep with us if it gets too late. Go on, now."

"All right. But call me if—"

"Amanda."

"Yes, ma'am." That tone always meant business, so Amanda sighed. "Tell the kids I'll see them later. I don't want to upset Eddie by seeing him and leaving again so quickly." The glare she received caused Amanda to laugh and hurry from the house.

AMANDA WAS HALFWAY to her SUV when Lorrie's voice stopped her.

"Mom, wait!"

Amanda turned to see her oldest jogging to catch up. "Honey, you don't have to go. We're probably going to be stuck at Shelby and Rebecca's for a while."

"That's all right." Lorrie tucked her hands into the front pockets of her jeans and walked in step with Amanda. "I really want to see Momma."

"Why?"

"Huh?"

Amanda stopped by the Expedition. "Sweetie, I love you more than anything in the world, but I also love your Momma. And I—"

"You're afraid I'll yell at her again?" Lorrie scuffed the toe of her sneaker along the front tire to etch the black surface with a lighter shade of dirt. "I was being stupid."

"You think so?" Amanda stepped around to lean against the vehicle, a few feet away from her daughter. "Why did you do it, then?"

"I dunno." When Amanda remained silent, Lorrie continued, "When you went to get lunch, Aunt Jeannie talked about when I was born. She said the stroke she had made her want to die, especially after my Dad was killed. And that she didn't even feel like my mom, ever."

"She said that?"

Lorrie continued to trace her foot in the dirt. "She said it was because she couldn't do anything for me, not even give me a bottle." She raised her head. "Was she really that sick?"

The woman Lorrie knew now was perfectly healthy. It was hard to picture her helpless and unable to move.

"Yes." Amanda rested her hand on Lorrie's shoulder as they both looked off into the distance. "I knew she was sad and upset, but I had no idea she felt so...lost. I should have been more supportive of her."

"She said you'd feel that way, that's why she never told you." Lorrie turned and looked into Amanda's face. "It's okay, Mom. I didn't tell you to make you sad. Did you know that Aunt Jeannie had a crush on Momma?"

Amanda blinked. "What?"

"Back then, I mean. She said it was a silly crush, just because Momma was so nice to her."

"Oh?" Amanda shook her head. "Um, no. We've never really talked much about that time. I knew that Lex would spend a lot of time with Jeannie. That's why we have paved walks from the house to the barn, and to Mada's. Jeannie was in a wheelchair and your Momma wanted to get her out of the house. So she had the walks poured."

"No wonder Aunt Jeannie liked her."

Amanda bumped her with her hip. "She still likes her, goofy." They both laughed, but Amanda sobered quickly. "Did Jeannie tell you what else your Momma did?"

"Ma'am?"

"Although Momma was completely swamped with running the ranch, she'd stop whatever she was doing and come in for lunch. She'd feed you and bring you in to visit with Jeannie."

Lorrie didn't appear convinced. "Every day?"

Sometimes, the girl was more like Lex than anyone else. The skeptical tilt to her head mirrored that of Lex, when she felt as if someone was trying to put something over on her. "Every day she could, yes. And when you'd wake in the middle of the night, she was the one who would get up with you."

"Really?"

"Yes, really. She'd rock you, walk with you and sing to you. Whatever it took to get you back to sleep."

Lorrie visibly relaxed. "Yeah, I remember sitting in her lap and her reading to me." She rested against the SUV. "Can we go see Momma? Please?"

AFTER AN ARGUMENT with Ron, Lex found herself on the road

to town. She knew she needed to start the treatment shots that would protect her against the rabies virus but she didn't want to go without talking with her wife. Unfortunately, Lex's cell phone battery was dead. And her charger was in the truck that Helen and Roy had taken home and Ron's was on his office desk. He promised to wait for the arrival of the sheriff, who Lex had contacted before her phone died. Jeremy would have to decide what to do with the strays before they were reunited with their rightful owner or enough time had passed so they could be auctioned.

She turned on the radio, not surprised to find it on an easy listening station. She often teased Roy about his taste in music, which leaned more toward soft rock and light jazz while her satellite radio was tuned to country. She hit one of the preset buttons and laughed as a Disney tune came through the speakers. "He's as bad as I am."

After another push, she found a station that played pop music from the eighties. "Good enough."

Lex hummed along softly to the music and enjoyed the scenic drive. The trees sported fresh leaves and the new grass beside the road grew in near-fluorescent matching green. Soon, she would have the men check out the other pastures to see if they had enough grazing so the cattle could be moved.

She soon crossed into the Somerville city limits. It didn't take long to get to Rodney's office. When she arrived, she was surprised to see a familiar Ford Expedition in the lot. "Crap. What's Amanda doing here?"

Lex had barely gotten out of the truck when Amanda met her.

Amanda put her hands on her hips.

Lex breathed a sigh of relief when her wife laughed. "I was going to call you, but the battery on my phone died."

"And your charger is in your truck, not Roy's," Amanda added in an exasperated tone. She moved closer and touched Lex's arm. "Are you all right?"

"I'm fine, I promise." Lex wrapped her arms around her wife and held her. "How did you know to come here?"

"We were on our way to meet you at Shelby and Rebecca's, when Jeannie called."

"Your sister is a damned gossip."

"No kidding. But for once, I'm glad." Amanda stepped out of the embrace, but kept one arm around Lex's hip. "Rebecca's already been treated, but Rodney had to give her an extra something for the pain, and she's resting in one of the examination rooms. After her shot, Shelby went in to stay with her."

They walked into the office together.

Lorrie was seated in the waiting room and rose to her feet when she saw Lex. "Momma!" She crossed the room quickly and embraced both parents. "Aunt Jeannie said you might have rabies." She didn't bother trying to hide her fear as she huddled close to them.

"There's a *very* slim chance of that." Lex kissed the top of her head. "I'm here to get a shot to prevent that from happening."

"I'm sorry for being mean to you, Momma. I promise never to do it again."

Lex closed her eyes for a moment to dispel the lump in her throat. "It's all right, sweetheart. We're okay."

The interior door opened and Ellie appeared. "Lex, I'm glad you're here. Rodney is ready for you." When Lex broke away from her family and started past her, Ellie gave her a pat on the back. "You just can't stay out of trouble, can you, cuz?"

"Nah. What fun would that be?" Lex turned to Amanda and Lorrie. "I'll be right back."

Amanda didn't want to leave Lorrie alone, and three people were a crowd in the tiny exam rooms. "We'll be here."

Chapter Twenty-one

MONDAY MORNING, SHELBY stepped out of the bathroom as she towel-dried her hair. She was surprised to see Rebecca still in bed, since she needed to be at work not long after her. Although she wasn't a morning person, Rebecca was responsible enough to drag herself out when she needed to.

"Hey, darlin'. You're gonna be late if you don't get up." She draped the towel on a chair and put on her underwear and jeans. "Rebecca?"

"I can't."

Shelby eased the blanket off Rebecca's face. "What's wrong?" She touched her flushed cheek. "You're running a fever."

Rebecca closed her eyes at the gentle touch. "I feel like I have the flu." She shivered and wrapped up tighter in the covers.

Shelby sat beside her. "Want me to call the feed store for you?"

"No, I'll get up. I can't afford to miss work. I've only been there a week." Rebecca sat up. "Oh, God." Her flushed cheeks paled and she covered her mouth. She flung the covers off and raced for the bathroom, barely reaching the toilet before she retched.

"Damn." Shelby followed her and dampened a washcloth. She knelt beside her lover and held her hair away from her face as her free hand dabbed the cloth along Rebecca's neck. Rodney had warned her of the side effects of the shot, but when Shelby was the only one that had been nauseous the day before, she thought they had gotten lucky.

Rebecca coughed and spit into the toilet before flushing it, then leaned back against Shelby. "Ugh."

"Let's get you off the floor." Shelby stood and carefully helped Rebecca up. She kept her arm around her waist as Rebecca shakily brushed her teeth. "You can't go to work like this. Let me give them a call, I know they'll understand."

"No, just give me a minute. I'll—" The toothpaste didn't set well with her queasy stomach. Rebecca shoved away from Shelby and ended up in front of the toilet, gasping for breath between dry heaves.

Once she was through, Rebecca felt as weak as a kitten. She didn't even argue when Shelby undressed them both and got into the shower with her. Shelby even surprised her by braiding her wet hair once they were in the bedroom.

"When did you learn to braid hair?" she asked as she fell back against the pillows.

Shelby grinned and tucked the blanket up around her chin. "No offense, darlin', but a woman's hair ain't all that different from a horse's tail, you know."

Rebecca gave her a weak glare. "Remind me to swat you when I'm feeling better. That was bad."

"I'll sure enough do that. But for now, I'm gonna call the store for you, and then give my boss a holler. I'm sure she won't mind me hanging around here today 'til you're feelin' better."

"You don't have to do that. I can probably take care of myself."

Shelby lightly touched the end of her lover's nose. "Too damned bad. I'm also gonna call the doc and see if there's anythin' I should do for you." She kissed Rebecca on the forehead. "You just lay there and rest. I'll run check on the horses after I make my calls."

"Better watch out, Shelby."

"What?"

"Someone might think you're getting soft, for being so sweet to me."

Shelby leaned close and whispered, "Only for you, darlin'." She gave her another light kiss on the head. "And I don't care who knows it."

"MELANIE, FINISH YOUR breakfast so you can wash up. Momma will be back from the barn soon to take you to the bus." Amanda wiped Eddie's face, causing him to fuss.

"No!" Eddie swatted the tray of his high chair and tried to squirm away from Amanda.

Amanda continued to clean his face. "Stop fidgeting. I'm not trying to kill you."

Lorrie, who had finished her breakfast earlier, came into the kitchen. "Can I go help Momma? My backpack is by the door."

"Sure. Could you please remind her that she's taking you to the bus? I have to get Eddie bathed and ready for his checkup at the pediatrician this morning."

"Yes, ma'am. Come on, Freckles."

The dog that was camped underneath Eddie's high chair, raised her head but didn't move.

"Greedy." Lorrie hurried out before Amanda changed her mind. Once she was off the porch, she glanced at the kitchen window before taking off toward the three-foot picket fence at a run. When she reached the gate, she placed her hands on top and vaulted over. As she landed on her feet, Lorrie raised her hands in the air to the imaginary cheers. "Thank you, thank you," she exclaimed as she trotted to the barn.

She stepped into the barn and looked around. The horses had all been fed, but her mother seemed to be absent. She was about to call out when she heard an unusual sound in the tack room. Lorrie followed the noise. She peeked around the open door and panicked. "Momma!"

LEX SAT ON a bale of hay, throwing up in a bucket. Her hair was matted against her forehead with sweat and her face was unusually pale. She raised her head. "Go back to the house, Lorrie. I'll be up there in a minute." Her voice was low and rough. "Please."

"Can..." Lorrie moved closer. "Can I help you?"

Lex swallowed as she shakily placed the bucket to the side. She took a clean handkerchief from her back pocket and handed it to Lorrie. "Could you wet this for me, please? I don't think I can get up just yet."

"Sure. Don't move." Lorrie hurried to the sink in the front of the barn. She returned and handed the wet cloth to Lex, who wiped her face and mouth.

"Thanks."

Lorrie stood close. "Momma?"

"Hmm?"

"Are you dying?"

Lex almost snapped off a snarky answer, but caught herself. Although Lorrie had grown up in the past year, she was still young. "No, sweetheart. I'm not." She cleared her throat. "Your uncle Rodney warned me that I might get a little sick from the shot he had to give me. I'll be fine in a day or two."

She closed her eyes and focused all her energy on not throwing up again.

"Maybe I should go get Mom."

"No!" Lex softened her tone. "She's got enough going on this morning. Run up to the house and make sure your sister is ready to go. I'll meet y'all at the truck, okay?"

Lorrie stared at her, as if she were about to argue.

"Go on. I'm fine, now."

Once she heard the outer barn door close, Lex slowly stood and took the bucket to the sink to wash it out. She cleaned her hands and splashed water on her face.

AMANDA GATHERED EDDIE'S diaper bag and two small toys for the trip to his pediatrician. She carried him and his bag down the stairs in time to hear the back door open. "Sounds like Momma's back from the bus stop."

"Momma, go." Eddie kicked his legs.

"Why am I not surprised? You always want your momma." Amanda pulled up short when she saw Lex. Her wife was pale and covered with sweat, although the March morning was cool. "Honey?"

Lex brushed her hair out of her eyes and sat on the bench by the door. "Hey. Kids are off to school."

"Momma!" Eddie squirmed until Amanda let him down. He toddled to Lex and tried to climb in her lap. "Up!"

"Easy, buddy." Lex slowly raised him to her knee, facing her. "Are you ready to go?"

He bounced a few times and giggled. "Momma, go."

Amanda sat beside them. "You don't look very well, honey. What's the matter?"

"Just a little queasy this morning. Rodney said it was possible with the shot. I just didn't expect to be losing my breakfast in the barn."

"Oh, no." Amanda rubbed Lex's back. "I'll call and reschedule Eddie's appointment."

"Why?"

"Because you're sick, and I'd like to be here to help you, goofball."

"That's ridiculous. I'll be fine." Lex couldn't stop the shiver that came upon her. "I'm going to go upstairs and take a shower, and you and this little guy here..." She bounced him on her knee. "Can go into town. If I need anything, I can always call Martha."

"Oh, yes. I can see that happening." Amanda held out her hands to Eddie. "Come on, cutie. Are you ready to go?"

Eddie laughed and bounced harder. "Go!" He grabbed Lex's shirt. "Momma, go?"

"No, Eddie, you go with Mommy. I'll see you when you get back."

"Momma." Eddie leaned against her and held on tightly. "Go, Momma."

Amanda picked him up. "Would you like to drop by and see Hunter?"

Jeannie's son was an endless fascination for Eddie.

"Baby!" he cheered, happy once again.

Lex stood. "You heard the young man."

"All right." Amanda touched Lex's cheek. "Promise me something, please?"

"Sure."

"Call Martha if you need anything?"

Lex rolled her eyes. "Well played, sweetheart. All right. I promise. Eddie, be good for Mommy, okay?"

He laughed. "Ha! Good."

Amanda patted Lex gently on the stomach. "He's definitely your kid."

"Ha." Lex poked her tongue out.

BY LUNCHTIME, LEX no longer felt sick to her stomach. She sat at Martha's table and finished the last of her roast beef sandwich. "That was great, Martha. Thanks."

"You're quite welcome, honey. I'm glad you liked it." Martha refilled both their tea glasses. "Have I thanked you lately for giving Charlie something to do? The man was driving me crazy around here." Her husband, a retired county sheriff, had become increasingly bored. Once Roy was given a walking cast, Lex had asked Charlie to drive him around the ranch, much to everyone's relief.

Lex wiped her mouth and sat back in her chair. "It was actually Amanda's idea. Once Shelby got a feel for things, it didn't make sense for Roy to keep riding with her. Besides, I think Helen was getting ready to bury him behind the barn."

"I wouldn't be surprised. Are you sure you're feeling okay? You still look a mite peaked."

"I'm okay." When she received the familiar glare, Lex held up her hands. "Okay, so I feel like I've been run over by a truck, and my arm hurts like hell where he gave me that blasted shot. Happy?"

Martha took a sip of tea. "Of course not, Lexie. Why don't you go lie down in the guest room?"

"No, that's not necessary. Shelby's at home with Rebecca today, so I really should—"

"You really should take care of yourself," Martha finished for her. When Lex rolled her eyes, Martha waggled a finger at her. "Did you happen to consider that your body is still getting past having pneumonia? That horrible shot couldn't have helped any. And you have to get another one, when?"

"Tomorrow."

"Exactly. So, you've got a choice. Either my guest room, or your own bedroom. Take your pick."

Lex was about to argue more, but a wave of lethargy rolled across her. "I think I'll head on home, while I can." She got to her feet and pushed the chair in. "Thanks."

Martha gave her a hug and escorted her to the front door. "That's what I'm here for, sweetie. To keep you in line when Amanda's not around." She rubbed Lex's back before giving her a gentle push onto the porch. "Go home, Lexie. And get some rest."

"Yes, ma'am." Lex saluted her. "I'm only agreeing because I had already decided to do it, you know."

"Of course."

REBECCA TIGHTENED THE blanket around herself and closed her eyes. She no longer felt nauseous, but the wound on her arm ached so badly it made her dizzy. Shelby had propped her on the couch with the television remote before she left to pick up a few things in town. "I should have never mentioned chicken noodle soup."

Her eyes slowly closed and she relaxed, until her cell phone rang. "Hello?"

"Becca? Honey, your father called me and said you weren't at work today. What's wrong?"

"Mom?" Rebecca sat up. "How did Dad know?"

Kathy Starrett clicked her tongue. It was a habit she had when talking about her spouse. "I haven't a clue. But don't try to change the subject. Are you ill?"

Rebecca bit her lip to keep from blurting the first thing that came to her mind. *No, Mom. I called out sick on my second week of work for the hell of it.* "I woke up sick this morning, but I'm feeling better, thanks."

"Are you running a fever? I hear there's a nasty virus going around."

"No, it's not a virus."

Kathy could not be dissuaded. "How do you know? Have you seen a doctor?"

"Mom."

"Honestly, Becca. I hate you living out there in the middle of nowhere. You need someone to take care of you."

Six years. For six long years, Rebecca had been hearing this refrain. She had a great relationship with both parents as she grew up. Even after she had moved in with Shelby, they had tried very hard to be supportive. But, as the years passed, they realized Rebecca wasn't going through a phase, and that she planned on staying with Shelby. During the past couple of years, their tolerance had begun to wane. "Mom, Shelby takes very good care of me."

"I'm sure she tries, dear. But she's not family."

As Rebecca's blood pressure continued to rise, the throbbing in her arm intensified. "She's as much family to me as Daddy is to you."

"There's no need to take that tone with me. I'm only worried about you." Kathy paused a moment. "While I'm sure you feel strongly about—" she almost choked on the name. "Shelby, you have no real commitment like your father and I do. What's to keep her from taking off and leaving you?" She sniffed in disdain. "Enough about her. You never answered me. Have you seen a doctor? You may need antibiotics."

"Yes, Mom. I've seen a doctor. That's why I'm sick."

Dead silence on the other end of the line.

"Mom?"

Kathy's voice was subdued. "Are you...pregnant? I know that most of your peers are married with children, but have you thought this through?"

"What? Mom! No!" Rebecca gathered her thoughts. "Um, Saturday, we found three abandoned horses. I was trying to get a halter on one of them and it bit me."

"Bit you? Becca, you should be more careful. There's no telling—"

"Yeah, I know. I went to the emergency room to have my arm looked at, then Amanda's brother-in-law gave me a shot—"

"Wait. Your friend, Amanda? The one that lives on a ranch? Her brother-in-law gave you a shot, for what? And is that even legal?"

Rebecca gritted her teeth. "If you would let me finish, Mom, I'd tell you."

Kathy didn't bother to hide her hurt feelings. "Fine."

"Okay, where was I? Oh. Amanda's brother-in-law is Dr. Crews. He has an office on Willow Street. Anyway, since we don't know anything about the horses, Dr. Crews started me on the rabies vaccine. That's what made me sick this morning. Shelby and Lex had to get shots, too. But Shelby was just a little achy today. Not throwing up like me. I'm not sure how Lex is feeling."

When her mother didn't say anything, Rebecca was afraid she'd hung up. "Mom?"

"Oh, I can talk now?"

"Mom, don't be like that. I'm sorry, but you kept asking me questions without giving me time to answer." Rebecca decided to play the pity card in the hopes of getting out of trouble. "And I'm not feeling good." She let a slight whine slip into her voice. "I'm sorry, Mom."

It worked.

"Oh, honey. That's all right. Do you need me to bring you anything?"

"No. Thanks, anyway. Shelby should be back soon. She went in to town to get a few things."

"She left you alone?"

"I'm not dying, or an invalid. As a matter of fact, I was thinking about going out and checking on our horses." Which, of course, was a lie. Rebecca had no urge to move from the couch.

"Don't go near those beasts! What if they attack you again?"

Rebecca couldn't help but laugh. "Horses don't attack people. Besides, the sheriff quarantined the horses. He's hoping to find the owner, or see if the one who bit me gets sick."

"Oh."

"Anyway, thanks for calling to check on me, Mom. I promise to call you soon, okay? Love you." Rebecca disconnected the call and turned off her cell, in case her mother called back.

"My father is as bad a gossip as an old woman!"

SHELBY WAS ON her way out of town when she took a wrong turn and ended up at the sheriff's department.

"Well, since I'm here," she told herself. "I might as well have a quick chat with Sheriff Richards."

She went inside and signed the visitor's log, then studied a bulletin board covered with information as she waited.

"Good afternoon, Ms. Fisher," Sheriff Jeremy Richards greeted her. He was around Shelby's age, with dark blond hair and brown eyes. At a little more than six and a half feet tall, Sheriff Richards cut an imposing figure in his uniform of dark brown pants and khaki shirt. He had been Charlie's second-in-command, and the obvious choice to succeed him. He shook her hand and gestured to the open interior door. "Let's go into my office."

"Call me Shelby." She followed him through the door. "Ms. Fisher makes me feel like a school teacher, or somethin'."

"All right, then. Have a seat, Shelby. How's your partner feeling?"

"Rebecca was a mite sick this morning, but she was feeling better when I left for town." She dropped into one of the visitor's chairs across from him. "Thanks for asking. Speaking of which, has that mare showed any more signs of rabies?"

Jeremy leaned back in his chair. "Ron called me this morning. The filly and the gray still seem healthy but the chestnut has begun to show signs of deterioration. We still don't know for sure."

"Damn it!" Shelby slapped her thigh. "Any luck on finding the owner?"

"No. I can't find a brand on file that matches the description on them, and no one in the state has reported them missing. In two weeks I can put them up for public auction, if you're interested."

Shelby stood. "What about the chestnut? You can't auction a diseased horse. Can we go ahead and have it destroyed, so we can test it for rabies?"

"We can't destroy the mare until we're certain she's terminal. It would open the county up to a lawsuit, if the rightful owner came forward. I'm sorry, Shelby. But until the vet tells me that there's no hope for her, my hands are tied."

"That's complete bullshit, Sheriff! How long will Rebecca have to worry?" Shelby placed her hands on the edge of his desk and leaned across it. "Are you going to wait until the fucking horse falls dead?"

Jeremy pushed his chair back and got to his feet. "Calm down."

Shelby had to tilt her head back to an uncomfortable degree to look into his eyes, but she was too angry to be afraid. "Don't fucking tell me to calm down! My partner is at home right now, sick, because of having to start the damned rabies vaccine. She cries herself to sleep at night, worried that she's going to die."

Tears burned her eyes and Shelby's demeanor changed. "Please, Sheriff. I'll do whatever it takes." She softened her voice. "What if the horse got loose? Disappeared? The county wouldn't be liable then."

He shook his head. "I can't authorize that, Shelby."

"Sheriff—"

"Wait." Jeremy rubbed his face and glanced at the open door. He walked around the desk and closed it then stood beside Shelby. "Look. I know you're a good friend of Lex's. Hell, we went to school together and she's like a sister to me. The thought of her going through those blasted shots so soon after she got out of the hospital worries me."

He sat on one guest chair and gestured to the other.

Shelby took a deep breath and released it before she sat on the edge of the chair. "Yeah. I don't even want to know how freaked Amanda is about all of this. She's more protective than a mama bear."

"No kidding. She's a fireball, that's for sure."

"Ha. That's puttin' it mildly."

Jeremy laughed along with her before sobering. "So, if that mare just happened to get worse, then the vet would put it out of its misery. Not that I'm advocating anything, mind you. Just having a conversation."

Shelby gave him a curt nod. "Right."

She slapped her hands down on her legs and got to her feet. "Thank you for takin' the time to see me, Sheriff. I appreciate it."

He shook her hand. "Anytime. Give me a call if you need me."

"Yeah. I'll do that."

THE SLIGHT DIP of the mattress woke Lex. She rolled onto her side and looked into the eyes of her wife. "Hey."

"Hey, yourself." Amanda mirrored her pose. "How are you feeling?"

Lex considered the question seriously before she answered. "Better, I think. What time is it?"

"A little after six."

"Wow. Guess I was more tired than I thought." Lex realized the house was quiet. Too quiet. "Where are the kids?"

"The girls went to town with Martha and Charlie to see a movie. Eddie was exhausted from his visit at Jeannie's and is sacked out in his room. He'll probably wake up at midnight, ready to play, but I didn't have the heart to keep him up."

Amanda brushed her fingertips along Lex's cheek. "You're hot."

Lex weakly grinned. "Nice of you to notice." Her grin faded as the light touch turned into a caress. "Mmm."

"I need to get you something for the fever, honey." But Amanda didn't seem in any hurry to move.

Lex's hedonistic moment was interrupted by the phone. "Figures." She rolled away from Amanda and picked up the phone. "Walters. Yeah, Ron."

She sat up and swung her legs off the bed. "Really? When?" She felt Amanda sit behind her and touch her back. "All right. Let me know as soon as you hear, okay? Yeah, I know. Thanks."

She hung up the phone and turned to her wife.

"Ron?"

"Yep. He went out to check on the chestnut mare and found her lying in her stall."

Amanda felt a moment of sadness for the loss of life, but then focused on the bigger picture. "And?"

Lex rubbed her face and exhaled slowly. "He's on the way to the testing lab in Austin, with the uh, specimen."

"It's getting late. Wouldn't it be better for him to go in the morning?"

"Remember who we're talking about here, sweetheart. Ron has

never been one to wait around."

Amanda leaned against her. "That's true. Especially when family's involved." She kissed below Lex's ear. "Hopefully we can find out something before y'all have to get another round of shots."

The warm tickle that ran down her spine had nothing to do with fever, and everything to do with the woman draped against her. Lex tried to focus on the conversation. "Um, huh?"

"How about," Amanda reached around Lex and unbuttoned her shirt, "we get this off you?" She placed another light kiss, this time on her wife's back. "And get you ready for bed?"

"Wait, what?"

Amanda laughed at her. "After you're ready for bed, I'll run down and grab you something to eat." She climbed off the bed and gently pushed Lex backward, until she was lying down. "Soup, or sandwich?"

Lex glared at her as she was tucked under the covers. "Sandwich, I guess."

"Peanut butter and jelly?"

The glare was replaced by a childlike smile. "With milk?"

"Of course." Amanda adjusted the blanket and kissed Lex on the forehead. "Be right back."

"THANKS, AMANDA. I appreciate you calling."

Shelby closed her cell phone and tucked it in the back pocket of her jeans. She scratched Patches' nose. "Looks like we'll find out one way or another by tomorrow. Have a good night, girl."

She left the barn and made her way across the yard. At the base of the steps, she turned and looked out across the acreage she and Rebecca owned. It was ten acres of mostly hills and trees, with less than two acres of flat land suitable for grazing. Shelby felt a deep pride at the improvements she and Rebecca had made through the years. "The best is yet to come, I reckon." She dusted off her jeans and went inside.

Rebecca turned and looked over the edge of the couch when her partner came into the living room. "How are the horses?"

"They're fine, darlin'." Shelby sat next to her and put her arm around Rebecca. "Patches said she misses you, but understands."

"Ha. You've spoiled her more than I have." Rebecca snuggled into her embrace. "I'm feeling better. But tomorrow I have to get the next shot, which will probably make me sick again."

Shelby hugged her. "Well, maybe not. I got a call from Amanda while I was in the barn. She wanted us to know that Ron found the chestnut mare dead this afternoon."

"Oh, no. That's horrible. Did he have any idea what caused it?"

"No. He ran a few tests, but then decided to load up the specimen and head for Austin."

Rebecca rubbed her hand on Shelby's stomach. "You don't have to sugar-coat it for me, hon. I know what they have to do to test for rabies." She sighed and rested her head against her lover. "I feel bad for the filly, though."

"She was gettin' close to weaning age, anyhow. And the vet had the chestnut quarantined, so they were already separated. So, hopefully we'll hear something before your doctor's appointment tomorrow afternoon."

"Maybe." Rebecca sniffled and tried not to cry. "I'm scared. If the horse died, it probably died from rabies. I don't know if I can go through being sick for the rest of the month, Shelby."

"Hey, now. We don't know nothin' yet. Let's try to keep a positive attitude, all right? By this time tomorrow, we'll have an answer. Whatever it is, we'll handle it."

Rebecca nodded. "Thanks, honey." She settled more comfortably in Shelby's arms. "I love you."

Shelby kissed the side of her head. "Love you too, darlin'."

Chapter Twenty-two

AMANDA WATCHED LEX'S hands clench the steering wheel until her knuckles were white. Her wife hadn't said more than three words since they had gotten Ron's call, asking them to come to his office. He had told them that he couldn't get away, but was supposed to hear from the state lab before three o'clock. He also had a few forms for Rebecca, Shelby and Lex to sign after the notification. "Honey?"

Lex blinked and glanced at her. "Hmm?"

"What's going through your mind?"

"Lots of things, I guess."

Wanting more of an answer than that, Amanda waited. At her wife's heavy sigh, she reached across the seat and lightly gripped Lex's arm.

"I'm worried about what Ron will find out. Odds are, the horse had been infected with rabies. And I really don't want to go through a whole month of those damned shots."

Lex turned to Amanda. "Kinda childish when I say it out loud. Especially since poor Rebecca has to worry about the bite she got *and* the shots."

"I don't think it's childish at all. Because I'm as worried about the results as you are." Amanda squeezed her arm. "I'm scared that the shots will screw with your immune system and put you back in the hospital. And I don't think I can handle that again."

Lex blew out a heavy breath. "Yeah, that sucked. And I'm lucky enough not to remember a lot of it." She took Amanda's hand. "I'm sorry you had to go through all of that, sweetheart."

"Me, too." They turned onto the street where the vet's office was located. "Looks like Shelby beat us here."

"Yep." Lex parked beside the older truck. "It's about a quarter 'til. Think he's got the results?"

Amanda got out of the truck and waited for Lex to do the same. "I hope so. Your appointment at Rodney's is at four."

SHELBY PACED THE small waiting room as Rebecca sat quietly and thumbed through an equine magazine.

The main door opened and Amanda walked in, followed by Lex. Amanda sat beside Rebecca and nudged her with her shoulder. "Hi."

Rebecca put the magazine down and gave her a forced smile. "Hi." She watched as Lex crossed to the other side of the room to speak to Shelby. "How's Lex feeling?"

"Anxious." Amanda leaned closer and softened her voice. "Scared,

I think. But you know we'll never hear it out loud."

"No kidding. Shelby's worse, if you can believe that." Rebecca giggled, which caused her partner to turn and look at her.

Lex tipped her head toward their significant others. "Bet they're talking about us."

"Oh, yeah." Shelby crossed her arms and stuck her tongue out at Rebecca, who laughed even louder. "Those two are dangerous together, Lex."

"Tell me about it."

The interior door opened and Ron appeared. "Hey, guys. Why don't all of you come back here?"

Trading looks amongst themselves, the four women followed him to an office, where Ron directed them to guest chairs. He sat on the edge of the desk and watched as Lex and Shelby held the two chairs for Amanda and Rebecca. "I really appreciate y'all coming by. Doctor Hernandez is out of town and I couldn't leave the office unattended."

"We most likely had to come into town, anyway," Lex answered for all of them. She had her hands on Amanda's shoulders while Shelby stood to one side of Rebecca's chair. "Unless you say differently."

Ron chuckled and crossed his arms. "Always right to the point, huh?"

"Some of us are," Lex chided him.

"All right, all right." His grin grew wider as he looked at her. "The chestnut did not have rabies."

Shelby paled. "What?"

Ron took a paper off the desk and handed it to her. "Here's the fax. Just the fax." When the other three groaned, he winked at Lex. "I've always wanted to say that."

"What does it say?" Rebecca asked Shelby.

"Tetanus," Ron answered for her. "I feel like an idiot. I should have thought of that, instead of jumping to conclusions."

Lex accepted the paper from Shelby and glanced at it. "The signs are very similar, Ron. And I'm the one that thought the wound was caused by an animal bite."

Shelby took the paper back from Lex and passed it to the vet. "A horse can die from tetanus, right?"

"Yes. I probably should have done a full autopsy after I found her, but I was in a hurry to test for rabies." He looked into her eyes. "But now that I know what it was, I'm surprised she succumbed so quickly."

Shelby tucked her hands into the back pocket of her jeans and met his gaze. "Yeah, I think everyone was surprised. It's a shame. Still, at least she's no longer suffering."

She gave him a slight nod before turning to her partner. "I guess I'd better get you back to work, darlin'."

Ron was almost certain what had happened to the chestnut, but since he'd had the body destroyed, he had no proof. "Let me get your signatures on an acknowledgment form and I'll let y'all go."

AMANDA SWUNG THEIR linked hands as they left the veterinary building. "I wonder what that was all about."

"Hmm?" Lex opened Amanda's door for her and helped her into the truck. "Oh. That little look between Shelby and Ron?" She hurried around and got in behind the wheel. "I have a pretty good idea."

"Do you plan on sharing, or just tormenting me with it?" Amanda asked as Lex backed out of the parking space.

Lex began to whistle until Amanda poked her in the ribs. "Hey, watch it. I'm trying to drive, here."

"More like trying my patience." Amanda thought about the exchange between the ex-rodeo rider and the veterinarian. "Oh, my God. Do you think that Ron believes Shelby had something to do with the horse's death?"

"What makes you say that?"

The truck slowed as it turned onto a residential street toward Anna Leigh's home. "You have to admit, the timing's right. Ron had told us the evening before that there had been no change in her condition, and then, all of a sudden, she's dead the next morning."

"Yep. He even mentioned that as the rate she was going, we'd probably have to take all the shots before we knew for sure." Lex parked on the street in front of the Cauble house, since there was a moving van in the driveway. "Is she moving today?"

"Who even knows, anymore? Ever since Daddy pissed her off by hovering, she's done what she's wanted to do without telling us about it. Not that I've been paying attention. My mind's been on more important things, lately."

Amanda started to open her door, but the look she received from Lex stopped her. After Lex helped her out of the truck, Amanda linked their arms. "You never answered me. Do you think Shelby killed that horse?"

Lex stopped and turned to look at her. "Truthfully? I wouldn't blame her if she did. If, God forbid, a stray horse bit you and then showed signs of rabies, I would have probably killed it on the spot."

"Come on, Lex. I know how much you love horses. I find it hard to believe you'd kill one."

"I do love horses." Lex rested her arms on Amanda's shoulders and looked into her eyes. "But I love you, more. And you, and our kids, mean more to me than anyone or anything else." She lowered her head and gently kissed her.

"Good grief! Don't you two ever stop?" Jeannie called from the front porch.

Lex put her arm around Amanda's waist as they walked toward her. "Of course not." When they were on the porch, she released

Amanda and kissed Jeannie on the cheek. "Is that better?"

Jeannie tried to shove her, but Lex didn't budge. "My God, you're a pain in the ass. Mandy, how do you stand her?"

"Labor of love." Amanda tugged Lex away by a belt loop. "Is Gramma inside?"

"Last time I saw her, she was upstairs showing the movers what order she wanted stuff taken and put on the truck." Jeannie followed them into the house. "Wait for me!"

ANNA LEIGH STOOD outside the master bedroom door. "I believe this room should be first, since it has the largest pieces. The northeast bedroom has the furniture for the guest room at the condominium and between the two there are less than a dozen boxes."

A male voice came from the bedroom. "Thank you, Mrs. Cauble. We'll take very good care of these things for you."

"Thank you, Mr. Wills."

Anna Leigh heard footsteps on the stairs and turned to see Amanda and Lex. "Hello, girls."

"Is there anything else you need from me, Mr. Wills?" she asked the mover.

"No, ma'am. We'll holler if we have any questions."

She nodded and returned her attention to Amanda and Lex. "To what do I owe this pleasure?"

Amanda put her arm around Lex. "We were in the neighborhood and thought we'd see how you were doing. Oh, and we found out that Lex won't have to have any more rabies shots."

"That's wonderful!" Anna Leigh hugged Lex and kissed Amanda's cheek. "I'm so happy for you, Lexington."

"Thanks, Gramma." Lex gestured to the bedroom. "I thought Dad said you were moving on Saturday?"

Anna Leigh let out an unladylike snort. "On the contrary. That's what Michael decided. He wanted to rent a truck and have the family move my things. As if everyone doesn't have better things to do. I, on the other hand, have made my own plans."

"Well, I'm sure I could have asked the ranch hands. I know the spring craft fair and barbecue is this weekend, so they'd be in town, anyway."

"No, Lexington. As much as I'd appreciate their assistance, I'm quite capable of hiring professional movers. These gentlemen come highly recommended. They've gotten most of the furniture from downstairs already loaded. At least the pieces I'm taking. Jeannie has offered to take care of everything else."

Amanda felt Lex inhale to argue, and she quickly jumped in. "That's wonderful, Gramma. You could be settled into your new place sooner. Smart."

Lex turned to her wife. "Yeah, smart."

"You girls are adorable. Are you able to stay for a few minutes? I have iced tea downstairs."

They followed her to the kitchen, where Anna Leigh took two blue disposable cups from a paper grocery bag. "I'm afraid all the tea glasses are already packed, but these should do."

Lex took them from her and filled them with ice. "They're fine, Gramma."

Jeannie came through the back door. "What happened to everything in the storage building?"

"I rented a storage space near my condominium. I assumed your family would need all the extra storage, dear." Anna Leigh sat between Lex and Amanda at the kitchen table. "The movers took care of that yesterday."

Jeannie refilled her cup and joined them. "Well, okay. But we could have handled that a little at a time and saved you some money, Gramma. I feel like we're kicking you out of your home."

"Nonsense. This was my idea, remember? But I'm glad you've decided to wait two weeks before moving. That gives me ample time to hire someone to do a thorough cleaning."

It was an old argument that Jeannie would never be able to win. "Gramma, I keep telling you that's unnecessary." She stretched her arms out. "I mean, look at this place. Even in the middle of packing and moving, I bet I won't find a speck of dust anywhere. It's ridiculous."

"You should just say thank you," Amanda added. "I've seen how you keep house, Jeannie. It will probably be the cleanest this house will be after Gramma leaves."

"I'm going to kick your a—"

"Jeanne Louise! Don't you dare," Anna Leigh warned.

Lex's laughter turned into a pained groan, when a sharp kick from Jeannie hit her shin.

When Amanda started to stand, Lex put a hand on her shoulder. "Down, girl." Once she was sure her wife wasn't going to climb across the table, she turned to Anna Leigh. "Gramma, are you absolutely sure this is what you want to do? Because we'd love to have you out at the ranch."

Anna Leigh patted her arm. "Yes, Lexington. I truly appreciate the offer but I must do this. The truth is, Jacob and I had spoken about him retiring from his woodworking. We had discussed downsizing so that we could enjoy one another's company without having to spend so much time maintaining this old house." She shook her head. "Perhaps if we had done so, sooner..."

Everyone at the table was respectfully silent as the older woman struggled with her emotions. Amanda and Jeannie stood at the same time and gathered their grandmother into a loving embrace.

LEX QUIETLY LEFT the table and stepped through the back door to give them privacy. She opened the door to the shop and went inside. The click of the light switch sounded loud, and she soon discovered why.

The room was completely empty, except for the remaining heavy-duty steel shelves along the far wall and the clean workbench nearby. The floor had been painted gray to cover the old varnish stains. "Wow," she said.

All of Jacob's tools and projects were gone. A cheery yellow paint covered the walls, leaving behind a clean smell that hid the odor of years of work. Lex felt her eyes burn. There was no sign of the man who had spent so much time here and she felt the loss hit her in the chest. "I'm sorry, Grandpa Jake." She rubbed her face and cleared her throat. "We'll do our best for her, I promise you." She shook her head. "At least as much as she'll let us."

ELLIE TOOK HER car keys out of the desk drawer and tucked them in her pocket. She walked down the tiled hallway and peeked into the doctor's office. "Is there anything else you need me to do, Dr. Crews?"

Rodney looked up from his paperwork. "Just the same thing I've always needed, Ellie." He put his pen down. "Your cousin is married to my sister-in-law, which makes us family. Please, call me Rodney."

"Sorry. It's a habit. I have no problem away from the office, but here, it's different."

He laughed and shuffled the papers on his desk. "All right. I guess that will have to do. And, no, I don't need anything else. Have a good night, Ellie."

"You, too." Ellie passed through the waiting room and locked the office door behind her. She was halfway to her car when she heard a voice behind her.

"Hey, baby. You doin' anything tonight?"

Ellie spun around. "Wha—"

Kyle, hands on her hips, was laughing. "You should have seen your face!"

"I swear, Kyle. One of these days, you're going to get it." Ellie turned away and continued toward her car.

"Ellie, wait!" Kyle jogged after her. "Come on, baby. I was just playing." When her partner quickly spun, held out her arms and screamed, Kyle stumbled backward and fell on her rear. "Shit!"

Ellie stood above her and laughed. "Not so funny when it's you, is it?"

"Well, actually, it is." Kyle got to her feet and brushed off her jeans. "I nearly pissed myself, you wicked woman." She put her arms around Ellie and kissed the tip of her nose. "Hey, wanna go to the junkyard with me?"

"Wow, such a romantic idea. I don't know if I could handle all that excitement."

Kyle took her hands and knelt on one knee. "Please, baby. Help me find a junker. We're going to raffle off tickets for people to destroy it. I'll make it worth your time."

Rodney happened into the parking lot at that very moment. "Oh! Um, excuse me. I didn't mean to interrupt."

Ellie looked down at her lover, who had a panicked look on her face. "Don't worry, Doctor... I mean, Rodney. Kyle was just trying to talk me into an exciting trip to the junkyard." She tugged on Kyle's hands. "Get up, loon."

Kyle stood and looped her arm around Ellie's waist. "Yeah, doc. My girl seems to think it won't be any fun. But, I ask you. Is there anything more interesting than finding just the right junker for the fair this weekend? The kids love paying to beat the hell out of something, and it's always one of the highest earners."

Now that his embarrassment had cooled, Rodney decided to play along. "Well, sure. I was just telling Jeannie the other day that we should take a trip out there for our anniversary."

He waved to them as he started toward his car. "Try not to have too much fun, ladies."

"I can't believe he thought that you were proposing to me. I'll never hear the end of this." Ellie tried to keep a low profile at work, as she did in everything. During the past year, Kyle had slowly pulled her from the self-imposed exile she had kept. But, at times Ellie felt her old fears come back to haunt her. She could almost hear her mother's voice, telling her that nice, Christian women never drew attention to themselves.

Kyle watched the emotions cross Ellie's face. "Would that be so bad, El?" At the confused look she received, she embraced Ellie. "Would it be so bad, to be committed to me? For me to be committed to you?"

"I...I thought we were." Ellie began to panic. "I mean, I never even thought about anyone else but you. Are you saying that you, umm —"

"No!" Kyle began to kiss Ellie's face lightly. "No, baby. You're it for me. I haven't even looked at another woman since before we got together, I swear."

Ellie relaxed in her arms and lowered her head to Kyle's chest. "Don't scare me like that."

"Sorry, El." Kyle released her and dropped to one knee again and held out her arms. "So, what about it? Want to make an honest woman out of me?"

"Are you serious?"

"Sure. Come on, Ellie. Let's get hitched. I know it won't be legal, but we can have a ceremony, maybe invite that crazy cousin of yours and the rest of the gang." Kyle stood and looked into Ellie's eyes. "Neither one of us are the hearts and flowers type, but I'd really like to put a ring on your finger so that everyone knows you're taken."

"Would..." Ellie lowered her eyes. "Would you wear a ring, too?"

"Damned right I would!" Kyle lifted Ellie off the ground and began to twirl in a circle. "Does that mean yes?"

Ellie laughed and put her arms around Kyle's neck to keep from falling. "Can we send my mother an invitation?"

"Baby, if it would make you happy, I'd take out a full-page ad in her hometown newspaper. C'mon, El. I'll find a car to destroy tomorrow. Let's go look at some rings."

"Why not?" Ellie kissed her and felt her feet touch the ground. "I love you."

Kyle returned the kiss. "I love you, too."

SEVERAL HOME DECORATING magazines, bookmarked with bright, yellow tabs of paper, covered the coffee table and sofa in the living room. Jeannie picked up one and flipped it open. She held it out to Amanda. "See? Don't you think this color would look good in the kitchen? Gramma picked it out."

"Really? Our grandmother chose—" Amanda squinted at the photo. "Lavender? For the kitchen walls?"

"Well, maybe not this exact shade," Jeannie admitted. "But, honestly. That kitchen has been plain old yellow for as long as we've been alive, Mandy. And with the white-washed oak cabinets, it's so eighties."

Amanda handed her the magazine. "What did Gramma say, exactly? Maybe I should go to the kitchen and ask her."

"If you're brave enough to be in there when she gets off the phone with Daddy, be my guest. I swear, I don't understand his problem." Jeannie sat on the edge of the sofa and flicked imaginary dust off her jeans.

"He's worried about her making a rash decision that she'll regret later."

After she gathered the magazines off the couch, Amanda stacked them on the table with the others and sat on the center cushion. "Doesn't it worry you, too?"

Jeannie slid off the arm and onto the couch. "Of course it does. That's why we're not going to sell our house, at least not right away. We wanted to pay Gramma market value for this one, but she said it had been paid for long ago, and between their retirement and insurance, she doesn't need our money." She bumped shoulders with her sister. "She made us promise to use our money to update this house."

"It's kind of hard to argue with her, isn't it?" Amanda bumped Jeannie back and leaned against her. "I just worry about her."

"I know, hon. Rodney and I do, too. He talked to some of the people in her new neighborhood. Two of her neighbors go to her church, and another is on the Ladies Auxiliary. They've been trying to recruit her for years."

Amanda laughed. "You make it sound so sinister. She's always been too busy with other things."

She sobered as she thought about those things, and how the most important reason for their grandmother not joining was no longer with her. "Maybe it's a good idea, after all."

OUT IN THE shop, Lex reached for the light switch, but was stopped by a cool hand on her own. She turned toward Anna Leigh. "Oh. Hi, Gramma. I was just, um, seeing if I needed to do anything in here."

Anna Leigh walked into the empty space as if she hadn't heard her. She stopped in the middle of the room and stared at the floor. "What do you think, Lexington? Have I lost my senses?"

Lex followed and stood beside her. She considered the question. "I believe, given the circumstances, you've held up incredibly well. As a matter of fact, I honestly don't think I could ever be as strong as you."

"Strong?" Anna Leigh shook her head and tried to hold back her grief. "I'm doing everything in my power to run from the memories." She crossed her arms and closed her eyes. "Even now, in this clean, repainted room, I can still smell his aftershave. And it tears me apart."

"I'm so very sorry, Gramma. I can't even begin to imagine your pain." Lex moved to hold Anna Leigh in her arms. "But I'll do whatever I can to help you through it."

Anna Leigh allowed herself to accept the strength of someone else. She tried so hard to be strong for her family, and it was a welcome relief to give up that control. She melted into the strong embrace and cried, pouring out her pain and anguish. Before she knew it, she and Lex were on the floor, holding onto one another in the space where she felt her life had ended.

LEX HELD ONTO Anna Leigh as if both their lives depended on it. She felt tears burn her eyes but held them back, determined to be strong. Had their situation been reversed, Lex knew beyond the shadow of a doubt that she wouldn't have handled losing her partner as well as this petite, soft-spoken woman had, and it scared her.

"I couldn't have survived," she mused softly.

"You'd be surprised at what you can do." Anna Leigh wiped her face with the back of her hand. "I went to bed that night, praying that I wouldn't wake the next morning. But when I did, I realized that I had to go on, no matter how horrible it was."

She accepted the handkerchief Lex offered. "Thank you."

Lex stood and helped the older woman to her feet. "Are you having second thoughts about moving?"

"Not at all. But I'm terribly tired of fielding the same arguments from everyone, especially Michael. I wanted to reach through the phone and throttle him." Anna Leigh patted Lex on the cheek. "Thank you for this, Lexington. You truly are a gift to our family."

Unable to hide her blush, Lex tried to shrug off the compliment. "Thanks. Um, would you like me to talk to him?" She winked. "Or maybe break his legs?"

Anna Leigh laughed and looped her arm with Lex's. "While both options are attractive, I'll handle my son, dearest. But thank you for asking. Now, I had better make certain Jeannie doesn't distract the movers. I'd like to be at my new home before dark."

THE TWO-BEDROOM CONDOMINIUM had all its furniture, as well as stacks of boxes, in every room. Amanda carried two plastic cups of iced tea around a tower of boxes and almost tripped over her sister, who was on her knees. Some of the tea sloshed from one of the glasses.

"Jeannie, what are you doing down there?"

"Waiting for you to pour tea on me, of course," Jeannie snapped, wiping the moisture from her face.

"Jeannie."

"Oh, all right." Jeannie got up and dusted the knees of her jeans. "I was trying to see what was beneath this carpet. I think Gramma would appreciate hardwood floors."

"You're something else. Has Gramma said anything about the floor?"

"Well, no. But—"

"Just stop. You've got enough to do with your two houses, Jeanne Louise. Leave poor Gramma alone. Have you seen Lex?"

Jeannie rolled her eyes. "Not since I caught you two making out in the truck while the rest of us were inside waiting for you." She pantomimed sticking her finger down her throat and made a gagging sound.

"I hardly call giving my wife a kiss making out. Jealous?" Amanda handed Jeannie one of the cups. "Here, maybe this will cool you off."

"Thanks."

Amanda tipped her cup at her sister before she continued her trek through the condo. She took in the open floor plan and the taupe-colored walls and tried to picture her grandmother spending the rest of her life here. Even with the familiar furniture, it was difficult. She moved from the living area to the kitchen, where she saw the heavy oak door open, but the exterior screen door closed. She glanced through the screen and saw her wife seated on the top step of the small, covered porch. Lex had her elbows resting on her knees and looked totally exhausted. Amanda slowly stepped outside and touched the top of

Lex's head. "Hey."

Lex looked up. "Hey. How's it going in there?" She took the offered cup of tea and drank half of it before setting it on the step by her feet. "Thanks."

Amanda sat beside her. "Gramma already has her bed made and the majority of her bathroom in order. I feel pretty useless."

"You're anything but that, sweetheart." Lex rested her arm across Amanda's shoulders. "I offered to unpack the kitchen and she sent me out here."

"Well, you do look pretty wiped. Maybe we should head home for the day."

Lex checked her watch. "Might as well. I'm sure your dad and Lois will be here before too long. This place isn't big enough for all of us. It's too late to cook dinner, but we could grab a couple pizzas on the way home."

"Sounds good." Amanda rested her head against Lex and closed her eyes. "It's been a hell of a long week."

"Yep."

The screen door opened. "There you are. Gramma said—" Jeannie stopped. "Are you guys all right?"

Amanda stood and turned to face her. "Not really. I think we're going to tell Gramma goodnight and head home." She pulled Lex up. "What were you saying?"

"Oh, um, yeah. Gramma wanted me send you home. She said, and I quote, 'Lexington needs her rest.' And I gotta agree, Slim. You've looked better."

Lex put her hands on her hips and glared at her. "What do you mean, I've looked better? There isn't anything wrong with me." She turned her stare to Amanda, who had swatted her lightly on the rear. "What?"

"In the past few months, you've fractured your arm, been in the hospital and then sick from a damned rabies shot. So, yes. We're going home, and you're going to bed."

Jeannie covered her mouth to keep from laughing at the indignant look on Lex's face. When Lex looked at her, she couldn't help but giggle. "She's got your number."

Lex climbed the steps and looked down on her sister-in-law. "Oh, yeah?"

"Yeah." Jeannie crooked her finger so that Lex would lean closer. When she did, Jeannie licked her cheek.

"Yuck!" Lex wiped at her face as, behind her, Amanda laughed so hard that she ended up sitting in the grass. "That was disgusting!"

Jeannie tapped Lex on the nose and headed back inside. "Teach you to mess with me."

As Amanda continued to laugh, Lex started up the steps.

"Hey, wait," Amanda called between giggles. "Lex!" She scrambled to her feet and jogged to catch up to her wife. "Aw, come on. You have to admit it was funny. She owed you one."

Lex held the door open for her. "Uh huh. Whatever you say." She stopped short to keep from bumping into Anna Leigh. "Oh, hi, Gramma. How long have you been standing here?"

The large smile on Anna Leigh's face was the perfect answer. "Well, at least you've already started the rabies vaccination, Lexington. That should protect you."

"Gramma!" Jeannie exclaimed.

Amanda hugged her grandmother. "We're going to head home. Give us a call if you need anything."

"I certainly will, dearest. Thank you." Anna Leigh kissed her cheek before holding her hand out to Lex. "And you, dear. Please get some rest."

Lex didn't argue about the politely framed order. "Yes, ma'am. I sure will."

She embraced Anna Leigh, holding on longer than usual. "I'll be back in town tomorrow. Would you like me to bring you lunch?"

"That would be lovely, thank you. Now, please. Run along. Michael will be here soon, and I want to have the guest room in order."

After Lex and Amanda left, Jeannie stood beside her grandmother. "Why are you worried about the guest room?"

"You know how your father is, dear. I'm certain he'll make a fuss and want to spend the night."

Jeannie laughed and nudged her. "Want me to short-sheet the bed?"

She enjoyed Anna Leigh's clear laughter and the arm around her shoulders.

Chapter Twenty-three

THE BACK PASSENGER door opened on the truck and Lex turned. "Hey, girls. How was school today?"

"Hi, Momma." Melanie kissed her cheek before settling in her usual spot. "We painted flower pots to sell at the craft fair. Mine has a sunflower on it."

"That's great. Be sure and show it to me on Saturday, so I can buy it." Lex waited until Lorrie closed the door and buckled her seatbelt. "How about you, Lorrie? Did you have a good day?"

"It was okay." Lorrie's glum expression changed into a smile. "Allie dared Trisha to shoot a pea out of her nose at lunch, but it got stuck."

Lex shook her head. "Is Trisha all right?"

"Yep. The nurse had to use tweezers to get it out. And now Allie has detention for a week." Lorrie rubbed beneath her nose and sniffled. "She's afraid she's going to be grounded when she gets home today. I hope not, because she was going to meet me at the craft fair so we could hang out."

Lex checked the traffic before driving away from the school. "What about Jerry?"

"He's not going. He told Allie it was dumb. Jerry is dumb, 'cause we always have a lot of fun."

Melanie had to add her two cents worth. "There's gonna be a petting zoo, with itty bitty horses. That's really cool."

"We see horses every day," Lorrie scoffed. "It's not that big a deal. Right, Momma?"

Lex shrugged. "Oh, I don't know. The miniature Shetlands are pretty cute."

Lorrie wouldn't be dissuaded. "I guess. But what good are they? You can't ride them, and they're too small to use."

"So what?" Melanie asked. "You can't ride Snow, and she doesn't do anything, either."

"Um, well." Lorrie frowned as she considered the argument. "She's for a project, Mel. That's different."

Melanie danced in her seat. "And the little ponies are for petting."

Lex had to cover her laugh with a cough.

Lorrie rolled her eyes, but seemed to concede. "Hey, Momma? How come you picked us up today? Not that it's not great," she added quickly.

"I dropped off the donated beef to the VFW so they could get it ready for the barbecue, and thought y'all might appreciate a day off from the bus."

"I like the bus. 'Specially if I get to sit on the back seat and bounce," Melanie said. "But I like riding with you more."

"Thanks."

When Lorrie sneezed, Lex grabbed a tissue from the console and handed it to her, never taking her eyes off the road. "Are you feeling okay, kiddo?"

Lorrie blew her nose. "Uh huh. Hey, Momma?"

"Yes?"

"Are we going straight home?"

"Can we get ice cream?" Melanie asked at the same time.

Lorrie gave her a dirty look and whispered something to her, which caused Melanie to grumble and reply just as softly.

Lex let them get it out of their system. She usually only jumped in when Lorrie was on the verge of losing her temper. "Sorry, girls. We need to head home. Maybe next time."

She'd had every intention of stopping, but Amanda had called and requested that they come directly home. "Ellie and Kyle are coming to the house, and they're bringing enough Chinese food to feed an army."

"With chopsticks?" Melanie asked.

"I don't know. Maybe." Lex checked the rear view mirror to see Lorrie's face. "How's that sound to you, Lorrie?"

"Will they stay long?" Lorrie asked. Seeing her mother's frown in the mirror, she added, "I want to show them Snow."

Lex nodded. "I'm sure they'd love to see her. Is she still trying to eat your pockets?"

Just thinking about the kid's playful habits made Lorrie giggle. "Not since you told me to leave her carrot bites in a bag. Now she looks behind me to see if I'm hiding them. Momma?"

"Hmm?"

"I just remembered something. I don't think I have enough feed to last until Saturday. Can we stop by the feed store?"

Lex usually drove into town on Saturday for supplies and Lorrie would get what she needed for Snow then.

"All right. That's a better idea, anyway. We'll be too busy on Saturday to do it. Good idea, kiddo."

Lorrie beamed at her. "Thanks, Momma."

BEFORE THE SECOND knock on the front door, Melanie scrambled through the house. "I'll get it," she yelled as she raced down the hall.

"Don't run," Lex warned from the living room. She sat on a quilt on the floor, stacking blocks with Eddie.

"Meemee, no go!" Eddie picked up a block and handed it to Lex. "Bok."

She stacked it with two others. "That's right, Eddie. Block."

Eddie giggled and knocked down the short tower. "Ha." He picked up another block and gave it to Lex. "Bok."

Melanie led Kyle into the room as Ellie was escorted to the kitchen by Amanda. "Look, Momma. Kyle's here."

"Hey, guys." Kyle walked in with Melanie and sat beside Eddie. "Hey, buddy. What are you doing?"

He picked out a block and handed it to her. "Bok."

As Kyle reached for the item, the light glinted on the ring finger of her left hand.

Lex caught her hand to study it. "Well, what do we have here?" She tsked as she looked at the shiny, platinum band. "I'm guessing this jewelry is one of the reasons y'all decided to bring dinner tonight?"

"Yeah." Kyle pulled her hand back. "It was one of those spur-of-the-moment type things, Lex. And we're planning on having a ceremony, but—"

Lex stood and put her hands on her hips. "Stand up, Kyle." Her expression was impossible to read. "Mel, why don't you take your brother to the kitchen? We'll be right there."

Kyle got up. "Lex."

"You know, Ellie's not just my cousin. She's more like a sister to me." Lex stepped closer. "And during the past year, I've seen quite a change in her."

Standing her ground, Kyle looked up into Lex's face. "I hope so, because she's made a big change in me, too."

"She has?"

"I love her, you know. More than I ever thought I could love anyone." Kyle stood as straight as possible and kept her hands at her sides. "So, go ahead. Do what you want."

As Lex swooped in and wrapped her arms around her, Kyle squeaked.

"Welcome to the family, Kyle. We've thought of you that way for a while, now. So it's nice to see you finally coming to your senses." Lex moved back and lightly swatted Kyle on the arm. "So, have y'all set a date for the ceremony?"

Kyle rubbed her upper arm and followed Lex to the kitchen. "Not yet."

"I'M GLAD YOU called, Ellie." Amanda took one of the bags from Ellie and placed it on the kitchen counter. "But you didn't have to bring dinner."

Ellie put her bag next to Amanda's and began removing containers. "It was Kyle's idea. She knows how much the kids love it."

"We all do." Amanda stopped what she was doing. "You look different."

"I do?" Ellie fought to keep the blush off her face, but from the warmth flooding her cheeks, she hadn't been very successful. She smiled and rubbed at her face, the ring on her finger shining brightly.

"Ellie? Is that what I think it is?"

Ellie nodded and held out her hand. "We picked them up last night."

"Ooh." Amanda took her hand and nodded at the simple platinum band. "Very nice."

"Yeah, well, we both have jobs that aren't conducive to anything big and flashy, so we thought these would be better."

Amanda dragged her to the table and pushed her into a chair. "Tell me everything. Who asked? Where were you?"

"Um, well, Kyle met me after work and asked if I'd like to go with her to the junkyard."

"No way." Amanda giggled at the deepening blush. "Seriously?"

Ellie played with the ring. "She was on her knee, begging. It was really funny, until Rodney came out of the office and saw her. After we explained what *wasn't* going on he went home, but—"

"Mommy, Momma said we were supposed to come help you," Melanie announced, as she led Eddie by the hand. "Her and Kyle was talking and sent us here."

Ellie exchanged worried looks with Amanda. "You don't think?"

"I don't know. Lex still surprises me sometimes. Mel, would you please run tell your sister it's time to eat?"

"Okey-doke."

Eddie toddled to Amanda. "Up." He was ignored until he added, "Pease?"

She put him on her lap. "That was very good, honey."

"Mmm." Eddie patted her leg. "Good."

Amanda turned to Ellie. "So, after Rodney left, what happened?"

"Oh, ah, I guess it got Kyle thinking along those lines, and she dropped back on her knee and proposed."

"Right there in the parking lot?"

Ellie started to laugh. "Crazy, I know. But it's really kind of perfect, for us. I mean, neither one of us are the mooshy, flowery type."

"Are you saying that I am?" Lex asked from the doorway. She came into the kitchen and kissed Ellie on the cheek. "Congratulations, cousin."

"Thanks, Lex." Ellie grinned shyly at her lover, who sat in the next chair and took her hand.

Amanda grabbed Lex's belt and tugged. "You have something against being mooshy?"

"No, ma'am, not at all."

"Moo." Eddie tried to add to the conversation. When everyone around him laughed, he said it again. "Moo!"

LONG AFTER THEIR company left and the children were tucked

into their beds for the night, Amanda snuggled against Lex in their bed. "That was really sweet of you to offer the ranch for their ceremony."

The only light in the room came from a night light in the bathroom which cast a soft glow across them.

"Well, I don't think that many churches in Somerville are open to a commitment ceremony." When Amanda draped her leg over Lex's, she tightened her hold on her. "I'm not going anywhere, sweetheart."

"Can't be too sure. You looked ready to bolt when Ellie asked you to give her away." Amanda giggled at her wife's indignant snort. "Don't bother trying to deny it."

Lex grumbled something unintelligible.

"Get over it."

"I think she did it just to see what I would say."

Amanda kissed her shoulder. "I think she did it because she loves you." The heavy sigh that answered confused her. "What's the matter?"

"Nothing. Hey!" A second poke to her ribs was all the encouragement Lex needed. "Do you think they're moving too fast?"

"Are you kidding?"

Lex shifted enough so she could look at Amanda, although the shadows made it difficult. "No. I think that Kyle is Ellie's first real relationship. Hell, for all we know, she's her first—"

Amanda covered Lex's mouth with her hand. "Don't even go there." She removed her hand and left a kiss in its place. "Honey, Ellie's a grown woman, and you know Kyle adores her. What more could you ask for?"

"I want Ellie to have what we have."

"What makes you think she doesn't?" Amanda propped her head on her hand so that she wouldn't get a crick in her neck. They were still so close that they were breathing the same air, and she found herself struggling not to get lost in Lex's eyes. "She looked pretty happy to me."

Lex softly traced her finger along Amanda's jawline. "I wish I would have had more time to talk with her before they left."

"You'll see her again Saturday at the craft fair. And, like they said, they're not as mushy as we are."

"I'm not mushy, or mooshy."

Amanda turned her head to kiss Lex's palm. "Of course not." At Lex's sharp intake of breath, she kissed it again. "You were saying?"

"Huh?" Lex rolled back and pulled Amanda with her. "Mooshy works for me."

Chapter Twenty-four

"WE'LL LEAVE IN about an hour," Lex told Lorrie, who was still buried beneath the covers on her bed.

Lorrie mumbled an acknowledgment, but didn't move.

"One hour," Lex reiterated before she walked through the bathroom to Melanie's room. She stopped and regarded the round lump under the polka-dotted comforter. "Melanie, it's time to get up."

"Mmm."

Lex sat next to the lump and gently shook it. "Sweetheart, if you want to go to the craft fair with me, you'll need to get up and get ready."

"Don't wanna go to school," Melanie whined. She rolled into a tighter ball away from Lex.

"I'm leaving in an hour. It's up to you whether you're with me." Lex gave the lump a gentle pat and left the room. She ambled down the hallway, gazing at the photographs that adorned the walls. Pictures of their children accounted for the majority, but there were some of her parents and grandparents, as well as candid shots of Michael, Lois, Anna Leigh and Jacob.

She touched the glass of one and a sad smile crossed her face. Jacob and her grandfather, Travis, were being chased from the kitchen by Martha after a holiday meal. All three were laughing and Lex remembered fondly how the two men kept getting in Martha's way as she tried to wash dishes.

"No!" Eddie cried from his room.

Lex sighed. "Wish me luck," she told the photos, before heading down the hall. Arriving at their son's room, she found Amanda in the rocker, wrestling with Eddie. "Need any help?"

Amanda stopped what she was doing. "Do you think you could get him to take this?" she asked, waving the medicine dropper.

"No!" Eddie swatted at the ibuprofen. "Uck!"

"What's wrong?" Lex took the dropper and squatted beside them.

"He's got the sniffles and is running a low grade fever."

Lex held out her hands and Eddie reached for her. "Why are you giving Mommy a hard time?"

"Uck, Momma." He made a face and shook his head. "Bad."

Amanda gave her one of her patented *see what I mean?* looks, but didn't say a word.

Lex rested Eddie on her knee. "Okay, buddy. Do you feel bad? Ucky?"

He whined and rubbed his eyes. "Momma."

"All right, then. This will make you feel better. Momma takes it when she doesn't feel good."

He looked up at her. "Bad."

"No, it's not bad. It's good." Lex made a show of tasting the medicine and barely kept a disgusted look off her face. "See?"

Amanda giggled but quickly covered her mouth when Lex's eyes turned toward hers.

Lex tried another tactic. "Don't you want to go to the craft fair? Sick little boys can't go."

Eddie shook his head. "No."

"All right. Guess you'll just have to feel bad." Lex stood and took Eddie to his bed. "I'm going to town with your sisters. Be a good boy while we're gone."

"Momma!" Eddie held onto the side rails of his toddler bed. He stomped his feet and looked to Amanda. "Mommy!"

Amanda stood beside Lex. "Do you want me to stay home with you, honey?"

"Mommy, good." Eddie fell back onto his rump and stuck out his lower lip. He looked at Amanda, then Lex. "Momma."

Lex held out her hands. "Come here, little man."

He reached for her. Once he was in the safety of Lex's arms, Eddie rubbed his face on her shirt and cried. "Momma, Momma."

"I know, son. It's going to be okay." Lex carried him to the rocker and sat. She rocked and hummed until his crying stopped and he was almost asleep. She quickly squirted the ibuprofen into his mouth as she continued to rock.

Eddie swallowed the liquid with minimal fuss. He tightened his grip on Lex and after a few minutes, nodded off.

"Maybe I should stay home," Lex whispered.

"No, you go ahead. I'll stay home with him this morning. If he's not feeling better by lunch, I'll call his pediatrician's service." Amanda took him from Lex and settled him in his bed. "How about the girls? Did you get them up?"

Lex followed her from the room. "I did what I could. You know that Mel could sleep through anything."

"True."

Lorrie stumbled from her room. She was dressed but her eyes were half-closed, and her hair stuck out from her head.

"Are we leaving?" She joined them at the top of the stairs and leaned into Lex.

"In a little while. I have to see to the horses, first." Lex placed her hand on Lorrie's shoulder. "You'll need to check on Snow before we leave."

"'Kay. I'll go to the barn with you."

Amanda tried to use her hands to tame Lorrie's hair. "I'll have breakfast ready when you get back, how's that?"

"Thanks, Mom." Lorrie stepped around Lex and opened the toddler gate. "Do you want me to help with the horses?"

"Sure." Lex waved to Amanda and followed Lorrie down the stairs.

ANNA LEIGH SIPPED her coffee as she took in her living room. The floral sofa, where she had spent so many hours snuggled with Jacob, didn't look right in the room. It fit along an empty wall, but the longer she stared at it, the more she noticed the frayed arms and sunken cushions. "I can't believe I actually brought that old thing with me."

The doorbell startled her, but she quickly recovered. She set her coffee on an end table before she crossed the room.

When she opened her door, she was tempted to slam it closed. "Michael. It's rather early, isn't it?"

He held his hands up. "I've already been reamed by my wife and both daughters. Can we call a truce?"

"Perhaps." Anna Leigh was still furious with her son. The night she moved, he had showed up after everyone else left, demanding to stay. She'd sent him home and hadn't spoken with him until now. "Do you plan to be civil?"

"Of course!" he snapped, before taking a deep breath to calm himself. "I'm sorry, Mom. Really. May I come in?"

Anna Leigh held the door open wider. "I have fresh coffee in the kitchen."

"Thanks." Michael stopped in the middle of the living room. "It looks nice, Mom."

She stood beside him and gestured to the sofa. "I must have been out of my mind to bring that old thing."

"Why? It's—" he paused and frowned. "Good grief, it looks like a herd of cats attacked it."

Anna Leigh burst into laughter. "That's certainly one way of looking at it."

"What happened to it? Did it fall off the moving truck?" Michael moved closer and ran his hand along one of the scruffy arms. "Maybe rolled down the street?"

"No. Apparently, it's looked this way for quite some time. I suppose the living room in the other house was large enough that we didn't notice."

Michael sat on the far cushion. "Has it always been this uncomfortable? I don't remember."

She joined him and shifted a few times. "I never noticed it, before. I'm certain it wasn't this lumpy when your father and I sat on it."

"Like you would have even noticed. It folds out into a bed, doesn't it?"

"Yes. Why?"

He shrugged. "Well, if you do plan on getting a new one, I could use this in my office. Just in case Lois makes good on her threat to kick me out of the house."

"Why on earth did she say that?"

"Probably because I was arguing with Jeannie at the time. I know I've been a complete ass through all of this, but I don't mean to be. I only want to help."

Anna Leigh touched his arm. "I know. But you must understand something. Although I depended on your father for many things, it wasn't because I had to. But because I wanted to. And there's no need for you to rush in and try to take his place. It's not only unnecessary, but horribly wrong."

"I realize that, Mom. Really. And I didn't come here this morning to start a fight, but to tell you that Lois and I are going out of town for a few days. Her Aunt Susan is in the hospital in Dallas, and she wants to be there for her. But you can reach me on my cell phone."

"Oh, dear. I'm terribly sorry to hear that. Please give my best to Lois. Is there anything I can do?"

He climbed off the sunken cushion and stood. "Not that I know of. But I'll check with Lois. Thanks. She's home packing, so we should hopefully be on the road in an hour."

Anna Leigh embraced her son, and allowed all the past hurts to fade. "Please keep me updated, dearest. I'll be at the VFW until around four, but should be home after that."

"I will." Michael kissed her cheek. "Save me a plate of barbecue?"

"Of course."

"YOU DIDN'T HAVE to drive me to work, Shelby. I know you've got things to do at home." Rebecca stared out her window at the passing scenery. "I'm sorry about taking the hours today. Especially since we had planned on spending the day together."

Shelby glanced at her before returning her attention to the road. "Darlin', I'm the last person who'd complain about workin' extra hours. Don't worry about it. Besides, you'll get off work at two. That's more than enough time for us to goof off at the craft fair."

"Still, you could be checking the fence right now, instead of driving me to work."

"Maybe I like spendin' the time with you. Ever think of that?"

Rebecca couldn't argue with that logic. "You win."

Shelby pushed Rebecca's purse closer to her. "Better write that one down. I don't win many."

"Smartass." After Shelby parked in front of the feed store, Rebecca reached across the seat and squeezed her arm. "Thanks for the ride."

"Anytime, beautiful. Call me if you get off earlier."

Rebecca got out of the truck. "I will. Love you."

"I love you too, darlin'." Shelby waited until Rebecca was inside before she drove away. She was curious about how the set up for the craft fair was going, so she changed her route.

As she came upon the town square, she saw a group of women carrying covered dishes into the VFW building. In the adjacent parking lot, several men stood around a huge iron grill on a trailer. The grill belched dark, mesquite-scented smoke.

"Wonder how many it'll take to cook everything? Probably all of 'em," she mused aloud.

Shelby slowed the truck and looked toward the grassy square, where the gazebo was decked out in bright green banners and with signs made by the high school students. Next to the gazebo, people had set up canopies for the craft booths.

"Well, what do we have here?" She parked as close as she could to the open area and got out of the truck. "That doesn't look straight," she yelled.

The person hammering the canopy stake into the ground dropped her hammer and turned. "Like you know what straight looks like," Lex snapped back. She laughed and held out her hand, which Shelby gripped and shook. "You here to be put to work?"

"Not hardly." Shelby tucked her hands in her back pockets. "How'd they wrangle you into this?"

Lex removed her baseball cap and wiped her forehead. "My wife volunteered me."

Lorrie arrived with a bottle of water. "Here, Momma. Oh, Mr. Page said when you're done, he wants you to meet him at the high school. Something about hauling more tables."

"Okay, thanks." Lex drank half the bottle before she set it on the ground by her feet. "So, Shelby. If you're not here to help, what brings you to town?"

"Rebecca has to work until around two. After that, I promised to take her to the craft fair, so I didn't see any sense in us having two vehicles in town. I'm almost finished checking my fence, so I should be done long before I need to be back in town."

Lorrie kicked at a clump of grass that had just begun to turn green. "You're lucky. There's nothing to do around here."

"I thought Allie was supposed to be coming," Lex asked. They had checked with Allie's mother, Wanda, who had decided not to ground her for the school prank.

"After lunch. If she gets all her chores done." Lorrie sighed. "I went to see if they needed any help in the kitchen, but Mrs. Sparks made me leave. She thought I was trying to steal cookies." She met Lex's gaze. "I wasn't, I swear."

Lex took off her leather gloves and rested her hand on Lorrie's shoulder. "I believe you, sweetheart. It's my fault. I used to swipe cookies from the party tables when I was your age. She got you confused with me."

"Oh." Lorrie giggled. "Did you get into trouble?"

"All the time."

Shelby stood by quietly, enjoying the interaction between the two. She could see how someone, especially a woman who had to be in her eighties, got the two mixed up. Lorrie was the spitting image of Lex, right down to the way she stood. But where Lex wore boots and western shirts, Lorrie dressed in sneakers and colorful girl's T-shirts.

"Hey, Lex. Do you think you could do without Lorrie for a while?" Shelby asked.

"I guess. Why?"

"I reckon two sets of eyes could check my fence a lot faster." Shelby turned to Lorrie. "That is, if you want to."

Lorrie's face brightened. "Really? Can I, Momma? Please?"

Lex rubbed her chin and appeared to think about it. "Well, I don't know. I've got three more canopies to set up, and you promised to help." She looked above Lorrie's head to Shelby, who covered her mouth with her hand to keep from laughing aloud. "What?"

"Nothin'."

"Uh huh." Lex put her hands on her hips. "All right. Just listen to Shelby, and do what she asks, okay?"

Lorrie enthusiastically nodded. "Yes, ma'am." She gave Lex a quick hug. "Thanks, Momma."

"Be good."

"I will."

Lex winked at her. "I was talking to Shelby."

"Smartass," Shelby muttered. "Come on, kid. We've got better things to do than goof off around here, unlike some people."

Lorrie appeared worried until she heard Lex laughing. "Okay. Bye, Momma."

WHEN SHE CROSSED the threshold into the house, Martha heard Eddie's cries. She headed toward the living room, where she found Amanda seated on the sofa, trying to calm him. "Gracious! What's the matter?"

"I thought maybe he was teething, but he keeps pulling at his ears."

Martha sat beside them and held out her hands. "Come here, sweetie."

Eddie slowed his crying and crawled into her lap.

"Poor little tyke. Have you called the doctor?"

Amanda leaned back and exhaled heavily. "I didn't even bother with the pediatrician, since it's the weekend. But Rodney called in something for him and Jeannie's bringing it out."

"You should have called me, I would have been glad to run in and get it for you." Martha held Eddie to her chest and hummed softly as she rocked back and forth.

"No, that's all right, Martha. Jeannie was coming out today, anyway. Teddy's spending the day with Rodney and she didn't feel like going to the craft fair by herself."

Martha's eyes lit up. "She's bringing Hunter?"

"Yes, Mada, you'll have another little one to spoil today." Amanda shook her head as Eddie quieted. "You've still got that magic."

When both girls were babies, Martha's magic would calm them when nothing else worked. "Melanie's upstairs cleaning her room before it's condemned. What's Charlie up to?"

"He's sacked out in front of the TV. I swear, men are more trouble than children, when they're bored."

Amanda heard a car in the driveway. "That's probably Jeannie. I'll run get her so she doesn't ring the doorbell."

She lightly brushed her hand across Eddie's hair before she left the room.

THE BLINDS WERE drawn and the curtain was closed, which kept the mid-morning sun from reaching the occupants of the queen-sized bed. Kyle, who was spooned behind Ellie, opened one eye and glanced at the alarm clock. "Crap."

"What?" Ellie mumbled, mostly asleep. She scooted back into her lover's warm body. "Mmm."

"Baby, it's almost eleven."

"Don't care."

Kyle moved Ellie's hair and kissed the back of her neck. "I thought you were looking forward to the craft fair."

"Rather stay in bed with you." Ellie rolled until she faced Kyle. "Oh, wait. The car smash. Do you have to be there?"

Now able to look into Ellie's eyes, Kyle kissed her on the lips. "Nope. I was in charge of getting the old heap. Someone else has to hand out the sledgehammers."

She stroked the soft skin along Ellie's back. "Of course, now we're both awake. I guess we might as well go to the fair, since there's nothing else to do."

"I can think of a lot better things to do." Ellie pushed Kyle onto her back and straddled her waist. "Can't you?"

"You know, now that you mention it, I can." Kyle rested her hands on Ellie's hips. Ellie was a very loving partner but she rarely initiated their lovemaking. Kyle was almost afraid to ask, but her curiosity begged for an answer. "You sure are frisky this morning."

Ellie paused and her face turned a deep shade of red. "I'm sorry, I didn't—"

"No, don't apologize." Kyle held her in place. "Believe me, sweetheart, I'm not complaining. Not at all." When Ellie's eyes filled with tears, Kyle tugged her down to lay across her body. "What's wrong?"

"You must think I've lost my mind." Ellie shifted so that she was lying beside Kyle, but put her head on her partner's chest. She took a deep breath and looked at her left hand, which lay on Kyle's bare stomach. "For the past year, I've been waiting for you to come to your senses and leave. But then you proposed."

She turned her head to stare into Kyle's face. Her voice was almost too soft to hear. "I never thought I'd find someone who loved me."

Kyle's heart ached at the tone in Ellie's voice. "Oh, baby."

"I know I'm no great beauty. Even my mother always said so."

"You're shittin' me, right?" Kyle asked, using her hand to raise Ellie's face so that she could see her eyes. "You're an incredibly beautiful woman, Eleanor Gordon." She gently kissed her. "I can't believe you looked past the grease under my fingernails and allowed me a chance to love you."

Ellie blinked away the tears and raised one of Kyle's hands to her cheek. "I love your hands. They're so strong, but I feel completely safe with them." She kissed Kyle's fingertips. "And with you."

"I'd never hurt you," Kyle whispered. She brought up her other hand and cupped Ellie's face. "I'd rather die than touch you in anger."

"That's why I know I'm safe." Ellie raised her head and kissed Kyle.

Chapter Twenty-five

A SUSTAINED RUMBLE, followed by excited barking caused Jeannie to raise her eyes to the ceiling. She and Amanda were in the living room, catching up. "Whose turn is it?" she asked.

"Mine, I think." Amanda glanced at Eddie, who slept peacefully on the loveseat.

"I'll watch him." Jeannie had been relieved of her son, Hunter, the moment she stepped inside the house. Martha had gleefully taken him to her home, in the pretense that he might disturb Eddie's rest.

As the noise continued, Amanda trudged up the stairs. She grimaced at the high-pitched bark that greeted her at the open toddler gate. "Freckles, stop."

The little dog dropped down so that her rear was in the air. She barked again, jumped one-hundred eighty degrees and pranced toward Melanie's room.

Melanie's door opened. "You can't catch me," Melanie shouted before she galloped toward Amanda, only to come to a screeching halt at her mother's glare. "Um, hi, Mommy."

"Here I come!" Teddy ran hard with Freckles right beside him. His eyes grew large as he stopped behind Melanie. "Mel started it."

Amanda held up one hand to forestall Melanie's argument. "I don't care who started it. We've told you several times to quit running and yelling in the house. It sounds like thunder downstairs."

"I'm sorry, Mommy." Melanie tried her best adorable smile. It quickly faded away when she didn't get the desired result.

"Either go outside to play, or find something quiet to do in your room. Because if I have to come up here again, neither one of you will be going to the craft fair this afternoon."

Melanie sidled up against her mother. "We'll go outside."

Teddy stood on the other side of Amanda. "Can we go to the barn?"

"No, sweetie. You have to stay in the yard." Amanda lightly rested her hand on Melanie's head. "And keep Freckles with you. It's a lot warmer now and you know how the snakes like to come out and sun on the walkways."

The rat terrier was great at warning them whenever a snake was in the vicinity, and would keep it occupied until an adult came to take care of the situation.

"Okey dokey." Melanie started toward the stairs. "Come on, Teddy. We'll see who can go higher on the swings."

Amanda followed them down and returned to the living room. "Did I thank you for bringing Teddy? He's certainly helping keep Mel occupied today."

"Hey, don't blame me. Rodney was all set to spend the day with him, until one of his patients ended up at the hospital in Parkdale."

"I'm not blaming anyone." Amanda sat beside her, stretched an arm across the back of the sofa and twisted so that they were facing one another. "I'm honestly glad he's here. Since Melanie wouldn't get up in time to go with Lex and Lorrie, she's been driving me crazy. We planned on going to town later, but that was before Eddie came down with his ear infection."

Jeannie giggled and mirrored her posture. "I had every intention of going to the fair this morning, but Teddy is just getting over his cold and I saw on the news that we have a slight chance for rain. To tell the truth, I was surprised that you let Lex out on her own."

"Yeah, well. I'm in no hurry to see Lex, especially after she gets through helping with the set up in town."

"Is everything all right between you two?"

Amanda laughed. "We're great. But I'm sure by now that she's a little pissed at me. I kind of volunteered her truck and services without telling her."

"Ouch. And we all know how much Slim enjoys running errands."

"She doesn't mind, really. And I had every intention of telling her, but it totally slipped my mind. And by the time I remembered, it was too late."

Amanda leaned back and relaxed. "I'm sure she's done with the hard stuff and is having a good time."

AT THE VFW, two women were arguing about the placement of two tables. The main hall had been cleared earlier, and they couldn't decide which direction the tables should face.

"Honestly, Kathleen. If we do it your way, how on earth will people be able to get to the buffet line?" the oldest one asked.

Her posture was permanently stooped, yet her eighty year-old eyes were sharp beneath her thick glasses. What little hair she had on her head was dyed a deep, chocolate brown and her gnarled hands gestured wildly to punctuate her point.

"We can get more tables set up, if you do it my way," Kathleen argued. Her brown hair was streaked with gray and cascaded in waves just past her shoulders. "Grandma, I'm sure Lex has better things to do than stand around and wait for us to make up our minds."

Kathleen had gone to school with Lex, although she had been a freshman when Lex graduated. She looked at Lex. "Isn't that right?"

Lex shook her head. "I'm not getting in the middle of this. But I have another truckload of tables I need to bring over. If y'all will just tell me where you want the first batch, I'll get out of your way."

Kathleen pointed to a wall nearest the back door. "How about stacking them there? The high school boys should be here soon, and we'll sucker them into setting them up for us."

"Sounds good." Lex touched the brim of her cap. "Mrs. Snyder. I'll be back in a short while with the rest."

She hurried away before the older woman could talk her into running more errands. As she stepped out into the mid-morning sun, she could feel the humidity weigh her down.

"I hope the rain holds off until after the barbecue, or at least until Shelby and Lorrie get back," she muttered.

SWEAT ROLLED DOWN Lorrie's cheek as she held the power pull steady while Shelby knotted the wire to the fence post. The hand-held winch made tightening the wire strands a lot easier, but it was still hard work.

It hadn't taken them long to find the break in the fence on the westernmost part of Shelby and Rebecca's property. An old tree had blown down and bent one of the steel posts.

"Shelby?"

"Hmm?"

"Where do you think those horses came from? I mean, we can tell they came through the fence here, but where were they before that?"

Shelby tucked the bullnose pliers into her back pocket and looked up. "Well, if you look right there, you can see where someone parked alongside the road. They most likely figured to dump the horses off and be long-gone before anyone found 'em."

"Oh." Lorrie glanced at churned dirt and grass on the other side of the fence. "So, they saw the fence messed up and just left? Why would they do that?"

"Times are a mite tough for some folks right now. Horses are expensive to keep, you know that."

Lorrie nodded. "Momma always talks about it, too. She said if it wasn't for the cattle she sells, she couldn't afford all the horses we have. But she also says that they're the best way to get around on the ranch."

"I reckon she's right about that. Although I'm glad I have a decent road around my fence line, 'cause my horses sure were skitterish today."

She took off her hat and wiped her sweaty forehead against her shoulder. The heavy humidity made for hot and sticky work.

"If they couldn't keep them, why didn't they just sell them?"

"That's the hundred-dollar question, ain't it? Either they didn't have bills of sale for them or maybe they were afraid they'd get in trouble for letting the horses get in such bad shape. Hell, for all we know, they stole 'em and then couldn't do nothin' with 'em. Maybe the sheriff will find out more and let us know."

"Sheriff Jeremy's nice, but I bet my pawpaw was a better sheriff. I've seen pictures of him, even before he was old." Lorrie grinned when

Shelby laughed. "Mada says he cut a dashing figure, whatever that means."

"It means she thought he looked good in his uniform."

Lorrie wrinkled her nose. "Eww. I didn't need to hear that."

"Aw, come on. I think it's nice that they love one another like that. Don't you?" Shelby unfastened the power pull. "I'll take this to the truck, if you don't mind picking up the bits of wire on the ground."

"Sure." Lorrie thought about how her grandparents acted. It wasn't much different from her parents. "Yeah, it's pretty cool," she said softly.

She bent to gather the pieces of wire that lay scattered along the ground, when a gust of wind nearly blew her off her feet. "Whoa." She heard the far off rumble of thunder and looked into the darkening sky. "I'm glad we got done before it rained."

Shelby placed the power pull in the steel toolbox that butted up against the cab of the truck. Before she could close the lid, the wind blew it out of her hand. "Damn!"

She turned and yelled, "Let's get a move on, Lorrie. I want to be back at the house before we get caught in this storm."

AMANDA ADDED ANOTHER diaper to Eddie's bag. She always packed too much, but she didn't want to be caught without one. That had happened to Lex once, and Amanda still laughed about the makeshift diaper her wife had made from her undershirt. Who knew that duct tape was so versatile?

"Mommy." Eddie stood beside her. He held up a bright blue toy truck.

"Thank you, sweetie. I'll add it to your bag." She heard the back door slam.

Footsteps pounded up the stairs. "Mommy," Melanie yelled.

Amanda closed her eyes for a moment. "Will your sister ever learn not to yell in the house?" she asked her son.

"Meemee no."

Amanda turned as Melanie stopped in the doorway. "Mel, you know better than to—"

"Mommy, Mada wants you to call her on the speaker. She says the phones don't work." Melanie went to Eddie and lightly patted the top of his head. "Hi, Eddie."

"Meemee, mine." He latched onto her shirt. "Meemee."

Amanda was about to ask Melanie to explain when she heard the wail of the weather radio in the kitchen. "Great. Mel, would you please keep an eye on your brother while I see what Mada needs?"

"Okey dokey. Come on, Eddie. Let's go to my room and color." She led him by the hand and kept her pace slow enough so that he could walk beside her.

Amanda followed them as far as the stairs, which she jogged down in a hurry after closing the gate. The back door opened and Martha stepped inside, followed by Jeannie and her children, with Charlie bringing up the rear.

"What's going on? I was just on my way to the kitchen to buzz you."

"Where's Eddie and Melanie?" Martha asked as her husband ushered the others toward the kitchen.

"Upstairs in her room. Why?" Amanda kept her hand on the banister, with her right foot still on the bottom step. "What on earth is going on?"

"There's a nasty storm heading this way and it's already knocked out the phone lines. We need to get into the storm cellar, just to be safe."

"I'll get the kids. Could you see if you could raise Lex on the radio? Hopefully they're already under cover." Amanda raced up the stairs. "Melanie! Bring your brother here, please!"

SHELBY FOUGHT THE wind as she tried to get them back to her house. "How you doing, kid?" she yelled. Big, fat drops of rain began to splat against the windshield. "Dammit!" She couldn't see the dirt road, which was bracketed by five-foot deep culverts on either side.

"I'm okay," Lorrie answered, just as loudly. She hand her left hand braced against the dash and her right hand on the door. When a strong blast of wind shoved the truck off the road, she screamed.

The gale-force wind caused the left tires to catch the shoulder of the road, where it flipped onto the driver's side in the ditch. Shelby was knocked unconscious as her head slammed against her window. Lorrie's frightened scream turned to a pained cry as she was thrown toward Shelby.

"I THINK WE'VE got enough tables and chairs," Lex told Weldon Page as they stood inside the high school gym. He was ten years her senior, and had been the assistant principal at the high school for twenty years.

"Maybe, but you can never be too sure. This past year, Mr. Miller was in charge, and he had to hear complaints from the Ladies' Auxiliary for months afterwards. I don't want all those old women calling me like that."

She laughed at him. "Chicken."

"Yeah, make fun of me all you want, but—"

Both of them were startled as a loud rumble of thunder caught them off guard. Lex looked up through the expansive windows that circled the top of the gymnasium. Heavy, dark clouds hid the sun.

"So much for hauling more chairs, Weldon. We'd better get back and see if they need any help securing stuff before the rain hits."

He followed her to the outside door. "You just don't want to load anything else into your truck."

"That's true." Lex opened the door, only to have the wind yank it out of her hand. "Damn. I think we need to hurry."

She tugged her cap down tightly on her head and headed for her truck at a run.

"Hey, wait for me," Weldon hollered. He tried to run behind her, but the strong wind made his progress difficult. They were halfway to Lex's truck when the sky opened and heavy rain pounded them.

Lex jumped in behind the wheel and slammed her door closed. Water dripped from her baseball cap and her clothes were soaked. When Weldon climbed inside, she turned and grinned. "Almost made it, didn't we?"

"You're crazy." Weldon wiped the water off his face with one hand. "Well? Are we gonna sit here and steam up the windows, or go back to the fair?"

Lex laughed and put the truck in gear. "I like you, Weldon. You're as much of an ass as I am."

As she drove away from the high school, the truck was rocked by the strong wind. "Damn. I hope the canopies hold up."

"Guess it depends on if you put the stakes in deep enough."

"Smartass." Lex used her hand to wipe the condensation off the windshield as she tried to see through the heavy rain. "I hope this blows over soon."

Weldon leaned closer to the windshield. "It's really coming down. Yow!" The truck lurched sideways due to the wind. A large tree branch fell in front of them. "Look out!"

Lex cursed and jerked the steering hard to the left. The truck skidded across the pavement and only the curb kept them from going across the sidewalk and into a private yard. "Holy shit, that was close."

"I knew you could handle it."

"Right. That's why you screamed like a little girl. I thought one of my daughters was in the truck with me." Lex tried to laugh it off, but her insides were still shaking from the close call.

As lightning hit a few miles ahead of them, the thunder rattled the windows on the truck.

"This is insane," Weldon remarked. "I'm glad we're safe in—"

When Lex turned the corner, the wind blew a small car against the truck. "Shit!"

She was so busy trying to move away from the car, that she didn't see the huge elm tree uprooted by the storm. It crumpled the hood of the truck and slammed into the windshield.

"THE WIND HAS really picked up," Kathleen remarked to Anna Leigh. They were side-by-side in the kitchen, preparing sandwiches from barbecue that someone had brought inside. "My grandmother told me she thought we were going to get a storm, but I hadn't heard anything on the radio about it."

Anna Leigh tore off a square of cellophane and wrapped the sandwich she had cut in half. "I'd listen to Bernice, dear. She's been right more often than not. What exactly did she say?"

"Well, before I took her back to her room at the home, she was talking about barometric pressure and such. Honestly, I thought she was just having one of her spells."

"Don't discount her words, Kathleen. She's rarely wrong, especially about—"

Something heavy hit the roof, causing the women in the kitchen to gasp. Evaline Cassidy, who was drying dishes, dropped a plate. The hard plastic rattled and caused her to blush. Her gray hair stood out like a beacon against her red face. "I'm sorry. What was that?"

"One of the trees must have lost a branch." Anna Leigh removed her disposable gloves and tossed them in the trash. "Perhaps we should go into the main hall away from the windows, just until this blows over."

Phyllis Chambers stood nearby, but she hadn't lifted a finger to help. She was the same age as Kathleen, but thought that such work was beneath her. "Honestly, Anna. Do you really think that's necessary?"

Another crash answered her, and she hurried out of the kitchen as fast as her legs could carry her.

"I think she has the right idea," Evaline added as she followed Phyllis.

"Come on, Mrs. Cauble. We'll go sit near the restrooms. That's where the strongest walls are." Kathleen linked her arm with Anna Leigh. "I believe Mary was out there, organizing the tables. Do you mind if I stay close to you?"

"Not at all, dear. Let's see if we can keep Evaline and Phyllis from killing one another."

LESS THAN A mile from the VFW hall, business was slow at McAlister's feed store. The manager, Tom Bennett, had sent everyone else home except for Rebecca. He sat at the desk in his office, in hopes of getting the deposit figured before she was scheduled to leave.

In the main part of the store, Rebecca used a feather duster to clean the shelves. She picked up a bottle of horse liniment and read the label.

"Good for horses and their humans? Oh, my God. That's scary."

She dusted the shelf and returned the bottles to their proper places. The sound of the wind and rain hitting the building made her think about her partner. "Wonderful. Just what we didn't need today."

She took her cell phone from her back pocket and hit the speed dial for Shelby. It rang several times before a recording came on that advised

Rebecca the party she tried to reach wasn't available. "Weird. It should have least gone to voice mail."

Lightning struck nearby, and the loud boom that followed caused her to jump. "Geez!"

Rebecca put her cell phone in the back pocket of her jeans. "I hope Shelby had enough sense to get under cover before the bad weather hit."

She cringed as the building creaked from the high winds. Her eyes tracked to the front picture window, where she could see various things blowing across the road. Trash, leaves and small tree branches flew by.

As she thought about Shelby, Rebecca crossed her arms to ward off a frightened chill. "I wish she was here."

She looked up as a loud noise came from above, just in time to see part of the ceiling come down. Rebecca's scream was cut off as she was buried in drywall, wood beams and the top of a monstrous tree.

"AMANDA, YOU NEED to get in here," Martha called from the door of the storm cellar. The wind had picked up and was throwing debris against the house. "Bring the damned hand-held with you!" She rarely cursed, but her worry now overrode her upbringing.

"I'm coming." Amanda hurried toward the kitchen. She carried her cell phone, the wireless handset to the house phone and two radios. "Were you able to reach Helen and Roy?"

Martha helped her down the steps so that Charlie could close the cellar door. "Right before we came over. They're safer where they are, since their house is in a lower-lying area. Helen latched the shutters in Roy's office, so they're well-protected."

Amanda sat across from Jeannie, who rocked Hunter to keep him from crying. Teddy, whose eyes were wide with fear, huddled on the other side of his mother.

"Mommy!" Eddie patted Amanda's leg and demanded to be picked up. Freckles stood behind him and whined.

She lifted him onto her lap and kissed his cheek. "Hey, handsome. Isn't this fun?"

"I'm scared, Mommy." Melanie had her right pinkie finger in her mouth, a gesture that only showed up when she was nervous.

Martha sat on the other side of Amanda and patted her lap. "Come sit with me, sweetie. We're perfectly safe in here. Right, Pawpaw?"

"Right." Charlie sat beside Jeannie and put his arm around her. "Everything will be just fine."

The house groaned as it was attacked by the hard wind.

"Are we gonna die?" Teddy asked.

Jeannie playfully bumped him with a shoulder. "Of course not, honey. This is the safest place in the world."

"What about Daddy?"

Melanie started to cry. "I want Momma."

Amanda agreed with the sentiment but she put on a brave face. "I'm sure everyone else is just as safe as we are." A loud thump above them caused her to look at the ceiling of the shelter. "We'll probably hear from them as soon as the storm passes."

THE DUPLEX SHOOK from the force of the wind. One of the bedroom windows shattered and blew glass and rain across the bed and its occupants.

"What the fuck?" Kyle yelled, awakened from a dead sleep. She had protectively rolled onto Ellie, who immediately wrapped her arms around her. Both of them were under the covers, until Kyle cautiously poked her head out.

"Kyle?"

"Hold on, baby. I'm not sure what happened." The rain continued to blow in. Kyle exhaled in relief when she realized the weather was to blame. "It's all right, just a storm."

She raised herself off Ellie. "A pretty nasty one, it seems."

Ellie wiped her hair away from her face. The electricity was off, and the heavy clouds made the mid-afternoon seem like evening. "My God, what's going on?"

Kyle tossed the glass-covered comforter onto the floor and wrapped the sheet around her lover. "Stay here while I grab us some clothes."

"You can't walk across the floor in your bare feet," Ellie argued.

"Well, I'm not sitting here naked in bed, waiting until someone comes to help." Kyle stepped on the blanket and carefully tiptoed to the closet. After she was dressed, she brought Ellie her clothes. "If I didn't know better, I'd swear it was a hurricane, or something. That wind sounds fierce."

Ellie quickly dressed and followed Kyle to look out the broken window. "I can't even see the house across the street. This is crazy." Another heavy thud shook the duplex. "Are we safe in here?"

A loud crash from the living room was all the answer they needed. "I never thought I'd say this to you, but let's get into the closet," Kyle said.

She tugged Ellie with her as she headed for the walk-in closet on the other side of the room.

Chapter Twenty-six

THE RAIN CONTINUED to pound the outside of the truck, which creaked with the force of the wind. Lorrie tried to keep from crying, but every movement of the truck caused her left arm, which hung lifelessly below her, to sway. Her seatbelt kept her in place but she was too far away to reach the still woman beneath her.

"S...Sh...Shelby?" She wiped the tears from her face with her good hand. "Shelby? Wake up. Please?"

She twisted in the seat, which moved her arm. She screamed as tears dripped off her nose.

The sound of Lorrie's distress brought Shelby around. She attempted to open her eyes, but only her right one would obey. "Ugh."

"Shelby?" Lorrie rubbed her fist under her nose to wipe away the tears. "Shelby, are you all right?"

"Uh," Shelby groaned as she tried to get her bearings. "Lorrie?"

Lorrie sobbed in relief. "I thought you were dead."

Shelby was able to move her head, but almost threw up at the motion. "Fuck."

"What's wrong?"

"Gimme a sec," Shelby ground out between gritted teeth. She concentrated on her churning stomach. She closed her eye and silently pleaded with herself to not get sick.

As she waited, she took stock of her condition. She was crushed against the driver's door and the pain coming from her left shoulder was almost as bad as the sharp throbbing from her head. Although it was dark beneath her, she could see muddy water that ran a few inches below them. She cleared her throat. "Lorrie? Are you okay?"

"My arm hurts really bad." As she spoke, the truck quit rocking. The rain continued, however. "I think the wind stopped."

"Good." Shelby slowly moved her right hand until she reached her belt. She took her cell phone out of the leather holster and used her thumb to push the keys. The off-key tones she heard made her want to cry. "Fuck. No phone service."

Lorrie crossed her right hand over her body. "Should I unbuckle my seat belt? Maybe I can help you."

"No!" Yelling made Shelby's head hurt worse and she was afraid she was about to embarrass herself by throwing up. "Let's just sit still for a minute and try to figure something out, okay? I don't want you to fall and hurt yourself more."

"I think I can turn and stand on the dash," Lorrie said, as she carefully raised her legs and braced them. "Then I won't fall, right?"

Shelby swallowed the bile that rose in her throat. She could feel a wet stickiness along the left side of her head, and fuzzily wondered what it could be. She was so focused on the pain that she didn't hear Lorrie's comments.

The click that announced the release of Lorrie's seatbelt was loud in the cab of the truck. An instant later, Shelby heard the girl scream in pain as she dropped from her seat.

THE ELECTRICITY FLICKERED off in the store as the storm raged around them. Tom felt as well as heard the crash in the front of the feed store and jumped out of his chair. He rushed blindly out of his office toward the main showroom.

"Oh, my God," he whispered.

The feed store, like many of the other older buildings in Somerville, was surrounded by large shade trees. The top of one of the biggest trees from the west side of the building had broken off and crashed through the roof. He ignored the rain that dampened his face as he moved into the room. His first concern was his employee. "Rebecca?"

He stepped cautiously toward the largest pile of rubble, where tree branches mixed with ceiling tiles and glass. "Rebecca, where are you?"

Tom slipped on the wet tile and fell to one knee beside the debris. He noticed a scratched, pale hand only inches away from him, and he shakily reached for it. "Rebecca, can you her me?" It was cool to the touch. "Hey."

The fingers wriggled and a weak voice called out, barely discernible above the sound of the rain. "Help me."

"I'm here." Tom tried to separate the branches so that he could see her, but it was too dark. "Don't move, okay? I'll go see if I can find someone to help me get this mess off you."

"Please don't leave me," Rebecca cried. She managed to turn her hand and grasped his with surprising strength. "I'm scared."

He lightly squeezed her hand. "I know. Um, can you tell if you're hurt?"

"I...I'm not sure." Rebecca's voice trailed off.

"Are you in any pain?" Tom almost leaped out of his skin when the wind slammed something against the building. "God."

Rebecca tried to pull her hand away. "Maybe you should be somewhere safer."

Tom used his free hand to wipe the water from his eyes and face then looked around. Part of the roof was missing and rain had soaked everything in sight. "Not much else can happen where we're at."

"Do you feel cold? I'm freezing."

"It's a little cool, with the rain and all. You just hang in there, all right? As soon as the storm passes, I'm sure help will be here."

"Could you do me a favor, Tom?" Rebecca's voice had softened to the point where he had to lean closer to understand her. "If something happens, could you—"

He shook his head. "No, no. Don't start thinking like that. Everything's going to be okay."

"I hope so. But, just in case, could you tell Shelby that I love her? Please?"

"Shelby? Her?" Tom released her hand. "You...you're gay?"

He hadn't gotten a chance to know Rebecca very well, but he had hoped to work up the courage to ask her out on a date.

"Tom? Please, don't leave." Rebecca began to cry. "God, I'm so scared." She wiggled her fingers. "Please? Tom?"

AS THE WIND and heavy rain slammed the VFW building, the five women huddled together in the darkness. The electricity had failed right after the storm started and the building had started to get warm and humid. They were underneath two tables that were pushed against the strongest interior wall. At one point, they heard the windows in the kitchen shatter, but no one made a move to investigate.

"I don't think I can take much more of this," Kathleen whimpered. She had admitted a paralyzing fear of severe weather just as the storm hit, much to the disdain of Phyllis. "I thought I could handle it, but I just can't."

"Sssh." Anna Leigh had her arms around Kathleen, who shook so hard it nearly rattled her teeth as well. "Listen."

The howling wind had stopped, and now the only sound was the hard rain on the roof. They could also hear the rain coming into the kitchen, and could tell that one of the main doors of the building had blown open during the peak of the storm.

Phyllis Chambers crawled from beneath her table. "Goodness that was intense." She brushed off her slacks and then looked at her hands. "I wonder how long it's been since anyone has swept or mopped around here."

"Really, Phyllis. I think we have more important things to worry about than dirty floors," Evaline chastised. She was a friend of Phyllis' mother and had plenty of dealings with the snotty younger woman. She held out her hand to Kathleen. "Come on out of there, honey. We're perfectly safe."

Kathleen accepted the helping hand and then turned to assist Anna Leigh. "Thank you for understanding, Mrs. Cauble."

Anna Leigh hugged her. "Please, dear, call me Anna Leigh." She turned to the other woman in their little group. "How are you doing, Mary? I know it had to be painful for you to be under there for so long."

"I'll live," Mary assured her. She was on the Ladies Auxiliary committee that had planned the barbecue, even though she had severe arthritis and couldn't always help. "I hope everyone outside was able to get to cover."

Phyllis snorted. "They could at least see the storm coming. We had no warning at all. No one even bothered to run in and tell us."

"Be that as it may, someone should go check," Evaline said, giving Phyllis a pointed stare. "Thank you for volunteering, Phyllis."

"Excuse me?"

Mary jumped in. "Come on. I'll go with you, and we'll see if anyone needs help." She grabbed Phyllis' arm and led her toward the open door.

"Wow, she's obnoxious," Kathleen whispered. "What's her major problem, anyway? She was ordering everyone around all morning."

Anna Leigh started toward the kitchen. "Do you mean Phyllis? She married a lawyer a few years ago, and now he's the county judge. Don't let her bother you."

"Where are you going, Mrs., um, Anna Leigh?" Kathleen hurried to catch up to the older woman.

"To see what kind of mess the storm made of the kitchen. Perhaps we can salvage some of the sandwiches, at the very least. I have a feeling it's going to be a truly long day."

THE RAIN FELL steadily on the overturned truck and the cadence lulled Shelby into a semi-conscious state. She could still hear Lorrie sniffling, but her crying had stopped a few minutes earlier.

"How're ya doin', kid?" she whispered.

Most of Lorrie's weight was on her left foot, which had gained purchase on the steering column. Her right foot was on Shelby's seat, inches away from the older woman's neck. "I think my arm's broke. It hurts to move it."

Shelby slowly raised her right hand to her face in an attempt to wipe the blood out of her eyes. Her mind was a muddled mess. "We can't be too far from the house. Think you can get out and call for help?"

"I'll try." Lorrie looked around. "Shelby?"

"Yeah?"

"I can reach the handle and roll down the window on my side, but I can't climb out with just one arm."

"Damn. That could be a problem." There was only one solution and she dreaded it. She released her seat belt. "All right. I'm going to need you to do something."

Lorrie stood above Shelby, holding her injured arm against her body. "What are we gonna do?"

"Do you think you can put both feet on the steering wheel or on the seat, so I can get up? Then I can boost you through the window and climb out after you."

"Okay." Lorrie kept her balance by bracing her good hand against the roof of the truck. It wasn't comfortable, but she was able to move around until she was out of Shelby's way. "Do you need any help?"

Shelby bit off a sharp reply. The girl was only trying to be useful. "Just ignore me for a few minutes, okay? I don't want your mom kicking my ass for using bad language around you."

Lorrie giggled. "Momma cusses a lot, too. And I've heard my mom say things she doesn't know I've heard."

"Yeah, I figured." Shelby took a deep breath and released it slowly. "Okay, here goes." She grabbed the steering wheel with her right hand and used it to leverage herself off the side window. The unsettling feeling of her sticky face peeling away from the glass caused Shelby's stomach to churn. She gritted her teeth as she struggled to a sitting position.

"Argh! Goddammit, that fuckin' hurts!" The shoulder that she had landed on throbbed to the point where she thought she might pass out. Shelby closed her eye and bit her lip to keep from fainting.

"Shelby?" Lorrie could now see the blood caked on the left side of Shelby's face. It slowly ran from her temple to her shirt and her hair was matted with drying clumps of blood.

"I think I'm gonna need your help, after all," Shelby gasped. She held out her right hand. "If I can just get my balance, I think I'll be okay."

Lorrie grabbed her hand and held on tightly as Shelby struggled to stand. She turned her head and noticed a crack along the back window. "Hey, look."

Shelby leaned against the truck roof and opened her one good eye, but her vision was too blurry. "What?"

"The back window has a big crack in it."

"How big?" Shelby ran her hand across the window, but with the leather glove on she couldn't feel anything.

"All the way across, I think."

Shelby blew out a heavy breath. "Finally, something in our favor. I'm going to try and kick it out. It would be a lot easier than trying to climb up through that little window."

"I can help."

"I reckon between the two of us, it should be easy."

Shelby tried to turn enough to use her leg, but the cab was too small. "Fuck. Okay, plan B. On the count of three, you kick and I'll ram it with my good shoulder." She closed her eye for a moment, inhaled deeply and then exhaled slowly. "One...two...three!"

"I THINK I like storms." Ellie sat in front of Kyle, who had her arms wrapped around her. "And I never knew closets could be so...romantic."

Kyle kissed the side of her neck. "Does this mean I don't have to take you out on our anniversary?"

Ellie tilted her head as she enjoyed the gentle kisses. "I don't care where we are, or what we do. You know that."

"Mmm-hmm." Kyle put her hands under Ellie's shirt and stroked her stomach. "Me either." Suddenly, something seemed different which caused her to stop. "Do you hear that?"

"Huh?" Ellie was lost in a sensual haze. Anytime her lover touched her, she melted. Kyle had been wonderful during the storm, holding her close and exchanging gentle kisses to keep her calm.

Kyle kissed Ellie's head and stood. "The wind's died down."

"Is that a good thing, or a bad thing?" Ellie accepted a hand up and put her arms around Kyle's neck. "Next time, we have got to have a flashlight or something, in here. I hate not being able to see your eyes."

"Yeah, I didn't think about the power going out. All I wanted to do was make sure you were safe."

Ellie found Kyle's lips easily in the dark. Once they broke apart, she laughed. "Depends on what I'm supposed to be safe from. The storm, yes. I was very safe. Making out in a dark closet? Not so much."

"I didn't hear any complaints."

"And you never will."

Kyle held Ellie's hand and led her from the closet. They both stopped when they saw the damage to the bedroom. "Whoa."

The bedroom was soaked from the rain, which continued to fall. Glass was everywhere, as were wet leaves and small twigs and branches. The white, microfiber-padded bench that sat beneath the window was drenched and covered with mud.

Ellie gingerly walked to the window and looked out. Although she was soon as wet as the rest of the room, she didn't move away. "Hey, Kyle?"

"Yeah?" Kyle stood beside her. "Wow. I wonder where that came from?" Just outside their window was a narrow section of wooden trellis. "I guess that's what broke the window, huh?"

"Probably." Ellie turned to take another look at the bedroom. "I hope everyone at the fair is okay. Lex and Amanda were going to take the kids."

Kyle kissed her on the forehead and retrieved her cell phone from the nightstand. "I'll give Amanda a call and see." She put her cell phone to her ear and frowned at the annoying buzz. "Tower must be damaged."

"Can we run by the town square and see if they're there?"

"Sure, baby. How about you get into something dry and I'll board up the window, okay? I think I have some plywood out in the garage."

Ellie grabbed her before she could leave the bedroom. "Thanks. But I don't see why I should change, especially since we're going right back out in this mess."

"Maybe because I'm overprotective?"

"Probably. But I love you for it." Ellie swatted her on the butt. "Go on. I'll try to get some of this mess cleaned up while you take care of the window."

REBECCA'S PLEAS WERE more than Tom could ignore. He took her hand and gave it a reassuring squeeze. "I'm sorry. It's really none of my business who you, umm, you know."

It wasn't as if he didn't know any gay people. Lex Walters had been coming to the feed store her entire life. But, Rebecca seemed different. Now that he was past the shock, he knew he had to help her.

"I...I'm so cold, Tom."

"I'm sorry. It's probably 'cause you're lying on the wet tile. Look, let me run back to the office and see if I can call someone to get you out of there."

Her grip kept him from leaving.

"Rebecca, I promise I'll be right back. But I can't move this tree or any of the other stuff without help."

She released his hand. "Please, hurry. I don't want to be alone."

Tom got up. "I'll be right back, I promise." He stumbled along the ruins and slipped on the wet tile, but finally reached the office. He picked up the phone but heard nothing but static on the line. He didn't want to return to Rebecca without something positive, so he left the office and headed out the back door to find someone to help.

BACK IN THE showroom, Rebecca couldn't stop shivering. She was lying on her stomach with her right cheek against the floor and she was chilled to the bone. "Tom?"

She waited for an answer, but between the rain that fell and the noises made by the damaged building, she couldn't hear anything. As the cold numbed her body, Rebecca found it hard to stay alert. Her eyes closed and her mind began to drift.

"I CAN'T BELIEVE all this damage was done by wind and rain. Good thing we keep our vehicles in the garage." Kyle was behind the wheel of her shop's truck, which she had borrowed until she could finish work on her own car's engine. "I've never seen so many beat up cars and broken windows from a thunderstorm before."

Ellie pointed to a house as they passed. "It looks like their roof is gone. Do you think a tornado did this?"

"I don't think so. But I wouldn't be surprised to find out we had hurricane-force winds. It's almost impossible to find clear streets."

"I really appreciate you taking me to the town square. I just want to make sure my family's safe."

"I'm worried, too. Besides, we can stop by the shop on the way. I want to check and see if we had any damage."

Kyle stopped when they came upon a huge elm that had fallen across the road. She put the truck in reverse until they came to a cross-street. "We'll have to go around by the high school."

Ellie ignored her mumbling and stared out the window. Tree limbs littered every yard and many of the cars had cracked or shattered windows. "Unbelievable." She held on to the handle above her door as Kyle drove onto the sidewalk to bypass another fallen tree. "Don't ever complain about my driving again, Kyle. At least I stay on the roads."

"Not much choice, baby. Besides, it's not like—" Kyle slowed when she noticed the stopped truck ahead. "Wow. Look at the size of that tree. I hope those guys got out okay."

Ellie unbuckled her seat belt. "We'd better go see."

"Hey, at least wait 'til I stop," Kyle yelled. She parked and jumped out to follow her lover. "Ellie, wait."

The closer she got to the vehicle, the faster Ellie walked. Even from the back, the large, green Dodge pickup looked familiar.

"Oh, no." She turned to Kyle, who jogged up beside her. "It's Lex's truck."

"Are you sure?" Kyle tried to look through the driver's window, but it was blocked by a limb. The entire front of the truck was crushed under the weight of the tree. "I can't see inside."

Ellie pointed to the door, where the edge of the Rocking W Ranch logo could be seen. "We need to see if she's in there."

"I'll check the other side." Kyle walked around the truck and moved a plastic child's playhouse out of her way. The passenger's side of the truck was obscured, and one of the larger branches had blocked the door. She turned and headed toward the rear of the truck. "I couldn't tell—" Kyle stopped when she saw Ellie in the bed. "What are you doing?"

"I think I can get through to the back window. The branches are thinner back here." Ellie disappeared into the foliage. "Kyle, do you have a screwdriver and a flashlight in the truck?"

Kyle didn't bother to comment. She went to her vehicle and searched through the attached toolbox, grumbling the entire time. She found a small crowbar as well as a flashlight and a handsaw. "Better than nothing, I guess."

Ellie stood by the tailgate and helped Kyle up when she returned. "A crowbar? Perfect! We can pry the sliding window open and I can squeeze through."

"Oh, hell, no! You're not climbing inside. We're just going to look and see if anyone is in there."

Ellie ignored Kyle's outburst and took the crowbar from her hands. Without another word, she squeezed through the branches and out of

Kyle's sight. "Hon? Could you bring the flashlight?"

"I swear, she's gonna be the death of me." Kyle struggled through the leaves and branches, only to see Ellie's legs and feet disappear through the window. "Ellie!"

Ellie popped back out and almost bumped faces with Kyle. "The branches have covered all the other windows, and with the rain and clouds, it's too dark to see inside."

"Maybe I should go in," Kyle offered.

"I'm a nurse. If there is anyone inside, they may need medical attention."

Kyle shook her head. "I don't want you to risk it. If the wind gets up again—"

"All the more reason for me to hurry." Ellie took the flashlight from her. "I'll holler if I need help, I promise." She quickly kissed Kyle's lips and turned away.

Kyle watched helplessly as Ellie disappeared into the cab of the truck. "Be careful," she called after her.

Inside, Ellie was on her knees in the back seat and shined the light toward the front. She could see a dark head on the flattened airbag on the driver's side. "Lex?" Ellie stretched over the seat and touched the driver's shoulder. "Lex, can you hear me?"

When she didn't get an answer, Ellie touched the side of Lex's neck, relieved to find warm skin and a strong pulse. "All right. Good." She turned the flashlight toward the passenger side of the truck to see a man in a similar state. His pulse was strong as well and she exhaled in relief.

Ellie turned to the back window and stuck her head out. "Lex is in here, along with some man I don't recognize. They're both alive, but unconscious."

"That's a relief. Let me get you out of there and we'll go find some help."

"I can't leave her here like this."

Kyle shook her head. "I'm sure as hell not leaving you here by yourself."

"You have to. I can't tell how serious their injuries are, and we need to get them out. And if they do wake up, I need to keep them still in case they have spinal trauma. I'm perfectly safe."

"No, El. Please don't ask me to leave you." Kyle hefted the saw. "I'll work on the branches by the door. Maybe we can get them out that way."

"Kyle."

"Let me try, okay? You've seen the damage around here. I'm sure the emergency services are overwhelmed."

"All right. I'm going to go back and keep an eye on them, in case they come to. Maybe I can find something to stabilize their necks."

"Holler if you need me."

Ellie reached through the window and wiped the rainwater off

Kyle's face. "I'll always need you. Be careful out there."

"I will. You, too." Kyle backed away.

THE RAIN HAD slowed to a drizzle, although to the two trudging through the mud, it didn't matter. Shelby's left arm was useless. She had her hand tucked into the front of her belt to keep it immobile, and each step brought agony to what she assumed was a broken collarbone. She glanced at Lorrie, who silently kept up with her. "How're ya, kid?"

"I feel stupid. Sorry I threw up on you." Once they had made it out of the truck, the two working together had splinted Lorrie's broken wrist. Lorrie cried so hard at the pain that she had vomited.

"Hey, don't worry 'bout it. Rain washed me right off."

Lorrie kept her eyes on the ground. "I bet you don't cry like a baby."

"I do, and have, on many occasions."

"Really?" Lorrie looked up and stumbled.

Shelby grabbed her shirt and kept her from falling. "Yup. Many times. Nothing wrong with it, kid. Everyone who has a heart, cries. I'd worry more about someone who doesn't show emotion."

"I guess I never thought of it that way. But I threw up on you! That's something little kids do."

"Nah. It's a natural reaction to hurtin'. Like I said, don't worry about it." As they crested the hill, Shelby pointed ahead of them. "See? We made it."

Lorrie sniffled and wiped her nose with the back of her hand. "Do you think Momma will still be in town?"

"I reckon she's out of her mind, worryin' 'bout you. We'll take Rebecca's car and find her, I promise."

Once they reached the back door, Shelby stopped. "Fuck."

"What's wrong?"

"I left my damned keys in the truck!" Shelby punctuated the sentence with a firm kick to the door, next to the knob. It burst open and slammed against the interior wall. "Rebecca's gonna love me for that."

Lorrie followed her inside. "You won't get into trouble? Momma gets into trouble when she breaks stuff."

Shelby took a set of keys from a bowl on the counter. "She's been after me for years to replace that door."

She went to the refrigerator and took out two cans of soda. "If you'll check the pantry, we should have a bag of cookies in there. Grab 'em and we'll head for town."

Chapter Twenty-seven

AMANDA FINISHED WITH Eddie's diaper as Charlie came into the living room. He had volunteered to check the roof and upstairs rooms for damage after the storm. "How bad was it?"

"Not as bad as I expected, the way the storm sounded." Charlie sat in the chair closest to Melanie and Teddy, who were busy drawing pictures. "As far as I can tell, you lost some shingles on the west side, but no major damage. The barns protected our place pretty well. There was some damage to the stables' roof, but the inside was fine."

"Thanks, Charlie." Amanda put Eddie on the floor and patted his rear. "There you go."

Eddie laughed and joined his sister and cousin. "Meemee!"

Melanie tore off a page from a coloring book and handed him a thick crayon. "Don't eat this one, okay?"

"Good," Eddie agreed.

Martha fed Hunter his bottle and made a silly face at him. "Cutie." She looked up when Jeannie came in with a tray of sandwiches and drinks. "Y'all are more than welcome to bunk with us, if you need to."

Jeannie placed the tray on the coffee table. "Thanks, Martha. I hope peanut butter and jelly is okay with everyone." PB and J's were one of the few meals that even she couldn't mess up. "I wonder if the storm was this bad in town. I still can't get Rodney on the phone."

"I'm half-tempted to drive in and see," Amanda added, before she left to wash her hands.

Martha handed Hunter to Jeannie and followed Amanda down the hall. "Usually I'd be the first one to tell you to stay put."

"But?" Amanda ducked into the spare bathroom and vigorously scrubbed her hands.

"But, I'm as worried as you are."

Amanda dried her hands and joined Martha in the hallway. "I thought Jeannie and I could ride in together, so we can check on Gramma and everyone else. But if Teddy goes, Mel will want to go. And if Mel—"

"Don't you worry about the kids. Charlie and I will take them to our place."

"All of them?"

Martha put her hands on her hips. "Are you saying I can't handle four children?"

"Um."

"That's what I thought." Martha patted her on the cheek. "Run upstairs and pack an overnight bag, just in case. We'll have a movie marathon this evening, and let the bigger kids camp out in the living room. Eddie can sleep with us and Hunter will be just fine in the portable crib. I'm glad your sister over packs diaper bags like you do. We've got plenty of formula and diapers for a couple of days."

Amanda gave her a quick hug. "Thanks. You're a braver woman than I, that's for sure." As she headed for the stairs, she heard Martha's parting shot.

"I raised Lexie, didn't I? How much harder can those four little angels be?"

"DAMN IT, LEX! Stay still," Ellie snapped as the paramedic placed the cervical collar around her cousin's neck.

Lex hadn't stopped complaining since she'd become conscious. Her right wrist was splinted and she awakened to find herself strapped to a backboard. "I need to call Amanda."

"The phone lines are down. Just relax and let these guys take care of you."

"How the hell am I supposed to relax, when I'm trussed up like this?" When Ellie came into her line of sight, Lex tried another tack. "I don't want Amanda to be worried."

Ellie rubbed her shoulder. "I promise, I'll get in touch with her. How's your vision, now?" When Lex first came to, she'd had trouble seeing anything.

"Still a little blurry."

"Well, that could be due to your broken nose, cuz. Or the concussion you probably have." Ellie felt, rather than saw, Kyle join them. She gratefully leaned into Kyle's body. "How's he doing?"

Kyle watched as they loaded Weldon into the back of the ambulance. "Not too bad. As far as they can tell, he's only got a broken leg." She moved to where Lex could see her. "How are you, Lex?"

"Fine." Lex tried to ignore the pain in her torso, which made it difficult to breathe. "I need to get home and check on my family. None of this is necessary." Lex blinked as something occurred to her. "Damn it. Ellie?"

"What?"

"Lorrie went with Shelby to help with her fence. Could you—"

Ellie followed as the firefighters took Lex toward a waiting ambulance. "We'll find her. Don't worry." As they loaded the stretcher, she turned to one of the men. "Which hospital are you taking her to?"

"Parkdale. The storm barely touched them there."

"Thanks." Ellie turned and fell into her lover's arms. Now that the rain had stopped and the clouds had lightened, she could easily see how badly the truck had been wrecked. "I can't believe that tree didn't kill them."

Kyle kissed the top of Ellie's head. "Yeah. I kind of freaked out when I saw the blood on Lex's face. You were great, though."

"I don't feel great, just drained." Ellie walked beside Kyle as they returned to the wrecked truck. Two uniformed men were trying to secure the doors. "Sheriff Richards, is there anything else we can do here?"

Jeremy turned away from his deputy. "No, we've got it." He handed Ellie a bag. "This is the stuff out of the glove box. I didn't want to leave it behind."

"Thank you. And thank you for getting help here so quickly."

"Well, having a woman jump in front of my cruiser gets my attention." He pointed to Kyle. "Next time, just wave. I could have hit you."

Kyle blushed. "All I knew is that we needed help, and yours was the first car I'd seen since we got here."

"You did what?" Ellie asked.

"Um." Kyle held out her hand to the sheriff. "Thanks for everything, Sheriff. Could you have Lex's truck towed to my shop?"

Jeremy shook her hand. "Sure." He listened to the chatter from the radio on his belt. "Sounds like we've got several of the surrounding towns sending help. I'd better head on to the square and check out the damage. Do you need anything else?"

Kyle looked at Ellie. "I don't think so. We promised Lex we'd find her daughter, Lorrie, and we'd appreciate it if you'd keep an eye out for her."

"She's with Shelby Fisher," Ellie added. "According to Lex, they were going to work on Shelby's fence."

Jeremy took a small notepad from his shirt pocket and wrote the information down. "All right. We'll keep an eye out for them. I'll also try to reach the ranch on the radio. If I know Charlie, he's probably monitoring our frequency for information."

"Great." Ellie shook his hand. "Thank you again, Sheriff. I can see why my cousin speaks so highly of you. Do you mind if we follow you to the town square? I'm hoping to find the rest of my family there."

"Of course. Let me tell Oscar what's going on, and we'll head out."

LORRIE'S MOUTH HUNG open at the devastation as Shelby tried to find passable streets in Somerville. "Did a tornado hit?"

"Looks more like the wind did most of this. It got up pretty high, remember?"

"Yeah, I guess." Lorrie stared at the fallen trees and trash that littered the yards and streets. "Do you think my mom is okay? She was outside when we left."

Shelby had been thinking that very thought. "Uh, well. I reckon your mom is a lot smarter than that. She's probably holed up somewhere safe, worried about you."

"What about my house? Everyone else was at home." Lorrie

pointed out the side window. "Look! That car is upside down!"

"It doesn't take much to toss one of those little things around. Hell, I bet you and me together could pick up one end."

After driving around another downed tree, Shelby thought about the huge trees that surrounded the feed store. Her thoughts drifted toward her lover and she sent out a silent prayer for her safety.

When the local hospital came into view, Lorrie glared at Shelby. "I thought we were going to find my mom." She had her injured arm cradled close to her body.

"We will, I promise. But you need to get your arm looked at."

"But—"

"Do you think I'm dumb enough to face either one of your folks without having you checked out, first? There's no telling how long it'll take to find them in this mess." Shelby circled the lot, unable to find a parking space. "If your wrist is broken, it needs to be set as soon as possible. I know all too well what happens if you don't." She showed Lorrie the two smallest fingers on her right hand, which were bent out of shape. "I tried to fix these myself and they healed wrong. Hurts like hell every time the weather changes."

"Yuck."

Shelby grinned. "And that's not even the worst of 'em."

She slowly cruised by the hospital entry and saw the line of people coming out the door. "Damn. I was afraid of that."

"What?" Lorrie looked at the hospital. "Oh. We're gonna be here forever."

"Nope." Shelby put the car in reverse. "We're goin' to Parkdale. Their hospital is bigger, anyway."

Lorrie's reprieve was short-lived. She dropped her head against the back of the seat. "Crap."

ACROSS TOWN, BATTERY operated floodlights cast a yellowish glow across the interior of the feed store. Tom watched the group of rescuers work to free Rebecca. He paced back and forth in an attempt to see their progress. While some of the tree limbs had been cut away and discarded, the heavier ones were still in place.

"Hold it, guys. That limb isn't stable," yelled a man stationed by Rebecca's head.

"Got it braced!" voiced another man. "Andy, bring me that board."

The next fifteen minutes seemed like a lifetime to Tom, who chewed on his fingernail as he watched the firefighters stabilize Rebecca's body and carefully remove her from the wreckage.

He moved closer as Rebecca was placed on the stretcher. In the surreal light, Tom could see the tears that ran down her face and disappeared into her hair. He touched her hand, which was strapped down with the rest of her body. "It's going to be okay."

Rebecca cut her eyes toward his voice. "Tom?"

"Yeah, I'm here."

"Could you?"

He leaned to hear her. "What do you need?"

She began to cry harder. "Shelby. Please find her."

"Um." Tom had to walk with the stretcher as they carried her from the store. "What about your family?"

"She is my family, Tom. Please."

The firefighter that held the top of the stretcher cleared his throat. "I'm sorry, but you're going to have to step back. We need to transport her."

"Okay." As he watched them load Rebecca into the ambulance, Tom wasn't certain what to do. He wanted to help her, but he didn't know the first thing about how to find or contact Rebecca's girlfriend. If he were honest with himself, he still had trouble thinking of her as a lesbian.

When the ambulance pulled away, Tom went back into the store. He needed to find a way to close it up so that he could leave, and he hoped he could decide what to do about Rebecca.

A LARGE CROWD had gathered at the VFW building, where Sheriff Jeremy Richards had set up a mobile command center. Butcher paper from the nearby grocery had been taped along one wall and people could use markers to share information there.

Anna Leigh and the other women were once again busy in the kitchen. Only this time, their food preparation was for those displaced by the storm and the volunteers who were busy trying to find the missing. She took a tray of completed sandwiches into the main hall and heard the sheriff's voice above the din.

"The more seriously injured are being routed to Parkdale. And before you ask, no, I don't have a list of casualties at this time. I do know we've had two reported fatalities so far, but we have a lot more buildings to check."

"How long are we supposed to be without power?" a voice from the group yelled. "There aren't many places that have generators, like this place." Other voices chimed in, raising the noise level.

Jeremy held up his hands to quiet the crowd. "I haven't gotten a call back from the power company, but they've assured me they're sending trucks to help repair the lines. We're the largest town that's been hit so far, so we've got top priority."

Anna Leigh stood by patiently as he answered a few more questions. Once he was finished, she handed him a sandwich. "You look like you could use this."

"Thank you, Mrs. Cauble." He unwrapped it, but stopped before he took a bite. "Oh! Hey, is Amanda here?"

"No, she's at home. Jeannie was going out to see her this morning, though. Why?"

He looked a little unsure, but took a gentle hold of her elbow and moved away from the crowd. "It's about Lex. She was in an accident, and was taken to Parkdale."

"Oh, goodness. How badly was she hurt?"

"I don't know for sure, but she was arguing with her cousin when they loaded her into the ambulance."

Anna Leigh couldn't keep from laughing. "That certainly sounds like Lexington. Perhaps I should try to drive out to the ranch. They may need help with the children."

"No, ma'am, I wouldn't advise trying right now. The roads are a mess. I just wanted to let you know, in case Amanda somehow gets in touch with you. Oh! Lex said that Lorrie was with Shelby Fisher. She works at the ranch. Do you know her?"

"I do, yes." She patted his arm. "Thank you, dear. When will it be safe to travel?"

"I guess it depends on where you need to go. Some of the major roads have been cleared by volunteers, but we've got a ways to go before all the residential streets are passable. If you need to get home, let me or one of my deputies know. We'll give you a ride."

"That won't be necessary, but thank you. I thought I could help around here at least a few more hours. Be careful out there, Sheriff."

He tipped his hat. "Yes, ma'am. Thanks for the sandwich."

Anna Leigh finished handing out the food and returned to the kitchen. Kathleen took the tray from her and guided her to a chair. "Are you all right, Anna Leigh?"

"Yes, I'm quite all right. Thank you. Have you heard any news of your grandmother?"

Kathleen placed the tray on the counter and squatted beside the chair. "As a matter of fact, yes. One of the volunteers passed by the home on his way here. He said that other than a lot of broken tree limbs everywhere, they're okay."

"That's wonderful, dear." Anna Leigh stood. "I believe I'll step outside for a breath of fresh air. I shouldn't be too long."

She left through the kitchen door and breathed a sigh of relief when it closed behind her.

It was still cloudy, but the rain had stopped sometime earlier, and Anna Leigh was surprised by how peaceful it was behind the VFW. If not for the amount of debris scattered around the area, she would be hard-pressed to tell that anything had happened.

She walked slowly around the building, taking her time to get her thoughts in order. She was so wrapped up in her thoughts that she almost missed the tiny mew. After a short search, Anna Leigh found the cause of the noise.

A small, soaked bundle of gray was huddled beneath a plastic garbage can lid. It raised its blue eyes up at the intruder and gave a half-hearted hiss.

Anna Leigh knelt beside the lid and held out her hand. "Well, hello there. Aren't you a brave little thing?"

The kitten wasn't much larger than her fist yet it cautiously sniffed at her fingers.

"That's right. I'm not going to hurt you." She allowed it to sniff for a moment, then carefully picked it up. "Goodness, you weigh next to nothing." When she held it close to her chest, she could feel it shiver. "You poor dear. I wonder who you belong to?"

Anna Leigh looked around the area to make sure there were no brothers or sisters lurking, before she continued along on her walk. "You must have gotten washed away from your home. I'm not quite certain what to do with you."

The more she talked, the calmer the kitten became, until it began to purr. "Aren't you a little heart breaker?"

She stepped around to the front of the building in time to see a familiar vehicle pull up in the yard.

Two women jumped out of the maroon Expedition and started for the main entrance of the VFW hall.

Amanda was the first to notice Anna Leigh, and she jogged to where her grandmother stood. "Gramma! I'm so glad you're all right!" She was about to embrace the older woman until she noticed what she held.

Jeannie followed her sister and stopped. "Gramma, what is that?"

"A kitten, of course." Anna Leigh shifted the animal and hugged Amanda with her free arm. "I'm so glad to see you. Is everything all right at the ranch?"

"Our roof was slightly damaged, but other than that, yes. We're all fine."

Jeannie got in a quick hug as well. "Where did you get a kitten?"

"I found it outside." Anna Leigh stroked the kitten with her thumb as she held it. "What are you two doing here?"

Amanda gently scratched the kitten's head. "Since the phones are out, we came to make sure everyone was okay. Have you seen Lex or Lorrie?"

"I just finished speaking with the sheriff, before I stepped outside." The stress of the day had caught up with Anna Leigh and she wavered.

Jeannie put her arm around Anna Leigh. "What's the matter, Gramma?"

"Amanda, dearest, I'm afraid—"

"No." Amanda took a step back.

"Lexington will be fine," Anna Leigh said quickly. "I spoke to the sheriff a short time ago."

Amanda stopped. "What happened?"

"The sheriff told me that Lexington was in an accident, but she should be all right."

"What about Lorrie?"

Anna Leigh continued to pet the kitten. "Lexington told him she's with Shelby Fisher. So I'm certain she's fine. But he said that they've taken Lexington to the hospital in Parkdale."

"When?"

"Just a short while ago. He's inside, trying to keep everyone updated."

When Amanda turned and headed for the door, Anna Leigh turned to Jeannie. "I'm sure Lorrie is perfectly safe."

"I'm sure she is, Gramma. Let's get you and your little friend inside, so we can find out more about Lex."

THE WHITE TILE ceiling still held no answers for the woman who had been forced to stare at it for the past half hour. Lex had given up finding patterns in the dots on the tile. She was still immobilized on the backboard, waiting to be seen by a doctor. "This is total bullshit," she said aloud.

"They told me a woman was being unreasonable in here. I should have known it was you." Rodney stepped into the examination room.

Lex tried to turn her head, but she was strapped down too tightly. "Rodney? What are you doing here?" Her voice was soft as she tried to keep from breathing too deeply.

"Isn't that my line?" he asked as he stood beside her head. "I was here with a patient when the storm hit Somerville. Since they got bombarded with casualties, I stuck around and helped in the emergency room." He read her chart as he spoke. "Why did you hit a tree, Lex?"

"Don't give up your day job. You'll never make it as a comedian." The friendly banter with her brother-in-law helped ease Lex's nerves, at least a little. "And for your information, the damned tree hit me."

He took out a penlight and shined it in her eyes. "Hmm."

"What?"

Rodney ignored her and studied her x-rays. "Are you in much pain?"

"I can handle it."

He rolled his eyes and switched out the film. "Let me try again. Are you in any pain?"

Lex muttered something.

"I'm sorry, what was that?"

"Okay, yes. I've got a god damned headache, my wrist is killing me, my back hurts and I think I've got some bruised ribs. Happy?"

Rodney lightly patted her shoulder. "Not happy, no. Are you claustrophobic?"

"Why?"

"Because we're going to need some better images of your head, torso and back, just to be safe."

"MRI?"

"Yes, I'm afraid so. Are you okay with that?"

Lex sighed. "Do I have much of a choice?"

He put the chart down and leaned above her, so that they could see eye-to-eye. "Of course you do. But, do you want to be the one who tells Amanda we didn't give you a thorough exam?"

"Are you afraid of my wife, Rodney?"

"Aren't you?" he asked as he laughed.

Her answer was unintelligible.

Rodney studied Lex's nose. "You're going to need that set, unless you want to go through the rest of your life looking like a boxer."

"Yeah, I figured. Hurts like hell. Speaking of Amanda, has anyone tried to contact her? I don't want her freaking out about this."

"I've tried a couple of times, but the lines are still down. Don't worry, I'll be the one to talk to her, so she's not given the wrong information."

Lex closed her eyes against the bright light of the room. Her headache was making her sick to her stomach. "I need to find out about Lorrie, too."

"What about her?"

"She's with Shelby at her place. It's west of town, which is the direction that damned storm came from." Lex clenched her fists. "I need to get out of here so I can find her."

The door opened and an orderly started inside. Rodney held up his hand to keep the orderly quiet. "Lex, I promise I'll do what I can to find Lorrie. But right now, I need you to relax and let us take care of you, okay?"

"Yeah. Oh, hey. How's Weldon?"

Rodney moved out of the way so the orderly could get to the stretcher. "He's going to be fine. He had a clean break. From what I understand, you both were very lucky."

"Be sure and tell my wife that, will you?" Lex asked as the orderly pushed her out of the room.

"DO WE HAVE to go in there?" Lorrie asked Shelby. "I just want to find my mom."

Shelby parked the car. "Yeah, we do. Your arm ain't gonna fix itself, and neither is my shoulder."

Lorrie got out of the car at the same time as Shelby. "Does that mean you're not going to leave me here by myself?"

"Of course not." Shelby could feel her last reserves ebb away as they walked to the doors of the emergency room. "I promise you, we're in this together. At least until your folks show up, all right?"

"Okay." Lorrie followed her through the doors. "Wow."

Shelby almost went back outside as they were assailed by dozens of voices, crying children and the blare of the hospital loud speaker. She gritted her teeth and continued to the admittance desk, where a lone woman struggled to answer the phone and enter data into the computer. "Excuse me, ma'am?"

"Take a number and take a seat, and we'll call you when we can," the woman answered, without bothering to look up.

"Yeah, but—"

"Take a number and take a seat," the woman repeated. She raised her head and gasped. "Oh, my. I'm sorry." She picked up a clipboard and handed it to Shelby. "Are you able to fill out these forms?"

Shelby took the clipboard. "Yes'm, I can do that." She tore a number from the machine. "Thanks." She looked around the waiting area, but didn't see any empty chairs. "How about we stand by the doors? At least it'll be less noisy there."

"Good. The noise hurts my head."

"Mine too, buddy." Shelby leaned against the wall and tried not to grin at Lorrie's attempt to mimic her. She looked at the clipboard and began to write when the bay doors opened, and a stretcher was brought in. "Watch out, Lorrie. We need to—" her mind went blank when she recognized the woman on the stretcher. "Rebecca?"

The stretcher rolled by Shelby, but not before Rebecca heard her name called. "Shelby?"

"Damn it! Lorrie, stay here, I'll be right back." Shelby dropped the clipboard and chased after them. "Hey, hold up!"

"Shelby!" Rebecca cried.

"For the love of God, will you guys stop?" Shelby yelled. Half of the people in the emergency area stopped and turned to look at her. She was still covered in mud, blood and everything else and was a frightful sight. "Please, wait."

They paused at the defeated tone in her voice. One of the attendants turned and saw Shelby for the first time. "Um, ma'am?"

Shelby moved past him and looked down at her lover. "What happened, darlin'?"

"Oh, God, Shelby," Rebecca cried. She tried to reach for her, but the straps kept her immobile. "Damn it."

"Easy, there." Shelby put her hand on Rebecca's. "You're gonna be okay."

Rebecca started to argue, but noticed Shelby's appearance. "What happened to you?"

"Just a little accident, nothin' major. You just worry about yourself, all right?" Shelby looked up at the men who brought her into the emergency room. "Can we go with you?"

"Are you family?"

Lorrie overheard them as she walked up. "They're my aunts."

"All right. But try to stay out of the doctor's way. They may have to send you back here, if they send Miss Starrett for tests."

Shelby didn't remove her hand as they left the noise of the waiting area behind. She kept her eyes on Rebecca's face. "See? It's—"

"Momma!" Lorrie broke away from them and ran down the hall, to where an orderly was pushing a stretcher. She skidded into the stretcher and hung onto the rail with her good hand. "Momma, what happened?"

"Hey, lil' bit. Damn, I'm glad to see you. How did you get here?" Lex asked.

"Shelby brought me. She's with Ms. Rebecca. What happened to you?" All of Lorrie's words came out in a rush. "Did you get hurt in the storm?"

"Whoa, sweetheart. Listen, your Uncle Rodney is in the room I just left. Go see him and let him know you're here, okay? I have to get some tests done, but I'll be back in a little while."

Lorrie started to cry. "I don't want you to go, Momma."

"It's okay, really. Your uncle is worried too, and needs to see you. Can you do that for me?"

Lorrie tried to stop crying. "I'm sorry, Momma."

"Hey, it's all right. Just go see Uncle Rodney. He'll bring you to me when I'm done, I promise."

"Okay." Lorrie let go of the stretcher, then chased after it again. "I love you, Momma!" she cried as Lex was wheeled into an elevator.

"I love you too, sweetheart," Lex answered, as the elevator doors closed.

Lorrie turned around and saw Rodney standing in the hall. She stumbled past Rebecca and Shelby and fell into her uncle's arms.

RODNEY TURNED AWAY from the x-rays and put his hand on his niece's shoulder. Lorrie was seated on the exam table, dressed in a clean hospital gown. "Looks like you and your momma will be twins for a while. But the good news is it's a clean fracture. You should be able to play softball in the fall."

"Will Momma be okay? She's been gone a long time."

"I haven't seen her film yet, but I think she'll be fine." He caught her as she swayed. "Why don't you lie back and close your eyes? I'll try to find out how much longer she'll be."

Lorrie yawned and allowed herself to be guided onto the pillow. "I'm not tired," she argued weakly as Rodney covered her with a thin blanket.

"I know." He watched as she fell asleep almost instantly. Her exhaustion, along with the light pain medication he had given her, worked quickly to relax her. Once he was certain she was out, Rodney stepped outside the room and carefully closed the door.

A harried young nurse met him in the hall. "Dr. Crews, there's two women in the lobby looking for you."

Rodney sighed and headed for the lobby. "All right, thanks." He stopped and turned around. "My niece is in room six. She's suffering from exhaustion and a fractured wrist, and I needed someplace for her to stay while her mother is having an MRI upstairs."

"I'll check in on her, Doctor."

"Thank you, I'd really appreciate it." When Rodney stepped through the doors that separated the waiting area from the examination rooms, he was surprised to see his wife and her sister walking toward him. "Jeannie? Are the boys all right?"

Jeannie hugged him as tightly as she could. "I'm so glad to see you. I was afraid..." her voice trailed off. "The boys are fine. They're with Martha and Charlie."

He finally pulled away from his wife and turned to Amanda. "I think I know why you're here. Lex is upstairs and Lorrie's in one of the exam rooms. Come on, I'll take you both back and try to fill you in."

AMANDA SLOWLY OPENED the door and stepped into the small room. She stood next to Lorrie and shook her head. "Just like your momma," she whispered as she lightly brushed her hand against her daughter's mud-stained forehead.

Lorrie opened her eyes and blinked several times, as if to clear her vision. "Mom?"

"I'm here, honey."

"Mom!" Lorrie rose and was quickly wrapped in Amanda's arms. She rested her cheek against Amanda's shirt.

Amanda sat on the table and tugged Lorrie into her lap. Lorrie was almost her height, but stretched until she fit comfortably. "Shh. It's going to be okay."

Jeannie lightly knocked on the open door and came inside. "Rodney told me that Lex is finished with the tests and is on her way to a room."

"Thanks."

Lorrie sat up and wiped her face. "Does that mean that she's gonna be okay?"

"They're pretty sure she will be," Jeannie answered. She sat next to Amanda and rubbed Lorrie's back. "How are you doing?"

"I'm hungry." She fought off a yawn.

Jeannie laughed and winked at her sister. "Let me see if I can find some scrubs that'll fit you, then we can run down to the cafeteria. Unless you'd rather wear that."

"Eww. No, I don't like dresses. And this one has a big hole in the back." Lorrie scooted off Amanda. "Can we go see Momma?"

"As soon as she's settled, I promise."

THE SOFT SNORE from Rebecca was the only sound in the hospital room. Shelby sat inches away and watched as her chest rose and fell. After the long series of x-rays and an MRI, it was determined that Rebecca had a spinal contusion. The doctors wanted to wait for the swelling to go down before they started treatment. She also had a nasty knot on the back of her head that they wanted to keep an eye on, so she was admitted and placed in a room.

Shelby scratched at the collar of the green scrubs that Rodney had found for her. They had to cut off her shirt to check her shoulder, which turned out to be a Type I separation and the nurse had made her throw away her filthy jeans, as well.

She leaned back in the plastic chair and sighed. The pain medication that Rodney had given her took the edge off her shoulder ache, but did nothing to slow down the barrage of thoughts that raced through her mind.

"I should have never left you alone today," she whispered. "I'm so sorry, darlin'."

"Shelby?" Rebecca rasped.

"Hold on." Shelby poured a small amount of water into a plastic cup and held the straw up to Rebecca's lips. "Easy, now."

Rebecca took a few sips. "Thanks." She studied Shelby's face. "You look terrible."

"Yeah?" Shelby leaned and lightly kissed Rebecca's lips. "You look wonderful."

"That bandage on your head must have affected your vision. Is it serious?"

Shelby touched the bandage on her left temple. It had taken eight stitches to close the gash, which she had completely forgotten about until now. She was thankful that she didn't have a concussion. "You know how I am. Hard-headed."

"That's true." Rebecca wriggled her fingers, which were immediately caught by Shelby. "I was afraid I'd never see you again."

"You can't get rid of me that easily," Shelby assured her. "All I could think about today was getting back to you to make sure you were okay. I did a pretty shitty job of that, though."

Rebecca frowned. "Are you kidding me? You're here, that's all that matters to me." She squeezed Shelby's hand. "When I was stuck under that stuff, and it was dark, wet and scary, I just pictured us snuggled on the couch together in front of a warm fire."

"Yeah?"

"Yeah."

Shelby scooted her chair as close as she could and kissed Rebecca again. "As soon as you're out of here, we'll do that. I love you, darlin'."

"Love you, too." Rebecca closed her eyes and sighed. "I'm so tired."

"Get some rest. I ain't goin' nowhere."

Shelby was content to hold Rebecca's hand and watch her sleep.

LEX WAS UPRIGHT in bed when there was a light knock on her door. "Come on in."

She grinned as the door opened and Lorrie hurried inside, followed by Amanda. "Hey, there."

Lorrie stopped short of the bed, until Lex patted the space beside her.

"Are you sure it's okay?" she asked.

"Yep." Lex held out her good hand and helped Lorrie up. The movement jarred her ribs, and she sucked in a short breath to keep from groaning. "See? Plenty of room."

She patted the opposite side. "How about you, Mom?"

Amanda laughed and sat on the edge. "This will do, thanks." She sobered and touched Lex's swollen face. "Broke your nose again?"

"Yeah. Not sure if it was the airbag, or the tree."

"Tree?"

Lex bit her lip. "Um, anyway, how's everyone at home?"

Amanda kissed her. "Good try. I'll let it go, for now. Everyone at home is fine." She moved back and touched the splint on Lex's arm. "How'd this happen?"

"Not too sure. But it's a clean break, so it should heal quickly." Lex looked at Lorrie's arm. "You too, huh?"

Lorrie shrugged. "Uncle Rodney said the same thing about mine. He also said that Shelby did a good job splinting it, which is why it'll be okay."

"She did? What happened to you two, anyway?" Lex asked.

Lorrie yawned. "The wind blew her truck into a ditch and flipped it." She leaned against Lex and closed her eyes. "Can I stay here with you, tonight?"

Amanda was about to argue, when Lex shook her head and said, "Sure, sweetheart. You can keep me company."

"Thanks, Momma." Lorrie turned until she was more comfortably snuggled against Lex's side. She closed her eyes and relaxed.

"Are you sure?" Amanda asked.

"Positive." After all the trouble she had been through recently with Lorrie, Lex wasn't about to throw away this gift. "Everyone else okay?"

Amanda kept her voice low, to keep from disturbing Lorrie. "Pretty much. I was finally able to get through to the ranch on my cell phone. Martha said, and I quote, 'tell Lexie I owe her a whuppin' for trying to drive during a storm.' End quote."

"Figures." Lex carefully raised her broken wrist. "Do you think this will protect me?"

"Not a chance." Amanda stood and stretched. "It's been a hell of a day."

Lex continued to stare at her wife, even after the stretch ended. "Huh?"

"I can see that thump on the head didn't do much damage." Amanda took the spare blanket from the foot of the bed and covered Lorrie. "I'm glad you're okay."

"I was more worried about you and the kids." Lex held out her good hand. "How much trouble do you think we'd be in, if you slept up here with us?"

Amanda laughed and took her hand. "Let's not give the poor nurses any trouble. They've been really nice to me."

When Lex faked a pout, she kissed her bottom lip. "Behave."

"Yes, ma'am. I love you."

"Love you, too." Amanda kissed her as gently as possible. "Time for you to get some rest."

"What about you?"

Amanda pointed to the small chair in the corner that converted into an uncomfortable bed. "That'll do, when I get ready. But I thought I'd check on Shelby and Rebecca, first."

"Good idea." Lex lowered the top of her bed a few inches so she could be more comfortable. "Give them my best."

"I will." Amanda tugged on Lex's foot beneath the covers. "You're worse than the kids. Go to sleep."

"Yes, Mom." Lex stuck her tongue out at Amanda and closed her eyes.

Chapter Twenty-eight

THE SQUEAK OF the breakfast cart woke Shelby from a fitful sleep. Her head, which rested against the plastic rail of the bed, throbbed and ached, as did the rest of her body. She glanced at Rebecca, who dozed peacefully. Shelby struggled to her feet. Every muscle she owned had stiffened overnight, and she had to bite her lip to keep from cursing. She looked up when she heard a light tap on the door.

Before Shelby could answer, the door opened and Rebecca's mother poked her head inside. She was an older, slightly heavier version of her daughter, with streaks of gray in her auburn hair and a few more wrinkles around her blue eyes. She ignored Shelby and moved to stand on the other side of the bed. After Kathy assured herself that her daughter was all right, she nodded to Shelby. "Thank you for calling us."

"You're her family," Shelby answered. "Sorry it was so late, but I kept tryin' 'til I could get through. Although she'll probably kick my a...uh, rear, when she finds out."

Kathy cracked a smile. "I'm sure you can handle her." She held out her hand across Rebecca's body. "I'm really sorry about how we've acted toward you, Shelby."

Never one to hold a grudge, Shelby took her hand. "Thanks, Mrs. Starrett. I'm sure that'll make Rebecca feel better."

"Mom?" Rebecca opened her eyes and noticed the clasped hands above her legs. "What's going on?"

Kathy squeezed Shelby's hand before she released it. "I was apologizing to Shelby for our behavior." She touched her daughter's cheek. "How are you feeling?"

"I hurt all over." Rebecca looked at Shelby. "Were you here all night?"

Shelby tried to shrug, but it jarred her shoulder. She masked her discomfort by adjusting the sling. "What makes you think that?"

"You're still in the scrubs they gave you, yesterday. And..." Rebecca looked at Shelby's head. "You have a red crease on your forehead."

"Um." Shelby tried to rub the mark away. "Would you like some coffee, Mrs. Starrett? I could give y'all some time alone."

Kathy shook her head. "No, that's all right. You don't have to leave. I just wanted to—"

"Mom? Would you give us a minute?" Rebecca asked.

"Sure. I'll be right outside." Kathy smiled at both women before she stepped from the room.

Shelby rested her good hand on the bed rail. "What's up, darlin'?"

"Will you do me a huge favor?"

"Anything."

Rebecca tried to raise her arm, but her back hurt too much. "Ow."

"Hey, take it easy." Shelby reached between the rails and covered Rebecca's hand. "What's the favor?"

"Go home."

"What?"

Rebecca carefully smiled. The motion pulled at the bruise on her cheek, but she ignored it. "Honey, you look worse than I feel. Please, go home and get a shower and some rest. I'm sure Mom wouldn't mind staying here, if that'll make you feel better."

"Are you tryin' to get rid of me?"

"Yes." Rebecca laughed then closed her eyes for a moment. "Ow. I shouldn't do that."

Shelby reached for the call button. "Do you need me to get the nurse?"

"No." Rebecca took a few shallow breaths before she opened her eyes. "But I do need you to take care of yourself, if only for me."

"A'right."

Rebecca was poised to argue her point. "What?"

Shelby touched the tip of Rebecca's nose. "You win. Besides, I could really use a shower. I itch in places that don't need to itch."

"I can just imagine. I'd do just about anything for a bath right now." Rebecca squeezed Shelby's hand. "I'll see you tomorrow?"

"You'll see me this evenin'," Shelby corrected. She leaned down and gave her lover a gentle kiss. "Get some rest, darlin'. I love you."

Rebecca blinked away the moisture from her eyes. "I love you, too."

Shelby used her fingertip to wipe Rebecca's tear. "Are you sure you want me to go?"

"I'm sure. I think all these drugs they have me on make me feel more emotional than usual. Go on, before my mother breaks the door down."

"Okay." Shelby opened the door and stepped into the hall. "Mrs. Starrett?"

Kathy met her not far from Rebecca's room. "Is everything all right, Shelby?"

"Yes, ma'am. Matter of fact, would you mind keepin' Rebecca company for a while? She's sending me home."

"Of course!" Kathy finally looked closely at Shelby. The hospital scrubs were too large for her slender body, which was covered in scrapes and bruises. Her eyes had dark circles beneath them, and her left eye was swollen from the bandaged injury. The gray sling that held her left arm didn't seem to fit correctly, either. "Are you all right?"

Shelby fought off a yawn. "I've had better days, that's for sure. Nothin' a little time won't heal, though. Thanks."

"All right." Kathy touched her unencumbered arm. "When something like this happens, it puts everything in perspective, doesn't it?" At Shelby's confused look, she continued, "When I heard that Rebecca had been hurt in the storm, I didn't care about anything else but her."

She lowered her gaze and focused on the tile floor. "We were just so sure that you were a phase she was going through. A way to get attention."

"With all due respect, Mrs. Starrett—"

"No, Shelby. Please. Even if I hadn't seen you by my daughter's side just now, I know we were wrong. Becca's told me again and again how much she—" Kathy stumbled through the words. "Loves you. It's hard to reconcile what I always hoped and dreamed for her, against what reality is, you know?"

Shelby nodded. "Yes'm, I do understand. And bein' at odds with y'all has really torn her up. But, at the same time, we've never been happier. I love her more than anythin' in the world, Mrs. Starrett. And that ain't never gonna change."

"I'm glad, Shelby." Kathy started toward Rebecca's room, then turned. "I thought we resolved that Mrs. Starrett stuff years ago."

"Yes, ma'am." Shelby nodded and graced her with a genuine smile, one she usually only shared with Rebecca. "Thanks, Kathy."

Kathy winked at her and went into Rebecca's room.

AMANDA PACED AROUND the small room, waving her hands and grumbling. "Of all the pig-headed, stubborn, lame-brained—"

"Sweetheart," Lex tried to interrupt.

"Stupid, foolish, moronic, idiotic—"

"Amanda." As her wife continued to stomp around, Lex balled up a piece of paper and hit her in the back of the head.

Amanda stopped and spun around, glaring at Lex. "What?"

Lex held out her hand. "Could you come here, please?"

"I don't know." Amanda put her hands on her hips. "Maybe I'm not through talking."

"Uh huh." Lex crooked her finger. "Talk over here."

Amanda growled, but moved across the room to stand beside Lex's hospital bed. "Yes?" She yelped when she was pulled onto the bed and across Lex's lap. "You're going to hurt yourself."

"Nah." The motion did make her back ache and her chest hurt but Lex ignored the pain and wrapped her arms around Amanda. "Now, what were you saying?"

"I know you're anxious to get out of here, but the doctors want to keep an eye on you for another day or so. They're concerned about the bruising on your chest."

Rodney had stopped by the room the night before to explain the results of the x-rays and MRI. Lex had two cracked ribs and significant bruising from the seatbelt. Although there was no sign of internal bleeding, they wanted to err on the side of caution, especially since Lex recently recovered from pneumonia.

Lex took a shallow breath and released it. "See? I'm okay. I've tried telling them that."

"Lex," Amanda placed her hand on her wife's chest. "It's not the bruises that concern them, it's what's under the bruises."

"Ah." Lex put her hand atop Amanda's. "One more day? Then I'm going home. I miss the kids."

She had awakened to find that Jeannie had taken Lorrie home with her and she still felt hurt by the loss.

"What if I bring Mel and Eddie for a visit this afternoon? Would that help?"

Lex stuck out her lower lip, which Amanda immediately kissed. They broke apart and Lex sighed. "Nah. There's no sense in dragging them all the way out here. I'll see them tomorrow."

"Maybe." Amanda gentled her point by a kiss to the forehead. "How's your headache?"

"Still going strong." Lex leaned into the kiss and closed her eyes. Amanda's light tracing around her swollen nose soothed her. "I look like hell, don't I?"

Amanda continued to place soft kisses on her face. "I." Kiss. "Think." Kiss. "You're." Kiss. "Beautiful." The final kiss was on Lex's lips, but was interrupted by a yawn.

"Sorry." Lex yawned again. "It's not you."

"I know." Amanda scooted off the bed and lowered it. "Time for your morning nap."

Lex groaned, both from the discomfort of changing position and her wife's words. "I just woke up."

"Then it shouldn't be too hard to go back to sleep." Amanda straightened the covers and brushed her hand across Lex's hair. "I'll see you this afternoon."

"'Kay." Lex struggled to keep her eyes open but emitted a low snore, instead.

Amanda shook her head. "I guess I'd better get used to that sound, at least until your nose heals." She kissed Lex's forehead again before leaving the room.

SHELBY LEANED AGAINST the back of the elevator and tried to keep from falling asleep. She let her eyes drift closed as the elevator stopped on the next floor and she nearly jumped out of her skin as someone touched her arm. "What?"

"I'm sorry, Shelby. Are you all right?" Amanda had peeked in on them last night, but both Shelby and Rebecca were sound asleep and she didn't have the heart to wake them.

"Uh, yeah." Shelby rubbed her face with her free hand and blinked a few times to get her bearings. "How's Lorrie?"

Amanda stepped into Shelby's personal space and carefully hugged her. "She's going to be fine, thanks to you."

"Don't thank me. It's a wonder I didn't get her killed," Shelby muttered once Amanda moved away. "How about Lex?"

"She's grumpy, which is a good sign."

The elevator opened on the ground floor. Shelby followed Amanda through the lobby and out into the morning air. She looked at the clear, blue sky and shook her head. "Hard to believe yesterday even happened, ain't it?"

"Sure is." Amanda stopped at the end of the sidewalk. "How's Rebecca? I was going to check on her before I left but I ran into you."

"She's hurtin', but she's tryin' to keep it to herself. The doc said her back is strained or sprained and they're worried about the swelling and a possible spinal contusion. So she'll have trouble movin' around for a while." Shelby scratched behind one ear. "I didn't want to leave, but since her mom showed up I figured they could use some time alone."

"That was sweet of you."

Shelby shrugged, or at least tried. She grimaced as the motion pulled on her shoulder. "Yeah, well. Kathy apologized this mornin' and it made Rebecca pretty damned happy. That's all that matters to me."

Amanda had heard Rebecca's side of the problem with her family. She and the younger woman had discussed it at length over coffee. "Where are you heading?"

"Home, I guess. Even with a change of clothes, I smell like a stock tank."

Amanda laughed at the comparison. It sounded exactly like something her wife would have said. "Is your house all right after the storm? Ours is going to need some work on the roof, but otherwise it's okay."

"Yeah. Other than the back door being busted, it's in good shape." Shelby straightened her posture in an attempt to wake up. "Can I walk you to your truck?"

"On one condition."

Shelby shuffled beside Amanda. "What's that?"

"Come to my sister's house with me. You can shower there and catch a nap. She's got plenty of room."

Shelby stopped. "Naw, that's okay. Y'all don't need me underfoot."

"Let me rephrase that," Amanda said, as she took Shelby's good arm. "You're about ready to drop, and you have no business trying to drive. Come with me and get some rest, and I'll bring you back up this afternoon. Deal?"

"Is that how you talk to Lex?"

"Yep. And she's smart enough to listen to me. Most of the time."

"Well, if you're sure I won't be any trouble, then."

"Not at all." Amanda unlocked the Expedition and climbed in behind the steering wheel. "You're not much smaller than Rodney, so I bet they even have some clothes you can borrow. Unless you're fond of those scrubs."

Shelby gave her a wry look. "They go great with the boots, don't they?"

As Amanda backed out of the parking space, Shelby cursed.

"What's the matter?"

"I need to head home and take care of the horses. They're probably chewing the barn to bits."

Amanda stopped Shelby from unbuckling her seat belt. "Let me have one of the guys do it. They need something to do."

"They have more than enough to do, Amanda. I'm sure there's plenty of broken tree limbs and shi— um, stuff to clean up at the ranch."

"Really?" Amanda continued to drive out of the parking lot. "Well, since I have you captive in my SUV, you have a choice."

Shelby couldn't wipe the grin from her face. She had witnessed Amanda's handling of Lex but had never been targeted by her. "What's that?"

"Either let me call the guys to take care of your horses or I'll drive you out there and we can do it together."

"You don't need to go to all that trouble. I can handle it just fine."

Amanda stopped the truck. "What's it going to be? Remember, I'm used to Lex. She's one of the most stubborn people I've ever met."

Shelby relaxed against the back of the seat as her energy left her. "I reckon Rebecca would disagree with you there. But, all right. Chet's been there with me a time or two. He'll know what to do."

"Smart woman."

Once they were headed toward Somerville, Amanda turned on the radio to a news station. "I hope this doesn't bother you, but I'd like to get an update on the weather."

"Sounds like a good idea."

> ...at least four people are missing and many injured in the storm that hit the small community of Somerville, yesterday afternoon. Two people drowned at Lake Somerville when their boat was capsized by the seventy-mile-an-hour plus winds and three more were killed in separate instances in the town proper. It's the first derecho in this part of the state in more than forty years, and many were ill-prepared for the fast-moving storm...

Amanda flicked the radio off. "My God. That explains a lot. One minute we had a few clouds in the sky, and the next all hell was breaking loose. The only reason we were prepared at the ranch was because of the weather radio."

She had only read about derechos. The widespread, fast-moving storm could cause destruction similar to a tornado. With winds that gust at least fifty-eight miles per hour, and several separate gusts of over seventy-five miles per hour, the swath of damage would cover more than two hundred forty miles.

She turned to Shelby. "You and Lorrie could have been killed. How did you know?"

"I heard some thunder and wanted to get her to the house before the bad weather hit. Just got unlucky that the truck was blown off the road when it was. I'm sorry, Amanda. I should have been more careful."

"Are you kidding? I'm just glad she was with you, instead of Lex."

Shelby shook her head. "What? No. Because of me, Lorrie's got a broken wrist. If she had been with Lex, she'd—"

"Been in the truck when it was hit by the tree," Amanda added quietly. "Who knows what would have happened to her, then." She took a cleansing breath. "So, thank you."

Shelby had nothing to say to that. "Then I'm glad she was with me. Thanks, Amanda." She closed her eyes and allowed herself to relax for the first time since the storm.

KYLE HAD NEVER seen the Somerville Hospital parking lot so full. She parked her shop's tow truck a block away and wearily hiked to the emergency room. After they had rescued Lex and Weldon, Kyle and Ellie had driven to the town square. They spent the rest of the day helping the injured. Afterward, Ellie had asked to be taken to the hospital so she could assist the overwhelmed staff. That was the last time Kyle saw or heard from her.

Once she had dropped Ellie off at the hospital, Kyle had gotten her company's tow truck and used it to give assistance as needed. Sometime before sunup, Kyle returned home to finish cleaning up their duplex. She had enough time to shower and change before driving to the hospital to pick up Ellie.

Kyle checked her watch and mentally cursed. Ellie was supposed to have called her before now. She stepped through the doors and glanced around. Most of the chairs in the waiting area were occupied, some by sleepers who waited for word of loved ones while others gathered in small knots to speak quietly amongst themselves. Kyle stood at the intake counter until the woman ahead of her walked away. "Hi. I'm here for Eleanor Gordon. She's a nurse who came in yesterday to help."

"I'll have her paged," the woman offered. She appeared as exhausted as Kyle felt.

"Thanks."

Ten minutes later, Ellie stepped through the doors from the

emergency area and glanced around. Her eyes quickly found Kyle. She hurried across the room and embraced her lover, mindless of the people around them. "I'm sorry I didn't—"

"Shh." Kyle kept her arm around Ellie's waist and led her outside. "Have you had anything to eat?"

Ellie rested her head against Kyle as they walked. "Hmm?"

"Food. Have you had any since yesterday?"

"I had a sandwich last night, I think."

When Ellie stumbled, Kyle tightened her grip around her. "I'll make you something when we get home. Eggs and toast okay?" Kyle felt Ellie's nod on her shoulder. "Then I'm putting you to bed."

"I'd like to go to Parkdale and see Lex. Besides, we still have some cleanup to do in our bedroom."

"Not anymore. I took care of it." Once they reached the truck, Kyle helped Ellie inside before jogging around to the driver's seat. "The window's still boarded up, but I was able to put clean sheets on the bed. I had to throw away the comforter, though."

Ellie rested against the back of the seat and closed her eyes. "You're amazing." She reached out blindly and smiled as Kyle took her hand. "I love you."

Kyle squeezed her partner's fingers before starting the truck. "I love you too, baby."

The drive home was in silence. Kyle let Ellie rest as she navigated the streets that had been cleared by volunteers.

"That's Amanda's SUV at Jeannie's house. Pull over, Kyle."

Kyle jumped at the sound of her lover's voice. "I thought you were asleep."

"No, just resting." Ellie had her hand on the door handle before the truck stopped. "Jeannie's house looks okay." She climbed from the vehicle and waited for Kyle. "I guess this area was away from the path of the storm."

"Yeah. It started a couple of blocks north of here." Kyle walked beside her as Ellie headed toward the front door. "Remind me to drive by Mrs. Cauble's after we leave here, okay? I want to make sure she doesn't need anything."

Ellie stopped short of the door and turned to Kyle. "You're just too sweet." She put her arms around Kyle's neck and kissed her.

THE DOOR OPENED and Jeannie cleared her throat. "Should I leave you two alone?"

Kyle jumped back as if she had been poked as Ellie laughed. "Hi, Jeannie. I'm sorry to bother you, but we saw Amanda's truck and decided to stop. How's she doing?"

"She's tired, but okay. Come on in." Jeannie stepped back to allow them inside. "Amanda's getting Shelby settled in the guest room. Do you want me to get her?"

"No, that's all right. We were on our way home," Ellie answered. "We'll get out of your hair."

Jeannie noticed how worn out both women were. "Amanda is going to start brunch in a few minutes. Why don't you come into the kitchen with me and have some coffee? We'll have more than enough food to go around."

Before her partner could argue, Kyle nodded. "Only if you'll let me help. I'm pretty handy in the kitchen, too."

"Thank goodness. I've been banned from my kitchen by my sister."

Jeannie pointed a warning finger at Ellie. She knew her husband had spoken of her misadventures to his staff, including Ellie. "Not one word."

AFTER SHE MADE certain Shelby was asleep in the guest room, Amanda moved down the hallway of her sister's home and opened the door to Teddy's room.

The light blue walls were complimented with navy curtains and posters of cartoon characters. Against one wall was a wooden desk with different action figures posed together. Next to the desk was a two-shelf bookcase, filled to overflowing with books and more toys. Across from both was a twin-sized bunk bed. Lorrie was curled up on the bottom bunk, mumbling in her sleep.

Amanda quickly crossed the room and sat beside her daughter. "It's okay, sweetie," she said, as she rubbed Lorrie's back. "Everything's all right."

"Momma!" Lorrie cried, waking up. She sat up and looked around the room in confusion. "Mom?"

"I'm right here, honey. You were just having a bad dream."

Lorrie tightly embraced Amanda. "It seemed so real."

"Do you want to talk about it?"

Lorrie shook her head. "It's too hard."

"That's all right, you don't have to." Amanda kissed her on the head. "But if you need to talk, I'm right here."

They sat quietly for a minute or two. Lorrie was the first to break the silence. "I was walkin' in the hospital, but it was dark and no one else was there," she whispered. "I heard a noise and went into this room, and—" She trembled and began to cry again. "Momma was lying on this bed, really still."

Amanda continued to rub Lorrie's back as she related her dream.

"When I," Lorrie choked out, "touched her, she was d...dead." She burst into tears and got as close to Amanda as she could. "I kept trying to get her to wake up, but she wouldn't."

"It was just a bad dream. Momma is doing fine. As a matter of fact, I thought that this afternoon, we could pick up your sister and brother and go visit her."

Lorrie moved back enough to see her mother's face. "Is she still okay?"

"She's grumpy, bored and misses all of you. I promised her if she'd do as the doctors tell her, we'd all come up for a visit."

"How long does she have to stay?"

Amanda kissed Lorrie's forehead in an attempt to erase the last vestige of terror from her daughter's mind. "Hopefully only one more day. They want to make sure her head and ribs are all right before they let her leave."

"How about her back? When she first came into the hospital, they had her tied in place. And something around her neck, too."

"Her back is okay, honey. She's going to be sore for a while, but the only real damage was to her wrist." Amanda lightly touched Lorrie's cast. "Like you."

Lorrie frowned and looked at her cast. "I...I don't know if I can go up there." She raised her head and blinked away the tears from her eyes. "I'm scared."

"Oh, sweetie." Amanda pulled her close. "You don't have to go. Momma will understand."

"But I want to see her."

"I know. Let's play it by ear, all right? Would you like to go to the ranch with me to get Mel and Eddie?"

"Is our house okay?"

"We have some roof damage, and one of the rear doors on the hay barn is broken." Amanda thought about the call she'd made to Roy before Lex awakened this morning. He assured her that the ranch was in better shape than they had thought, and that two of the ranch hands had covered the damaged roofs with tarps. "But yes, everything's okay."

Lorrie's stomach growled, causing them both to laugh. "Sorry."

Amanda touched the end of Lorrie's nose. "I was going to ask you if you were hungry, but I think I already have my answer. Why don't you go wash your face and then meet me in the kitchen?"

"Aunt Jeannie's kitchen?"

"Don't worry. I love you too much to subject you to her cooking." Amanda stood and hauled Lorrie out of bed. "Just don't tell her I said that, okay?"

"Okay." Lorrie giggled and hugged her. "I love you, Mom. And I think I want to go see Momma at the hospital, too."

"That's my girl." Amanda lightly swatted her on the rear. "I love you, too. Hurry up, before Aunt Jeannie decides to poison, I mean, cook for us."

Chapter Twenty-nine

SHELBY YAWNED AS she walked toward the hospital entrance. She had made the drive from their home to Parkdale twice a day for the past week. Each morning, she took care of their horses before the forty-minute trip to visit Rebecca. Shelby stayed until the nurses sent her away, then returned that evening until they forced her to leave. The only upside was that she and Kathy had become better acquainted.

She stepped off the elevator and nodded politely to the nurse as she passed the desk. "Mornin', Miz Charlotte."

"Good morning, Shelby. I'm going to miss seeing you here."

Shelby stopped and looked at her. "What? Does that mean Rebecca's gonna be released today?"

"Dr. Patterson signed her release and gave instructions to her family a short while ago. I was surprised you weren't here."

"Her—" Shelby bit off the curse. "Thanks, ma'am." She headed for Rebecca's room.

When she reached the open door, Shelby heard Rebecca's father's raised voice.

"I don't know why you're being so stubborn, Rebecca."

Shelby moved into the room and stepped around him. "Mornin'."

She insinuated herself between Greg and the hospital bed so she could kiss Rebecca's cheek. "How're you doin', darlin'?"

"Much better, now that you're here." Rebecca cupped her hand behind Shelby's head and pulled her in for a proper kiss.

Greg cleared his throat. "I was just suggesting to Becca what a good idea it would be for her to stay with us while she recuperates."

Shelby straightened and turned to look at him. "How do you figure that, Greg?"

She felt Rebecca's hand on her back, which was the only thing that kept her from yelling at him.

"Well, the doctor said she'd need to go to physical therapy every day for the next couple of weeks. And since we live in town—"

"Physical therapy? Every day?"

Rebecca tugged on Shelby's belt to get her to turn around. "Because of the weakness in my legs." She glared at her father. "I wanted to surprise you with the news that I'm being released this morning."

"That's great to hear, darlin'. The boys from the ranch already helped me build a ramp to the back door for you, so we're good to go."

Greg would not be dissuaded so easily. "And you're going to drive her into town every day? What about your job?"

"I'm on paid leave 'til my shoulder heals," Shelby answered. She had initially argued with Lex about it but now she was glad she had the leave to fall back on. "And yeah, I'll do whatever I need to do for Rebecca."

Kathy came through the door waving a bag. "Sorry it took so long, Becca, but—" She silenced when she felt the tension in the air.

"Good morning, Shelby. I ran out to the car to get the new sweats for Becca to wear home." She gave Shelby a careful hug and kissed her daughter's cheek. "I bet you're excited to be going home."

"I sure am. Thanks for the clothes, Mom."

"I was glad to help." Kathy stood beside her husband. "How is your shoulder, Shelby? Is it still giving you much trouble?"

"It's feelin' better every day, thanks."

"I'm glad to hear it. Becca, do you need me to help you change?"

"Um." Rebecca looked at Shelby, then her father.

"I think I can manage it, Kathy," Shelby said.

When Kathy's expression deflated, she added hurriedly, "But it would be great if you could come out to the house. Maybe show me some things that are easy to cook? I really don't want to send Rebecca back to the hospital from eating my cookin'."

Rebecca exhaled in relief. "That would awesome. Could you, Mom?"

"Of course, honey." Kathy turned to her husband. "I told you."

He shrugged and stared out the window.

Kathy went on to explain. "Greg thought we should have Becca stay with us. I told him it wasn't a good idea, because the bedrooms are upstairs." She nudged him with her shoulder. "But you know how guys are. We'll leave you to get dressed, Becca. Shelby, give me a call once you get settled at home."

She gave her daughter a gentle hug and kiss on the forehead.

"I sure will, Kathy. Thanks." Shelby couldn't help but grin at Greg. "See you later."

Greg ignored her and kissed Rebecca's cheek. "Love you, sweetheart."

"I love you too, Daddy."

Shelby closed the door behind the couple and leaned against it. "That was fun." She exhaled heavily and sat at the foot of the bed. "Your dad sure was full of himself today."

"I don't know what's gotten into him, lately. Every time he'd come to visit, he would start griping about one thing or another."

"Maybe it's his time of the month."

Rebecca giggled. "Poor Mom."

"Yeah." Shelby stood and took the clothes out of the bag. "Let's get you dressed and out of here, before they change their mind."

AMANDA HEADED UPSTAIRS after seeing the girls off onto the school bus. She could hear her wife talking, so she followed the sound toward Eddie's room. She stopped at the doorway and bit her lip to keep from laughing at the conversation.

"Big boy," Eddie said.

"I know you're a big boy, son. But you still need to wear socks and shoes." Lex tried to slip a sock onto his foot but he jerked it away.

"No."

Lex sighed. "Come on. I promised to have you dressed before your Mommy got back."

Eddie turned his head and grinned. "Mommy!"

"Yeah. Now don't give me—"

"Mommy!" Eddie squealed again, kicking Lex's hand away and climbing to his feet on his bed. "Hep!"

Amanda came into the room and stood beside Lex. "Are you giving Momma trouble?"

"No."

Lex rested her casted arm on the edge of his bed. "I think his idea of trouble and mine aren't the same."

"Eddie, why aren't your shoes and socks on?" Amanda asked him. "Don't you want to be ready when Mada and Pawpaw come over?"

"No." Eddie backed away from his parents. "No go, Mommy."

Lex started to say something, but stopped when Amanda touched her back.

"Why don't you go downstairs and see if we have enough coffee. I'll finish with him." Amanda leaned closer to Lex and kissed her cheek. "I'm sorry I forgot about you being down a hand. It's hard enough wrestling with him with two good ones."

"All right." Lex lightly touched Eddie's stomach. "Behave, Eddie." She laughed as he grabbed her finger. "Now what are you gonna do?"

"Momma, no go." He tugged until he lost his grip, then toppled back onto his rear. "Momma!"

Amanda picked him up and kissed him. "We'll see Momma in a minute, as soon as you get your socks and shoes on."

"No."

Before she could get pulled into the argument, Lex kissed the top of Eddie's head. "Be good." She kissed Amanda's cheek. "You, too." As she left the room, she heard Amanda laugh.

"We'll have to show Momma who's good, won't we?"

LEX CHUCKLED AND moved gingerly down the stairs. She had gladly put away her cane two days earlier, but still walked slowly in deference to her healing body. As she hit the bottom of the stairway, the back door opened.

Martha entered the house and allowed Charlie to help her remove her sweater. She looked up and noticed Lex. "You look a little too happy this morning."

"Too happy? What does that mean?" Lex followed them into the kitchen. She nudged Martha away from the counter. "Sit. I'll bring the coffee over."

Martha glared at her, but joined Charlie at the table. "How long will you and Amanda be gone?"

Lex brought four mugs and the insulated carafe to the table. She poured everyone coffee before she took her place across from Martha. "Not too long. I'm hoping we'll be done by the time the girls are out of school, so we can pick them up."

"Mada! Pawpaw!" Eddie toddled into the kitchen with Amanda not far behind. He grabbed a handful of Martha's slacks and tried to pull himself into her lap. "Hep."

She hefted him up and kissed his chubby cheeks. "How's my boy?"

"Mmm." Eddie wrapped his arms around her neck and gave her a slobbery kiss on the chin.

Amanda laughed and sat beside Lex. "Be careful, Mada. His newest trick is to lick instead of kiss. I think he's been playing with Freckles too much."

As if she had heard her name, Freckles raced through the pet door and into the room. She danced around the table to see if anyone had goodies for her. When none were forthcoming, she trotted to the corner by the pantry and curled up in her dog bed.

"Lellels," Eddie screeched. He slid from Martha's lap and headed for the dog.

Freckles raised her head and sighed, but didn't move as she was tackled by the rambunctious child.

"Eddie, be gentle," Lex warned. "Don't hurt Freckles."

"Love Lellels." He left a gooey kiss on the dog's head.

Amanda laughed and stood. "Since he's found something else to focus on, I think it's a good time for us to head to town." She rinsed out her coffee mug and placed it in the dishwasher. "Do either of you need anything while we're there?"

Charlie stretched his arm behind Martha, who leaned into his embrace. "Not that I'm aware of. Are you sure you don't need my help?"

"All the heavy work is done," Lex assured him. "We're just going to be there for moral support, more than anything else. And maybe to keep Jeannie from doing anything in the kitchen."

Amanda swatted her on the arm. "Be nice. She's very excited about moving into Gramma's house. I doubt she'd do anything to jeopardize that."

"Who's being ornery, now?" Lex walked to the dog bed and picked up Eddie. "Be good for Mada and Pawpaw, okay?"

He giggled when she blew raspberries on his cheek. "Momma, no."

Lex put him down, but not before one more kiss. "I love you, Eddie."

"Love Momma," he answered with a big smile, before returning his attention to Freckles.

Lex cleared her throat. "Well, okay. Guess I can't put this off any longer."

Amanda knelt beside the dog bed to give Eddie a kiss as well. "You've been itching to get away from the house all week."

"Ha. I have not."

"Have to."

Martha rolled her eyes. "Children!"

"Have not," Lex whispered. She kissed the top of Martha's head. "Bye."

Not to be outdone, Martha lightly swatted Lex on the rear as she stepped away. "Don't make me get my spoon after you."

When Amanda laughed, Martha added, "You, too."

"Hey!"

Martha shook her finger at them. "You two try to stay out of trouble. I know that'll be hard for you, but at least try."

"I don't know what you're talking about," Lex scoffed. "Come on, sweetheart. Let's go." She held the back door open for her wife. "Have not!"

She quickly closed the door.

JEANNIE FLOPPED ONTO the sofa beside Anna Leigh and blew out an exhausted breath. "Moving sucks."

"Yes, it does." Anna Leigh patted her arm. "Perhaps this will be your last move."

"Oh, yeah. They're going to have to drag me out of here, feet first," Jeannie quipped, then gasped in horror. "Oh, my God. I'm so sorry! That was awful of me."

Anna Leigh shook her head as she stared off into the distance. "Nonsense. You shouldn't have to guard your every word, dearest. Jacob wouldn't have wanted that, and neither do I." When Jeannie rested her head against her shoulder, Anna Leigh hooked her arm around her granddaughter. "As hard as it has been, we have to keep living our lives."

"I miss him," Jeannie whispered.

"As do I. But I believe your grandfather is here, watching over us." Anna Leigh hugged Jeannie and sat up straight. "And he'd thump us both for sitting here, moping."

A knock at the open front door caused them both to turn, as Lex and Amanda stepped into the house. Lex balanced several white, thin boxes on her cast as Amanda hefted a cardboard box.

Amanda stopped at the entry to the living room. "Hey there. Is the kitchen presentable?"

Jeannie stood. "Mostly. Why?"

"Because we brought goodies," Lex answered.

"Oooh." Jeannie moved forward. "Donuts!"

Lex stepped around Amanda and started for the kitchen. "If you're nice to me, I'll let you have one with sprinkles." She jerked and came close to dropping the boxes when Jeannie pinched her rear. "Watch it, woman."

"Lexington looks much better," Anna Leigh commented to Amanda, once the kitchen door had closed behind Lex and Jeannie.

"She is, mostly. Her back is still hurting her, but she won't let me schedule a follow up appointment with her orthopedist. How are you handing all this?"

Anna Leigh gently smiled. "I'm quite all right with it, truly. This old house needs a happy family. I'm thrilled that Jeannie decided to move so soon."

Amanda laughed and held the kitchen door open for her grandmother. "Lex swears she did it for the attention."

"Did what?" Jeannie asked, her mouth full of donut. Multi-colored sprinkles dotted her chin and shirt.

Lex handed her a paper towel. "Moved so soon after the storm. Here, you look like one of the kids."

Jeannie stuck her tongue out at Lex, chewed donut and all.

"You're disgusting." Amanda sat at the table. "Gramma, are you sure we're related?"

She took a chocolate glazed donut and sat it on the napkin in front of her.

"Most definitely." Anna Leigh used a napkin to remove a glazed donut from the box. She nibbled at it delicately, but didn't elaborate.

Lex laughed and sat beside her wife. Amanda continued to tease Jeannie so Lex took the opportunity to steal a bite from her donut.

"Hey, get your own." Amanda snatched the other half and held it away from her.

"You are my own," Lex stated, which caused Jeannie to make gagging sounds. "What?"

Jeannie rolled her eyes as she finished off her donut. "You're disgustingly mushy, Slim. I think my sister has corrupted you."

For a moment, Lex didn't say anything. She wiped the chocolate from her lips and stood as she stared at Jeannie the entire time. "Maybe I should show you what you're missing," she said in a soft voice. She held her good hand out to her sister-in-law.

"Um." Jeannie looked at Amanda, who shrugged. Acting braver than she felt, Jeannie took Lex's hand and was pulled to her feet.

Lex dipped Jeannie backward and held her there. She brought her face close to Jeannie's until they were almost nose-to-nose.

"I bet you've always wanted this," she whispered.

Jeannie's eyes grew large as Lex's lips descended.

With a wicked grin, Lex bypassed Jeannie's lips and blew a wet chocolate raspberry on her cheek. When Jeannie squealed and struggled, Lex was unable to hold the position and they both tumbled to the floor.

Amanda stopped laughing long enough to help her wife up. "Are you okay?"

"Never better." Lex stood and stretched. She looked at Anna Leigh, who held a hand over her mouth to mute her laughter. "How about you, Gramma? You ready for a spin?"

Anna Leigh shook her head. "I believe I'll pass, Lexington. But thank you for offering."

Jeannie climbed to her feet and wiped her cheek with her hand. "You're so gross, Lex. I'm gonna get you for that."

"Promises, promises." Lex swatted her on the butt. "You asked for it."

"I did not!"

The kitchen door opened.

"What on earth is going on in here?" Kyle asked.

"Jeannie's been picking on Lex," Amanda answered, as the trio took their places once again. She pointed to the boxes and the extra cups of coffee. "We brought sustenance."

"I've always liked you." Kyle stepped into the kitchen and opened the top box. "Oooh. I love chocolate glazed."

She went to the sink and washed her hands.

Anna Leigh scooted her chair back so that the other side of the table was accessible. "Why don't you take a break? You've been working non-stop."

"Thank you, A.L." Kyle had never been comfortable calling the older woman by her given name, so the initials were her way of compromise. "Everything's in place upstairs, and the guys just left."

"Oh. Okay. I was going to pay them—"

Kyle waved Jeannie off. "They didn't mind helping, so don't worry about it. But they had other plans later, and wanted to head home to clean up."

She sat on the other side of Anna Leigh and exhaled heavily. "Since everything is already done, I need to call Ellie and tell her not to bother coming here after work."

"She can still come, if she wants. I was thinking of cooking a roast for lunch," Jeannie said. "Rodney was only going to have the clinic open for half a day."

Frightened sets of eyes glanced around the table at the announcement. Anna Leigh was the first to find her voice. "I didn't see a roast in the refrigerator."

"No, but I think I have one in the deep freezer. Somewhere."

Amanda shook her head. "Jeannie, it's after ten. You can't cook a frozen roast in a couple of hours."

"Of course I can," Jeannie scoffed. "I'll just turn up the oven.

Right, Gramma?"

"I'm afraid it doesn't work that way, dear. Haven't you read that book I gave you?"

Jeannie rolled her eyes. "Gramma, I don't need a beginner's cookbook."

When Lex choked on her coffee, she swatted her. "Stop that."

Lex coughed a few more times while Amanda rubbed her back. She finally cleared her throat. "Two words, Jeannie. Boiled potatoes."

"That wasn't my fault!" Jeannie whined. She turned to Kyle. "Somehow the burner on the stove got set to high, and the pot burned dry. I had it set lower, I know it."

"The fire department didn't believe her, either. They showed up when the potatoes caught fire and smoke billowed out the back window," Lex helpfully explained to Kyle.

Amanda covered Lex's mouth. "What we're trying to say, Jeannie, is that maybe it would be easier to order out for lunch. Lex and I can go pick up some barbecue."

Lex nodded, since her mouth was still covered. She licked Amanda's hand, which earned her a dirty look from her wife. But it also gave her a chance to speak when the hand moved away. "Right."

When everyone became quiet, Anna Leigh turned to Kyle. "Have you and Eleanor decided when and where your ceremony will be?"

"Um, not exactly. I mean, well, we don't want it to be some huge, drawn out affair." Kyle looked to Lex and Amanda. "We figured to just have a few family members around as the vows were read. Nothing fancy."

Amanda reached for Lex's hand beneath the table. "Our offer of having it at the ranch is still open. Right, Lex?"

"Sure," Lex agreed. "Do you want us to talk to Reverend Hampton? He presided over ours."

Kyle shook her head. "No, thank you. Ellie really doesn't want to have anything to do with religion. She totally freaked out when I asked her."

"That makes sense," Amanda mused. "If I had her mother, I'd probably feel the same way."

Ellie's mother was a religious fanatic that had disowned her only daughter after finding out she was gay. They hadn't spoken since.

"Yeah. I guess I'm lucky that my folks moved to Virginia. They cut me out of the family when I was in high school."

Anna Leigh patted Kyle's arm. "We're very happy you're a part of our family, Kylie."

"Thanks, A.L." Kyle covered Anna Leigh's hand. "That means a lot to me." Kyle looked around the table at the family she had acquired when she and Ellie had gotten together. "It's a great family to be a part of."

Jeannie decided to lighten the mood. She bumped her shoulder against Lex's. "Most of the time, it is."

"Watch it, woman," Lex warned.

"Or what?"

Amanda leaned in front of Lex to stare at her sister. "Or I'll finish it."

"Thanks, sweetheart." Lex put her arm on the back of Amanda's chair and made a silly face at Jeannie. "As we were saying, Kyle, check with Ellie. We'd love to host your ceremony at the ranch."

Kyle nodded. "I will, thanks." She finished her coffee and stood. "If y'all will excuse me, I think I'll go home and get cleaned up, before Ellie gets off work."

After Kyle left, Anna Leigh stood as well. "I believe I'll run home and check on Derry. She's not used to being home alone for very long."

"Gramma, you've only had her a week. She can't already be that spoiled." Jeannie balled up a napkin and tossed it toward Lex. "And I wish you would have named her something more normal."

Anna Leigh shook her finger at her. "Nonsense. The little dear survived the first derecho to hit Somerville. I think Derry is a perfect name."

"So do I. It's better than your idea," Amanda said to Jeannie.

"Fluffy is a perfectly good name for a cat," Jeannie defended.

Lex batted away the napkin that Jeannie threw. "Ha. Not for a short-haired cat, Jeannie. Why not just call her Dog?"

Amanda got out of her chair. "Come on, honey. Let's walk Gramma out."

"Sure." Lex allowed herself to be led from the kitchen as Jeannie took another donut from the box.

"Mushy," she muttered, before devouring the donut.

SHELBY TUCKED THE blanket around Rebecca's legs once she got her partner settled comfortably on the sofa. She struggled to control her anger as she listened to Rebecca's side of the phone conversation.

"No, Terry. I don't care what your friend looks like, or how much money he makes. I'm very happy with Shelby."

Rebecca brought the phone away from her ear and sighed. She listened again as her brother ranted.

"Stop it! I don't care what you think. You didn't bother to come see me in the hospital, so why should I allow you to visit now? Please. You're an assistant manager at a hamburger joint. It's not exactly the most important job in the world. Yes, I realize that Austin isn't next door, Terry."

She held the phone out at arm's length and rolled her eyes. "I haven't heard from him in more than a year, and suddenly he cares?" she whispered to Shelby.

"Want me to have a go at him?"

Rebecca shook her head. "I can handle him, but thanks." She put the phone to her ear. "Shut up, Terrance. No, I said shut up!"

Once her brother quieted, Rebecca took a deep breath and released it slowly. "If all you want is to bitch at me about my life, then don't bother calling again. We have this conversation every time you bother to call. I'm with Shelby, and I'm going to stay with her until we're old and gray. Got that?"

She hit the disconnect button and tossed the phone to the other end of the couch. "He's such a jackass."

Shelby sat on the arm of the sofa. "Sorry, darlin'. I know you were upset when he didn't visit you in the hospital."

"It wasn't that, exactly. I just get tired of having to defend our relationship with the people who are supposed to love me. I mean, it's an ongoing thing. We've been together for six years. When is it going to stop?" She looked up to see the anguish in Shelby's eyes. "You're not a phase, Shelby. You're my life."

"I know. And I hope you realize it's the same for me."

Shelby kissed the top of Rebecca's head. Something occurred to her and she stood. "Be right back, okay?"

Rebecca watched Shelby go into the bedroom. "All right."

SHELBY PASSED TO the closet and moved the clothes to one side so that she could reach the small, metal box in the far corner. She opened the box and dug through the few photos and trinkets from her life. "Ah."

Beneath the folded rodeo playbills and the letters from her aunt, she found a balled handkerchief. She removed the handkerchief and closed the box.

After she stood, Shelby unfolded the cloth and stared at the contents. Her hand shook as she picked up the two thin, gold bands. "I hope I'm doin' the right thing, Pop," she whispered. "It sure didn't turn out so good for you."

She tightened her fist around the rings and tucked the handkerchief into her back pocket.

When Shelby returned to the living room, Rebecca frowned. "Hon? What's wrong?"

Shelby shook her head and sat beside her lover. "Ain't nothin' wrong, darlin'. Um." She looked at her closed hand. "I'm kinda late with this, but it ain't because of you."

She raised her head and looked into Rebecca's eyes. "I might not say it all the time, but you're the best thing that's ever happened to me, you know."

"You tell me more than enough, Shelby. I can always see it in your eyes." Rebecca gasped in surprise when Shelby dropped to her knee beside the couch. "What—"

"I reckon you could have just about anybody you'd want, Rebecca. I'm uneducated, foul-tempered and stubborn. But I swear to you, I'd die before I'd hurt you." Shelby took Rebecca's left hand and held it in hers. "We can't do this legal-like, but I'd be honored if you'd be mine, and wear this ring."

"Shel—" Rebecca couldn't stop tears from welling when her lover shakily held out a gold ring. "Is that?"

Shelby swallowed. "Yeah. It was my mom's. She left it when she took off, and my dad kept it. I figured maybe we could give it better luck."

Rebecca sniffled and nodded. "I'd like that."

Her hand was shaking as badly as Shelby's, and it took more than one try to get the ring on her finger. "It's a perfect fit."

"I had it sized a couple years back," Shelby admitted. "I just never got up the nerve to ask you."

"Why were you scared?" Rebecca looked at the ring on her hand. "You weren't afraid I'd say no, were you?"

Shelby shook her head. "If there's one thing I've ever been sure about, it's you, darlin'. But I remember what hell my parents went through and didn't want to do that to you."

Rebecca tugged on Shelby's hand. "Get up here."

Once she had Shelby next to her, she leaned in close and slowly kissed her. When Shelby deepened the contact, Rebecca tangled her fingers in her lover's hair. Once they broke apart for air, Rebecca said, "How's that for an answer?"

"I dunno. Maybe we should talk about it some more." Shelby grinned and kissed her again.

Chapter Thirty

AMANDA HELD THE back door open for Rebecca, who moved slowly with the aid of a cane. "It's so good to see you! Would you be more comfortable in the kitchen or the living room?"

"Probably the living room," Rebecca admitted.

"Bibba!" Eddie greeted from the kitchen. He sat in his high chair and waved his spoon in the air. "Mommy, Bibba!"

Amanda rolled her eyes. "Let me get him cleaned up and I'll join you. Would you like some coffee?"

Rebecca stopped at the kitchen door to catch her breath. She had stopped using her wheelchair only a few days earlier and still tired easily. "How about I join you in the kitchen, first?"

"Sure. Do you need any help?"

"Bibba!" Eddie slammed his fist on the tray. "Bibba!"

Amanda took the empty bowl and spoon away. "No, I've got it. Eddie, behave." She unbuckled him from the chair and sat him on the counter. "How do you manage to get so much of your breakfast on you?"

"Ha."

Rebecca settled in a chair. "I never thought walking from the truck would be so tiring."

"I was surprised to see you moving so well." Amanda used a wet paper towel to get the worst of the oatmeal off her son.

"Mommy, no!" Eddie shook his head to avoid the towel. "No! Bad!"

Amanda ignored his pleas and continued to wipe away the food. "Almost done." She kissed his forehead and set him down. "See? You survived."

Eddie toddled toward Rebecca. "Bibba!"

"Careful, Eddie. Miss Rebecca has an owie," Amanda warned him. "Be gentle."

He paused and looked at Amanda, then back to Rebecca. "Owie?"

"It's okay, sweetie. Come here." Rebecca held out her hands and laughed as he charged forward. She helped him climb onto her lap. "There you go."

Eddie grabbed her shirt and kissed her cheek. "Good." He settled on her lap and stuck his finger in his mouth.

Amanda brought two mugs of coffee to the table and placed one in front of her friend, but out of Eddie's reach. "Here you go."

She noticed the light glint off Rebecca's hand. "Well, hello. What's that?"

Rebecca blushed but held her hand out for inspection. "Shelby gave it to me last week."

"She did? How sneaky!" Amanda nodded her approval at the simple ring. "I like it. Does this mean what I think it means?"

"Yes, it does." Rebecca smiled and stared at her ring, as if she still had trouble believing it was real. "She got down on one knee, and everything."

Amanda patted her hand. "That's wonderful. Are you going to have any kind of ceremony?"

"No. We've already said what we wanted to say to one another. A ceremony isn't going to change anything for us." Her smile disappeared. "And if we had one, I'd have to invite my family. Mom would want some big production, and my father and brother would probably drive us all crazy."

"I'm sorry."

Rebecca shrugged. "My dad has been acting strange for the past year or so, and Terry's always been a jerk. They're not going to change, and I'm tired of messing with them. Mom has been great, though. She brought us at least a weeks' worth of meals and sent Shelby to the barn when she complained." She laughed at the memory. "Shelby was offended at the thought that she wasn't taking good care of me, but Mom told her to get over it."

"Poor Shelby."

"AND THEN SHE had the nerve to send me out of my own house." Shelby tossed the clean hay onto the floor of the stall.

Lex coughed to cover up her laugh. "Serves you right." She opened another bale. "Sometimes you just gotta keep your mouth shut and take it, especially where family's involved."

"What would you have done, if Amanda's mother had just come into the house and took over?"

"Um, well." Lex leaned against the opposite stall and crossed her arm. "That's different."

Shelby stopped and removed her hat. She wiped her forehead against her shoulder and sighed. "Damn, I take a couple of weeks off and now I'm out of shape." She leaned against her pitchfork. Her arm still ached, but she refused to give in to it. Instead, she worked herself harder, much to Rebecca's dismay. "And how is it different?"

"'Cause Amanda's mother was a freakin' psycho. If she had tried to take control of my house, I'd have called the sheriff."

"Oh." Shelby took off her gloves and scratched her neck. "Kathy means well, I guess. It just pissed me off that she thought I wasn't takin' good care of Rebecca."

Lex opened her mouth to say something, when she noticed Shelby's ring. "That's nice."

"Huh?" Shelby paused and realized where Lex stared. "Oh. Yeah." She shrugged and blushed. "It was my old man's."

"Is Rebecca wearing one, too?"

"Yeah. My mother's." Shelby stared at the floor of the barn. "I was tired of her family thinkin' we were just roommates or a fling she'd get over. So I gave her a ring and promised to always be there for her." She raised her head and gave Lex a hard look. "Ain't nothin' wrong with that, is there?"

Lex shook her head. "Not at all, my friend. I'd say there's a lot right about it." She walked closer and held out her hand. "Congratulations."

"Thanks." Shelby shook her hand and grunted in surprise when Lex hugged her.

"When's the big day?" Lex asked after she stepped back.

Shelby looked genuinely confused. "Big day?"

"Yeah. You know, the ceremony?" Lex stretched as she walked across the barn to sit on a bale of hay. "Wedding bells?"

"Uh, no." Shelby shook her head as she joined Lex. "Ain't happenin', buddy."

Lex braced her back against the wall and stretched out her legs. "Why the hell not?"

"Neither of us want that kind of fuss. Rebecca would end up killing her family and I don't feel like visitin' her in prison."

"Really?"

Shelby removed her hat. "Yeah. Her mom is okay, but her dad would raise holy hell, I'd imagine. And don't even get me started on that little bastard brother of hers. I'd love a chance to take him out behind the barn and kick his ass."

"Ah. Well, that sucks."

"Yeah. But I still feel like the luckiest person alive." Shelby scoffed at her sentimentality. "Stupid, huh?"

Lex shook her head. "Not a bit. It'd be stupid if you didn't feel that way." She quietly reflected on her own life. "Pretty damned amazing, if you ask me."

"Yeah."

THE GRAY KITTEN flipped in the air, as it batted at imaginary foes. Anna Leigh chuckled as she sipped her coffee. Derry had been just what she needed after Jacob's loss. The small bundle of fur would never fill the gaping hole his death had left, but at least she had a reason to get up every day. She checked the clock on the stove and stood. Before she could move, there was a soft knock on her front door.

Not long after her husband's death, she had begun to share breakfast and coffee on weekday mornings with someone she had come to consider a good friend. She set her cup down and picked up Derry.

"Right on time." Anna Leigh's smile widened when she opened her door and came face-to-face with her visitor. "Good morning."

"Good morning, A.L." Kyle held a paper bag in one hand, and

small catnip ball in the other. "I brought your favorite today."

"Apple fritter?" Anna Leigh asked, as she traded Derry for the bag. "They're still warm."

Kyle nuzzled the kitten and followed his human into the kitchen. "Yes'm. Timed it just right."

She sat in what had become her usual chair as the older woman poured her a cup of coffee. Kyle had learned the hard way not to offer to get it herself. After clearing out Jacob's workshop, she realized she enjoyed Anna Leigh's company, and started making excuses to drop by. Now she came before work every morning. She set Derry on the floor with the ball and graciously accepted the steaming mug. "Thanks."

"Certainly." Anna Leigh removed the two fritters from the bag, placing each on a paper plate. "How was your weekend?"

"Busy. I was informed on Saturday that I'm going to have to find something besides jeans to wear." Kyle shook her head. "I think that Ellie's been hanging around your granddaughters too long, A.L. She's getting a little crazy about the whole thing. It's only two weeks away and she's getting frantic."

Anna Leigh laughed at the look on her young friend's face. "Well, Mandy has a good head on her shoulders. But Jeannie—" she stopped to consider her words. "She's always been more, shall we say, fanciful."

"Nice save." Kyle raised her cup in salute.

"Behave." Anna Leigh couldn't stop her smile. "You are a bad influence on me, I believe."

Kyle buffed her nails on her work shirt. "I try."

She sobered and nervously brushed her hand across her hair, which stood up in short spikes. "Um, I also found out something else. Ellie asked Lex to give her away, since she's the only family that'll be there."

"That makes sense. Does that bother you, dear?"

"No! Um, not at all. I'm glad she has Lex. Amanda is standing beside her, as her best woman, I guess." Kyle took a deep breath and looked directly into Anna Leigh's eyes. "Would you stand beside me?"

Anna Leigh almost dropped her fork. "Me?" She shakily placed the bite of fritter on the plate. "Don't you have someone else you'd rather have?"

Kyle took the older woman's hand. "I know a lot of people, A.L. But you're just about the best friend I have, outside of Ellie."

"Then I'd be honored, Kylie. Thank you."

Anna Leigh leaned across the small table and kissed Kyle on the cheek, which caused the younger woman to blush.

HER DESK FACED the back wall, so Ellie had no idea that someone had come into the small office she shared with the bookkeeper and the other nurse. She had her head down as she tried to make out Rodney's written instructions on a patient's file.

"I wish we'd go digital," she grumbled.

"Good luck with that," Jeannie answered cheerfully. "My husband hates technology. He'd rather go back to the days of house calls and horse-drawn carriages."

"Ah!" Ellie tossed her pen in the air and covered her chest with one hand. She turned the chair around and gave her boss's wife a dirty look. "You scared me."

Jeannie moved a stack of files out of her way and sat on the edge of the desk. "Why are you hiding in here?"

"I'm not hiding, I'm working." Ellie retrieved her pen from the floor. "What are you doing here?"

"I came to get you." Jeannie took the pen away from her. "Come on."

Ellie shook her head. "What? No. Wait. I have to work."

"Nope. You've got the day off. Let's go." Jeannie tossed the pen on the desk and held out her hand. "We've got stuff to do."

"But—"

"No butts. You've got two weeks to get your dress. I've already taken the liberty of asking my father to do the photographs."

Jeannie hauled Ellie to her feet and gently pushed her toward the door. "We'll stop by your place first, so you can change."

AN HOUR LATER, Ellie stood in the fitting room of Jeannie's favorite boutique, which was a tiny, overpriced store in Parkdale. She looked down at her body, clad only in the white, sensible underwear she always wore. Her figure had filled out during the past year. A layer of muscle now covered her slender body, due to the activities her lover had introduced to her. On their days off, they hiked or bicycled, something that Ellie would have never thought she'd enjoy as much as she did.

"Hey, try this one." Jeannie draped a full dress over the door.

Ellie took the dress and unzipped the back. She stepped into it and pulled the lace sleeves across her shoulders and looked into the mirror. The person staring back at her was a stranger. "What the hell am I doing?"

"Did you say something?" Jeannie asked. "It's gorgeous, isn't it?"

"Uh, well." Ellie frowned at the rows of lace across her chest and shoulders as the ivory, satin skirt flared out well away from her body. "It's something, all right." She carefully removed the dress as her good sense returned. "Jeannie, we need to talk."

"Wrong size?"

Ellie quickly got into her jeans and T-shirt. She opened the door and handed Jeannie the dress. "You can put this back."

"Okay. Was it too big?" Jeannie waved the sales clerk to them and passed the dress off to her. "I'm sorry, we'll have to try something else, I guess."

Ellie shook her head as she stepped into her canvas shoes. "No, we won't. I'm sorry we wasted your time."

She tugged on Jeannie's sleeve. "This is all wrong."

"What do you mean? Ellie, wait." Jeannie gave the clerk an apologetic look and jogged after Ellie. "Hey, hold on." She finally caught up with her outside. "What's the matter?"

"This has gotten way out of hand," Ellie said, waving her hands around. "It was fun at first, but it's not what Kyle and I talked about."

She started toward Jeannie's SUV, which was parked nearby. "We wanted a small little gathering, just family. But thanks to my stupid cousin, we have a minister."

She had been totally against anything to do with organized religion since breaking free of her mother's influence. But after meeting the reverend who presided at Lex and Amanda's ceremony, she had agreed to have him involved.

Jeannie hurried behind her. "But what about the cake and the caterer?"

Ellie stopped at the SUV and rested her arms against the hood. She lowered her head until it was on her arms. "That's not us. I don't think Kyle even cared about having a ceremony." She looked at Jeannie. "I got so caught up in it all that I almost forgot the most important thing."

"What?"

"Kyle," Ellie softly answered. "She's probably afraid that I'm going to make her wear some fancy dress, like you almost roped me into."

"Now, wait a minute. I didn't—"

Ellie held up her hand to stop her. "I know you didn't mean anything by it, but honestly, Jeannie. Can you really see me in that lacy thing you had me try on?"

Jeannie thought about it for a moment before she started to laugh. "You'd be about as comfortable in that as your cousin." She poked Ellie. "Why did you go along with me, then?"

"I dunno." Ellie leaned against the truck and crossed her arms. "Maybe I liked hanging out with you."

"Hey." Jeannie stood beside Ellie and put her arm around her. "We're already family. And, to tell you the truth, I get along better with you than I do my own sister."

"You two do go at it, don't you?"

"God knows I love her, but she can really get on my nerves," Jeannie admitted. "Since I don't have to be home for a few hours, let's go get some pie from the diner. You can tell me what you really want your ceremony to be like."

"All right. But I'm buying."

Jeannie laughed. "I never said you weren't."

She stuck her tongue out and jogged around the SUV.

LOUD MUSIC BOUNCED off the concrete walls of the shop, drowning out the muttering from beneath the late-model Ford truck. Kyle fought with the cross-threaded nut until it snapped free and caused her to skin her knuckles on the undercarriage. "God-damnit!"

She tossed her wrench on the floor and used her legs to wheel out from under the vehicle. She stopped in surprise when she noticed a familiar pair of shoes. "El?"

Ellie knelt in front of Kyle and shook her head. "Why don't you wear your mechanic's gloves?" She took a tissue from her jeans pocket and held out her hand. "Let me see."

"It's not that bad," Kyle argued weakly, as her lover dabbed at her bloody knuckles. She sat quietly as Ellie cleaned the scrape.

"Where's your first-aid kit?"

"Our what?"

Ellie gave her a look. "The boo-boo box."

"Funny." Kyle climbed to her feet. "We have one in the bathroom. I guess I might as well wash up."

"What are you doing here? I thought you had another day of power shopping with Jeannie," she asked as they walked across the shop.

"That's what I came to talk to you about." Ellie followed her into the restroom and waited until Kyle locked the door. The small room had a single toilet and a sink, along with a metal cabinet that hung on the opposite wall. Ellie opened the cabinet and snorted. "A greasy, half-empty box of old bandages and some dried-out medical tape?"

Kyle shrugged her shoulders as she scrubbed her hands, mindful of the oozing injury. "I bought the bandages myself a couple of years ago. Most of us keep them in our tool boxes, anyway."

"Ugh." Ellie gingerly took the box of bandages from the cabinet and set them on the edge of the sink. "Let me see your hand." She tsked as she used a paper towel to dab the wound as dry as possible.

"Are you ever gonna tell me why you're not out with Jeannie?"

Ellie covered the injury with a bandage and lightly kissed it. "There. Now it's properly germy." She looked into her lover's eyes and shook her head. "I'm so sorry, Kyle."

"Huh? For what?"

"The past couple of weeks. I got all caught up in Jeannie's excitement, and didn't even bother to ask you what you wanted. I feel like a jerk."

Kyle stroked Ellie's cheek with her fingertips. "Hey, it's all right. You seemed like you were having such a good time, I didn't mind at all."

She kissed Ellie gently. "As long as I'm not expected to wear some crazy-assed dress, that is."

Ellie laughed at the thought of her lover in the gown Jeannie had her try on earlier. "You have nothing to worry about. In fact, I've told Jeannie to back off and let you and I handle it. I thought we could dress comfortably, with just our family around. Nothing fancy."

"Are you sure?"

"Definitely." Ellie put her arms around Kyle's neck. "If Jeannie wants a big ceremony, she can get remarried."

She laughed when Kyle swung her around the bathroom.

"Have I told you lately how much I love you?" Kyle asked.

She stopped spinning and kissed Ellie until someone started beating on the door.

Chapter Thirty-one

AMANDA PEERED THROUGH the kitchen window to the backyard. The morning sunlight glinted off the dozen or so folding chairs set beneath the trees. She watched as Lex fussed with the placement as Roy and Chet stood nearby.

Martha stepped behind Amanda and looked out the window. "Is she still at it?"

"Yes." Amanda turned away from the window. "You'd think it was our wedding, the way she's carrying on." She leaned against the counter and crossed her arms. "I really can't blame her, though. Ellie's more like her sister than her cousin, and I know she wants everything to be perfect."

"That's true. And how on earth did y'all convince Ellie to have the reverend preside? Last I heard, she wanted no part of it."

Amanda laughed and pushed off the counter. "Lex didn't give her much of a choice. She grabbed Ellie at lunch a couple of weeks ago and took her to see Reverend Hampton in person."

"I'm sure that went well." Martha opened the window. "Lexie, quit being such a pain in the patootie. I'm sure Roy and Chet have better things to do than watch you rearrange the same chairs over and over."

Lex turned toward the house. "It's only four hours until—"

"I can tell time, girl. Go find something else to do." Martha closed the window before Lex could argue. She turned to Amanda, who had a wide grin on her face. "What?"

"Nothing."

Martha's stare was enough to make Amanda raise her hands in surrender.

"I had already told Lex the same thing you did, and you saw where it got me. So I found it pretty funny when you hollered at her."

Martha's glare softened into a smile. "She's a handful, isn't she?"

"Every day." Amanda sat at the table and took a sip of her coffee. "Not that I'd change a thing about her. Well, maybe her tendency to find trouble at the drop of a hat."

"Good luck with that." Martha joined her at the table. "Where's Eddie?"

"Upstairs."

Martha almost choked on her coffee. "Alone?"

"No, both girls are up there, too."

"Honey, are you sure that's wise? After what happened last week?"

Amanda laughed. "I think Mel learned her lesson. She promised not to leave him alone, no matter what."

Melanie had been after her parents to give her more responsibility and Lex was the first to give in, asking their youngest daughter to keep an eye on Eddie. Mel swore she had only been gone for a moment, but by the time she found him, the toddler had dumped all his socks in the toilet that she and Lorrie shared and tried to flush them away. It had been a very expensive error in judgment but Amanda was willing to give Melanie another chance.

Amanda listened for a moment. "Although, now that you mention it, it does seem to be too quiet." She got up from the table. "If my wife comes in the house, tell her to take a chill pill, will you?"

"I surely will. And if you'll excuse me, I believe I'll run home and check on my overnight guest. Ellie was up late last night, talking to Kyle on the phone."

"You should have sent her here. She could have kept Lex company. I caught her downstairs at two o'clock this morning, playing games on the computer."

Martha waved to her and went to the sink to rinse out her coffee cup. She noticed Lex still messing with the chairs. "Crazy thing."

ONCE SHE WAS upstairs, Amanda looked in Eddie's room, which she found empty. She walked down the hall and noticed that Melanie's door was open.

Melanie and Eddie were in full tea party mode. Both were wearing floppy, straw hats. Eddie had a purple feather boa around his shoulders and Melanie wore her old princess Halloween costume.

"Okay, Eddie. Now drink out of your cup, like this." Melanie pretended to sip from the plastic teacup.

"No!" Eddie waved his empty cup around before he slammed it on the table. "No."

"It's just pretend, Eddie. Mommy won't let me use real tea."

Eddie pounded the plastic table with his cup. "No!" He shook his head until the hat fell. "Ha! Bad, Meemee."

"Eddie, you can't have a tea party without the hat. It's just not right." Melanie bent to pick it up, only to be hit by a flying cup. "Eddie, stop it."

"Meemee, ha!"

Amanda decided to intervene before there was an all-out brawl. "How's it going?" she asked as she stepped into the room.

"Mommy!" Eddie upturned his chair in his eagerness to get to her. "Meemee, bad." He tossed the boa to the floor.

Melanie pushed her hat back on her head. "He's not playing right, Mommy."

"Well, little boys aren't known for their tea party manners, honey."

Amanda lifted Eddie and rested him against her hip. "Have you been giving your sister a bad time?"

Eddie chewed on his index finger for a moment then pointed it at Melanie. "Bad."

"No, Eddie. Meemee isn't bad. She just wanted to play with you." She smiled at her daughter. "Thanks for watching him. I'll take him off your hands, now."

"That's okay, Mommy. He didn't like wearing the hat, anyway." Melanie gathered Eddie's castoffs and adjusted her hat. "I'll wait until he's older."

Amanda solemnly nodded. "That's probably a good idea."

She rubbed noses with Eddie, who giggled. "Let's go see what Lorrie's up to."

"Leelee good."

MARTHA VEERED FROM the paved path and ended up behind Lex, who stood beneath the tallest oak tree, staring upward. "What are you doing now?"

Lex startled, turned. "Hey, Martha."

"Don't you 'hey' me, Lexie. What's going on under that hat of yours?"

"Uh, well." Lex removed her black Stetson and scratched her head. "I was thinking of trimming that one branch, 'cause it sticks out some."

Martha's hands went to her hips as she glared at Lex. "Oh, really? And why would you do that today?"

Lex shrugged, looking more like the teenager Martha had raised than the mother of three children of her own. She set her hat low on her head.

Martha crooked her finger. "Come here."

"Hmm?" Lex leaned closer, until her ear was grabbed in a vice-like grip. "Ow! Dammit, Martha. Let go!"

"Now, you listen to me," Martha whispered. Out of the corner of her eye, she saw Roy and Chet quickly escape through the gate. "You're going to stop all this nonsense and settle down."

She released Lex's ear. "You have a choice."

Lex rubbed her ear. "What choice?"

"You can go in the house and relax, or you can come with me and help Ellie get ready for her ceremony. Hers, not yours."

"I know that. I just want everything to be perfect for her." Lex followed Martha through the yard and out the gate. "She deserves it, after everything she's gone through."

Martha stopped and looked back at the yard. She had to admit it looked nice. Lex and the boys had decorated the top of the fence with floral garland. Beneath the tree was a trellis arch, similarly adorned. "Honey, do you think that Kyle loves her?"

Lex appeared shocked at the question. "Of course, she does. What kind of—"

"Nothing else matters to her, I'm bettin'."

"Oh." Lex grinned and swatted Martha on the rear. "Pretty smart, aren't ya?"

Martha shook her finger at Lex. "You were good training, kiddo. Come on, let's go check on Ellie."

AMANDA AND EDDIE both knocked on Lorrie's door.

"Leelee! Naw naw!" Eddie said as he slapped the door.

There was a furious shuffling sound behind the door before it opened and Lorrie appeared. "Hi."

Eddie squirmed. "Down." When he wasn't released, he added, "Pease?"

Amanda set him on the floor and laughed as he waited for Lorrie to move aside. She noticed the handset to the cordless phone in her daughter's hand. "I'm sorry, did we interrupt?"

"Um, no. I was just talking to a friend. We're done, though." Lorrie stepped back. "Come on in."

Eddie laughed and charged ahead. He saw Freckles curled up on the end of Lorrie's bed and made a beeline for her. "Lellels!"

Lorrie chased after him and scooped him up before he could pounce on her dog. "Hey, want to sit at my desk and draw?"

"Lellels," Eddie cried, until Lorrie's words registered. "Dwaw?"

"Yep."

As Lorrie attended to Eddie, Amanda looked out the window. She watched as Martha grabbed Lex's ear, which caused Amanda to laugh.

Lorrie soon joined her. "What's so funny?"

"Just Mada keeping your Momma in line, as usual." Amanda put her arm around Lorrie and brought her close. "How are you doing?"

"I'm okay." Lorrie turned into the embrace and wrapped her arms fully around Amanda. She had recently gone through another growth spurt. The top of her head was even with her mother's eyebrows and she rested her chin on Amanda's shoulder. "I think it's cool that we don't have to dress up today."

Amanda laughed and kissed her cheek. "Me, too. Do you want to come downstairs and keep me company while I get things ready in the kitchen?"

"Um, can I come down in a little bit? I promised my friend I'd call her back."

"Sure." Amanda almost commented on the blush that covered Lorrie's face, but decided against it. "Let me just grab Eddie and get out of your way then."

Lorrie shrugged. "He can stay here, Mom. I'll bring him downstairs with me."

Amanda blinked, but didn't say anything. She wasn't about to look a gift horse in the mouth. "All right. Thanks."

She left the room and closed the door. "Pod person. That's got to be it."

CHARLIE PULLED UP short as he met Lex and Martha on the front porch of the cottage. "I was just on my way into town to pick up the cake."

"Do you want me to go?" Lex asked.

"Nah, I can handle it." Charlie clapped her on the shoulder before he kissed his wife's cheek. "Anything else you can think of, hon?"

"I believe we have everything. Be careful." Martha brushed her hand down his arm as he walked away.

Lex heard the small sigh escape from Martha's lips as she watched her husband walk to their SUV. "Is everything okay?"

"Hmm?" Martha seemed to gather herself together. "Everything's good. I just sometimes get caught up in thinking."

She went inside and headed for the kitchen. "Why don't you see if Ellie's up, and I'll check the coffee."

"Martha?"

The older woman turned around in the kitchen doorway. "I'm fine, Lexie. These past few months have reminded me how lucky I am, that's all."

Lex understood exactly what Martha meant. She often spent time thinking the same thing. "Yeah."

She stepped forward and put her arms around Martha and gently squeezed.

Martha returned the hug and then swatted Lex on the rear. "Now, go on. We don't want Ellie sleeping through her own ceremony, do we?"

"Yes, ma'am." Lex kissed the top of her head and darted out of the way before she could retaliate. "Whatever you say, ma'am."

"Brat."

Lex chuckled all the way down the hall. She stopped in front of the closed guest room door and listened, but didn't hear a sound. Her light knock went unanswered, so she tapped louder. "Hey, Ellie. Rise and shine!"

"Go 'way," a grumpy voice growled.

"You'd better be decent, 'cause I'm coming in," Lex warned, right before she opened the door. She was hit in the face with a pillow as she crossed the threshold. "Good morning to you too, sunshine."

The lump under the blankets groaned and Ellie poked her head out. "Since when did you become so damned cheerful?"

Lex laughed as sat on the edge of the bed. "It's a gorgeous day. The sun is shining, the birds are singing and one of my favorite people in the world is exchanging vows in just a couple of hours."

"Yeah, well." Ellie popped up with a panicked look on her face. "A couple of hours? What time is it?"

Lex looked at her watch. "A little after ten."

"Oh, my God!" Ellie threw the covers off and was on her feet in a flash. "Why didn't someone wake me sooner? I've got so much to do! I haven't showered or — "

"Calm down, cousin. Everything's already set up, Charlie's picking up the cake and I'm here to help you get ready. It's not like you have to put on a fancy dress, or something."

Ellie dropped back onto the bed. "Why did I agree to this circus, anyway?"

"Don't worry about it. Just think about how much fun you're gonna have on the honeymoon." Lex laughed at her cousin's blush. "Aww, that's cute."

"Shut up." Ellie swatted Lex with her spare pillow. She wasn't prepared for the retaliatory hit. "Hey!"

The battle started in earnest, as both got to their knees on the bed and pounded one another with pillows. They laughed.

ANNA LEIGH SAT on her new sofa as the kitten in her lap purred. Her hand kept a smooth motion on its fur.

"You're going to have to come out of my guest room at some point," she said, her voice loud in the quiet house.

"I know." Kyle walked into the living room and held her hands out away from her body. "I'm just not sure about this."

"Oh, Kylie. You look wonderful."

Kyle looked down at her clothes. Her jeans were faded and fit like a second skin, and the black, ribbed T-shirt hugged her muscular body. "I know Ellie wanted me to wear this, but I feel like I'm under dressed."

"Hmm." Anna Leigh placed Derry on a cushion and stood. She slowly walked around Kyle and hummed to herself. "Did she say why?"

Kyle blushed and lowered her head as she mumbled her answer.

"I'm sorry, dear. What was that?" Anna Leigh stood behind Kyle and tried to keep from laughing.

"She likes the way I look in a tank top and jeans."

"I don't blame her. You do cut a dashing figure."

The comment caused Kyle to rub her face with one hand. "Oh, God."

Anna Leigh took pity on her and patted Kyle on the back. "Go put your socks and shoes on, and I'll have a calming cup of tea waiting for you in the kitchen."

"Shoes?" Kyle glanced at her feet. "Damn." She scampered back to the guest room.

Anna Leigh was almost to the kitchen when she heard Kyle yell.

"I can't find my socks!"

Reversing her course, Anna Leigh followed the panicked voice. When she reached the room, she saw Kyle bent at the waist, looking under the bed.

"I can't get married without socks," Kyle cried. "I'll never hear the end of it from Ellie." She had her shoes in one hand while she used the other to balance against the bed. "I could have sworn I brought my damned socks."

Anna Leigh cleared her throat as she took the boots away from Kyle. "Are they white tube socks?"

"Yes!" Kyle rose so quickly she almost slammed into the older woman. "Do you see them?"

Anna Leigh held up the boots, which had a pair of white socks stuffed into one of them. "Do these look familiar?"

"Good God, I'm an idiot. Thanks, A.L." Kyle sat on the edge of the bed to finish dressing. "You're not going to tell anyone about this, are you?"

"Oh, I don't know. I'm sure Eleanor would enjoy this story."

Kyle shook her head. "You wouldn't, would you?"

Anna Leigh winked at her. "That should give you something else to think about," she teased before she turned away.

Chapter Thirty-two

ELLIE CROSSED THE small living room and peered through the front window. "What time is it?"

"Thirty seconds after the last time you asked," Lex responded drolly. "Calm down."

Her phone beeped and she glanced down at the display. "Ellie, come sit down for a few minutes, before you wear a hole in Martha's carpet."

"I see Lorrie out there. Maybe I should go—" Ellie squawked when Lex grabbed the back of her shirt. "Damn it, Lex!"

Unperturbed, Lex none-too-gently pushed her cousin toward the closest chair. "Sit down."

"Do you always have to be such a jerk?" Ellie brushed her hands down her white silk shirt. "Are you sure these jeans look okay with this shirt?"

The new, black jeans she wore molded perfectly to her body, much to Ellie's embarrassment. She wasn't used to standing out. She usually dressed to blend in with everyone else.

Lex perched on the end of the coffee table, which put her directly in front of Ellie. "For the one-hundredth time, it's fine. Now that I have your attention, I need to talk to you about something."

"What? Is it Kyle? Is she okay?" Ellie tried to stand, but a firm hand on her shoulder kept her grounded. "Lex?"

"She's fine. Your clothes are fine. Everyone and everything," Lex sighed, "is fine." She took a deep breath. "I know you wanted me to stand by you today, but—"

Ellie's eyes grew wider. "Oh, no. You can't back out, now. I need you."

"Are you sure about that? Wouldn't you rather have someone closer to you?"

"Lex, the only one closer to me than you, is Kyle. And she's kinda busy."

Ellie didn't notice the man coming out of the kitchen until he spoke.

"I see how I rate," he joked. "I fly all the way from California, and this is the thanks I get?"

Ellie nearly bowled Lex down as she charged the newcomer. "Snot face!"

William Gordon, Ellie's younger brother, caught her as she leaped into his arms. "It's so damned good to see you." He buried his face against her shoulder to hide tears of happiness.

"Oh, my God. I can't believe you're here. How did, I mean, what—"

He pointed to Lex. "Ask my fairy godmother about it."

Lex held up her hands. "Oh, no. I didn't do it. Amanda did." She pointed at him. "And don't be calling me a fairy."

Ellie laughed through her tears. "You've been called worse."

She looked into her brother's eyes. "When did you get here? How did you get here?"

"Mr. Bristol picked me up at the airport." William kept one arm around Ellie's shoulders. "Why didn't you tell me that you were getting married? We just talked on the phone last week."

"I know, but I didn't want you to waste your money on airfare. And you've told me before how you can't afford to lose any time from work." She touched his cheek. His blond hair was short, but in a more respectable style, and his nose and eyebrows were no longer adorned with metal rings. "What happened to all the crazy jewelry you used to wear?"

"I outgrew it." He squeezed her again. "I've missed you."

Lex stepped by them. "I'll see if Martha needs any help in the kitchen."

She shook William's hand before making her escape. "It's good to finally meet you."

"Thanks. I really appreciate everything you've done for my sister."

"Family means a lot down here," Lex said. "That means you, too." She winked and left.

William shook his head. "Wow, sis. Photos don't do that woman justice."

"Forget it, Billy-boy. She's very taken."

"Hey, I didn't mean it that way. It's just that she's kind of, you know, intense."

Ellie laughed at the redness in his face and poked him. "Uh-huh."

She pulled him into a one-armed hug. "Damn, I still can't believe you're here." Spying the clock on the mantel, she gasped. "Oh, God. It's time."

Martha stepped out of the kitchen. "For goodness' sake, girl. Don't just stand there with your mouth hangin' open. Get yourself out there!"

"Yeah, you look like a ghost," Lex added helpfully from behind her. "Try not to pass out before the I-do's, Ellie."

"Shut up, Lex." Ellie glared at her, then swatted her brother when he laughed. "You too, Billy."

KYLE NERVOUSLY SHIFTED from foot to foot as Anna Leigh brushed imaginary lint from her shoulder.

"I can't believe I'm this nervous," Kyle muttered. "What do you think that says about me?"

"I believe it says that you're taking the commitment seriously, dear. That's a good thing."

When Ellie and her brother came through the gate, Kyle turned and stared.

Anna Leigh tapped her on the back. "Breathe, Kylie."

"Uh." Kyle had always thought Ellie was a beautiful woman. Today her light brown hair framed her face like a fine portrait. Ellie's pale, brown eyes seemed to always look directly into her soul and give her the peace she always craved.

Kyle had felt like an outsider her entire life. She had never fit in with her gregarious family, preferring solitude to the awkward silences her presence would bring. She loved her family, and would be the one they always went to when they needed something, but when she finally came out to those that professed to love her, their outrage and disdain tore her apart. But the day she was chewed out by a feisty nurse in the driveway of a duplex was the day her life changed for the good.

Lex snapped her fingers in front of Kyle's face. "Don't go passin' out on us."

"What?" Kyle's eyes never left Ellie, who continued to move closer to her. "Where'd she get those clothes?"

"I took her shopping," Amanda whispered. "She looks great in black and white, doesn't she?"

"Oh, yeah."

"Please, take your places," Reverend Hampton directed. He stared at Lex until she sat on the front row with Lorrie and Melanie.

Lex leaned close to the girls. "Where's Eddie?"

"With Mada." Lorrie pointed her thumb over her shoulder. "She's back there sitting by Pawpaw."

"Oh. Okay, thanks." Lex turned to look and couldn't keep from grinning. "I'll be right back."

She jumped up and hurried to the third row, where Martha and Charlie were talking quietly with a new arrival. "Hubert!"

Hubert Walters stood and wrapped his arms around his sister for a mighty hug.

"You're looking a lot better than I expected." He had been kept up to date on her injuries via Amanda.

"Thanks." Lex pulled away and lightly poked his stomach. "Why didn't you tell me you were coming?"

"I asked Amanda to keep it a surprise, in case I couldn't get away."

Lex nodded. "How's your father-in-law? Any better?"

When Reverend Hampton loudly cleared his throat, everyone, including Lex and Hubert, quickly settled onto their chairs. "Thank you all for being here today."

He smiled at the two women in front of him. "Kyle and Ellie. Are you both ready?"

Kyle looked at her lover. "Ready as we'll ever be, Reverend. Right, El?"

"Rrr," Ellie had to clear her throat. "Right." She ignored the laughter of her friends and family, and kept her eyes on Kyle. "Yes."

"Very well. Let's get this started, shall we?" He took a deep breath and opened his bible.

"Wait." Kyle caught everyone off guard by her interruption. She never took her eyes off Ellie. "I know we said we didn't want to say our own vows, but I've changed my mind."

Ellie's expression was a combination of surprise and understanding, with a healthy dose of love tossed in. "Me, too."

The reverend chuckled and closed his bible. "Well, that's wonderful."

Kyle gently gripped Ellie's hands. "I've always said I wasn't the hearts and flowers type. But, standing here with you today made me realize that I lied. I may not have started out that way, but being with you has changed me."

Her quirky grin brought a matching one from her lover. "You made me realize what love was all about, El. Your love has given me permission to be who I am, not who I thought others wanted to see."

She kissed Ellie's knuckles. "I love you."

"I love you, too," Ellie whispered. She blinked the tears from her eyes and stared at their joined hands. "I never thought I'd find someone like you, Kyle." She shrugged and sniffled. "I'd resigned myself to going through life alone. I mean, I never thought I was good enough for someone."

She shook her head when Kyle opened her mouth to argue. "No, I realize now, thanks to you, that I am." She squeezed Kyle's hands. "I hope you always know how very much I love you, Kyle."

"That was quite beautiful, ladies." The reverend smiled broadly and stood a little straighter. "True love is a joy to see. It doesn't matter who we are, only that we care and understand. May the two of you know this feeling for the rest of your days."

He paused and nodded. "Well, go on. Seal the deal with a kiss."

Ellie's face turned beet red, but she leaned forward and met Kyle halfway. The roar of blood pulsing through her ears was soon drowned out by the cheers of her family, which she ignored as her arms circled Kyle's neck.

VOICES OVERLAPPED IN the crowded living room, which drowned out the soft music that floated through the air. The happy couple sat close together on the loveseat, with their hands entwined and their eyes locked on one another.

Kyle whispered into Ellie's ear, causing her to blush. They shared a private laugh, much to the amusement of another couple nearby.

"Aren't they cute?" Amanda asked her wife, who was on the sofa beside her.

Lex nodded. "It's great to see Ellie so happy. Although I'm a little worried about her brother hanging out with Ron. No telling what kind of trouble they'll get into."

"Ha. You know as well as I do that Ron does whatever Nora tells him to do. He's completely and totally wrapped around her little finger." Amanda snuggled closer and sighed. "As much as I love our family and friends, I wish this day was over."

"Yeah, I know what you mean." Lex stretched her legs out. "Do you think anyone would notice if we headed upstairs?"

"Just what do you have in mind?"

Lex leaned closer until their faces were inches apart. "After all these years, I still have to tell you?"

Amanda kissed the tip of her nose. "Of course not. I just like to hear you say it."

"Good grief," Jeannie lamented as she plopped onto the sofa arm beside her sister. "You two are worse than them." She hitched her thumb toward the newlyweds. "Have you seen my husband? We need to go rescue Lois from our boys."

"I don't know why you didn't just bring the boys with you." Lex put her arm around Amanda and poked Jeannie. "Unless you're using them as an excuse to leave early."

"Excuse? Who says I need an excuse, Slim?" Jeannie tried to poke her back, but was pushed off the arm of the couch by Amanda. "Hey, watch it!"

She crossed her arms and glared at her sister. "What did you do that for?"

Amanda sweetly smiled at her. "Do what?"

Jeannie pushed her into Lex. "You suck."

Before Amanda could retort, Lex covered her mouth. "Jeannie, I think your dad is calling you."

"He is?" Jeannie looked around the room and spied Michael taking pictures by the fireplace. She pointed to Amanda. "This isn't over, brat."

Amanda waggled her eyebrows and licked Lex's palm.

"Ew. Damn, why did you do that?"

"That's what you get." Amanda checked her watch. "Let's see if we can clear some of these people out of here."

She stood and held her hand out to Lex. Once they were both on their feet, she moved to the center of the room and faced Ellie and Kyle. "Can I have everyone's attention, please?"

The room quieted, except for Eddie, who sat on Hubert's lap and seemed to be telling him a story. Hubert shrugged and grinned, which delighted the toddler.

Amanda shook her head and directed her comments to the newlyweds. "I know you two asked that no gifts be given today, but you know Lex and me well enough to understand that we'd find a way around that, right?"

Ellie laughed and leaned her head against Kyle's shoulder. "I should have known."

"We're not going to need batteries, are we?" Kyle joked, causing her partner to blush.

Lex rested her arm across Amanda's shoulders. "Nah. Well, maybe." She grunted as her wife elbowed her in the stomach.

"As I was saying," Amanda continued. "We wanted to make sure you started off on a good note. So we all pitched in for this." She handed an envelope to Ellie, who passed it to Kyle.

"Go on. Open it," Amanda urged, when Kyle stared at the seal.

"All right." Kyle fiddled with the edge until she was able to use her finger to tear it open. She pulled out several sheets of paper and handed them to her partner.

Ellie read the papers and looked up. "You're kidding me, right?"

"What is it, baby?" Kyle asked. "Holy shit. No way!"

She steadied Ellie's shaky grip on the papers. The first page was a detailed itinerary of a four day, three-night trip to San Francisco. "This...this is too much. I can't afford to take this much time off."

Kyle's boss, J.B. Davis, laughed. "I think we can survive a few extra days without you, Kyle." He raised his bottle of beer in their direction. "Consider the time off with pay as my little present."

When Ellie looked at Rodney, he held up his hand to forestall her argument. "Same here, Ellie. It's the least I could do. Enjoy yourselves."

"Wow." Ellie shook her head and rubbed her eyes. "This whole day has been like a dream."

"Don't dream too long," Lex teased. "A limo will be at your place early tomorrow morning to take you to the airport."

Kyle stood and helped Ellie to her feet. "Looks like we've got some packing to do, baby."

"I guess so." Kyle hugged Amanda as Ellie took a few steps and embraced her cousin. She closed her eyes and held onto Lex for a long moment. "Thanks for everything. I don't know how to repay you for today."

"Be happy, Ellie. That's the best payment." Lex kissed the side of her head. "Now, get out of here, before I become a blubberin' mess."

Ellie laughed and backed away. She saw the sparkle of tears in Lex's eyes. "Yeah. If you start, I'll join you."

She moved in and hugged Amanda. "Thank you," she whispered.

"My pleasure." Amanda squawked when Jeannie goosed her. "What?"

"Quit hogging them," Jeannie ordered. "Let the rest of us have a turn."

When she felt a hard swat on her rear, Jeannie spun around. "Mandy! I swear—" she saw her husband grin. "Roddy?"

He shook his head. "I don't know what you're talking about." He nodded his head to the right, where Michael stood with his camera.

"Daddy?"

Michael took her picture as the rest of the room continued to laugh. He backed away slowly until he reached the hallway then quickly disappeared.

It took them close to fifteen minutes to walk from the living room to the front porch, but neither Kyle nor Ellie seemed to mind. Ellie stood on the steps, fending off the well-wishes of Lorrie, Melanie and Jeannie as Kyle stayed a few feet away and enjoyed the gentle laugh of her partner.

"It was a beautiful ceremony, Kylie."

Kyle turned and nodded. "Thanks, A.L. And thank you for standing with me."

Anna Leigh smiled. "It was entirely my pleasure, dear." Her smile turned wistful. "Have a wonderful time."

"We will." Kyle took Anna Leigh's hand and gently squeezed it. "I'm going to miss our morning coffee."

"Oh, please. You won't have time to miss babysitting an old woman." Anna Leigh touched her cheek. "Enjoy every moment with her, Kylie. Cherish each second."

Unable to speak, Kyle nodded. She pulled Anna Leigh into a firm embrace and held her. "I swear to you that I will."

AFTER THE FINAL guest departed, Lex closed the door and sighed. She loved her extended family, but too much of a good thing exhausted her. She shuffled into the living room and flopped onto the sofa beside Amanda. "Remind me again why we host these things?"

Amanda lazily turned her head from the cushion she was propped against. "Because we have the largest house, I think."

"Or we're the biggest suckers," Lex countered with a yawn. "Good lord. I feel like I've been brandin' cattle all day."

Amanda snorted. "Thanks for that visual."

"Huh?"

"I pictured my sister, hog-tied and screaming, getting a brand on her butt."

Lex laughed along with her. "She'd probably bellow like an old brood cow," she added, causing Amanda to laugh louder. She changed her voice to a high-pitched whine. "Mooo, Mandy!"

"Oh, God," Amanda wheezed. "Stop before I pee my pants." She tumbled onto Lex and continued to giggle.

As her laughter quieted, Amanda moved around until she was tucked against her wife's side, with one hand lightly stroking Lex's stomach. "You realize that the next time I see her, I'm gonna lose it, don't you?"

"Me, too." Lex shifted so she could rest her cheek against Amanda's head. "This is the best way to end the day."

Amanda sighed. "Amen."

She closed her eyes and slowly relaxed. "It's a shame Hubert had to go back to Oklahoma. I was hoping he could spend a few days."

"Yeah. He seemed anxious to get back to Ramona. To be honest, I was surprised he drove all the way down here, with her father so ill."

"He wanted to surprise Ellie. And speaking of surprises, what do you think of Billy staying with Ron and Nora?"

Lex yawned again. "I think Nora's got her hands full. They sure seemed like long-lost brothers, though. It'll be good for both of 'em. They're about the same age, and Martha raised Ron well. I don't think Ellie needs to worry about her brother."

Billy was Ellie's half-brother, as she had been fathered by Lex's uncle, before he died in Vietnam. Her mother married Anthony Gordon, who had been the only father Ellie had ever known. A hidden picture and old letters sent Ellie searching for her paternal family, and she never looked back.

She kissed Amanda's head. "Speaking of kids, ours seem a little too quiet."

Amanda opened her eyes and stared at the ceiling. "Lorrie said she didn't mind watching Eddie, right?"

"Yep. Last I heard, she was gonna read to him. He likes when she acts out the characters in his books. Although she'd probably stop if she knew we knew about it." Lex paused and listened. "This is spooky."

"Maybe we should sneak upstairs and check on them." Amanda started to get up, but Lex pulled her down. "What?"

Lex wrapped both arms around her and nuzzled Amanda's neck. "Let's trust Lorrie, sweetheart. She's smart enough to call for us if she needs us."

She pulled Amanda's blouse free from her jeans and grinned as her wife gasped at her touch. "I'm sure we can find something to do down here."

"Yeah, oh." Amanda arched her back as Lex's warm hand slipped beneath her bra. "I thought you were tired."

"I'm never too tired for you." Lex rolled until Amanda was lying on the couch. She lowered her face and looked into her wife's eyes. "I love you."

Amanda stretched her arms so that she could lock her hands behind Lex's neck. "I love you, too." She pulled Lex's head down.

"Momma, Lorrie's being mean to me," Melanie yelled from the doorway.

Her announcement startled her parents. Amanda jumped, which caused her to knock Lex into the floor.

"Ow! Dammit!" Lex growled. "Mel, what have we told you about yelling inside?"

Amanda hurriedly adjusted her top and sat up. "What's going on?"

Melanie sniffled and walked around the couch. "Momma, why are you on the floor?"

Lex gritted her teeth to keep from saying something she'd regret. She accepted Amanda's assistance and got to her feet. "I think a better question is why are you downstairs tattling?"

"Um." Melanie chewed on the end of her index finger as she thought of an answer. In the Walters' household, telling on someone was as wrong as being the one being told on. "I wanted Eddie to play dolls with me, but Lorrie said no."

Lex squatted beside her so they were eye to eye. "And why did she say no?"

Melanie looked to Amanda for help, but her mother just shook her head. "Um. She said, he wasn't...uh. Umm." She stopped to think. "'Cause Lorrie's mean."

"If I go up there," Lex began. "What will I find?"

"Umm." Melanie took a few steps back. "They're in Eddie's room on his bed." She walked around the sofa and peeked over the top. "Lorrie's reading, and they won't play with me."

Amanda touched her hand. "I think you need to go to your room and think about what you did, Melanie. We'll be there in a few minutes."

Melanie looked at Amanda, then turned her sad face to Lex. "Momma?"

Lex stood. "You heard her, Melanie. Upstairs."

Once Melanie had slunk from the room, Lex pulled Amanda off the couch and into her arms. "Do you want to be the good guy or bad guy, this time?"

Amanda chuckled and swatted Lex on the butt. "I'm always the bad guy, honey. You crumble every time she looks up at you with those big, tear-filled eyes."

"I can't help it," Lex muttered. "She looks just like you."

"What are you saying?"

Lex slipped away from Amanda. "Uh, I mean, she has your eyes."

"Uh-huh." Amanda stalked her across the room. "Come here, Lex."

"I think I'll run check on Eddie," the largest chicken on the Rocking W Ranch said as she hustled out of the room.

Amanda laughed as she followed behind at a more leisurely pace. Life with Lex was always interesting. She wouldn't change a thing.

Other Carrie Carr titles in the
LEX AND AMANDA SERIES

Destiny's Bridge - Rancher Lexington (Lex) Walters pulls young Amanda Cauble from a raging creek and the two women quickly develop a strong bond of friendship. Overcoming severe weather, cattle thieves, and their own fears, their friendship deepens into a strong and lasting love. ISBN: 1-932300-11-2

Faith's Crossing - Lexington Walters and Amanda Cauble withstood raging floods, cattle rustlers and other obstacles to be together...but can they handle Amanda's parents? When Amanda decides to move to Texas for good, she goes back to her parents' home in California to get the rest of her things, taking the rancher with her. ISBN: 1-932300-12-0

Hope's Path - Someone is determined to ruin Lex. Efforts to destroy her ranch lead to attempts on her life. Lex and Amanda desperately try to find out who hates Lex so much that they are willing to ruin the lives of everyone in their path. Can they survive long enough to find out who's responsible? And will their love survive when they find out who it is? ISBN: 1-932300-40-6

Love's Journey - Lex and Amanda embark on a new journey as Lexington rediscovers the love her mother's family has for her, and Amanda begins to build her relationship with her father. Meanwhile, attacks on the two young women grow more violent and deadly as someone tries to tear apart the love they share. ISBN: 978-1-932300-65-9

Strength of the Heart - Lex and Amanda are caught up in the planning of their upcoming nuptials while trying to get the ranch house rebuilt. But an arrest, a brushfire, and the death of someone close to her forces Lex to try and work through feelings of guilt and anger. Is Amanda's love strong enough to help her, or will Lex's own personal demons tear them apart? ISBN: 978-1-932300-81-9

The Way Things Should Be - In this, the sixth novel, Amanda begins to feel her own biological clock ticking while her sister prepares for the birth of her first child. Lex is busy with trying to keep her hands on some newly acquired land, as well trying to get along with a new member of her family. Everything comes to a head, and a tragedy brings pain — and hope — to them all. ISBN: 1-932300-39-2

To Hold Forever - Three years have passed since Lex and Amanda took over the care of Lorrie, their rambunctious niece. Amanda's sister, Jeannie, has fully recovered from her debilitating stroke and returns with her fiancé, ready to start their own family. Attempts to become pregnant have been unsuccessful for Amanda. Meanwhile, a hostile new relative who resents everything about Lex shows up. Add in Lex's brother Hubert getting paroled and an old adversary returning with more than a simple reunion in mind and Lex begins to have doubts about continuing to run the ranch she's worked so hard to build. ISBN: 978-1-932300-21-5

Trust Our Tomorrows - Set six years after *To Hold Forever*, life at the Rocking W ranch is constantly changing. Lex and Amanda are back, struggling through a drought and trying to raise their two daughters as best they can. Lorrie is now ten and gets into as much trouble as Lex ever did, while six-year old Melanie is content to follow along. When someone from the past returns and asks for an unusual favor, will Lex and Amanda agree? And, considering the favor, can they refuse? ISBN: 978-1-61929-011-2

More Carrie Carr Titles:

Something To Be Thankful For

Randi Meyers is at a crossroads in her life. She's got no girlfriend, bad knees, and her fill of loneliness. The one thing she does have in her favor is a veterinarian job in Fort Worth, Texas, but even that isn't going as well as she hoped. Her supervisor is cold-hearted and dumps long hours of work on her. Even if she did want a girlfriend, she has little time to look.

When a distant uncle dies, Randi returns to her hometown of Woodbridge, Texas, to attend the funeral. During the graveside services, she wanders away from the crowd and is beseeched by a young boy to follow him into the woods to help his injured sister. After coming upon an unconscious woman, the boy disappears. Randi brings the woman to the hospital and finds out that her name is Kay Newcombe.

Randi is intrigued by Kay. Who is this unusual woman? Where did her little brother disappear to? And why does Randi feel compelled to help her? Despite living in different cities, a tentative friendship forms, but Randi is hesitant. Can she trust her newfound friend? How much of her life and feelings can Randi reveal? And what secrets is Kay keeping from her? Together, Randi and Kay must unravel these questions, trust one another, and find the answers in order to protect themselves from outside threats – and discover what they mean to one another.

ISBN: 1-932300-04-X
Available in both print and eBook formats.

Diving Into The Turn

Diving Into The Turn is set in the fast-paced Texas rodeo world. Riding bulls in the rodeo is the only life Shelby Fisher has ever known. She thinks she's perfectly happy in her world of one night stands until she goes to a rodeo/fair and meets spoiled barrel racer Rebecca Starrett. Suddenly, Shelby's life feels emptier, and she can't figure out why. The two women take an instant dislike to each other, but there's something about Rebecca that draws the silent and angry bull rider to her. It's not long before Rebecca's overtures pays off, and a grudging friendship occurs. Against a backdrop of mysterious accidents that are happening at the rodeo grounds, the women's friendship develops into something more. But when Shelby is implicated as the culprit to what's been happening will Rebecca stand by her side?

ISBN: 978-1-932300-54-3
Available in both print and eBook formats.

Piperton

Sam Hendrickson has been traveling around the Southwest for ten years, never staying in one place long enough to call it home. Doing odd jobs to pay for her food and gas, she thinks her life is fine, until fate intervenes. On her way to Dallas to find work for the upcoming winter, her car breaks down in the small town of Piperton. Sam's never concerned herself over what other people think, but the small minds of a West Texas town may be more than she bargained for - especially when she meets Janie Clarke. Janie's always done what's expected of her. But when she becomes acquainted with Sam, she's finally got a reason to rebel.

ISBN: 978-1-935053-20-0
Available in both print and eBook formats.

Heart's Resolve

Gibson Proctor, a Park Police Officer for the Texas Department of Parks & Wildlife, has returned after twenty years to the rural area she once called home. She's able to easily adapt to the slower pace of the farming communities that surround the town of Benton, Texas, and tries her best to handle the expectations of her family, as well. Gib's comfortable existence is set into a tailspin when she unwittingly offends Delaney Kavanagh, the fiery-tempered architect who's in charge of repairing the spillway at Lake Kichai.

Although Delaney is currently in a relationship, she can't seem to get the amiable officer out of her mind. Not used to the type of attention she receives from the chivalrous woman, Delaney keeps waiting for the "real" Gib to show up. Will she ever accept Gib's acts of kindness as truth, or will she be content to stay in a relationship where she has to fight for everything?

ISBN: 978-1-61929-051-8
Available in both print and eBook formats.

Other Yellow Rose Titles You May Enjoy:

Hard Lessons
by J. M. Carr

June Cunningham was four years old when her parents were brutally murdered. Now as a brilliant young engineering student, she falls in love with the killer's next intended victim.

Irene Hawkins is the estranged wife of a self-absorbed financial executive whose greed knows no bounds.

June has learned to live without family and Irene has learned to deny her feelings. When they come together, everyone learns more than they ever expected.

ISBN 978-1-61929-162-1
Available in both print and eBook formats.

The Gardner of Aria Manor
by A.L. Duncan

Janie O'Grady is a woman quite adapted to her life and circumstances as they are, living in New York City during the Great Depression. A hint of cynicism clouds the cold winter streets and keeps the rum runners strange bedfellows to the Irish mob's bounty in and out of speakeasy's, daring to brush shoulders with the neighboring Italian mobs. At a moment where Janie fears for her life she is presented with circumstances which seem like a harsh nudge from the heavens to decide her own destiny.

Feeling there is no other choice, Janie makes the fateful decision to change her identity and move to the Devon countryside on the coastal shores of England, as a Head Gardener to a 17th century manor, where déjà vu and the intrigues of a past life and murder mystery overshadow her life in the big city.

This tale invites you to peek into the pages of one woman's life and follow her incredible story of self-discovery of a very different kind; where looking back at one's past includes connecting the threads of passions and desires of a life lived before. A life lived where one's odyssey must wait to complete the circle in the next life.

ISBN: 978-1-61929-158-4
Available in both print and eBook formats.

Jess
by Pauline George

Jess is a modern day lesbian Lothario who was so hurt from an emotionally damaging relationship that now she doesn't let anyone get close. She protects herself by keeping her relationships short and sweet. When Jess's sister Josie challenges her to get to know a woman before she jumps into bed with her, Jess is intrigued. How hard can that be?

Although she's a serial monogamist, Jess has deep-seated morals that will be tested to the limit by her carefree acceptance of Josie's challenge. When she falls for her sister's best friend Katie, she suddenly finds her life upended, and she's left wondering if she actually has what it takes to have a lasting and fulfilling relationship. Is she destined to spend her life bed-hopping? Will her ever-growing attraction to Katie be the catalyst for romance, or will Katie's indecision about her life prove to be Jess's downfall?

ISBN: 978-1-61929-138-6
Available in both print and eBook formats

White Dragon
by Regina Hanel

The story of Halie Walker and Samantha Takoda Tyler continues a year after they first met in Love Another Day. Halie's efforts to reestablish a career while still recovering from previous injuries consume her time and focus, leaving Sam far from the center of her attention and their relationship under emotional strain. Adding to their troubles, someone unknown begins a campaign of attacks. Sam's horse Coco winds up missing, their home is vandalized, and worse. As anxiety builds, Halie's childhood friend, Ronni Summers, provides welcome support, but no one can figure out who is involved in the attacks.

Ronni's brief encounter with Cali Brooks taunts her dreams, but finding her potential soul mate again proves most difficult. As Thanksgiving approaches, a series of events bring Cali into Sam and Halie's life, and almost into Ronni's. New and old friends join together on Thanksgiving Day, but snowfall cuts the gathering short. What follows brings not only the White Dragon, but also revelation, love, and death; the question is: which is brought to whom?

ISBN: 978-1-61929-142-3
Available in both print and eBook formats

The Game of Denial
by Brenda Adcock

Joan Carmichael, a successful New York businesswoman, lost the love of her life ten years earlier. Alone, she raised their four children, always cherishing her deep love for her wife. Her memories of their life together come back even stronger as one of their daughters prepares to marry. Joan and her four adult kids fly to Virginia to meet the groom's family and attend the ceremony at the small horse farm owned by the mother of the fiancé.

Evelyn "Evey" Chase, also a widow, has secrets in her past, and her memories of her dead husband aren't pleasant. She's concerned about meeting her future daughter-in-law's family, certain that she and her three kids will have little in common with the wealthy New Yorkers. Besides, the thought of two women in a relationship bringing up a family together makes her uncomfortable, even though her daughter-in-law assures her that lesbianism is not hereditary or catching.

When the two women meet they are drawn to one another in a way neither anticipated, and the game of denial begins. Evey fights her attraction and doesn't realize the effect she has on Joan. Joan tries to shake off her feelings, seeing them as a betrayal to the memory of her wife. Besides, isn't Evey Chase straight? After Evey and Joan share an intimate moment at the wedding reception, they are both emotionally terrified and Joan flees. Will Joan overcome the feeling of betraying her former mate and stop denying her desire to be happy again? Can Evey finally face her past in order to accept the love of another woman and the desire to live the life she had once dreamed of?

ISBN: 978-1-61929-130-0
Available in both print and eBook formats

OTHER YELLOW ROSE PUBLICATIONS

Brenda Adcock	Soiled Dove	978-1-935053-35-4
Brenda Adcock	The Sea Hawk	978-1-935053-10-1
Brenda Adcock	The Other Mrs. Champion	978-1-935053-46-0
Brenda Adcock	Picking Up the Pieces	978-1-61929-120-1
Brenda Adcock	The Game of Denial	978-1-61929-130-0
Janet Albert	Twenty-four Days	978-1-935053-16-3
Janet Albert	A Table for Two	978-1-935053-27-9
Janet Albert	Casa Parisi	978-1-61929-015-0
Georgia Beers	Thy Neighbor's Wife	1-932300-15-5
Georgia Beers	Turning the Page	978-1-932300-71-0
Carrie Brennan	Curve	978-1-932300-41-3
Carrie Carr	Destiny's Bridge	1-932300-11-2
Carrie Carr	Faith's Crossing	1-932300-12-0
Carrie Carr	Hope's Path	1-932300-40-6
Carrie Carr	Love's Journey	978-1-932300-65-9
Carrie Carr	Strength of the Heart	978-1-932300-81-9
Carrie Carr	The Way Things Should Be	978-1-932300-39-0
Carrie Carr	To Hold Forever	978-1-932300-21-5
Carrie Carr	Trust Our Tomorrows	978-1-61929-011-2
Carrie Carr	Beyond Always	978-1-61929-160-7
Carrie Carr	Piperton	978-1-935053-20-0
Carrie Carr	Something to Be Thankful For	1-932300-04-X
Carrie Carr	Diving Into the Turn	978-1-932300-54-3
Carrie Carr	Heart's Resolve	978-1-61929-051-8
J. M. Carr	Hard Lessons	978-1-61929-162-1
Sky Croft	Amazonia	978-1-61929-066-2
Sky Croft	Mountain Rescue: The Ascent	978-1-61929-098-3
Cronin and Foster	Blue Collar Lesbian Erotica	978-1-935053-01-9
Cronin and Foster	Women in Uniform	978-1-935053-31-6
Pat Cronin	Souls' Rescue	978-1-935053-30-9
Verda Foster	The Gift	978-1-61929-029-7
Verda Foster	The Chosen	978-1-61929-027-3
Verda Foster	These Dreams	978-1-61929-025-9
Anna Furtado	The Heart's Desire	1-932300-32-5
Anna Furtado	The Heart's Strength	978-1-932300-93-2
Anna Furtado	The Heart's Longing	978-1-935053-26-2
Melissa Good	Eye of the Storm	1-932300-13-9
Melissa Good	Hurricane Watch	978-1-935053-00-2
Melissa Good	Moving Target	978-1-61929-150-8
Melissa Good	Red Sky At Morning	978-1-932300-80-2
Melissa Good	Storm Surge: Book One	978-1-935053-28-6
Melissa Good	Storm Surge: Book Two	978-1-935053-39-2
Melissa Good	Stormy Waters	978-1-61929-082-2
Melissa Good	Thicker Than Water	1-932300-24-4
Melissa Good	Terrors of the High Seas	1-932300-45-7
Melissa Good	Tropical Storm	978-1-932300-60-4
Melissa Good	Tropical Convergence	978-1-935053-18-7
Regina A. Hanel	Love Another Day	978-1-935053-44-6
Regina A. Hanel	White Dragon	978-1-61929-142-3
Jeanine Hoffman	Lights & Sirens	978-1-61929-114-0

Jeanine Hoffman	Strength in Numbers	978-1-61929-108-9
Maya Indigal	Until Soon	978-1-932300-31-4
Jennifer Jackson	It's Elementary	978-1-61929-084-6
K. E. Lane	And, Playing the Role of Herself	978-1-932300-72-7
Helen Macpherson	Love's Redemption	978-1-935053-04-0
J. Y Morgan	Learning To Trust	978-1-932300-59-8
J. Y. Morgan	Download	978-1-932300-88-8
A. K. Naten	Turning Tides	978-1-932300-47-5
Lynne Norris	One Promise	978-1-932300-92-5
Paula Offutt	Butch Girls Can Fix Anything	978-1-932300-74-1
Surtees and Dunne	True Colours	978-1-932300-529
Surtees and Dunne	Many Roads to Travel	978-1-932300-55-0
Vicki Stevenson	Family Affairs	978-1-932300-97-0
Vicki Stevenson	Family Values	978-1-932300-89-5
Vicki Stevenson	Family Ties	978-1-935053-03-3
Vicki Stevenson	Certain Personal Matters	978-1-935053-06-4
Vicki Stevenson	Callie's Dilemma	978-1-61929-003-7
Cate Swannell	A Long Time Coming	978-1-61929-062-4
Cate Swannell	Heart's Passage	978-1-932300-09-3
Cate Swannell	No Ocean Deep	978-1-932300-36-9

About the Author

Carrie Carr calls herself a true Texan. She was born in the Lone Star State in the early sixties and has never strayed far from home. Currently a resident of the Dallas-Fort Worth Metroplex, she lives with her partner of fifteen years, Jan, whom she legally married in Toronto in September, 2003.

As a technical school graduate and a quiet introvert, publishing her fiction — lesbian-based — was something she never expected.

"Living on a farm probably influenced me the most because I had to use my imagination for recreation," she says. "I made up stories for myself, and my only regret is that I didn't save the ones I had written down and hidden away when I was growing up."

Her writing also brought Carrie her greatest joy – her wife, who wrote her when she posted *Destiny's Bridge* online. They've been together ever since. When Carrie's not writing, she spends her time keeping up with their three dogs, Nuggie, Daisy and Ribbie, and getting into trouble while geocaching.

VISIT US ONLINE AT
www.regalcrest.biz

At the Regal Crest Website You'll Find

- The latest news about forthcoming titles and new releases

- Our complete backlist of romance, mystery, thriller and adventure titles

- Information about your favorite authors

- Current bestsellers

- Media tearsheets to print and take with you when you shop

- Which books are also available as eBooks.

Regal Crest print titles are available from all progressive booksellers including numerous sources online. Our distributors are Bella Distribution and Ingram.

CPSIA information can be obtained
at www.ICGtesting.com
Printed in the USA
LVOW12s1545270317
528625LV00002B/476/P